WHAT ALICE KNEW

*A Most Curious Tale of
Henry James & Jack the Ripper*

PAULA MARANTZ COHEN

sourcebooks
landmark

Published by Sourcebooks Landmark, an imprint of Sourcebooks, Inc.
ISBN 978-1-61129-256-5

Printed and bound in the United States of America.

To Alan,
my first story man

ACKNOWLEDGMENTS

My thanks to the following people who offered background, ideas, or editing help with the manuscript: Simeon Amon, Victoria Amon, Rosetta Marantz Cohen, Maria Esche, Michael Harris-Peyton, Peter Lynch, Neeti Madan, and Jean-Michel Rabaté.

I owe a special debt of gratitude to my husband, Alan Penziner, and to my children, Sam and Kate Penziner, who provided useful comments and unfailing, if sometimes exasperated, support.

AUTHOR'S NOTE

I WROTE THIS BOOK in order to bring to life historical characters and events that I have come to know through my reading. But as this is a work of fiction, imaginative material has necessarily been added and factual material altered to accommodate the plot.

CHAPTER 1

London. 1888.

ENRY JAMES WAS DRUNK.

The room where he was dining looked familiar, but he could not place it. There was an oak sideboard, elaborately carved, and a cupboard containing a collection of fine porcelains. The plate was bone china, the silver heavy and apparently old. There was a landscape (was it Corot?) near the door, a set of prints (Rowlandson?) on the side wall, and a portrait by someone of talent over the mantel. It was a good house, though how good was a matter of whether the portrait was by van Dyck of an esteemed ancestor or by Sargent of a more contemporary personage (he was too bleary-eyed to look), and whether the silver had been passed down or purchased secondhand.

Henry was seated at a large, well-appointed table at which he vaguely recognized some of the guests. Mrs. Drummond was to his left, and Lady Dalrymple to his right (unless it was the other way around); Oscar Wilde was gesticulating at the far end; and across was Edmund Gosse, if it was Gosse, bent over his soup. There were others he was certain he knew, except he could not summon up their names. Not that it mattered. Real places and people were the germs that fertilized his novels, but a certain level of distractedness (helped by a certain quantity of wine) left an opening for the imagination.

"What do *you* think, Mr. James?" asked the woman to his left—Lady Dalrymple or Mrs. Drummond—the face blurred in his vision. He had almost finished his soup, a very nice beef bouillon, and would have liked to answer the lady (whoever she was) if only he knew what she was talking about.

Fortunately they were interrupted by Wilde, engaged in one of his familiar critiques of someone who wasn't there.

"I can't say I think much of Stevenson's work," Wilde pronounced. "It's thin. The stage adaptation of *Jekyll and Hyde* owes its success to the actors; the book lacks depth and amplification. If the man weren't so ill, I would be harsher. And if he were dead, which they say he will be in a year, I would be more generous."

"Dead? Who's dead?" shouted an elderly gentleman across the table.

"No one, yet," said Wilde, "but in time, all of us. Though some sooner than others," he added, sotto voce, to the handsome young man seated next to him.

Henry pushed away his soup. Secretly he agreed with Wilde about Stevenson. How was it that Louis had gotten his *Jekyll and Hyde* produced for the stage? Henry's lifelong dream was to have his own work adapted for performance, but when he approached the theater people, they said his novels were not dramatic. This was nonsense; they were extremely dramatic if one read them carefully.

"Stevenson's tale chilled my blood," asserted one of the pretty, more impressionable women.

"Then your blood, exquisite though it is, is easily chilled, madam," chided Wilde. "Lopping a man in half so that the animal is turned loose is an obvious sort of conceit and entirely unrealistic. Much better if the monster doesn't look like a monster at all, but like an angel, the point being that the worst atrocities are committed not by animals but by men, and often men of apparent refinement."

A stout American woman in heavy brocade looked up from her soup. "I can always tell a person by his face," she announced, casting a supercilious glance around the table.

Henry winced. Although he had lived in London for years, he still took the arrogant stupidity of his countrymen personally. The stout American woman was married to an oil man or a lumber man, referred to as though they were made of these substances, which perhaps they were. One never saw the men, only their wives, who were everywhere, elbowing their way into the best houses.

"I pride myself on my ability to read faces," the American woman continued, raising her chin to reveal a set of emeralds whose vulgar splendor caused Henry to avert his gaze. "I have only to look in a person's eyes, and I know his character." She cast a flirtatious glance in the direction of the handsome young man sitting next to Wilde, who raised an eyebrow back.

"I question your infallibility, madam," countered Wilde. "The best actors are always the best villains. And evil often comes in seductive guises. Think of Duessa in Spenser's *Faerie Queene*, her monstrous nether parts hidden under beautiful drapery."

"Nether parts—where?" demanded the elderly gentleman, excitedly.

"I have no idea what you are referring to, Mr. Wilde." The American woman shrugged. "But I am certain that it would not change my mind."

Henry drained his glass. There it was: the most dire attribute of the new money was its complacency. It wore its ignorance like a badge of honor.

"What do *you* think, Mr. James?" asked the woman to his left. He wished she would leave him alone, though she was to be commended for valuing his opinion. He took a sip from the glass in front of him that had been refilled. "I don't believe in the existence of evil *per se*."

He spoke slowly, taking care not to slur his words. "I believe that men, and women"—he nodded politely to the woman—"may be prompted to commit acts of thoughtlessness, even cruelty, in pursuit of some greatly desired object, and that repetition of such acts, given the persistence of certain influences, may create a kind of reflex of mind. The act, in short, grows habitual; the conscience dulls. One might call this the evolution of a depraved personality. But that would be an oversimplification."

"Everything for you is an oversimplification," noted Wilde.

"But you've written about evil, haven't you, Henry?" asked Gosse (if it was Gosse).

"Evil, as I conceive it, is in the effects of the action, not inherent in the perpetrator," Henry recited, surprised to be able to put it so succinctly.

"Your position ignores the more heinous sorts of human cruelty," countered Wilde. "The Whitechapel murders, for example. Are you going to argue that the perpetrator is not an evil man? That his murders are the result of complex motivation?"

"It's not the sort of thing that interests me," said Henry shortly, starting in on the oysters that had made an appearance on his plate.

"You are wrong not to be interested in those poor women," said the female to his left. "That's precisely why they continue to be killed. If it was one of us, the perpetrator would have been caught long ago."

Henry thought that his sister, Alice, would say the same thing, and the thought momentarily humbled him. He bowed his head, finishing the oysters and watching as a portion of sweetbreads au jus replaced them.

"The police think the Whitechapel murderer is at large, mixing among us," said the handsome young man seated next to Wilde.

"He's a lunatic!" declared Du Maurier (was George here? mused Henry; had they come together?) "You've read the letters he wrote to the newspaper. No sane man would write with such odd taunts and turns of phrase."

"On the contrary." Wilde took this up. "The letters suggest a literary side to the fellow. But then, all of us literary fellows are mad, aren't we, Henry?"

Why must Wilde ask such questions? Henry thought with irritation. He waved away the asparagus that was being offered by the boy at his elbow, but allowed a small helping of the potato salad. "I'll admit that we all have our peccadilloes," he responded finally, "but some of us are more excessive in that way than others." He cast a disapproving glance at Wilde's foppish waistcoat.

"But excess is a matter of context," protested Wilde. "You are, in certain contexts, as excessive as I am. The number of words you employ, for example. True, you are subtle, but there is lunacy in subtlety. Perhaps our murderer is being subtle too, if we only knew the context in which he is operating."

"Now you're being too subtle for me," said Henry, finishing the potato salad and wishing he had taken more.

"The letters to the papers are certainly curious," noted Du Maurier, returning to this point. "Whoever heard of a murderer naming himself Jack the Ripper? It's almost comic, in a morbid sort of way."

"Yes," acknowledged Wilde, "the man has a dramatic flair."

"And some of his locutions," continued Du Maurier. "The 'ha ha' that he puts in the letters, for example, taunting in the most unambiguous terms. It makes one's skin crawl."

"It reminds me of Whistler's laugh, you know," said the young man next to Wilde, winking at the American woman. "He laughs like that: 'ha ha.'"

"Quite true; that's Whistler," agreed Wilde. "You do it well." He nodded approvingly at the young man. "Let me try. 'Ha ha.' You do it better. Do it again."

"Ha ha," repeated the young man.

Everyone laughed.

"Where is that great pretender?" asked Du Maurier. "I mark a distinct absence of preening in the room."

"He's on his honeymoon in Paris," said the young man. "He married his architect's widow, Beatrice Godwin."

"Beautiful Beatrice, rich as Croesus," intoned Wilde.

"Shaw is an ass!" asserted the elderly gentleman suddenly.

"We're not speaking of Shaw, but of Whistler, Monty," corrected Wilde.

"Whistler is an ass too," put in Du Maurier. "Keep him away from me."

"That shouldn't be a problem," proffered the young man next to Wilde. "After his honeymoon he intends to settle in Paris, where he feels he will be more appreciated. It's a commendable plan, in my opinion. His art has swayed too far toward the Japanese, and he needs to be recalled to the French influence."

Henry glanced at the young man for voicing such an informed opinion. He could not place him, but then, his mind was jumbled; a headache had set in. He had a meringue à la crème on his plate along with a chocolate crème and a maraschino jelly. Was he eating too much? Alice maintained that he was and was growing stout. "Corpulent" was the term he preferred. He motioned for the champagne, which he imagined might settle his stomach.

The cheeses had made their appearance, and the sardines. "No sardines, please; they disagree with me." Why had he said that? It was more than a servant needed to know. He was always doing that—saying too much. He ought to be more reticent, especially with the servants.

Wilde had embarked on another subject. "We must have a dramatic evening next time," he proposed, and with a nod to the young man beside him: "We can do our music hall turns."

"But will there be more murders?" asked the American woman, who obviously had no interest in music and preferred the more macabre topic.

"Undoubtedly. If this Ripper fellow is caught and put out of commission, then someone else will have to take them up. Your response is indicative, madam. We have come to view the murders as entertainment. Of course, to keep us interested, they will have to become more gruesome."

"Oh no!" exclaimed the pretty, impressionable woman.

"Sadly, yes," said Wilde. "It is in our nature to enjoy atrocity so long as it continues to shock and remains comfortably removed from our own lives. It takes an exceptional sensibility to feel beyond the parameters of self. I know very few so constructed, and I am not one of them."

Henry acknowledged to himself that he was not either, though his sister, Alice, was. "An apricot," he instructed the boy who was holding the platter of fruit off to the side. It occurred to him, as the apricot was placed on his plate, how much the servants would enjoy the leftovers. So much food! Would they carry it off to their homes? Where did they live? In the East End, where the murders had happened? And what, he wondered, did this boy's mother do—washing or sewing or something less reputable? He would not think about it. "A touch of the Madeira," he instructed the boy.

The ices were being served, and he noted, with a leap of pleasure, that they had pineapple cream, his favorite.

"Will they catch him?" inquired the American woman. "Will he be brought to justice?"

"Justice," Wilde sneered. "What is justice?"

"The gallows, I should think."

"Perhaps they will find him if he is a crazed lunatic and bring him to the gallows—but is there justice in that? What would a lunatic care or know about being hanged? And if he's not a lunatic, then no doubt they won't catch him. It's an unsatisfying set of alternatives."

"You should write about it, Mr. James," insisted the woman to his left.

"I don't write about such things," said Henry. "They are too—"

"Vulgar." Wilde completed the thought.

Henry did not disagree. His work was a means of keeping the more unseemly aspects of life at bay. Each member of his family had found a way to do this: his older brother through theoretical constructions, his younger brothers through the anesthetic of alcohol and gambling, his sister by taking to her bed. Overall, he preferred his own method: the evasion of art.

He began to eat his ices and tried to make his mind focus on where he was, but he felt dizzy, and the rumblings in his stomach distracted him. He had had too much wine; the sweetbreads (unless it was the oysters) had disagreed with him. He wished he were in his rooms in De Vere Gardens, where Mr. and Mrs. Smith, his invaluable servants (with whom he must learn to be more reticent), would put him to bed. Tomorrow he would work. He had a new project in view—a story about a couple who existed in ghoulish symbiosis, one sapping energy and personality from the other. Marriages, as he had observed them, were brutal arrangements; he was glad he had no truck with them.

But—his mind darted beyond the complacent thought, as it so often did in its drive to complicate—*who* was exempt from brutality? His own imagination was brutal; no knives or hatchets, but brutal nonetheless. He knew it was so, thinking of what he did. In his own way, he knew all about hacking to pieces. Which was why the murders in the East End, horrible though they were, did not shock him. They had their source in the same kind of anger and fear and resentment that coursed through him. He had learned to control such things, to channel them by putting pen to paper. But that excess of words, that devotion to subtlety, wasn't it, in its own way, mad? Yes, much as he hated to agree with Wilde, he knew that lunacy was a matter of context, and the line separating the novelist and the murderer was not as great as one might think.

CHAPTER 2

HENRY OPENED HIS EYES with a start. He had dozed over his ices, and he now saw that the table had been cleared. A few disorderly souls were loitering in the corner of the room, but the other guests had already taken their leave and dispersed into the night.

He rose and made his way unsteadily to the side door. His stomach had begun to rumble loudly, making him eager to exit the premises as quickly as he could.

Gosse's manservant opened the side door at Henry's request (but wasn't Gosse's man portly, while this one was spindly and with an insinuating eye?).

"Pressed for time," he muttered as he stumbled out. "Relay thanks to the host—or hostess."

Did Gosse's man wink at him? Servants were getting cheeky these days. His own, though not entirely reliable, were not cheeky—at least he didn't think so.

He moved quickly out of sight of the smirking manservant. He would find a hansom cab to take him home, but first he would walk, to clear his mind and settle his stomach. He should never have eaten the oysters.

He began moving briskly, in itself a novelty, since he was generally slow and sedentary, at his desk writing or driving about with women, but pains had erupted in his stomach, inspiring an urge to quicken his pace.

What if he had to—? Why had he not remained inside, where he could have—?

Perhaps he would vomit. That would be preferable—the lesser of evils, so to speak. The reality of his physical being, that whole unseemly apparatus of human plumbing, pressed itself on his consciousness. He felt a piercing pain in his abdomen that put him in mind of the stabbings discussed over dinner. Those women in the East End, their bowels ripped open, were horrible to think about. Yet now he must think about bowels, as he felt the pain ripping him from the inside. Was all suffering the same, indigestion as intense as the cut of a knife? The body was the great leveler. A thought to be pondered, though not now.

He would have to rid himself of the contents of his stomach; the certainty of this gripped him. He looked around at the well-appointed houses and neatly swept stoops he was passing. If he were in Mayfair, he might find his way to St. James Park, where he could locate a spot behind the shrubbery to do his business. The prospect of relieving himself, unseemly though it was, made him walk faster, and soon he could see that he had left the manicured streets and entered a new and unfamiliar area.

There was no greenery here. He had not been in Mayfair, perhaps, but in Chelsea or Bloomsbury, which abutted less pleasant parts of the city. Indeed, he was walking on a street that had little to recommend it. The lamps were fewer, and the curbs were mostly piles of rubble. What he could see of the houses were low, mean structures, their shutters broken, with little show of light inside. There was more movement on the street, however, though not festive movement; figures skulked and jostled up against him. He could not make them out but did not like the look of them.

He became aware of foul odors emanating from the pavement. Garbage was strewn about, and he stumbled over trash, his foot landing squarely in a pile of offal. The stench wafted up to his nostrils and made his stomach turn over more violently. He realized, to his horror, that his bladder had leaked, and the front of his trousers was wet. Disgust at his own person took hold; he was at the mercy of his body. A greater awareness then gripped him: he was at the mercy of his surroundings as well. He glanced at the low buildings and skulking figures and then at the narrow, trash-strewn streets, hoping to hail a carriage, but no vehicle was in sight. He had always sought control, in his life and his writing, but here he was, suddenly alone in a strange neighborhood, his mind clouded by wine, the figures around him alien and threatening. The sense of exposure, the sort of quivering vulnerability that he had always sought to avoid, swept over him, causing him to shudder violently. "Fine gentleman on an errand," he heard someone call out. "What's yer hurry?"

He ought to slow down. He was drawing attention to himself, walking so fast. But he couldn't. The stabs of pain in his abdomen were intense and the waves of nausea coming more quickly.

These people must hate him, he thought, lowering his head. Wasn't he portly and prosperous looking? Why shouldn't they want to rob him, or worse, take a knife and cut into his soft belly? What had they to lose? If only he felt more like himself, he could show his authority in his bearing and, if necessary, his speech; these people were cowed by authority. But in his present state, he could not walk properly or speak or even think about anything but the terrible uproar inside him.

"Don't run away, Mister." A woman's face, bloated with drink and garishly painted, appeared in front of him. Despite the cold, she was wearing practically nothing, her breasts pushed up like mottled melons from a tattered corset. He tried to shove her aside, but she held tight to both his arms, and her face and body, rancid with the odor of sex and sweat, pressed up against him.

"No," he muttered, "not interested."

"I kin make you interested, sir; just you gi' me a second." She rubbed against him forcibly, and with the pressure on his belly, he felt a lurch of nausea that caused him to retch, spilling the contents of his stomach—oysters, sweetbreads, the lot of it—on to her breasts.

The woman jumped back with a shriek. "Pig! Filthy pig! Look what he done, puking his dinner on me! Fine gentleman, got me filthy with his puke!"

People on the street turned around to look. Henry tried to move away but felt the woman block his passage, continuing to scream and point, the colorful stew of his vomit dripping from her front.

A man with a cap pulled low over his ears appeared, elbowed the shrieking woman aside, grabbed Henry by the arm, and pushed him to the ground. He felt the mud and gravel against his cheek as he lay facedown on the pavement, waves of nausea surging through him. The man with the cap tried to get into his pockets, and instinctively, Henry clutched the watch chain that had been his father's, holding it close to his body and refusing to be turned, as he continued to retch onto the pavement. His body was in such a state of upheaval, under assault from without and from within, that his only thought was that this, certainly, must be the end of his mortal life.

Out of nowhere, a voice cut through the din. He could not make out the words, but he could hear the manner of locution: a gentleman's voice, refined but forceful. With it, the chaos in which he had been engulfed receded. The woman's screaming ceased; the hands that had been pulling at his jacket loosened and let go. He was helped miraculously to his feet and given a handkerchief to wipe his mouth. The door of a hansom cab was opened; he was handed in and asked his address; money was passed to the driver.

The next thing he knew, he was in front of his flat in Kensington.

The uproar in his bowels had begun to subside, and his head, though it ached badly, had begun to clear. He staggered from the carriage, the Good Samaritan's handkerchief still clasped in his hand. Through the haze of his returning consciousness, he noted that it was of very good cambric and wafted a faint scent of lavender.

CHAPTER 3

A YOUNG MAN MADE A clattering entrance into the small, airless room in Boylston Hall where Professor William James had just finished a lecture on English philosophy (Locke, Berkeley, Hume) at Harvard College in Cambridge, Massachusetts. The young man's tie was askew, and a light sweat had formed on his brow, evidence that he had been climbing up and down stairs looking for Professor James, whose academic interests had shifted so often over the past few years that no one seemed to know where in the Old Yard he could be found.

Now, having finally located the elusive professor, the young man thrust a missive into his hands and explained, between short breaths, that it had been delivered by special courier to the Office of the Dean that morning, where an immediate response was awaited. The letter, which William opened at once, given the importance that seemed to surround it, read as follows:

Office of the Commissioner
Metropolitan Police
Scotland Yard
4 Whitehall Place
October 1, 1888

Professor William James
Department of Philosophy
Harvard College
Cambridge, Massachusetts

Dear Sir:

It has come to our attention from a variety of reliable sources that you are engaged in important research in the new science of the mind. In light of this expertise, we find ourselves prompted to solicit your help. You have perhaps heard, through the reporting of your own newspapers and from your contacts abroad, of the cruel and repulsive Whitechapel murders, the devilish work of a creature (I hardly deem him a human being) who calls himself Jack the Ripper. Five murders of an especially ghastly and unusual sort have occurred to date, and there is every indication, according to our officers at Scotland Yard, that more such murders are likely to occur in the next several weeks. It therefore behooves us, in light of this possibility, to seek the aid of your scientific acumen, your training as a physician, and most significantly, your unique understanding of the human mind in its deviant manifestations, and request that you review the facts of this case with an eye to discerning what may have escaped the perception or eluded the understanding of our otherwise well trained and industrious investigators. We acknowledge that the failure on the part of our investigative body to resolve this case has caused some consternation among the general populace and has been a source of dismay to our governmental body at the highest levels. We feel, in short, that we must put aside any false pride, the excrescence of an undue nationalist sentiment, that might impede us from reaching across our national borders to a citizen of that young country which once fell under the beneficent domination of our crown.

We have enclosed relevant background material on the case for your perusal, along with a voucher for your passage on the Cunard Line, of which we sincerely hope you will avail yourself as soon as you receive this missive. Although we cannot reimburse you for your services to the degree that you no doubt richly deserve, please rest assured that the moral debt incurred by Her Majesty, by the prime minister, and by myself will, if you should be so gracious as to respond to our appeal, be great indeed.

I close in the hope that you may present yourself, as soon as it may be possible to effect a transatlantic voyage, at our offices in Scotland Yard, where you will be granted access to any and all information regarding this profoundly troubling and intractable case.

Yours sincerely,
Sir Charles Warren,
Metropolitan Commissioner of Police

CHAPTER 4

ALICE JAMES SAT PROPPED up by two pillows in the large wooden bedstead in her flat on Bolton Street, Mayfair. An autumn breeze lifted the curtains of the windows behind the bed, sending a pleasant chill into the room. The Japanese lacquered lamp on the bed table was lit, and a fire was in the grate, so that the walls flickered with a soft, pink-tinged glow.

Alice was not a pretty woman, but her face exuded intelligence and a good deal of unsentimental kindness. It was a round face, with the high forehead and deep-set eyes of all the James children. But her eyes were brighter and more alert than those of her brothers, which tended to a vaguer, more distracted gaze.

She was the most Irish of the children and, since settling in London, had acquired the hint of a brogue, as though intent on making her loyalties clear at once. She also voiced these loyalties directly whenever she could: her admiration for Gladstone, her passionate support for Irish Home Rule, and her outrage at the condition of workhouses and orphanages. She read three newspapers a day, received a steady stream of visitors, and wrote frequent letters to Parliament and regular entries in her diary. The rest of her time was spent prostrate from a headache, a fainting spell, or an attack of nervous palpitations. And since these debilities struck unexpectedly, she had found it convenient, except on special occasions (a birthday dinner for her brother Henry, an exhibition of John Singer Sargent's work) to remain in bed.

Today, though ensconced as usual in that place, she had gone to some trouble with her appearance. Her hair was neatly combed and shining from a special rinse that had been sent to her from Paris. She wore a crisply pressed nightgown with a bed jacket and night bonnet of white piqué. She was sitting up very straight against the pillows, her hands clasped tightly over the coverlet, as her eyes darted happily back and forth between the two visitors seated on either side of her bed.

On the right side, in an armchair angled to take in the view through the open windows, sat her brother Henry. There was a bandage affixed to the left side of his face, the result, he had explained brusquely, of an accident with his razor.

"Clumsy of you," noted Alice.

"Quite," said Henry.

Alice looked at him quizzically but said nothing. His uncharacteristic terseness suggested that there was more to the injury, but she knew to respect his privacy, as he knew to respect hers.

Ever since she had moved into this apartment on Bolton Street, a five-minute carriage ride from his rooms in Kensington, they had come to an excellent understanding of each other. As children, they were separated by an unbreachable wall of differing family loyalties. Alice had been assigned to her father and her oldest brother, William, and Henry had belonged to his mother and his aunt Kate. The division meant that they had viewed the world from different angles. As Henry observed, "It's as though, as children, we saw things lit from only one side, and that now, being together, we can see them completely illuminated. It's a special kind of binocular vision."

"We should use our binocular vision to do some good," Alice had noted, her sense of the suffering larger world being acute. "And think if we had William's vision too, how well we would see. We could solve the deepest mysteries!"

Now, miracle of miracles, William was with them! He had telegraphed a few days earlier that he was making the crossing, without specifying why, and had burst in upon them that afternoon, greenish and disheveled from a bout of seasickness, but full of his usual nervous exuberance. After embracing Henry (with a concerned nod to the bandage and an amused pat to his brother's waistline), he had pulled a chair up to the other side of Alice's bed and examined her closely for a few moments. She was reminded that he had trained as a physician, though he had never formally practiced medicine.

"You look very well," he finally concluded after studying her.

Alice laughed. "You should never tell a professional invalid she looks well. It's the last thing she wants to hear."

"But you do. You look the best I've seen you look since Father died."

"It's living near me," Henry boasted.

"Or away from me," noted William wryly.

Alice waved her hand, pleased to be fought over but not wanting to see her brothers begin their familiar sniping. "First," she asserted, "I'm not well. Second, if I am, it's not because of either of you; it's the London air."

"So American air isn't good enough for you?" demanded William. "There's nothing better than American air. It's the best air in the world!"

"The problem," Henry soberly addressed his brother, "is that American air is *too* good. Alice and I can't take it. We need to breathe our air second-hand in the conservatory and the drawing room."

"That's ridiculous," said William.

"Whether the air is good or bad is not a subject worth quarreling about," interceded Alice. "I'm just glad you've come. I never feel entirely myself when I'm not with you both. The three of us are like an old plate that was broken and glued back together. You see the cracks and know you can't use the plate, but when you see it on the shelf, it's a joy to behold."

"I like that." Henry nodded.

William considered the metaphor. "I admit we're all damaged—cracked, if you insist on putting it that way. We've all had our share of…" He paused, searching for the right words.

"Desperation, despair, and doom?" suggested Henry.

"Yes." William nodded gravely. He had indeed had his share of these things—his long black moods when he couldn't work or even read a book. There had been one episode of true madness, followed by the long years of wandering in the wilderness, fleeing from his first career as a painter, giving up on medicine. But in the end, he had found his way, turning his own warring impulses into a subject of study, transforming weakness into strength. He had married, had children, and settled into a productive life. Given his own success, he was convinced there was hope for others. The mind, no matter how wild or resistant, could be trained or willed or seduced into some sort of compliance.

"But there's no reason for you to be in bed." He completed his thought, peering down at his sister disapprovingly. "We've ruled out a physiological basis for your illness. It's purely a case of mental adjustment. I've been developing ideas that might be useful to you, habits of thought—mental gymnastics, so to speak—that can alleviate the tendency toward pathological thinking and which, combined with diet and exercise—"

"It looks bad for his reputation that you won't get well," interrupted Henry. "He's supposed to be an expert on the mind, but he can't cure yours. It's like the shoemaker's children having no shoes."

William ignored his brother's remark and continued. "I see no reason why you should *resign* yourself."

"I don't *resign* myself," said Alice impatiently. "I just don't care to do mental gymnastics. I don't have the stomach for it, or rather, the head. Besides, you both have your vocations; I won't be cured of mine."

"She has a point," noted Henry. "She has everything she wants within reach; everyone comes to her. And she is free to say whatever she pleases, since an invalid is granted complete latitude. As I see it, she has arranged things beautifully."

William glared at his brother. "It's ridiculous for her to stay in bed all day; don't try to make it sound creative. It may be fine for your novels, but in life we want people walking around." He turned to his sister. "I have several ideas that may get you on your feet—"

"You will never get me on my feet."

"You were fine after Mother died."

"I had to take care of Father."

"So you stay in bed because no one needs you to take care of them?"

"That would be too simple."

"Henry needs you."

"Henry has never needed anyone. He has his work; his characters are his family. The rest of the time, he has his admirers, mostly women of a certain age who serve very good dinners. As for you, William, you ceased to need me when you married your Alice."

There was a momentary silence as the brothers exchanged glances. William had married an appropriate woman. Their mother had practically picked her out—she even had the same name as his sister. It was as close to marrying inside the family as one could get. And yet it wasn't. Alice James had had her first breakdown soon after William's marriage; Henry had fled to Europe; Wilky and Bob had begun their downward spiral into depression and alcoholism. But it wasn't "William's Alice" (as they referred to his wife inside the family) who had done it. It was *all* the things that had happened: the trauma of civil war, the need to find useful work, the simple fact of growing older. It was change itself that was to blame. The family was not a sturdy artifact, not even a simple breakable one like a plate. It was a supremely intricate and fragile structure, so intricate and so fragile that any change of pressure or temperature was bound to make it crack. Not that it was a bad thing. Henry, of all the children, saw this fact most clearly. If the family had not given him up, if the seismic shift had not happened, he would never have written a word, never have felt the need to create imaginary worlds to replace the world of his childhood.

Alice quickly moved to reassure William. "But you were right to marry. Sisters are fine for a while, but a man wants a wife and children. Except Henry, of course. He doesn't go in for that sort of thing. And me."

"You could have married," noted William glumly. "You still could. There's Norrie's son; he always liked you."

Alice snorted. "Norrie's son! No one can stand him! Why is it people think women will share their beds with men they wouldn't want to sit next to at dinner? But Norrie's son aside, marriage holds no appeal for me. I wouldn't marry if the man were…" She tried to think of someone who would be impressive to marry. "The Prince of Wales or even John Sargent, if he asked me. And John, if not the prince, is one of the pleasantest men I know."

"John doesn't go in for marriage either," noted Henry.

"That's true," agreed Alice. "Nor his sister, which may be why we like them both so much. But I'm speaking hypothetically, to make the point that I am not interested in marriage or anything associated with a normal life in the world. Please don't argue with me about it anymore."

William knew from her tone that the subject was closed.

There was silence among them for a few moments as Alice arranged the pillows behind her head, pulled the coverlet up under her arms, and took a sip from a glass of port on her bed table. "Now," she finally said, turning to William, her eyes growing brighter, "tell us why you are here. Your Royal Society lecture isn't until January. Have you been invited to give another talk?"

"No." He spoke carefully. "It's a different kind of invitation. A very unusual one."

"Tell us!" said Henry.

"Yes," said Alice, "tell us!"

William reached into his vest pocket and extracted the letter from Police Commissioner Warren. He passed it to Alice. Henry shifted to the side of the bed and positioned himself so that he could peer at the letter over her shoulder.

They read for a few minutes in silence. "Extraordinary!" Henry finally exclaimed, adding, "I trust the fellow is more adept as a policeman than as a literary stylist."

Alice, however, was not amused. She sat up very straight against her pillows and spoke quietly. "I've read about the Whitechapel murders and been dismayed by the lack of progress the police have made on the case. But now, finally, they have done something right; they have sent for you, William. It is a surprising step but an astute one, and I commend them for it. We can now stop these poor women from being killed."

Henry and William glanced at each other and then exclaimed together, "*We?*"

"Yes." She nodded. "It occurred to me, as I read William's letter, that the solution to these horrific crimes requires the three of us. 'Tri-ocular vision,' I would call it." She paused, as if working out an equation. "Henry, to observe the social world where I sense the murderer lurks and to plumb his friends and acquaintances for gossip. William, to study the physical evidence through his contact with the police and to supply psychological analysis where needed."

"And *you?*" William asked in amused wonder. "What will *you* do?"

"*Me?*" She leveled her intelligent gaze at her brothers. "I will review what you gather…and solve the case."

CHAPTER 5

THE MORNING AFTER HIS arrival, William rose early, washed, dressed, and took his own breakfast in the small kitchen of Henry's flat. He had agreed to stay with his brother for fear of giving offense, and Henry had insisted that he stay for the same reason. Both would have secretly been happier had he stayed somewhere else.

Outside in the gray London morning, he waved down a hansom cab and asked the driver to take him to Whitechapel. It was still too early for his appointment at Scotland Yard, and he thought it might be profitable to use the time to visit the scene of the murders.

"Doing a little sightseein', sir?" asked the driver as they pulled up to the corner of Whitechapel High and Commercial Streets at the heart of the district. William did not answer. It rankled to be mistaken in his motives, perhaps because he suspected those motives himself. Yet he was always suspecting his own motives, wasn't he? It was how his mind worked; it was what lay behind his best accomplishments: the drive to prove that he was not the dubious sort of person he secretly imagined himself to be.

As he stepped out of the carriage and began to walk, he was struck by the contrast of this part of the city to the area from which he had come. Kensington was sedate and extremely quiet. Whitechapel was full of chaotic life and noise, its streets teeming with fish peddlers and flower girls, organ grinders and men with placards advertising the latest music hall attractions. It occurred to William that some of the people hurrying around him might have known the murdered women, given them a farthing out of pity or shared a drink, or even consorted with them for pleasure. Perhaps the murderer himself was brushing past at this very moment or standing in the shadow of a building, seeking his next victim.

He proceeded briskly for another block down Whitechapel High Street. Away from the main thoroughfares, he could see more clearly the squalor and human misery that pervaded the area: the dark, airless alleys where men and women were leaning against walls or lying on the ground, their senses dulled by drink or opium. Soot and horse offal were piled in the courts between the tenements, whose doors were open to provide a bit of air. Inside, the dim interiors were like rabbit warrens, crammed with people lying on sacks or piles of straw. Even passing quickly, William was repelled by the odors that wafted out—damp and mildew mixing with the reek of excrement from unemptied chamber pots and stopped-up privies.

He turned into a narrow alley marked Mitre Square. The map Warren had sent indicated that Catherine Eddowes, the last Ripper victim, had been killed and mutilated here. As he approached the end of the alley, he saw that a pail was positioned near the curb with a ragged sign propped in front, on which was scrawled "On this spot Katie Eddowes was merdrd. Arms for her chilren."

"Arms for her children." William felt a welling of sadness. Newspaper accounts had reported that all the victims had once been married, though abandoned by their husbands because of drink and dissipation. Had there been children too? In the areas through which he had passed, he had seen many children, filthy and neglected, holding hats or with cupped palms, begging a few farthings from passersby. His throat tightened at the memory of his own child, his little Hermie, who had died of whooping cough before his first birthday. Then, with the rapidity of morbid association to which he was prone, he was seized by guilt for having left his other children, as he so often did, to pursue his work, and also, he acknowledged to himself, to escape the suffocating intimacy of family life. He shook himself, as if determined to throw off the weight of debilitating thought, and then dug into his pocket and dropped a coin into the pail for the Eddowes family.

There was a hollow ring as it struck the metal. If there had been other coins there before, they were gone now, as this would be too, within the hour, he thought. Was he being unjust in assuming this fact? His sister would say that poor people were not more dishonest than other people; they were simply poorer and therefore obliged to steal.

Walking back to Whitechapel High Street, he turned onto Mansell Street, where shops with Hebrew letters on the windows lined the road. Groups of men in long coats and skullcaps stood mumbling in corners, and women in head scarves hurried by, holding the wrists of children who had ringlets covering their ears. He walked briskly through the area and paused only near a collection of bookstalls that had been set up in one corner of the street. A scattering of fashionable young men were looking through the volumes, hoping to find that rare edition of Milton's sonnets or Dryden's plays that had escaped the professional estate brokers. William was tempted to join them in browsing, but it was approaching the time for his appointment at Scotland Yard. Instead, he motioned to a hansom cab that had parked across the street, as if waiting for him to decide to leave the area. How often, he wondered, did men like himself visit here to indulge some secret vice and then motion to a cab to whisk them away?

CHAPTER 6

THE ADMINISTRATIVE HEADQUARTERS FOR the London police was situated among other unimposing gray buildings surrounding a barren courtyard. The one exception to the drab scene was a large, well-appointed barouche parked in front, the letters *CW* carved in gilt on its door. William assumed the barouche belonged to Sir Charles Warren, the London police commissioner.

As William entered the foyer of the building, he noted that the paint was peeling from the walls, and the gas fixture on the ceiling was crooked and emitted very little light. The general air of shoddiness surprised him. In America, the police headquarters for a major city, no less the country's capital, would be immaculately maintained, a signal to the citizenry of a zealous and energetic attitude toward the eradication of crime.

"I'm here to see Commissioner Warren," he explained to the officer seated behind a battered desk.

"Sir Charles is in conference," the officer responded curtly, barely glancing up from his paperwork.

William took a step forward and cleared his throat. "I am Professor

James of Harvard College with an appointment to meet with Sir Charles Warren. I have just made the crossing from America at his request."

The response was immediate. "Terribly sorry, sir!" The officer pushed his papers aside and spoke obsequiously. "I'll inform Sir Charles at once." He scampered off, supporting William's hypothesis that, for the English, the propensity to be supercilious was equaled by the propensity to grovel, and that both behaviors emanated from the same place.

The man returned quickly and ushered William into a room very different in its appearance from the shabby outer area. Two men were seated at a polished mahogany table. There were gilt-framed portraits on the walls and a green and gold damask drape on the window. The table had been set out with a silver tray, on which was placed a bottle of whiskey and an assortment of sandwiches.

The man at one end of the table had a red face, a large, overly waxed mustache, and a well-tailored uniform with a profusion of ribbons and medals. He was seated comfortably in an upholstered chair, pouring himself a glass of whiskey as though he was in his club or at home in his drawing room. William was reminded of the pictures he'd seen of British officers camping out in style in the African bush.

On the other end of the table sat a small man with a neatly trimmed mustache. He wore shirtsleeves slightly worn at the cuffs. It was hard to tell from his expression what he was thinking, but his back was very straight, and there was the slightest suggestion, given his position on the edge of the chair, that he wished to be off doing something else.

"Ah, the American professor," said the large man, raising himself partially from his seat and extending a hand, not very far, so that William had to lean forward to reach it. "Charles Warren here. We greatly appreciate your willingness to cross the Atlantic to assist us. I was just telling Inspector Abberline here that we would do well to send more men to interrogate in the East End, where, I'm sure, our perpetrator lurks in some tawdry hovel or musty cellar. My own speculation leads me to assume that he is a barber or perhaps an indigent surgeon or butcher, given the testimony of Dr. Phillips, our esteemed police surgeon, on the expert way in which these poor women were dispatched."

William thought he saw a grimace skim the features of Abberline.

"Be that as it may, our attorney general has instructed us to pursue even the more remote avenues of possibility. To this end, we sent for you. Inspector Abberline spoke highly of your work in…the area in which you work…and assures me that your expertise could, conceivably, be helpful. We must, in short, leave no stone unturned."

William nodded his head. "Your obedient stone," he said gravely and caught a flicker of amusement cross the face of Abberline.

"What's that?" said Warren, who had been refilling his glass, which he raised to William before he could respond. "Some spirits, sir, after your arduous journey?"

"No, thank you," said William. "Given that I am on an abbreviated visit, I should like to begin work on the case at once."

"Certainly, certainly," said Warren. "Inspector Abberline will tell you everything you need to know. You have my full approval to go anywhere and see anything. If nothing else, you will be able to report that you have been privy to the inner workings of the famed Scotland Yard. And don't feel undue pressure with regard to the case. It's a knotty one, you know, and if we do not solve it, it means only that it cannot be solved." At this, Warren rose to leave. "I am at your disposal, sir, should you need me," he said, "but Abberline here is a capable second." He gave a short nod in the direction of the inspector, who also rose from his chair. "No, stay where you are." Warren waved regally. "I shall have your men show me out."

As soon as he was gone, Abberline, who had seemed frozen in his upright posture until now, jumped up with alacrity and strode over to the closet, where he took out his coat. "I will take you to see her if you like."

"What's that—who do you mean?" asked William.

"Catherine Eddowes," said Abberline brusquely. "The last victim. You can still see her. She's been on ice for more than a week, and they plan to bury her tomorrow. It won't be pretty, but as you're a scientist with medical training, I thought it would be useful. I'm going over to the mortuary now."

William expressed eagerness to accompany the inspector and, after a short hansom cab ride, found himself walking through the dank halls of the London morgue. He was not unfamiliar with morgues. While in medical school, he had been lectured on muscular disease at the Boston City Morgue, and on the process of rigor mortis at the morgue of Harvard Medical School. But both places had been relatively benign settings, more reminiscent of a hospital or a laboratory, with scrubbed floors and whitewashed walls.

The London morgue was entirely different. The building was in a state of extreme decrepitude, the stone walls crumbling and mildewed. As William followed Abberline through the dingy corridors, a feeling of oppressive gloom descended on him. Hard as he tried to push the image from his mind, he was reminded of the nightmarish episode of his youth, when, lying in bed, he had sensed the presence of a monstrous creature, the very embodiment of undiluted evil, lurking in the corner of his room. That creature, though a figment of his deranged mind, had resembled a real figure he had once seen as a child, and that had impressed itself indelibly in his memory. He had been walking with his father on a street in New York when he had noticed a young man, practically naked, huddled at the side of a building. The man was shivering and covered with sores, and when they had approached nearer and were about to pass him by, the man had suddenly bared his teeth and growled with animal ferocity, turning his face upward so that it seemed to engulf William's vision. The image had engraved itself on his consciousness, so that he never forgot it. It had returned in his illness and, since then, had presented itself to his imagination as what the devil must look like, the devil in the form of a ferociously desperate and suffering human being.

It was just such a figure, he thought now, that had lain in wait for the poor women of Whitechapel, and he was about to see one of these women after she had been visited by this diabolical creature.

For a moment, he felt prompted to tell Abberline that he must turn back; he could not view the body after all. But as soon as the thought occurred to him, he knew that he would not act on it. His fears were psychic phantasms, and horrifying though they were, his rational will could dispel them. If he could face down his imaginary demons, then he could face the remnants left by what a real one had done.

The main area of the morgue was poorly lit, the air heavy with the odor of must and incipient rot. Death was palpable, not just in fact but in that more pervasive sense that reached out to include oneself. One felt not only that the people taken here were once alive and now were dead, but that this would be one's own fate too. It was rare that one believed, more than abstractly, that death would come, but here one understood, felt in one's bones and sinews the inevitability and certainty of it.

In the large dim room, two bodies were in the process of being "prepared." One, a young woman who had drowned, lay on a wooden plank, her nightgown still tangled with her limbs. Her long, lank hair covered most of her face. The very struggle that she had endured in the act of dying was there, dramatically rendered in her face and body. The other, an old man, lay on a table, wholly exposed to view. He was being washed down like a side of beef by an emaciated young man with an iron around his leg.

"Who's that?" asked William, glancing at the man, who appeared to be neither a nurse nor an orderly.

"One of our convicted felons," said Abberline matter-of-factly. "They do the rounds of mortuary duty, cleaning the corpses and whatnot."

William looked surprised. "Are they trustworthy for matters of such…delicacy?"

"That's debatable." Abberline shrugged. "If I could, I would discontinue the practice, but it's been mandated by Sir Charles as the most efficient use of criminal labor. It's had some unfortunate repercussions in this case, I should note. I was not here when the first victim was brought in, and it seems she was washed and her clothes discarded, valuable evidence lost. Since then, I've given strict orders that nothing be touched or done away with, but these people have a tendency to ignore what they're told."

William looked with distaste at the disreputable fellow washing the corpse and gazed around the room, with its worn and grimy appurtenances.

Abberline nodded, following William's gaze. "Yes, the facility is not good. But changes in this area happen slowly here. We make do with what we have. Step this way, please."

He led William through a small recess to another room, where bodies that needed to be specially photographed for purposes of record keeping were displayed before being removed for burial. This room was even more oppressive than the outer area, the sense of claustrophobic enclosure added to the foul odor of rotting corpse. As William entered, he noted that a curtain had been hung in the corner. Abberline walked over to it and then motioned to a chair in front for William to be seated.

"Best to get off your feet for this," he noted. "It's not a pretty sight, and I've found that viewers take it better sitting down."

William sat, and Abberline pulled the curtain.

The image took a few seconds to take in. At first it looked like a fancy leather jerkin was hanging from a hook, but a moment brought the recognition that it was not a coat, but a body suspended from a collar around the neck. It was Catherine Eddowes, who had been hung in this way for the purpose of photographic recording. What made the body hard to identify was the maze of stitching, where it had been reassembled, in light of the extensive slashing. Black thread crisscrossed the abdomen and breasts, the neck, and most grotesquely, the face, delineating the gashes that the murderer had made under the eyes. There was a zigzag of black thread at the left side of the head as well, where a severed ear had been reattached.

"As you see, she was cut up considerably," said Abberline without inflection. "None of the others were so extreme."

"Do you agree with Warren, that the cuts show…facility…in the use of a knife?" asked William haltingly, after taking a few seconds to gain his bearings. He concentrated his attention on the crisscross of stitches on the abdomen of Eddowes's body, which struck him, despite his limited experience with surgery, to be excessive for the purpose of removing internal organs.

Abberline walked over to the body and paused. "No," he said finally. "This is not the work of a trained surgeon or even a butcher. The cuttings are not directed toward the excision of the organs, though that is the result. They are largely gratuitous, vicious, and undirected, as far as I can see."

"But they seem to reflect a certain pattern," said William, forcing himself to stand and move closer to the body to examine the stitching, which seemed to move out in spokes from the navel. He kept his head down and tried to take small breaths from his mouth, not wanting Abberline to see that the mixture of the odor and the image before him was making him faint and nauseated.

"It's true the lines repeat themselves here," said Abberline, his finger tracing the parallel lines of the stitching, "almost like the killer were stabbing rhythmically, operating in a trance or a methodical sort of frenzy, which I suppose would conform to a certain style of lunacy. It's what may have caused the medical examiner to assume some sort of medical expertise. The slashes under the eyes, too, are symmetrical, and for no apparent reason. Dr. Phillips postulates that he may have had in mind removing the eyeballs, but then the slashes would have been higher up, and gouging rather than slashing would have been in order."

"It's a ghastly sort of evisceration," noted William, standing back and forcing himself to gaze squarely at the grotesque spectacle of the hanging body. "Perhaps the goal was to appall future viewers. Like us."

"It's possible." Abberline nodded. "The letters suggest an inclination to frighten and taunt. It's confusing and one of the reasons I thought that your psychological expertise might be of help."

William looked at Abberline and felt a wave of affection course through him. He knew that a portion of his regard for other people came from knowing that they held him in regard. He also knew he was not unique in this; most people responded well to those who responded well to them. It was how bonds beyond the family were established and how altruistic action often received its impetus. "I will do what I can," he promised.

The two men stood silently staring at the body before them. So strong was the underlying force of human physiognomy that, despite the massive mutilation, William felt he could discern what Catherine Eddowes had once looked like. She was about his age, in her early to midforties, and would have been an attractive enough sort of person, correcting for poor nourishment and dissipation. Indeed, it struck William, as he gazed at the figure before him, that he could make out not only what this person had once looked like as a woman, but also what she had looked like as a child before that. Perhaps he saw the child in the woman's corpse because his dead son was so present to his imagination. Or perhaps it was having just seen his sister and having recalled the child she once had been behind the bedridden woman she had become.

It occurred to him as well that Catherine Eddowes might have been such a child as his sister, a little girl who tagged behind an older brother, pushed aside when other, more enticing forms of entertainment diverted his attention. Girl children were often neglected and ignored, so it might have been with Katie Eddowes (hadn't the sign referred to her that way?), but with the added element of poverty to degrade her. As she grew older and began to develop as a woman, she would have been drawn to men for money and a fleeting sense of intimacy; the inevitable abuse would have followed. In her squalor and desperation, she would have turned routinely to strangers, and finally, to one who might have seemed kinder and more interested than usual. This man would have led her into a dark alley, where suddenly, his gentleness disappeared: a vicious look in the eye, a glint of a knife, and then the sudden pain of being cut, before the blankness of unconsciousness set in.

An imagined life and death for this woman flashed through William's mind, and he recalled the placard over the pail: "Arms for her chilren." If she had had children, where were they? Would they know that their mother was a grotesquely stitched corpse hanging from a hook in a London morgue?

He sat back down on the chair, leaning forward, his head in his hands, knowing that he was close to being sick.

Abberline stood respectfully silent for a few minutes. Finally he spoke in what was a surprisingly passionate tone for a man normally so formal and inexpressive. "It makes you wonder about the nature of human beings," he said. "Made in the image of the divine, they tell us in church, but no God made the one who did this."

William looked up. For all the disgust he felt at the image before him, he was roused to oppose Abberline's words. "I must differ with you there," he asserted with surprising force. "It is my conviction that a divine spirit exists in us all, which transcends—even redeems—such viciousness."

Abberline gave a dry laugh. "I'd like to believe you," he said, closing the curtain on Catherine Eddowes's corpse, "but I can't say I do."

CHAPTER 7

H AD PHILIP WILKINSON—HENRY crossed out "Wilkinson." *Something more Dickensian*, he thought.

Had Philip Wiltingham not been sent to Algate Market (check spelling) *by his wife*...No, not his wife. That would suck the life out of the character before the story got started.

Had Philip Wiltingham not been sent to Algate Market (check sp) *by his sister to buy the lamb chops for her dinner party that night, and had he not ducked into the building when he saw Joseph Donner* (Donning? better), *an insufferable bore to whom he had lost fifty pounds at cards*...too much information there, about the losing at cards.

Had Philip Wiltingham not been sent to Algate Market (check sp) *by his sister to buy the lamb chops for her dinner party that night, and had he not ducked into the building when he saw Joseph Donning, an insufferable bore to whom he owed fifty pounds, approaching in the other direction, he would never have found the body.*

Henry paused and took his watch out of his pocket. It was after seven o'clock, time to prepare for dinner at...he must check his date book to see where he was invited to dinner that night.

He put down his pen and surveyed the parlor of his flat, where his desk had been set up in the corner. The room was to his liking, with its silvery damask chairs, pale gray wallpaper, and long, elegantly draped windows.

He got up and crossed the room, touching the peonies in the vase on the mantel and straightening the bust of Benjamin Franklin that William Dean Howells had sent him as a reminder of his American roots. It was dusty, Mrs. Smith being remiss again. He proceeded to his room, passing the spare room that William was occupying during his stay. He could see that clothes were strewn on the floor and the daybed was unmade.

He went into his dressing room and rinsed his face in the china bowl with its sprinkling of wilted rose petals (not replaced, he was dismayed to note, since the morning). He changed into his dress shirt, taking care with the fastening near his neck where he had once pinched himself and drawn blood. He chose a dark gray waistcoat, black trousers, and a pearl gray cravat. He recalled the charcoal striped trousers from the other night, which he had to discard in the trash bin behind his building. No need to think about that.

He knew that Mr. Smith, retained in the combined role of valet and butler, ought to be on hand to help him dress. There was no denying that the two who served him, for all their exemplary qualities, were not up to par when it came to doing what they were hired to do. Secretly, however, he was pleased for the opportunity to dress himself. It was an aesthetic pleasure to put his outfit together—an elegant, leisurely assemblage of pieces, not unlike the assemblage of words in the construction of a well-turned sentence.

He chose the silver cuff links that had belonged to his father. He had worried that William would want them, but William did not appear to care. As they moved into middle age, his older brother had become even more oblivious, if possible, to everything except his work and, at sporadic intervals, his family. The patterns of their boyhood had persisted but mutated as well. William had always been the more daring and insouciant of the two, but Henry, once timid and negligible, had come into his own. He was proud to think that his brother occasionally took notice of how well regarded he had become in certain circles, how nicely his particular brand of courtliness conformed to the manners of the British gentry among whom he had chosen to live.

He heard the door open and a rustle of garments in the front hall. Mrs. Smith had come in. He glanced at his watch…late again. He must have a talk with her about her laxness with regard to hours—and other things. As for her husband, his chronic absence was certainly annoying, especially since he was being paid a considerable stipend to be present.

Henry walked tentatively into the front hall, where Mrs. Smith was busily hanging up her mackintosh and shaking out her umbrella. The umbrella was leaving a large puddle near the door.

"Don't worry, sir. I'll mop it up," said Mrs. Smith cheerfully. She was always promising to do things that she never got around to doing.

Henry looked at his watch and coughed. "Your husband is…indisposed?" he asked.

"He's walking Mary home," said Mrs. Smith blithely. "Worries himself sick with that Jack the Ripper loose. Can't say I'm not without worries myself. Mary's the age he likes, you know."

Henry considered this. "Doesn't Mary live in Lambeth?" he asked. "This Ripper creature…operates…in Whitechapel."

"For now he does," said Mrs. Smith, "but he'll be in Lambeth soon enough. He'll be wanting a wider berth."

Henry nodded at this geographic logic. "But he's killing women of a certain type," he added. "Mary's not…" He paused. Perhaps Mary was. He didn't know much about Mr. and Mrs. Smith's daughter beyond the fact that she was often their reason for being elsewhere. He had met her once. She was a blowsy, unkempt young woman; the word "slatternly" came to mind, which was why he had stopped himself so abruptly in noting that Jack the Ripper's victims tended to be of an unsavory sort.

"For sure, he's killing off those types now," said Mrs. Smith, as though she had access to the modus operandi of the killer. "They always start low and work their way up."

"Ah!" said Henry, wondering how far up Mrs. Smith imagined Mary was.

"These sorts aren't easily satisfied," Mrs. Smith continued sagely. "There's the lustful part, of course, but they don't go after us women just for that."

"No?" said Henry. He was uncomfortable with the line the conversation was taking but still eager to hear more.

"No," asserted Mrs. Smith. "It's for we're weaker and more sensitive-like, as sets 'em off. I once been with a man who beat me most every night, not 'cause I did him no harm, but as he thought to be rid of his own weakness that way. Couldn't be the man he wanted, so he blacked my eyes to make him feel strong. Thank God I got away afore he killed me. Mr. Smith'll drink himself to a stupor, but he don't see no need to beat me, God bless 'im."

Henry coughed uneasily, wondering if he was expected to praise Mr. Smith for this. Still, there was something to what Mrs. Smith said. "Manliness"—he disliked even the term—had always been a source of frustration and difficulty for him. He had found ways to cope, but he supposed there were others whose resources were less…developed.

"It's an interesting observation, Mrs. Smith," said Henry, nodding absently. "I'll have to tell my brother to consider it in his investigation of the case for Scotland Yard." He spoke without thinking, instinctively trying to assert his authority, only to realize that he had been dreadfully indiscreet; this was hardly a matter to be shared with a servant, or with anyone for that matter. Why couldn't he keep his mouth shut? Mrs. Smith's eyes had opened wide in hearing of William's involvement in the case, and Henry hurried to change the subject. "I'll be going out now, Mrs. Smith. I don't know when my brother shall be back, so please have his room made up as soon as possible."

"I was just about to do that," said Mrs. Smith with a touch of huffiness. "By the by, sir"—she resumed a more congenial tone—"there's a note dropped off for you yesterday by Mr. Wilde's man. I kept it with me for safekeeping." She reached into her pocket and drew out a small envelope, which she handed over with a flourish.

Henry removed the note from the envelope. It was an invitation to a dinner party next week at Wilde's club. At the bottom was a scrawled message. "Surprise guest!—and music hall turns, as promised." What was that about? Oscar was always making allusions to things one was supposed to know, but didn't. Though, of course, he would accept the invitation. Whatever surprises Wilde had in store, there was also sure to be good conversation and good wine—both tended to flow copiously in Wilde's proximity.

"Will you be dining at home tonight?" asked Mrs. Smith obsequiously.

She knew he was not dining at home, thought Henry; he had said he was going out and was dressed for the purpose—without the help of Mr. Smith, he noted to himself. But his mood had improved, and he was willing to play along. "No, no, not tonight," he assured her. "But please prepare something for my brother. No need to make a fuss. Professor James is parsimonious in his diet."

"As you like, sir," said Mrs. Smith, as though she would have been glad to prepare an elaborate meal. "I'll go make up his room now if you'll excuse me. I hope I'm not being forward to say this, sir, but it's a shame the professor don't share your habits." She cast a sly glance at Henry, who could not hide that he was pleased by the remark. He had always been neat, where his brother, to be frank about it, was slovenly.

After Mrs. Smith left the room, Henry took a cloth from the kitchen and wiped up the puddle from her umbrella. He then went to his desk, glanced down at the sentence he had written, crumpled the paper, and threw it in the basket near his chair. Why should he write about something like that? He had been instigated to do so because William was being so smug about working for Scotland Yard. And there was the lady at Gosse's (was it Gosse's?) who had encouraged him. His mind veered off. The ghastly events of that night remained cloudy in his memory. It was fortunate that his consciousness had been muted by drink (the irony of this was not lost on him), and that he was free of any vivid recollection of pain or fear that might have derailed his social relations or, worse, his work.

Yet something from that night nagged persistently at his memory. It was not the attack itself but something that had occurred earlier. He closed his eyes, trying to remember, but all he could summon up was a blur of faces around a table. If there was a germ there—the kind of hint that so often sparked his stories—he could not recall what it was.

No, he would not write about murder, but he would take an interest in the case and help where he could. The observations of Mrs. Smith had left an odd resonance. He felt a vague kinship with the murderer—he had felt this before, but when?—a sense that the impulses that drove this deranged creature to kill were not so very different from those that drove him to write. He had learned early on how to transform frustration into a fantasy of fulfillment, to turn life into art. To catch Jack the Ripper, he understood, was to effect a reverse transformation, to uncover the frustrated desires that found their perverse fulfillment in murder.

CHAPTER 8

WILLIAM AND ABBERLINE WERE seated in a small cubicle in Scotland Yard, where they had repaired following the viewing of Catherine Eddowes's corpse. It had been Abberline's idea to review the photographs of the other victims in the hope that William might see something of value that had been missed by the police. The inspector had become convinced that the key to solving the case lay not in material evidence but in something more ineffable—what was called, in certain circles, "the psychological aspect." It had been his idea to consult William, a suggestion agreed to by Sir Charles, a man always willing to be accommodating so long as he did not have to do any work himself.

Abberline took a folder from the cabinet and opened it on the table where he and William were seated. The folder contained photographs of the Whitechapel victims. There were two photographs included for each of the four murders: one of the victim found at the scene and one of the victim on a slab in the London morgue.

The first set of photographs was of Martha Tabram, killed August 7. In the one taken at the scene, the woman was sprawled on the ground, so drenched in blood it was impossible to tell where she had been stabbed.

In the second photograph, one could see clearly the crazy quilt of jagged slices to her abdomen.

"I'd like to eliminate this case from our investigation," said Abberline, pointing to the second photograph by way of explanation. "The stab wounds to the stomach are not symmetrical, as in the subsequent cases, and the weapon used appears to be a bayonet rather than a knife, which produces neater incisions. Finally, the throat wasn't cut, which appears to be the cause of death in all the other cases." He jabbed his finger at Tabram's neck with a certain violence, which indeed showed no mark, though the face itself was contorted in a terrible grimace. William looked away for a moment as Abberline continued. "There's a determination to see Tabram as the first Ripper murder, perhaps to ratchet up the number of his crimes, perhaps to alleviate the need to seek out another killer. It's an ongoing problem. The public, and many in authority as well, try to press into service acts of violence that are clearly the work of other hands. Pin it on this Ripper fellow and be done with it." He snorted contemptuously, as though familiar with the rationalizations and dodges of his colleagues.

William felt compelled to add another perspective. "It's human nature to want to find pattern," he noted. "Once we begin to think there is one, we are likely to see it reinforced. It's the drive to create order out of chaos."

Abberline, disinclined to this more forgiving view, had moved on to the photographs of Mary Ann Nichols, known as Polly, murdered August 31. He pointed to the relevant points in the morgue shot, speaking with authoritative coolness (William imagined Abberline had gone over these photographs many times already and had become numb to their horror). "Throat cut in simple execution style, symmetrical wounds to the stomach, opening of the abdominal cavity and exposure of the viscera."

He flipped to the third set of photographs of Annie Chapman, killed on September 8. "Throat cut. Symmetrical abdominal cutting. Exposure of viscera. Uterus removed." He paused to editorialize. "Our killer is becoming more ingenious…and more invasive. But the pattern, as you see, remains similar to the Nichols case."

He moved on. "Elizabeth Stride, killed in the early morning of September 30. Throat cut. That's all." He gave a dry laugh, as though struck by the irony of referring in such a way to a cut throat. "It might not seem to fit the pattern," he continued, "since there are no other mutilations, but it's clear that the murderer was interrupted in his work. Note the state and disposition of the body." He turned to the photograph taken in the morgue and pointed to where the victim's dress was ripped but not torn off the body, and then shifted to the photograph at the scene, where the body was shown slumped, face forward, suggesting it had been pushed down in haste. "What also supports this hypothesis, of course, is that the Eddowes's murder occurred less than an hour and a half later. Frustration at the earlier interruption would also account for the level of brutality here." He displayed the photograph of Eddowes on a slab in the morgue, which had been taken before the stitching up of the wounds. The head was twisted to the side, almost severed from the trunk; great flaps of skin were exposed on the face; and the abdomen was a thicket of standing flesh. The killer had carved up that area of the body with frenzied completeness.

Abberline droned out the details. "Throat cut, extreme and symmetrical cutting of the abdomen and the face, uterus and kidney taken away, left ear partially severed—something new there, suggesting that our murderer may have in mind additional variations to come." He had spoken without emotion, but a sigh escaped him at the prospect of what those variations might be. He quickly resumed his professional tone and moved on to conclude, "There are marked similarities in the pattern of cutting in Nichols, Chapman, Stride, and Eddowes, not to mention affinities in their age and occupation. They were all in their late thirties and early forties, all prostitutes. All were in dire physical condition, not necessarily underfed, but unhealthy. Our man likes to prey on weakness."

"Did the murderer commit on them acts of a…sexual nature?" asked William carefully. He was prone to prudery, despite his medical training, and had noted that his European colleagues were less tentative on this score.

Indeed, Abberline responded bluntly, "No. The women were found in suggestive positions, legs exposed and spread, but there was no indication of sexual intercourse, neither in vaginal tearing nor in the presence of the expected fluids."

"What you describe seems to suggest a desire to possess and penetrate these women, but apparently not in the sexual sense."

Abberline nodded. "Possibly a case of severed or maimed organs on the part of the killer."

"Perhaps," mused William, "but my sense is that he would not commit these acts unless some additional expressive route were inhibited or blocked. The form of the killings is indicative of more than sexual frustration. Or sexual frustration instigated by something else."

He gazed down at the photograph of Catherine Eddowes, with its grotesque flaps of skin, and thought of the stitched image he had seen in the morgue. Somehow the photograph was even more disturbing than the actual body. It was not a sharp image, yet the graininess contributed to the horror of its effect. He was reminded of the mourning photograph taken of his son Hermie before the burial, a carefully staged shot of his little boy tucked into bed, just as he might have been after he had been kissed good night. That picture, meant to be a beautiful keepsake, had given William terrible dreams, and his Alice had finally hidden it, for fear that it would precipitate another breakdown.

A photograph was a kind of haunting, he concluded, a representation of a reality not literally present. And the photograph of a dead person was a double sort of haunting. As for these murdered women, their photographs were also testimony of their society's neglect and abuse. Strangers would look at them years, perhaps even decades, hence and be haunted by them. It was a grotesque sort of immortality.

He was flipping back through the pictures, musing about these things, when a young officer entered the room, walked quickly over to Abberline, and whispered in his ear.

The inspector's face grew taut as he rose quickly from the table. "There's been another murder…or at least, the suspicion of one. I try not jump to conclusions, but it's imperative to investigate. You're free to come along."

He was already halfway out the door before William grabbed his hat from the hook and followed rapidly on his heels.

CHAPTER 9

THE TWO MEN ARRIVED by police carriage at the corner of Hanberry and Latham streets and descended with their destination still a block away. A large crowd had gathered in the vicinity, drawn by the rumor that another Ripper murder had taken place, and Abberline decided it would be faster to get to the scene on foot. While the inspector, whom the officers recognized, was ushered quickly to the front, William was left behind to make his way forward alone. As he moved through the crowd, he saw that a number of policemen were pushing people back in a brutal, unthinking manner. It struck him as an example of the psychological dimness that operated on so many levels in governance and that, left unchecked, could incite revolutions.

He explained his presence to one of the policemen, who took him by the elbow and led him through the crush of onlookers. There were catcalls of "Who's the fine gent?" and "What's he seeing Jenny for, when us who knew her can't get a glimpse o' the poor girl?" He finally made his way to the front, where a phalanx of policemen were attempting to shield the view in front of the alley where the body had been found, kicking away the smaller children who were attempting to peek through their legs.

William's escort said a few words to one of these sentinels, and an opening was provided for him to slip through.

He had already been shocked at the sight of Catherine Eddowes's stitched body and of the grotesque photographs that Abberline had shown him of all the victims, but what greeted him now was more deeply moving. It was death in its most profoundly immediate form. The chief inspector was standing with two officers, along with a white-smocked gentleman whom William assumed to be the medical examiner. They stood around the body of a young woman lying on the pavement near the alley, behind a row of tenements. One of the woman's legs was extended, the other leg bent. One arm lay near her body; the other was outstretched, the palm open. The posture was oddly graceful, almost balletic, and the effect was enhanced by the appearance of the face pressed to the pavement in profile. The dead woman could not have been more than thirty years old, with finely etched features and an abundance of auburn hair that lay spread like a luxurious drape to one side of her head. But what gave the image its most compelling aspect was that around the head and merging with the thick hair was an almost perfect circle of blood. There was no indication that the clothes had been disarranged or ripped, and from the angle at which the face lay, it looked entirely unblemished. William assumed that the woman's throat had been cut on the side on which she was lying, so that all one saw was the roseate halo of blood. She might very well have been a rather plain sort of person in life, but in death, laid out in this dramatic pose, there was something breathtakingly beautiful about her.

As he gazed at the body, he noticed that the outstretched arm was turned up, exposing a thick scar on the wrist above where the delicate fingers lay unclasped.

He approached Abberline, who was standing with the physician over the body.

"Sorry to have brought you out for this," said Abberline. "One of my men heard her throat was cut and assumed we had another Ripper murder on our hands. I encourage them not to make assumptions, but it's difficult, given the climate at the moment."

William looked down at the body again. "What happened to her?" he asked.

"Suicide," said Abberline succinctly.

"How do you know?"

"All the standard indicators: the disposition of the body, the knife found there." Abberline pointed to a spot where a mark had been made on the ground. Nearby, one of the officers was holding what looked like a medium-sized kitchen knife wrapped in a rag. "And of course, she's tried it before." He motioned to the scar on the woman's wrist.

"I see all that. But the method seems so unusual."

"Not really, among these people, sadly enough," noted Abberline, "though it's more the women who do it. The men drink themselves into a stupor and stumble under a carriage or fall off a bridge, but the women tend to be more efficient. It's a gruesome death, and it takes a sort of nerve. One almost has to admire them for it."

"But why did she do it?"

"Why? Not hard to find an answer to that. Because life got too hard, too much poverty and hopelessness. Look at the neighborhood. They say she wouldn't bring herself to do what so many of the others do—sell herself to live. So this is what comes of it. It's a sad state of affairs that when they can live by their bodies, they die at the hands of a lunatic killer, and when they can't, they die by their own hands."

The wagon had arrived to take the corpse to the mortuary, and several of the officers turned the body over. A kerchief was placed around her neck to hide the wound, and the woman was moved gingerly onto the cart. Something about her ethereal beauty inspired reverence and caused even the coarse officers to handle her gently and arrange her clothing carefully around her.

Several onlookers were speaking to Abberline, explaining that the woman, Jenny Stoddard was her name, was a ladylike sort of person, but too sad for this world. "There was the death of the first child," said one large matron with a gruff but not unkind manner. "She cried for months—too long to mourn a child. Then, when another came, we thought she'd rally, but she didn't. If anything, it made her worse, reminded her of the other one she'd lost. She did what she could for him at first, but her heart wasn't in it, and then she just stopped caring. The husband wasn't a bad sort, but he had no patience for her weeping. He took off. After that, she tried to do away with herself, but her boy found her, and they patched her up. But now, she done it, and it's just as well. He won't be no worse off with her gone than he was with her here, poor soul."

"Where's the child?" asked William, though as soon as he asked, he wished that he hadn't.

The woman pointed to one of the doorways, where a boy stood watching. He looked about ten, though he was undernourished, and William imagined he was probably a year or so older. His face was drawn and expressionless, but his eyes looked perceptive, and for a moment William thought he saw something like relief in them. Was it a relief to have his mother, perennially sad and useless, finally gone out of this world?

Looking at the boy made William's throat constrict. The thought of his own beloved and pampered child dead, and of this child, so neglected and impoverished, alive—what did it mean? Whose will was behind it? On what basis could William cling to the spiritual belief of which he had spoken to Abberline? Wanting to leave the scene, he nonetheless found himself walking over to where the boy was standing. "It's your mother there, I hear," he said gently, feeling it best to be direct.

The boy looked at him a moment before speaking. "She wanted to do it, and she done it," he finally said.

"I'm sure she's in heaven and at peace," said William.

"I dunno 'bout that," said the boy. "But she won' be crying no more. That's somethin'."

"And what about you? What will you do with her gone?"

"Same as I done with 'er 'ere." The boy shrugged.

"Did you live with her?"

"Naw, she coulden have me. Not much room in that basement she lived in, and it made 'er sadder to see me, so's I stayed with the ol' lady." He pointed to the top of the building in whose doorway he was standing. "She can't walk, so's I bring 'er things, whatever I can get 'er for dinner, and she lets me sleep on 'er floor."

"And how do you get money to eat?"

The boy shrugged again. "I dunno. I ha' my ways. And I don' eat much. I once had a job with one of them greengrocers, but he went out of business. The ol' lady says I'm smart enough to fin' somethin' respectable if I grows a bit. They don' like 'em as small as me for mos' things."

"I'm sure you'll grow to a good size," said William, wondering how the boy would ever grow if he didn't eat.

"Can I ask you somethin', sir?" said the boy, obviously feeling that he had met that rare creature, a respectable person who listened to him when he spoke, and that he ought to take advantage of it. "What's for me to do in the way of buryin' 'er? That's been on m' mind since they found 'er. She diden care for me, but it wasen her fault. She were still my mother. I want she be buried proper and not in one of them graves where they put all the bodies in a heap together."

William looked at the boy. He wished he could be rid of him and be alone, back in his study in Cambridge, Massachusetts, where he could lose himself in his books or, as he sometimes did, put his head on his desk and weep. His Alice was an exceptional woman who knew when to console him and when it was best to leave him alone. But here he was in the middle of London, and it wasn't the loss of Hermie or his own father and mother or the burden of his own existence that he had to deal with, but this poor soul with more misery than anything he had ever suffered. What was the use of all the philosophy he'd read and the thinking he'd done when confronted with so simple a piece of human misery? He drew a breath. "What's your name, boy?" he asked quietly.

"It's Archie, sir. They says as it stands for Archibald, after my dad, but I don' think on him, so I's as soon go by Archie."

"Well, Archie, I'd be glad to arrange for the burial." William tried to take a straightforward tone, so as not to seem to be acting out of some ulterior motive. "I'll tell the coroner myself that you want a proper funeral for your mother."

"But I can't pay nothin', sir," said the boy.

"It will be on loan from me," said William, sensing an awkwardness attached to his offering to pay outright. "You could pay me back and make more by doing some work for my sister. She isn't well, and it would be a source of special gratification to me if you could assist her with household chores. She lives in another part of town, though, and you may not know how to get there."

The boy's eyes grew bright. "There ain't a place in London I don' know, sir. I been to the poshest places—jus' to see what they're like," he hurried to explain. "You tell me where's to go to make a farthin', and I'll do it."

William scribbled Alice's address on a piece of paper and then paused before handing it over.

"I can read, if that's what you're thinkin'," the boy assured him. "The ol' lady taught me. You won't regret givin' me a chance, sir. I promise. I ain't gonna kill myself like my mum, so I'd just as well find some way to live."

CHAPTER 10

"THE MUTTON IS EXCELLENT," said Henry. "Cooked to perfection and seasoned superbly. The potato fritters are a nice touch too."

"You can thank Katherine for that," said Alice. "She supervises Sally in the kitchen and has taught her American cooking."

"Of course, in America they'd be corn fritters," noted William. "I love corn fritters, Katherine," he told the woman sitting next to him, who nodded placidly.

Katherine Loring was a tall woman in her midthirties, with a plain, pleasant face. Although she had no disposition to talk unless she had something to say, she did like to listen, making her an ideal companion to Alice, who had, in the course of the past few years, developed a fierce dependence on her. William and Henry understood that the relationship worked, apparently for both parties, and had tacitly agreed not to question it. The one exception, if it could be called that, was in Henry's recently published novel, *The Bostonians*, in which a female friendship was unflatteringly portrayed. When confronted, Henry had denied that his fiction bore any relationship to life, and Alice had decided to take him at his word or not care that he was lying. She and Katherine *did* exist in a possibly unhealthy symbiosis. William had once insinuated that she could not get well because it would deprive her friend of the job of nursing her. To this, she had responded, "It's expected in a marriage for the two partners to depend on each other in complementary ways. If I were a man, I could go out and do something in the world, and then Katherine could take care of me the way your wife takes care of you. But since I can't do that, I let her take care of me this way."

There was no countering such simple and elegant logic.

"You should teach Sally to make corn fritters," William counseled. "That is, if you can get corn in this country. Can you get corn here, Henry?" He turned to his brother.

"I really don't know, William. I am not the devotee of corn that you are."

"I'll have to ask John Sargent. I'm sure he likes corn."

Alice, who had barely touched the mutton or fritters on her tray and was instead nibbling on a piece of cake, cut the discussion short. "So the woman's death yesterday was suicide and not murder?"

William had tried to forget the image of the beautiful dead woman and had no wish to discuss what had happened, but he realized, suddenly, that he had forgotten to tell Alice about the boy. "The woman had a son," he explained quickly, "ten or eleven years old. A bright-seeming sort of boy, extraordinarily resilient and eager to be of use. I said you might have some errands for him to do." He spoke apologetically, realizing that Alice might find it presumptuous that he had made arrangements without asking her. "I know it's an imposition, but his situation is pitiful. He sleeps on the floor of an elderly cripple and scavenges for both of them. And with his mother dead there in front of his eyes—"

Alice cut him short. "Of course, you were right to send the boy to me," she reassured him with a wave of her hand. "There's not much work for him here, but I can always find something for him to do. He can wash down the front steps and scrub the walkway. Those tasks supply endless labor, since they are no sooner done than they have to be done again."

"So many things people do are useless," noted William. "Their only purpose is to demonstrate that one has the time to do them or the income to have them done."

"But it's the gratuitous that constitutes civilization," objected Henry airily.

"There is such a thing as too much of the gratuitous," countered William.

"And who's to determine what is too much?"

"We have only to follow Aristotle: 'Everything in moderation.'"

"I'm afraid that maxim would not produce much art," asserted Henry, growing more adamant. "One isn't likely to write or paint very well on a Fletcher diet." He was referring to the strict regimen of food and exercise that William and his wife followed and had tried to impose on him, needless to say, without success.

"To return to the subject at hand," said Alice, interrupting an argument that she knew was capable of producing hurt feelings on both sides, "tell us, William. Have you and your police inspector come to any noteworthy conclusions about this Jack the Ripper?"

William considered the question. He had returned to headquarters with Abberline after viewing the body on Latham Street and had met with Dr. Phillips, the divisional police surgeon in charge of the case. Phillips continued to forward the opinion that had been voiced by Sir Charles that the murderer had knowledge of anatomy. "The general belief is that he is a doctor, perhaps a coroner's assistant, or at the least a butcher," reported William. "Abberline and I disagree."

"You see no surgical acumen involved in the cutting?"

"No. Just because the bodies have been cut and organs removed does not necessarily mean that the murderer knew what he was doing. Indeed, the amount of *gratuitous* cutting"—he glanced pointedly at Henry—"suggests the opposite. What struck me upon looking at the poor mutilated body of Catherine Eddowes was that the wounds reflected no sense at all of the body in its depth, but a powerful if demented sense of the body as a surface. As Abberline pointed out, the knife follows in certain broad, repetitive strokes. They are utterly uneconomical with regard to surgical procedure, but they still reflect a kind of pattern, though not one proper to a doctor or a practiced butcher."

"So you're saying that the murderer may be viewing the body from a context which is not clinical but has its own logic."

"Precisely."

"A ritual murder, perhaps? Something with political or religious symbolism attached?"

"Possibly. There was the incident, which you may have read about in the papers, of a message written on the wall near the site of the Eddowes murder. It was a strangely worded piece of writing." William flipped open his notebook and thumbed through until he arrived at the desired page. "'The Jews'—spelled here, J-u-w-e-s—'are the people who will not be blamed for nothing.' Those were the words written on the wall."

"Perhaps the work of a Jewish cabal," Henry suggested.

"Please!" said Alice irritably. "It's obviously *not* the work of Jews, but of someone venting hatred against Jews."

"But the wording of the message *is* odd," said William. "It sounds like a formal proclamation."

"On the contrary," protested Alice vehemently, "its syntax is common to the lower orders of society."

"And how do you know that?"

"I know because I read the newspapers and listen to people." As she spoke, she picked up the little bell on her night table and rang it. "But I don't need to argue this with you. I can demonstrate."

A few seconds after the ringing of the bell, a strapping girl of perhaps sixteen, whom Alice and Katherine had hired from one of the local orphanages, came bustling into the room.

"Did you call, mum?" asked the girl, making an awkward curtsy.

"Yes, Sally dear. Would you mind if I ask you a few questions?"

"I'm not agin you asking me nothin', mum."

"You've been here six months now, dear, and I must say you've done fine work. Do you think you would like to stay on?"

"I woulden want to be goin' nowhere, mum."

"So you would like to stay?"

"I'm far from unhappy, mum."

"Let me be perfectly clear on the matter now. You're satisfied with your employment?"

"Oh yes, mum! That's what I said. Everything at your house is so lovely and refinedlike, and you treat me so nice and polite. I'll be grateful till my dying day, mum."

"Well, you've been a great help in the household, Sally, and a great comfort to me. Now there may be a boy coming by to help you with some of the housework. I know there's not much for him to do, but he's a poor soul who needs to be occupied. His mother did away with herself, you see. I trust you'll be kind to him."

"I woulden be nothing else, mum, seein' as I'm a poor soul myself."

"Thank you, Sally. And by the way, what are we having for dinner tonight?"

"The oysters with mushrooms, as Miss Katherine taught me, if yer not agin it, mum. I know Mr. James likes it. I think he diden say no to two helpins last time."

"The oysters with mushrooms?" recalled Henry, pleased. "I think I didn't say no to three helpings, now that you mention it."

"You mayn't be wrong there, sir."

"Thank you, Sally. I think that will do for now," said Alice.

"Extraordinary!" exclaimed William, after the girl left. "I'll have to write a paper on the use of the double negative locution in lower-class British speech."

"It could be a boon to your social reformers," said Henry. "Teach the unfortunate to speak in positive declarative statements and eradicate poverty."

"There's something to that, you know, language as social destiny," mused William. "I wonder what Spencer and the Darwinians would make of it—"

"Yes, well, you can debate the linguistic fine points of the impoverished classes another time," Alice intervened. "I was only proving the point that the message you mentioned was probably written by an illiterate cockney with a conventional grudge against the Jews. The Jews and the Irish are always useful scapegoats when there's no one else to blame."

"But there was also the odd spelling of the message," noted William. "As I said, Jews was spelled J-u-w-e-s. Warren thinks that it may be some secret reference, perhaps from some book used in the inner circles of the race."

"Nonsense!" asserted Alice angrily. "It's simple illiteracy. Besides, the point could be easily checked. Don't you know any Jews you can query on the subject, Henry?"

"I could ask Lady Asbury. She was Jewish once."

"Not Lady Asbury!" said Alice. "She's the last person who would know. Either the chief rabbi of London or Samuel Isaacson, who owns the pawnshop down the street. But certainly not Lady Asbury."

"Perhaps the murderer is an anarchist," Henry proffered, changing tacks. "Very unpredictable sorts of people. Or a member of one of the purity leagues. Some of those women are lunatics; give them a knife—"

"I believe your imagination is running away with you," chided Alice brusquely. "As I see it, the idea of a conspiracy is unlikely. The letters printed in the newspapers make no mention of a cause or an allegiance. And there hasn't been any of the secret insignia or code words that such groups go in for. No—as I see it, the murders are the work of a singular, demented individual. But even a demented mind must have a motive in order to kill with such regularity and pattern."

"Yes." William nodded. "There is generally a method in madness if one supplies the right context. Knowing childhood influences, forms of abuse, disappointments, rivalries, and so forth can provide the logic for seemingly incoherent behavior. There is never an effect without a cause."

"That's a law to be respected in the writing of fiction," piped in Henry, who was feeling left out. "It's Louis Stevenson's problem, in my opinion. His effects exceed their causes."

Neither his brother nor sister appeared to care.

"When you see the letters, perhaps you'll be able to supply the context and deduce the cause," Alice instructed William. "Pay special attention to the quality of the paper and the ink. Look for patterns in the formation of letters. Note the sentence formation, the use of fragmentary exclamations, and repeated words."

"I think, as a trained scientist, I know what to look for," William responded. "I am familiar with standard methods of research and investigation."

"Yes, but it's always good to be reminded. And you're not trained in the investigation of murder."

"And you are?"

"No," acknowledged Alice, "but I've had more time to think about it. I lie in bed and imagine what might have happened. I have been doing such things since childhood."

"Are you saying that you have feared being murdered by us?" Henry laughed.

"Yes, and of murdering you," she added gravely. "It is in the nature of the nervous invalid to create such extreme scenarios. We get ill because imagining them is enough to scare us out of all action."

William considered the comment. "And Jack the Ripper is somehow empowered to live out the fantasy that frightens the neurasthenic. He is the obverse of what you are, your imagination turned real."

"Yes," said Alice, "which is why I am the person to catch him."

CHAPTER 11

WITH LUNCHEON CONCLUDED, WILLIAM rose and announced that he was going back to the East End. "Half of problem solving has to do with posing the right questions," he explained. "The other half with listening to the answers. It's what I learned teaching undergraduates, which qualifies as a form of detective work, the goal being to figure out how to make mostly uninterested students learn. I hope to bring some of this skill to the interrogation of witnesses. After that, I will proceed to Scotland Yard to examine the letters." He nodded to Alice, whom he knew was eager for a full report on this aspect of the case.

"Bring them back with you," she ordered.

"It's highly unlikely that they'll allow them to leave headquarters."

"Try!"

William waved his hand in exasperation. His sister made him feel duty bound to fulfill her requests, even when they were utterly impractical. He didn't know whether it was respect for her opinion or deep-seated guilt that made him so solicitous of her. Whatever the motives, he knew that, if he could, he would bring the letters back.

As he moved into the foyer, he was surprised to find his brother beside him, buttoning a cashmere topcoat and reaching for a bowler hat and silver-tipped cane.

"I thought I'd come along," Henry explained casually. "Very important to cover the throat," he noted, tucking a silk scarf around his neck. "Most vulnerable part of the anatomy."

William stiffened. Henry, with his Savile Row wardrobe and effete manner, was bound to be out of place among the poor people of Whitechapel. Besides, he didn't want his little brother tagging at his heels. He had discouraged it when they were boys, and the same reflex made him discourage it now.

"I know what you're thinking, that I'd be in the way," said Henry placidly, anticipating William's protest. "But it's not as though you're going off to play ball or something strenuous and manly in that line. I've lived in this country for a while, you know. I have a sense of the people."

"In the East End? Among the squalid tenements and boardinghouses of the poor? Really, Henry, they're not the sorts with whom you eat your dinners."

"No, they're the sorts who serve me my dinners. I have observed them; indeed, I have talked to them. You'd be surprised how even the lower orders hold to ideas that Americans don't understand."

"And aren't *you* an American?"

"Not really. Not anymore. I have thrown off the yoke of my native country, or if you prefer, I have assumed the yoke of my adopted one. Which is to say, I think I could be useful to you in your present mission."

William paused, sensing that Henry was not about to give way. "All right, you can come," he conceded in the manner of the slightly coerced but magnanimous older brother. "Just don't lord it over these poor people. And keep your sentences short."

Henry smiled but said nothing. He secretly believed that of the two of them, William was the greater snob. As a professor at Harvard, his brother dealt almost exclusively with intellectuals and scholars, people who lived a relatively comfortable and cloistered life. He, on the other hand, consorted with a far more eclectic mix of people: old-moneyed dowagers; newly minted millionaires; aspiring, often impoverished, artists; not to mention domestics of various sorts who were constantly on hand to carry his bags or serve him his meals. He was convinced he had the broader, more ecumenical view of human nature, despite the fact that William saw himself as the man of the people.

The brothers took a hansom cab to George Yard, where Martha Tabram had been stabbed two dozen times. William had the address of one Rosie Tynan, who had told the police she saw someone she thought was Martha speaking to a gentleman on the evening of the murder. Rosie Tynan's house was empty, and the neighbors had, like vultures over a corpse, descended to take it apart. The glass in the windows was gone; the steps broken up; the shutters pulled off. William knocked on the house next door, where a disheveled woman, gripping a crying child tightly by the arm, informed him curtly that Rosie had left the area. "Went south 'cause she got sick of it all," said the woman, motioning with her free hand to the area around her. "Don't know if it's better where she is, but it coulden be worse."

"Did she ever talk to you about seeing Martha Tabram before her death?" asked William.

"Naw," said the woman. "She hardly knew what she seen, and the police badgered her till she knew less. That's what they do; they get hold of something they think will make things easy for them, and then they try to make you say what they want. Rosie seen nothing but some woman, who she thought might be Martha, speaking to some gentleman near the corner by the pub. Martha spoke to gentlemen all the time; it was her living." The child began to cry loudly, and the woman paused to pinch its arm, along which there was already a string of bright purple bruises. "You woulden learn no more from her than you done from me."

Leaving George Yard, William and Henry walked farther east to the upper end of Whitechapel Road to look for Patrick Mulshaw, who had said he saw someone suspicious near the site of the Polly Nichols's murder. Mulshaw, however, was gone too, according to a man standing at the corner with a tray, on which were arranged an assortment of tobacco butts. "Who knows where he's at?" The man shrugged. "Probably went up to Belfast. Pat said there weren no point hangin' round here; he'd do as well to starve to death with his own people."

William looked at the informant, whom he realized was in a striking state of emaciation and whose livelihood apparently was made by selling the cigarette butts that he picked up from the street. William put a pound on the tray and hurried off, only to have his brother catch up with him a few minutes later, breathing heavily.

"That was very rude of you!" exclaimed Henry with annoyance.

"Giving the poor man money?"

"Running off and leaving me there to deal with his excess of gratitude. He took hold of my waistcoat and wouldn't let go. Wanted me to take all his cigarette butts, and I had to assure him that we were Americans and didn't smoke. Next time you want to be altruistic, please don't leave me holding the bucket—or, as it were, the butts."

During the next hour, the brothers wandered through the area, where none of the witnesses associated with the Annie Chapman or Elizabeth Stride murders could be found, though they did unearth a young woman who had gone to dinner with Catherine Eddowes early in the evening of her murder and who said that there had not been any rendezvous arranged for later, as far as she knew. "Katie met her gentlemen where she could, and took care of business on the spot," the woman asserted. "It wasn't her way to plan ahead."

William fleetingly wondered if the failure to plan ahead in such matters was another facet of what the great Darwin would argue served to winnow the species of its less adaptable specimens.

As the brothers moved through the neighborhood, William noted that Henry remained quiet. Not that there was anything for him to say, but since when had that ever stopped him before? Occasionally one of the respondents would address themselves to him, which gave William the annoying suspicion that they thought his brother was the higher-ranking official.

"That's all the witnesses I have on my list," he finally concluded somewhat apologetically after they had trudged through the maze of streets for several hours. They had arrived near the spot where Catherine Eddowes had been killed, and William noted that the pail with the placard was still there. He walked over and, once again, dug in his pocket and dropped in a coin.

"Perhaps a little random investigation would be helpful," suggested Henry, looking around at a group loitering nearby. There were several young women, their blouses all but unbuttoned, and a shifty-eyed youth, who seemed on hand to retrieve the coin just dropped into the pail as soon as the men turned their backs.

William nodded at the suggestion and addressed the motley group. "Do you know the family?" he asked, motioning to the sign over the pail. "Do you know where we can find them?" He had checked the police records and had noted that there was no mention of a family for Catherine Eddowes.

The women with the unbuttoned blouses looked at him blankly, but the shifty-eyed young man stepped forward and responded in an aggressive tone. "What's it to you?" he asked, spitting a wad of tobacco onto the pavement in front of the brothers and narrowing his shifty eyes.

William was about to turn away in disgust, when Henry addressed the man sharply. "We have reason to want to meet with the family," he said in a crisp, authoritative tone. "Kindly tell us where we can find them." As he spoke, he put his hand in his pocket as though suggesting that reimbursement for information would be forthcoming, though the gesture seemed as much threatening as potentially generous.

The young man's posture straightened. "They's not here, sir," he said. "They's been out of the area since Lord knows when; it's to gather the coins that the people put that up." He indicated the sign.

"You, you mean," said Henry sternly.

"Not me," said the man defensively. "I sometimes stop by to see what's been put in, but it weren't my idea."

Several older women who had gathered on the steps of the building nearby approached, and the shifty-eyed young man, who must have decided he was out of his depth, sought their assistance. "These gents say as they have matters to discuss with Kate's family," he explained to one of the older women.

She had a square red face and a stout build and looked like she could wrestle half a dozen men to the ground if it were required of her. A flowered apron was the only indicator of some link to domesticity. "Katie had no family," the woman said shortly. "What she had, gone off to Liverpool years ago, poor girl. What would you be snooping here for, anyway? The police are always snooping. Never gettin' anywhere for it, though."

"We're not police," William reassured her. "We're Americans."

Some members of the group nodded, as though they understood these sets to be mutually exclusive. "Maybe you'll shoot the bastard who did this," one of the women said. "You Americans at least know how to bring 'em to justice."

"Bang! Bang! Shoot 'em up," said a man without teeth, who had appeared out of nowhere. He looked at William, whose disheveled appearance was probably not reassuring, though perhaps he could pass for a cowboy.

Henry moved in to clarify. "We are here in an unofficial capacity to help with this sorry case. We are convinced, you see, that the American point of view may shed light on what may have been overlooked."

There was more nodding among them. Henry's courtly manner and clipped enunciation had drawn the respect of the crowd, and William realized that he had been wise, after all, to let his brother accompany him.

"Them Americans are smart," called out one of the women. "Even the poor ones are rich over there."

"We're seeking additional views on what happened," said William, taking the lead now that Henry had eased the way. "Anyone who might have theories or information that they wouldn't want to share with the police, we'd be pleased to hear. We promise to keep what we're told in confidence as far as possible."

"Maybe Mary Wells'll talk to 'em," suggested one of the women. "She knew Polly Nichols."

"Mary wouldn't open 'er mouth to the police," said another woman, "ever since they arrested her Tom for pilferin'."

"Mary's Tommy?" said someone else in the group. "Everyone knows 'e got sticky fingers."

"She don' deny it, only says 'e didn't steal that time; they hung it on 'im 'cause he took the horse the week before. 'Er boy may be a thief, she says, but that don' mean they can say anythin' stolen, 'e done it. That's corruption, she says, and it's worse than stealin'."

"She has a point," said William.

"She might speak to you," said another woman, "seeing as you're American and she has that daughter in America."

"Where does her daughter live in America?" asked Henry.

"She's in some city. Milarky, I think it's called."

"Milarky?" asked William.

"She probably means Milwaukee," said Henry. He then addressed the group. "It's a fine city in the great state of Minnesota."

"Wisconsin," William corrected his brother under his breath.

"Yes," continued Henry, undeterred, "we've spent quite a bit of time in Milwaukee. We might even have met her daughter."

"In that case, you should talk with Mary for sure. She'll want to hear any news about Tessie. She's around the corner, two houses on this side.

It's the one with the yellow curtains. And she'll be wearing a red apron. She goes in for the colors. What with Tessie gone and Tommy 'n prison, it's the least she can do to keep 'er spirits up."

CHAPTER 12

MARY WELLS WORE THE red apron that had been predicted, and she also had on a crisp white cap and a freshly laundered white blouse. Her home, though modest and not in the best repair, was neat and welcoming. She had opened the door wide enough at the brothers' knock so that they could see inside, but she stood squarely blocking the entry and squinting at them suspiciously.

William was surprised at the economy with which Henry proceeded to make his case for an interview. "We are American citizens here to lend a hand in the resolution of the Whitechapel murders at the request of your queen. Your name was given to us as someone who might be of help. I should add that we are on a limited visit to London, since we have work to do at home in our great city of Milwaukee."

The woman, who had been staring at them blankly at the beginning of this speech, suddenly broke into a smile. "You live in Milarky?" she exclaimed.

"Yes, we do, though we're often asked to perform special errands outside our fair city."

"My daughter lives in Milarky!" said the woman excitedly. "Tessie Wells is her name. Might it be possible that you know her?"

William shot Henry a look, but he appeared not to notice.

"Tessie Wells; let's see." He surveyed the mother's appearance quickly. "Medium height, light brown hair, snub nose, rather pretty?"

"That's her!" exclaimed the woman. "You know her?"

"I think I know her slightly." Henry nodded vaguely. "I believe I saw her with some friends of mine at a very nice restaurant not long ago. I'll make sure to send my regards when we return."

"Oh my word, to think that you live in Milarky and know my Tessie. Please come in. So Milarky is a lovely city, is it? Tessie writes me that she's happy there. She even found a man who goes to work every day."

"Yes, it's quite common in the city for the men to work," noted Henry.

"We wonder if we can ask you some questions regarding the death of Polly Nichols," interrupted William, feeling that Henry had perhaps gone too far in the direction of extolling a city he had never visited and of expressing knowledge of someone whom he had never met. "We're told that you knew the girl and might share information with us that you were unwilling to give the police."

"The police be damned!" asserted the woman. "They took away my Tommy. He's no angel, but they could at least charge him with something he actually done."

"Quite true," said Henry. "One would want to be accused correctly."

"They said he stole a china plate, can you imagine?" continued the woman in an incensed tone. "Tommy has no use for a china plate! A horse, maybe, a barrel of ale, I could understand. But a china plate? It's as false an accusation as you could ever lay on a man."

"We'll do our best to look into it," said Henry, as William gave him another warning glance.

"If you would, I'd be indebted to you," said the woman, casting her eyes up at Henry with a look of adoration that William found particularly annoying.

"Polly Nichols," repeated William, "we're told you have some thoughts about her activities that might have bearing on her death."

"Well," said the woman doubtfully, "I can't say if it means anything."

"Let us be the judge of that, ma'am," said Henry in his most ingratiating tone.

"Well…it's just that I know Polly went somewhere a few evenings a week, and wherever it was, she got paid for going there."

"Is that surprising?" asked William.

"It wasn't what you think." The woman shook her head. "Not that Polly didn't have business in that way too. But this wasn't favors; it was something else, only she wouldn't say what."

"Do you know where she went?"

"No," sighed Mary. "But I know it weren't far. I know 'cause she walked, and once I saw her come back after only an hour or so. She had her cardigan buttoned wrong."

"That would suggest—"

"Yes, I know, but she said express it wasn't that. It was more of a highbrow sort of thing, she said. But she'd promised not to say more. I don't know if it got to do with her death, and it probably don't. You find all kinds that prowl around here and have odd tastes. Polly wasn't one to judge."

"But she said it was something highbrow?"

"Yes. Can't say what she meant by that."

"Well, if anything more occurs to you, please let us know," said William, scribbling his name and Henry's address, 34 De Vere Gardens, Kensington, on a sheet of paper and handing it to her.

She looked at it doubtfully.

"It's *his* lodging," said William, a bit miffed. "He's here for a longer duration, and I'm staying with him."

The woman's concern appeared to be assuaged, and she addressed Henry again in a supplicating tone. "You'll say hello to my Tessie when you see her, won't you? And as I think on it, wait here." She hurried from the room and returned in a moment with a package wrapped in brown paper. "It's just a cardigan I made and a jar of one of her favorite jellies. I'd be more than obliged if you could get them to her. Here's her address." She extracted a postcard from the pocket of her apron and handed it to Henry, along with the package that she had obviously prepared in advance in the hope she could find someone to mail it for her.

"It would be my pleasure," said Henry. "Your daughter is fortunate to have such a devoted mother." He took the package and bowed his head gallantly.

After they left, William looked at his brother with exasperation. "Now what are you going to do with that?" He motioned to the package.

"I'm going to send it to Howells, who will make sure the girl gets it. Howells knows people, you know."

"Your capacity to lie with aplomb disturbs me."

Henry bristled. "I don't lie," he protested, "I make things up. There's a great difference between the two. I may not have literally *been to* Milwaukee, but I have visited the city in my imagination; I may even have created a character who lived there. I shall write the girl a note to be delivered with the package, in which I extol the virtues of her mother. I will get a complete report from Howells's emissary as to how she is doing. I am not as socially indifferent as you think. I daresay I see people more clearly in their human context than you, who are continually seeking to insert them into a theoretical one."

"You were helpful," admitted William grudgingly. "Thank you for accompanying me."

"You're welcome," said Henry, trying not to show that the acknowledgment touched him. He had achieved a modicum of success with his novels, and he had a profile of sorts in society. But William had always treated him dismissively, had viewed his life as frivolous, and had denigrated his writing, if only by failing to read it. These things pained Henry deeply, though he pretended not to care. For more even than social acclaim and fortune, more even than literary immortality, he desired the good opinion of his older brother.

CHAPTER 13

NOT LONG AFTER HENRY and William left Alice's flat, Sally entered her employer's bedroom to announce that Mr. and Miss Sargent were downstairs. "They say to tell you as you don't have to see 'em if you don't want, as they don't want to disturb you if you're resting."

It was a typical sort of message from the Sargents, who were always extravagantly polite and unassuming. They had a long-standing friendship with the James family and treated Alice with particular reverence because of their instinctive belief that she was a uniquely gifted person. As a result, even today, when Alice had planned to review newspaper clippings of the murders, she was willing to put aside her work and welcome their visit.

"Show them in," she instructed Sally, "and bring us some tea."

A tall man and a small woman with a slight limp entered the room. Emily Sargent ran to kiss Alice and Katherine and then immediately began helping arrange the furniture. She had been the victim of a debilitating spinal disease in childhood and had suffered years of pain, but it did not appear to have embittered her or slowed her down in the least. On the contrary, she was the most loving and congenial sort of person, energetically devoted to her friends, but most devoted of all to her brother, whose talent she worshipped.

Everyone agreed that John Singer Sargent's ability to paint as freely as he did and to shrug off any criticism that came his way was because he had his sister to take care of everything and sing his praises all day long.

Emily also had enormous respect for the relationship of Alice and Katherine and was the one person, even above Henry, they allowed to enter the sickroom when Alice had one of her "spells." "Emily is a creature who makes me temporarily put aside my spiritual skepticism," Alice liked to say. "I feel sure she is modeled on the angel you see in the background of those paintings, the one who makes sure that the Lord doesn't trip on his robe. Of course, John is an angel too."

Indeed, John Sargent, a towering figure who stooped slightly when he walked, as though not wanting to assert his height too aggressively, had a quality of such gentle goodwill about him that even those of his peers who, for reasons of jealousy or aesthetic prejudice, were scornful of his work, found themselves disarmed when they met him. The Jameses spoke of these friends as one would of family members who had been raised in a different part of the world and spoke a different language. The Sargents were not cerebral people and would as soon listen to music or, in John's case, paint or play the piano, as talk. Not that he was simple—he spoke half a dozen languages without an accent and knew his way around every city in Europe. But his very cosmopolitanism made him a kind of innocent. Alice's father had traveled far and wide in search of the proper place to educate his children, finally settling in Cambridge, Massachusetts, as the best he could do, but Sargent's parents had merely traveled, with no destination in mind, and had never settled anywhere. John Sargent had thus been spared the pressure of expectation that the Jameses had suffered. He had started drawing when he was a boy and simply kept on doing it.

While Emily was occupied with pulling the armchair nearer to the bed and arranging the curtains, John sauntered over, embraced Alice, and kissed Katherine's hand.

"How is your mother?" asked Alice. She knew that their father had died in April, a loss that both Emily and John had handled with equanimity, as had their mother, though she had maintained the convenient social prerogative of a long mourning. Alice sometimes envied her friends for having a father who had effaced himself so completely during his life that his death was a gentle slipping away. Her own father had been a towering presence, and his death three years earlier had been a crushing, incapacitating blow, not just for her, but also for her brothers, who dwelled on it continually and were constantly trying to get over it—without succeeding.

"She's getting along," said John mildly.

"She always asks about you and can't wait to be in a condition to visit," added Emily.

It was hard for Alice to imagine that Mary Sargent was not in a condition to visit, and assumed that she was simply not in the *mood* to visit, which was, upon consideration, the same thing.

"Please sit," said Alice, motioning to the chairs beside her bed.

Sargent lowered himself into the armchair, stretching his long legs out in front of him, while Emily, in her usual compulsion to be helpful, ignored her hostess's command and began preparing the tea that Sally had brought in.

"I'm afraid you just missed Henry and William," explained Alice, once the tea had been served. She added casually, "William's here to help investigate the Ripper murders for Scotland Yard."

Emily clapped her hands in delight, and even Sargent, constitutionally phlegmatic, opened his eyes in surprise.

"You must keep this entirely confidential," warned Alice. She knew she could depend on Sargent to say nothing, but Emily, rather like Henry, was an excitable person, likely to blurt things out inadvertently.

"We'll be quiet as a tomb," Emily assured her.

The door opened a crack, and Archie peeked in. The boy had reported to the house that morning and seemed to have taken to his new responsibilities with alacrity. He entered the room boldly; he was holding two blankets in his hands. "Sally says as how Madame James might be needin' a blanket as it's a bit chill in here today," said the boy, looking at the group with the unselfconscious gaze possible only in a total innocent. "She tol' me to bring this wool'un here, but I says as it's too rough for her ladyship, and the mohair's the one I'd like."

"Quite right," said Alice, casting an amused glance at the Sargents. "Her ladyship prefers the mohair."

"I knows it!" exclaimed Archie triumphantly, bringing the blanket to Alice and, though Emily seemed eager to take it, insisting on draping it over the bed himself.

"Archie is a new addition to the household," explained Alice to her guests. "William engaged him to help Sally out."

"Really?" said Emily. She knew that Sally did not need help.

"These are two friends of mine." Alice addressed the boy: "Miss Sargent and Mr. John Singer Sargent. Mr. Sargent is a painter."

"A painter?" said the boy. "I likes pictures!"

"Very good." Sargent nodded. "Liking pictures is good."

"What pictures is it the gentleman paints?" asked Archie. "I likes them pictures they paste on the walls to tell o' what's playin' at the music halls. But I don't know as gentlemen does those."

"You'd be surprised what gentlemen do," said Sargent. "Posters are the least of it. But I'm in a different line myself. I paint pictures of real people."

"Real people?" queried the boy. "Like me?"

"Most certainly like you. You would make an excellent subject."

"People pay Mr. Sargent a great deal of money to paint their portraits," clarified Alice.

"I coulden do that," said the boy.

"Nor would I expect it," said Sargent. "I don't paint only for money; I also paint for pleasure—subjects that interest me."

"Like that," said Emily helpfully, pointing to a small painting over the table that Sargent had given Alice for her birthday. It was of a young woman in a red cloak standing in the portal of a building.

"Tha's beautiful!" breathed the boy, gazing at the painting intently. The woman had a dark, delicately pretty face. He moved closer and studied the figure a moment. "She looks like me mum," he finally said.

"Archie's mother passed away recently," explained Alice.

"Poor child!" murmured Emily.

John had risen from his chair and stood beside the boy, looking at the picture. It was one of his gifts to be able to relay sympathy and understanding without saying a word. In the present instance, he focused his attention on the painting, but in such a way as to include Archie in the act of assessment. They might have been two casual connoisseurs touring a gallery together. "The lady was a very interesting subject," he noted, then squinted a bit. "Don't you think it looks dull?"

"I woulden know," said the boy. "It looks beautiful to me."

"And to me," seconded Emily.

"I'll brighten it up with a coat of varnish," said Sargent, ignoring these opinions, as he would more expert ones, and taking the painting off the wall. He turned to the boy. "A little dressing up always helps."

"I sees as that's so," said Archie, looking down at his own new clothes, which had been bought with Sally at a haberdasher that morning.

"It doesn't really change what's there," continued Sargent sagely, "but most people don't know that. I've made many a mediocre work appear better with a coat of varnish."

"Nothing you do is mediocre, John," insisted Emily, turning to Alice proudly. "He just had his portrait of Mrs. Marquand sent over for submission to the Royal Academy show. It's said to be a masterpiece."

John waved his hand dismissively. "It's a flattering likeness, which, to the subject at least, qualifies it as a masterpiece."

"Oh no," protested Emily. "You paint your subjects exactly as they are."

"Yes." Sargent nodded. "Only six inches taller and with good teeth."

Alice laughed. "You have, in my opinion, come up with the perfect formula for success as a portraitist. If your subjects are impossibly old and ugly, you make them look like dowager empresses, and if they're young and vacuous, like blushing roses. How, I wonder, would you paint me? Would you make me wise or beautiful?"

"I would not need to make you either." Sargent laughed. "You are already both!" He had returned to his chair, although not before producing a farthing and a piece of candy, which he slipped to Archie before he left the room.

"I won't argue with your flattering assessment of me," said Alice, "especially since you might have leverage with my brothers. They tend to be skeptical of my wisdom, if not my beauty."

"Oh, they'll come around," said Sargent, stretching out his legs and closing his eyes. "You'll see to that. Now if you'll excuse me, ladies, being in the presence of so much wisdom and beauty has tired me out. And since I'm sure you have a great deal you want to gossip about, I think I'll take a nap."

CHAPTER 14

WHEN HENRY AND WILLIAM returned to Alice's apartments that evening, Archie was on hand to take their coats. "If you'll step this way, I'll show you to the apartment of Madame James," said the boy with an exaggerated bow.

William seemed nonplussed by this childish formality, but Henry, with a greater understanding of how custom and ritual served to uphold the social structure, responded with a grave nod. "We're much obliged to you, young man."

"Archie, get back here and stir the pot!" shouted Sally from the kitchen.

"If you'll excuse me, sirs, I'm called to duty elsewhere," explained the boy. "Milady's chambers is through that door, if you'd be so good as to find your own way." Having apparently suffered the ire of Sally already and not wanting to repeat the experience, he ducked out of sight.

Henry laughed after the boy left. "It's a great thing to lift the lower classes."

"I suppose," said William doubtfully, "though I suspect it only teaches a more elaborate form of servitude. The whole system offends my ideal of democracy."

"Your ideal of democracy would not work in this country. Your cutlery would be stolen and your daughter carried off before you had a chance to launch one of your progressive schools."

"A rather cynical way of looking at things."

"Not cynical; realistic. You speak continually about the importance of context. Well, context works in social settings as well. One doesn't apply democratic ideals without an understanding of the history and customs of a people. Here, change happens incrementally, and giving the boy a uniform and a chance to stir the pot in Mayfair is a great leap forward from pilfering and worse in the East End."

William did not argue.

When they entered Alice's bedroom, their sister was sitting in her bed, munching on a piece of celery. "It's supposed to be good for the digestion, only I hate it," she grumbled, at which she threw the celery across the room, where Katherine, who had been sitting reading a newspaper, calmly picked it up.

"I hope your visit to the East End was productive," continued Alice, as though throwing celery were a perfectly normal part of her everyday activity.

"I'm afraid we didn't learn much," said William, "though we had one intriguing interview with a woman who knew the second victim, Polly Nichols. She said that Polly used to visit a gentleman a few times a week in the area."

"But isn't that what such women do?"

William cleared his throat; his sister's directness still embarrassed him. "Not insofar as Polly told our witness that she was being paid to do something else."

"And what was that?"

"Unfortunately, we don't know."

Alice looked annoyed. "Then you ought to find out, hadn't you?"

Before more could be said, Sally entered the room with a large casserole dish containing the oysters with mushrooms, and some time was spent ladling out portions.

As they were being served, Alice turned to Henry. "Did you write anything interesting this afternoon?" she asked politely.

"As a matter of fact," said Henry, pleased to expound, "I have begun a new project, the dramatization of one of my works."

William made a slight choking sound, and Alice shot him a look. "A play, how nice." She nodded. They ate without speaking for a few moments, until finally, Alice broke the silence, speaking to William of what clearly interested her most. "I assume you spent your afternoon at Scotland Yard examining the letters. Did you bring them for me to look at?"

William put down his fork and took a sip of wine. As he did so, he touched his jacket pocket in a reflexive gesture.

"You have them!" exclaimed Alice. "They've let you borrow them!"

"I really don't know what you're talking about," said William, bringing his napkin to his lips and opening his eyes in mock innocence.

"You see how he gives himself away?" Alice directed herself to Henry. "He can't lie. He's afraid he'll go to hell if he does."

Henry shook his head. "I don't think that's it. He tries to lie, except he's bad at it. It's why he could never write fiction—and doesn't appreciate mine."

"Enough!" interrupted William. "I admit I have the letters, or at least a few of them. Abberline's men went through the lot and identified those they felt to be authentic. I've been given permission to examine them at my leisure. Obviously they're confidential."

"Phooey," said Alice, waving her hand. "Let me see them!"

"I really can't do that. The letters were released to me as a special consultant to the police commissioner."

"And I am a special consultant to *you*," declared Alice, "and a highly sensitive one. If you don't show me the letters, I'm sure to get a headache and have a fainting spell."

William gave his sister a withering look. "That's...beneath you!"

"No, it's not!"

He paused and, still glaring at her, took an envelope out of his pocket and handed it over. There was silence for a few minutes as Alice perused the letters while Henry peered over her shoulder. There were a dozen or so assorted sheets, some on full pieces of vellum, some on scraps of paper or postcards.

"Why do you assume these are authentic?" Alice finally asked.

"It's not a definitive assumption. There are a hundred or so letters received at Scotland Yard and the Central News Agency alleged to be from Jack the Ripper, and more come in each day. Abberline has confided that at times he wonders if *any* are genuine. But the experts he has employed believe that these, at least, have a claim to validity by virtue of their content and style." He leaned forward, extracting a sheet from the group. "This one, for example, dated September 25 and postmarked September 27, was addressed to the Central News Agency, forwarded to Abberline, and not published until October 3."

Alice took the letter from him. It read as follows:

Dear Boss
I keep on hearing the police
have caught me but they wont fix
me just yet. I have laughed when
they look so clever and talk about
being on the right track. That joke
about Leather Apron gave me real
fits. I am down on whores and
I shant quit ripping them till I
do get buckled. Grand work the last
job was. I gave the lady no time to
squeal. How can they catch me now.
I love my work and want to start

again. You will soon hear of me
with my funny little games. I
saved some of the proper red stuff in
a ginger beer bottle over the last job
to write with but it went thick
like glue and I cant use it. Red
ink is fit enough I hope ha. ha.
The next job I do I shall clip
the lady's ears off and send to the
police officers just for jolly wouldn't
you. Keep this letter back till I
do a bit more work then give
it out straight. My knife's so nice
and sharp I want to get to work
right away if I get a chance.
Good luck.
Yours truly
Jack the Ripper
Don't mind me giving the trade name.

And at a right angle to the note was written at the bottom:

wasn't good enough
to post this before
I got all the red
ink off my hands
curse it.
No luck yet. They
say I'm a doctor
now ha ha.

"The reference to Leather Apron is to a criminal with that nickname who was associated with the murders but has since been cleared," explained William. "It's a reference that warrants additional looking into," he noted, more to himself than to the others.

Alice glanced through the remaining sheets. "Here's the postcard that they printed in the papers," she said, holding it up so William could see what she was referring to, and then peering at it more closely. It read:

I wasn't codding
dear old Boss when
I gave you the tip.
Youll hear about
saucy Jackys work
tomorrow double
event this time
number one squealed
a bit couldn't
finish straight
off. had not time
to get ears for
police thanks for
keeping last letter
back till I got
to work again.
Jack the Ripper.

William again provided the commentary. "That was also sent to Central News and was postmarked October 1. The reference is to the double murder of September 30. Elizabeth Stride, throat cut, but no further violence done her, followed a few hours later by the extensive stabbings to Catherine Eddowes. It is true that one of the latter's ears was partially severed, suggesting that the murderer was attempting to follow his intention in the former letter."

Alice had taken up a third letter on a larger sheet and scrutinized it, with Henry leaning over her shoulder.

> *From hell,*
> *Mr. Lusk*
> *Sor*
> *I send you half the*
> *Kidne I took from one women*
> *prasarved it for you tother piece I*
> *fried and ate it was very nise I*
> *may send you the bloody knif that*
> *took it out if you only wate a whil*
> *longer*
> *signed   Catch me when*
> *you can*
> *Mishter Lusk*

"The man certainly could use a spelling primer," noted Henry. "Who is this *Mishter* Lusk?"

"Mr. George Lusk," explained William, "president of the community's Vigilance Committee, whose assistance to the police the murderer was apparently very proud to thwart. The letter was received only a few days ago, along with a small parcel containing half of a left kidney. Catherine Eddowes's left kidney was indeed missing. There is no proof, given the timing of these letters, that they could not have been written based on newspaper accounts, hearsay, or even presence near the scene upon the discovery of the bodies. The organ too could have been obtained from another source. Still, the handwriting in these letters shows marks of similarity which, though hardly definitive, are noteworthy."

"I see no consistency in the misspellings and punctuation," noted Alice. "It looks like someone making up the mistakes as he goes along."

William nodded. "They're erratic, extravagant sorts of mistakes: 'sor' for 'sir'; 'knif' for 'knife.' He drops the *e* but keeps the silent *k*. It's what I call 'disingenuous illiteracy,' the spelling and syntax errors of someone who knows language but wants to appear ignorant."

Alice had been fingering the letters ruminatively. "This one is on good vellum," she noted. "Is there a stationer's mark?"

"What?" asked William.

"The imprint that they put on stationery of a particular brand. It's not readily perceptible, but held to the light, you can see it."

William looked interested, if slightly annoyed. "I don't know that either Abberline or I took note of that. It would be hard to trace a piece of vellum in London."

"That depends on the quality. And certainly, if it's good quality, it would help locate the killer as someone who circulates outside the East End." She held the paper up to the light on her bed table and pointed to a mark that read "Pirie and Sons." "It would be worth finding out how much of this paper they sell and the nature of their clientele. And if you had a suspect, you could check to see if his other correspondence comes from this particular stationer."

"Good point," said William, a touch sheepishly. "Are you going to illuminate anything else?"

"It seems interesting that the pens are different colors."

"As the first letter said, he tried to use blood but substituted red ink instead."

"True, but this ink on the postcard appears to be purple or brown. More than one colored ink was used, it would seem."

"Part of the fantastic nature of the creature," said William.

"Yes, but the inks themselves. Where did he get them?"

"I don't believe that they're hard to find."

"But not in a cheap stationer's."

"It supports my theory that the man is not a poor illiterate," said William a bit smugly. "I've already suggested as much. The handwriting, even when it seems to be primitive, is too good. And the spelling seems too mannered in its inaccuracy to be genuine."

"Hmm," said Alice. "What's this?"

"What?" William asked. He had begun to feel defensive in the face of his sister's astute observations.

"This mark near the bottom."

"I noted that." William nodded. "Abberline and I assume that it's glue. It's clear and shiny, slightly raised. It might suggest that the writer is in one of the trades, a cobbler or furniture maker, for example."

"Possibly," said Alice. "And this?" She pointed to a smudge on another letter.

"It looks like dried blood," said Henry, leaning closer.

"Does dried blood look this way?" Alice asked William, assuming that, with his years of medical training, he could validate this fact.

He paused. "Not really. I made a note to look into it. The police assume it's blood, given the context, but blood generally dries darker. But if it's not blood, I don't know what it is."

"If it's not blood, then what it is, is interesting," said Alice a bit sharply. "I should like to study the letters this evening."

"I don't think so," said William, taking them from her, replacing them in the envelope, and putting them back in his pocket.

"Were you planning to look at them tonight yourself?"

"No, not tonight. I have an appointment with Professor Sidgwick of Cambridge University."

"Oh no!" groaned Alice.

"Henry Sidgwick is a noted philosopher and classical scholar. A giant in his field."

"Also a spiritualist crank."

"Alice!"

"I can't help it. The man is president of the Society for Psychical Research—I believe that is the title chosen to dignify an interest in Ouija boards and crystal balls. For someone of your intellect and reputation to be drawn to that sort of thing is an embarrassment. I know that you mourn your Hermie; the loss of a child is more painful than any wound a human creature can suffer. But grief is no excuse for idiocy."

"I will not listen to you speak this way."

"All right. Just leave me the letters and go ask the spiritualists to solve the case."

"I am not asking the spiritualists to solve the case. I'm just leaving the window open."

"I never leave my windows open; surest way to catch a head cold," commented Henry, but neither his brother nor sister were in the mood for his whimsy.

Alice glared at William. "Leave *your* window open, but close mine—bolt it, please," she said sharply. "I don't want some sniveling ghost rapping on my walls and chattering about how Father buttoned his jacket or Mother held her knife. If you want to talk that sort of palaver with a Cambridge don, you have my blessing. But I want the letters."

William looked at his sister, took the envelope out of his pocket, and handed it over. "Keep them tonight. But be careful with them."

"I'll be sure to wash my hands." Alice sat back on her pillows, looking pleased. "So now that that's settled, what do you say to a cup of Moroccan coffee? Violet Paget brought the beans back from her last trip to the Orient. We could throw in a little eye of newt."

William scowled and got up from his chair. "I'm afraid I have to skip the coffee. I promised Sidgwick I'd meet him at the Oxford and Cambridge Club."

"I have tea if you prefer," said Alice. "I'm told the leaves are very informative."

William, sensing that mockery of an escalating sort was in the air, grabbed his hat and strode to the door.

"But if I can't tempt you, then at least we can plan our next rendezvous." She lowered her voice dramatically. "'When shall we three meet again?'"

Henry took it up, laughing. "'In thunder, lightning, or in rain?'"

"Oh shut up, both of you!" said William, slamming the door behind him.

CHAPTER 15

WILLIAM LEFT ALICE'S FLAT and began to walk toward the site of his rendezvous with Henry Sidgwick. The prospect of meeting Sidgwick, with whom he had corresponded but never met, excited him. Both men were eminent in their fields of philosophy and shared, along with their respect for rational mind, a sense of great, uncharted vistas beyond the scope of the rational. People like his sister had no appreciation for this sort of thinking; they were grounded in practical reality. But William knew that the vast majority of human souls hungered for a belief in the unseen but feared how such belief might be perceived. Henry Sidgwick had the courage to look foolish.

William was entertaining these thoughts as he walked up Piccadilly toward Regent Street, where he intended to cross and make his way to Pall Mall. It was early evening, and large numbers of the workforce had left their place of employment. There were robed barristers and suited scriveners, men in shirtsleeves who had come out of the pubs, and ascotted gentlemen on their way to their clubs for drinks. There were elegant ladies who had just finished tea in Mayfair and governesses pushing their prams. The weather, as was usual for London, was overcast, and a light rain fell, enough to produce the bedraggled look that was characteristic of the English crowd. Some had their umbrellas up, though the rain was light enough that many simply walked quickly, collars up, hats pulled down.

The crush of humanity felt novel to William. Boston was a large city but not a hectic one, and even there, he confined himself to the more rarified enclave of Cambridge, and within that, of Harvard College. This was where he lived with his family, where he carried on his work, taught, and entertained visitors. This was where he had established a fortress to protect his intellectual and personal aspirations. It was a site at once circumscribed and supremely free.

Thrown into the hubbub of the London streets after a workday, he was struck by the reality of teeming human life that his daily existence tended to obscure. The difference, he also realized, was the difference between the New World and the Old. In one, the sense of the individual was paramount. "We are all endowed by our creator with certain inalienable rights," he quoted to himself proudly. In the other, the individual was submerged, not just in the density of population but the sheer weight of history. As an American, he had shed his old-world heritage as though he had nothing behind him beyond a vague loyalty to Ireland. He could stretch his arms and legs and do whatever he pleased. But here, the past was always present, pushing up against you in coats of arms and family estates, in portraits and heirlooms, and in the web of relations, near and far. Even among working people, the past hung heavy. They were pressed into age-old traditions and customs, following along, doing what was expected, doing what was always done. The idea of following the past because it was the past repulsed him, though he also knew that history was the resource, the supple clay, that he relied on for his intellectual life and that he needed to produce his work.

He felt this duality now as he made his way through Piccadilly. London was truly the center of the Old World, in which the weight of the past and the richness of the past combined, where diabolical minds could operate unseen, and where the greatest, most penetrating intellects could be found and unite in brotherhood. It was exciting, this Manichaean city, this conjunction of evil and good, animal stupidity and godlike intellect. Yet he was glad, as he glanced around him at the scuttling populace, that he did not have to live here for any length of time.

He arrived at the crossing at Piccadilly Circus with its circle of racing vehicles and lurching crowds. A policeman was directing the traffic, flicking a gloved palm to direct the throng to cross the thoroughfare and then holding it up stiffly to indicate that they should wait. The carriages were clattering past, including a large curricle with four horses, which the driver was whipping faster, so as to make the corner before the need to stop.

William was standing with the crowd at the curb, waiting for the signal to cross, when suddenly he felt a quick but powerful shove to the center of his back that propelled him into the street. The jolt to his body was so sudden and so unexpected that he barely had time to realize what had happened. At one moment he was standing idly on the corner; at the next, he was lying in the dirt with the curricle about to bear down upon him. There was an enormous din, a chaotic clatter of wheels, and a piercing braying of horses as the carriage, its spokes stirring dust up into his nose and mouth, swerved to avoid hitting him. He could hear cursing as the driver, who had been in such a hurry, careened to the side of the road. William, meanwhile, lay dazed, his face pressed into the mud and gravel, until he was pulled to the side and helped to his feet. His suit and face were covered with dirt.

The officer directing the traffic had run up. "Are you daft!" the officer shouted, pushing him angrily onto the curb. Then, seeing that he was a gentleman and an American, took a more conciliatory tone. "You Americans got to watch yourselves," he said, making a show to dust off William's jacket. "We lose more of you that way than even we would like.

Keep back from the street and look both ways, I tell your people, if you don't want to be sent home in a box."

William murmured a vague thanks for this piece of wisdom and took a moment to regain his bearings and review what had happened. Looking back and recalling the jolt that had hurtled him into the street, he could not be sure if it was the definite pressure of a hand pushing him forward or merely a jostling elbow or carrying case that some careless member of the crowd had swung in his direction. The whole incident was a blur, though the pressure, as he recalled it, had seemed definite and purposeful. Regardless of its meaning, malevolent mischief or accident, there was no possibility of tracing its source. The crowd in which he had stood had already moved on, and whoever or whatever had pushed him was lost in the vast sea of undifferentiated humanity.

CHAPTER 16

Nora and Henry Sidgwick were waiting for William in the large front room of the Oxford and Cambridge University Club overlooking Pall Mall. Nora Sidgwick, the former Nora Balfour and sister of the eminent politician, was a tireless advocate on behalf of female suffrage. Learned in the fields of history and literature, she had helped found and was about to take on the principalship of Newnham College, the first women's college at Cambridge University.

Her husband, Henry Sidgwick, was one of the foremost philosophers of his day. Early in his career, he had been a member of the Cambridge Apostles and had broken with the Church of England, but after a short hiatus when he was stripped of his professorship, according to university rules, he had been reinstated as an honorary fellow and then as a chaired professor. He had built his reputation in the field of ethical philosophy, where he had managed to reconcile the utilitarianism of Bentham with the idealism associated with more romantic and aesthetic currents in English thought. But his real interest—if "real" was the proper term for it—was as a founding member and current president of the Society for Psychical Research, the organization devoted to the scientific exploration of spiritual phenomena for which Alice James had expressed so much disdain.

As William entered the room, he noted that the Sidgwicks, whom he recognized from photographs, were seated at a central table and that groups of men at the other tables were glancing in an unfriendly fashion in their direction. There were perhaps four or five such groups, several older, venerable-looking types William vaguely recognized from academic conferences, and some younger ones he imagined to be university men. All were staring angrily at the couple at the center of the room and whispering among themselves.

Spotting William as he approached, Sidgwick stood up and waved a greeting. He was a large, bearlike man with an unruly beard; he seemed to exude goodwill and affability, making the angry stares of his peers that much more puzzling. His wife, Nora, seemed equally pleasant, if less effusive. She was a small, delicately pretty woman some years younger than her husband, with an alert, confident manner. Neither, however, seemed to notice William's disheveled appearance or the fact that he had a large mud stain on his sleeve. It struck him that it was typical of such people, their minds fixed on the larger issues of philosophy and social justice, to miss the details of ordinary life. He had been prepared to discuss the accident that had sent him practically under the wheels of the curricle, but it seemed that he would not have to do so. He was grateful for that, for he was eager to put the incident out of his mind.

He shook Sidgwick's hand warmly and congratulated Nora on the strides she had made in the area of female education. It was a cause that he publicly championed but privately questioned. He knew that his sister would have benefited from such opportunities, but then, she was the exception. His wife, like most women he knew, preferred her quiet, domestic role to a larger, more active one, which was just as well; how could he do his work if she had research of her own? It was a selfish thought, but he would not feel guilty for it.

As he sat down with the Sidgwicks, he noted that the other members of the club continued to glare in their direction. He could only imagine that they were registering their distaste for Sidgwick's spiritualist interests, though the thought struck him as odd. Since when would such an interest provoke animosity? Ridicule, yes; scorn, possibly, but venom?

"Have a cognac," said Sidgwick cheerfully. "Or better, a whiskey. That's what I'm drinking. You need it to fortify yourself against the rancor that surrounds us."

"But why such rancor?" asked William. "You and Nora are respected figures in your fields. I'd think they'd be eager to talk with you."

"Normally they would be," said Sidgwick blithely, "but not now. It's Nora's presence in this room that enrages them. The Oxford and Cambridge Club has been designated an all-male bastion, and she refuses to honor the gentleman's code." He pointed to a youth in livery cowering in the corner. "When the waiter over there politely informed her that ladies were not welcome, she told him that he would have to call a constable if he wished to remove her."

William nodded. It was clear now. He knew, from experiences in America, that the female issue was a lightning rod among even the most enlightened men, for whom superiority to the other sex was the one thing to which they felt entitled; their very definition of masculinity seemed to turn on it. He sometimes wondered if it was a requirement of a democratic nation to maintain this one site of hierarchy as a kind of structural support, much as a house must have one weight-bearing beam. From a rational point of view, of course, it was nonsense, as oppressive and unfair as any other sort of enforced hierarchy, but as a practical fact, he had sympathy for it, if only because his gender disposed him that way. "Is it in the club bylaws to exclude women?" he asked. He was used to the reflexive tendency to invoke university regulations as though they were universal laws.

"It is," responded Sidgwick, "and this is precisely what Nora hopes to change. The club was formed to serve the graduates of Oxford and Cambridge. Newnham is Cambridge's first female college, just as Girton is Oxford's, but the bylaws have not been amended to reflect this, and Nora, as head of one of these female institutions, protests the fact strenuously."

Nora, who sat by while her husband explained her position, did not appear to be protesting strenuously, but she did look very charming as she nodded in agreement. "I stumbled on the idea while reading your Henry Thoreau," she said languidly. "He refused to pay his taxes. I'm acting on the same principle."

"Not an exact analogy," acknowledged Sidgwick, "but close enough."

"Henry Thoreau went to jail," noted William.

"Nora's intention precisely," said Sidgwick. "She feels it would be good publicity for the movement. Unfortunately, she can't get anyone to arrest her."

"Englishmen are cowards," explained Nora. She glanced around the room, and the men who had been staring at her immediately averted their gazes.

"We British tend to hope the cold shoulder and the venomous stare will do the work of prescribed legislation, which is why reform grinds exceedingly slow in this country," said Sidgwick.

"Since I don't think they have the courage to arrest me, I might as well leave," said Nora, sighing. "It's a pleasure to meet you, Professor James. I look forward one day to meeting your wife. Perhaps you will visit us in Cambridge. The Newnham girls are very good with children, so she could rid herself of the albatross of childcare and enjoy herself."

William assured her he would relay the message, wondering whether his Alice had ever considered childcare to be an albatross.

"And send my regards to your sister," she added. "I hear she is not well. She might find some relief in spiritualism. We would welcome her as a member of the SPR."

William explained that his sister was too much of a skeptic to entertain ideas beyond the realm of the empirical.

"Well then," said Nora, "perhaps we can find common ground elsewhere. I have also heard that she has a strong feeling for social justice. Perhaps she can come sit with me and weather the stares of the ossified members. It would be a nice touch to have an invalid who could barely walk thrown out of the club."

"That *is* the sort of thing that would appeal to her," agreed William, "if she could get up the strength to get out of bed."

"The prospect of being thrown into the street might be an incentive for her to do so," said Nora shrewdly. She had risen from the table and begun putting on her cloak.

The eyes of every man in the room registered relief as they watched her leave, and as soon as she was out the door, the young waiter came over to take the men's drink order.

William turned to Sidgwick, pleased finally to be able to speak in person with someone he had long admired. "A great honor to meet the author of the *Methods of Ethics*."

"The admiration is mutual," Sidgwick responded. "Most illuminating, your treatise on habit. It is, as you rightly say, the foundation for moral character—on the one hand, ensuring discipline and virtue; on the other, blinding us to wonders that may exist beyond our daily routine. Which is why we must not let the skeptics close our eyes to the possibility of other worlds and the otherworldly."

"'There are more things in heaven and earth...'" agreed William. It was the premise on which both men rationalized their interest in psychical phenomena. "You are not deterred after that fiasco with Madame Blavatsky?" he asked gingerly. He was referring to the alleged medium Sidgwick's group had discovered, but who was found to have fabricated a large swath of her personal history.

"That *was* a disappointment." Sidgwick sighed. "But I still hold that the woman possesses extraordinary capabilities; a little charlatanism ought not to be a complete disqualification."

William nodded. It was precisely his view. One fraud, even fifty or a thousand, did not mean that the subject was closed. All you need is one white crow to destroy the assumption that all crows are black.

"And now, what brings you to London, my dear fellow?" asked Sidgwick with a pointed look that seemed to know the answer, supporting the general assumption that he had psychic powers of his own.

"I'm here to investigate the Whitechapel murders." William had not intended to give a reason for his visit, but the question had been so direct and so knowing that he felt he could not evade it.

Sidgwick's eyes brightened. "I suspected as much," he exclaimed, slapping William heartily on the shoulder. "How surprisingly intelligent of those duffers at Scotland Yard! You're just the person we need to shed light on the case. And I must say that our meeting today is a happy accident—if there is such a thing as accident. It happens that I have access to"—he cleared his throat—"evidence…that you may find uniquely useful."

"Don't tell me you have someone channeling the dead women of Whitechapel!" exclaimed William.

"Not *all* the dead women, James, my friend. Only *one*: Annie Chapman, the second victim."

"Annie Chapman was the *third* victim," corrected William.

"No. The one they're putting out as the first, Mary or Martha someone, was killed by someone else. Or so Mrs. Lancaster claims."

William was reminded that Abberline had his doubts that Martha Tabram was a Ripper murder victim. "And your source, Mrs. Lancaster, can put us…in touch…with Annie Chapman?"

"Under the proper circumstances, it appears that she can. She is, I should note, a very respectable sort of lady; her husband does something in the foreign office. One of her neighbors, whose daughter attends Newnham, alerted Nora of the woman's trancelike states. We brought her to Cambridge for a week for study, and the results, while hardly definitive, were, if I may say so, promising." Sidgwick settled back in his chair as though savoring the details of what he had to impart. "Her control is a ten-year-old girl, beaten to death by her father not far from where the Nichols woman was killed. Police reports check this out. Certainly worth your looking into, given the purpose of your visit, I should think."

William agreed. He had not expected to consult a psychic medium about the Whitechapel murders, but Sidgwick had thrown one in his way, and he was not about to miss an opportunity to pursue truth when it presented itself.

"Would the lady be available for a...meeting?" He hesitated to use the word "séance," cognizant of the vicious ribbing he would get from Alice.

"I've no doubt something could be arranged, no doubt at all," rumbled Sidgwick. "She promised to be at my disposal anytime she was needed, day or night, so to speak. A very accommodating sort of woman—not the most prepossessing, I admit, but one can't be picky there—but accommodating, which is not something you can say for all of them."

"Well then," said William, considering what would be best. "Could you ask her to come to my sister's apartments tomorrow at around seven?" He made the proposition, knowing that Alice's flat would suit the purpose, though knowing as well that to tell his sister about the arrangement might prove more daunting than communicating with spirits from another world. Nonetheless, he scribbled the address on a sheet of paper and handed it to his friend. "I assume you and Nora can be there."

"I'm afraid not." Sidgwick sighed. "We're returning to Cambridge tonight; Nora is organizing a suffrage rally at the college. She's been working on the thing for months—sashes, placards, all the standard paraphernalia. Must be there for moral support—spouse's job, you know."

"Of course, of course," said William, wondering if he gave his wife the moral support that was a spouse's job.

"But I'm sure Mrs. Lancaster will be fine without us. A fresh set of witnesses always helpful, you know."

William agreed, thinking how the presence of Alice would provide an additional element. She was more than a fresh witness; she was a zealous skeptic.

Sidgwick was no longer concerned with channeling spirits. He had begun nodding pleasantly toward some of the men who had been shooting daggers at him and Nora only half an hour earlier. He pointed them out for William's benefit. "That's Crutchlow over there in the corner, faculty at the University of London. First-rate on Aristotelian concepts of virtue. And Pumley, the pockmarked one with the withered arm, foreign service, excellent piece in the *Times* last week on the Scottish Enlightenment. Young Pomeroy is to his right, very promising medical man at St. Barts, working on valves of the circulatory system."

A few of these personages had wandered over. "William James of Cambridge, Massachusetts," Sidgwick announced to the assemblage.

One of the younger men jumped forward and pumped William's hand with enthusiasm. "William James! What an honor to meet you, sir! I greatly admire your work!"

William was about to ask whether he was referring to his work in psychology or in philosophy, when the young man offered his own explanatory commentary:

"Wonderful story of yours about that American girl who comes to England and makes a mess of things. Well observed! Psychologically astute! I couldn't put it down!"

CHAPTER 17

AT TEN MINUTES TO seven the next evening, Mrs. Lancaster was standing in the foyer of Alice's flat. "I like to be punctual," she announced blandly, "which means I take into account the possibility of delay and thus tend to arrive early."

The announcement was not what one might have expected from a spiritualist medium as Alice imagined her. She had in mind bangles and scarves as well as a greater vagueness regarding time, and was, in truth, a bit disappointed with the unfestooned and uninflected person of Mrs. Lancaster.

Alice had spared William the difficulties he had imagined when he announced his intention of holding a séance in her apartment. Partly it was because of her guilt for being hard on him the day before. Partly it was because she was curious to see what a séance was like. She had heard about such things from her friends, and it all sounded very foolish, but it *was*, after all, a sort of adventure, even if a bogus one. If she could not climb a mountain or ride a horse, she could at least sit at a table as alleged spirits played with the lamps and banged on the walls.

To prepare for the event, she had gotten out of bed and dressed in the Chinese silk robe her aunt had sent her for her last birthday. It was an indeterminate sort of garment—something between an evening gown and a dressing gown—that had the advantage of being comfortable and hiding a body debilitated by erratic nourishment and lack of exercise. It had the additional value of giving her the free use of her limbs, should she want to move them under the table in an effort to explore (she had read about these psychic ladies and knew something of their modus operandi). She had thrown on a string of her mother's pearls and had Katherine put up her hair in an elaborate chignon. In a word, she looked ready to preside over the séance herself.

The contrast, in fact, to the actual medium was noteworthy. Mrs. Lancaster was wearing a long, mustard-colored dress, an unflattering shade under any circumstances (Alice's favorite color was pink), but particularly so given the woman's sallow complexion. She was tall and angular, with the kind of unprepossessing features that one associates with a New England schoolmarm: thin lips, bushy eyebrows, and a nose that was extremely long and aquiline and of the sort likely to get very blue at the tip during the winter. She moved her mouth only slightly when she spoke, suggesting that she had bad teeth and, given the nasal quality to her voice, possibly a serious sinus condition. She had on a pair of worn black shoes that looked too large for her feet. Not at all the sort of woman one would have imagined channeling spirits, Alice thought, though with the secondary observation of the inveterate skeptic that this was precisely the get up that a shrewd operator in this line might choose to put her audience off their guard.

The round table normally in the corner of Alice's bedroom had been moved into the adjoining study, where Katherine did household accounts. The room had been cleared of its books and papers, and five chairs had been arranged around the table. Mrs. Lancaster immediately took the seat facing the door, and Henry and William, who had been standing off to the side looking uncomfortable, sat down next to each other opposite her. This left Katherine to sit on Mrs. Lancaster's left and Alice on her right. There had been some discussion about inviting the Sargents, but it was finally agreed that the fewer participants, the better. Sally had been told to remain in the kitchen and keep an ear open in case she was needed.

Mrs. Lancaster indicated that the lights in the room should be dimmed and the shades drawn. The result was dark, though not as black as Alice had heard some mediums required in order to work.

"We must all hold hands," said Mrs. Lancaster, taking Alice's hand in her bony fingers. "The spirits find it consoling to know that we are united."

"Is there music?" asked Henry. "I like a bit of music."

"No music," said Mrs. Lancaster curtly.

Henry coughed and then sniffed slightly. "Can I get out my handkerchief, or will that bother the spirits?"

"Shh," said William. "You don't have to play the prima donna all the time. Just sit still and be quiet."

The group remained silent for a few minutes.

"I don't know that I'm getting anything," said Mrs. Lancaster. "There is a great deal of negative energy in the room."

"Maybe if I could blow my nose?" asked Henry.

"Blow your nose, for God's sake, and be done with it," snapped William.

Henry blew his nose, and the group returned to silence.

Suddenly there were two loud raps that Alice felt must have come from under the table. She moved her leg quickly against Mrs. Lancaster's and felt a tremor in the muscles of the woman's calf, though so slight, it seemed hardly enough to produce the loud noises she had just heard. There was no time to explore further, for Mrs. Lancaster began to shake violently. She continued to hold Katherine's and Alice's hands, but the shaking grew so violent that everyone around the table was pushed from side to side.

"Oh my!" said Henry. "I'm not cut out for so much exercise."

"Shh!" said William.

Mrs. Lancaster's teeth began to chatter, and her eyes rolled back in their sockets. If she had not been much to look at before, she was definitely not a pretty sight now.

"Perhaps we should call a doctor," murmured Henry.

"Shh!" said William.

Mrs. Lancaster sat bolt upright, her eyes wide open. Her face, harsh and bony in its natural outline, appeared to soften. Her eyes grew bright, and her mouth shaped itself into a pout. In an uncanny eruption, a child's voice suddenly cried out, "I wants some cake! I wants some cake!"

Everyone looked at Mrs. Lancaster in wonder.

"Mayn't I have some cake?" the voice cried again.

"It seems she wants cake," murmured Henry.

"Mayn't I have some cake, mum, please?" The voice, which had been demanding, had turned to a plaintive whine. "It's cake I want; please, Mum, please!"

Alice, who had been staring raptly at Mrs. Lancaster's transformed features, called out to Sally, who appeared in the doorway, and at the sight of the medium's contorted visage, looked like she was about to faint.

"No need to be frightened, dear," said Alice, who herself sounded a bit shaky. "Please go to the cupboard and bring some of that lemon cake that Mrs. Woolson brought over the other day."

Sally disappeared and returned with a platter with a cake on it.

"Put it in front of the lady," instructed Alice, so that Sally, her hands trembling, deposited the cake in front of Mrs. Lancaster and then quickly ran from the room.

"There's your cake, dear," said Alice. She took hold of Mrs. Lancaster's arm and directed it toward the cake. Mrs. Lancaster placed her hand in the cake and began to shovel it into her mouth. She kept shoveling until the cake smeared her face and the front of her dress.

"Someone needs to learn some manners," murmured Henry.

"Shh!" said William.

After several minutes of cramming the cake into her mouth, Mrs. Lancaster leaned back. "Good cake," said the child's voice.

"I'm glad to hear it," said Alice. "Now tell us your name, little girl," she said.

"I's Cassie Bartram," said the voice.

"And how old are you, Cassie?"

"I be nine or ten, not sure which one," said the voice.

"And why are you here?"

"I comes here sometimes to speak through this lady. Don't know why I do, but she's easy to go through when I's something I need to say."

"And you have something you need to say now?"

"I do. I do. It's from Annie—that's a lady here I know who had a hard time of it. She been good to me, and so I said I'd do as I can for her over on this side."

"What do you need to tell us about Annie?"

"I gotta tell that she been killed. Like me. On'y worse than me. Me dad, he jus' hit me real hard, and it kinda busted my head. It weren't that he meant to kill me; he just got mad like he always done, but this time he hit too hard. But Annie, she got stabbed with a knife. That's worse than hitting."

"Where was she stabbed?" asked Alice.

"Well, first in the neck, and then he cut her up down below in the privates."

"She told you that?" asked Alice.

"That she did. Said as he cut things out of her horrible."

"And what did the man look like who did this? Did she tell you?"

"He was dark and kinda small and spoke in that funny language them people speak."

"A Jew, you mean?" asked Alice.

"I guess as it was, since he spoke them funny words, and he may've had the horns too, though she weren't sure about that."

The voice stopped, and Mrs. Lancaster shook again, more violently than before.

"What is it, Cassie? Is there something wrong?" asked Alice.

The voice suddenly grew shrill and upset. "No, no, I says it wrong! That wasn't it as I wanted to say!" Mrs. Lancaster's face contorted as if struggling to break free of something. "It was his hands I wanted to tell of. They was pretty hands, small and delicate-like—white, but not the fingers. They was stained."

"With blood?" asked Alice.

"No, not blood. More black or sootish. Maybe tar or somethin' like."

There was more violent shaking, and Mrs. Lancaster frothed at the mouth. Something viscous emanated from her lips. She coughed a few times and took her hand away from Alice's. The medium's voice returned to its flat and nasal tone. "There it is: Annie Chapman." Reaching up into the air, she grasped hold of a small image, seen in the dim light to be a picture of a woman—Annie Chapman, it appeared to be, if one had seen the woman's face in the newspaper. As Mrs. Lancaster held the image a moment in front of her face, it just as suddenly disappeared.

"That's it. It's done," said Mrs. Lancaster drily. "You can turn the lights on now."

Katherine turned on the lights. Everyone was silent for a few moments.

"Impressive!" William finally said.

"Strenuous!" said Henry.

"Very interesting," said Alice. She addressed Mrs. Lancaster. "I want to thank you for giving us your time." She went over to the desk drawer and took out a bank note, which she handed to the woman, who nodded stiffly in response and turned to go.

"Not quite yet," said Alice. "Would you mind, please, removing your shoes?"

"Excuse me?" said Mrs. Lancaster, looking offended.

"Remove your shoes. It shouldn't be difficult. They look rather loose."

"I will not remove my shoes!" declared Mrs. Lancaster.

"Then I must assume that you have practiced upon us through that means," said Alice. "I have read about an American spiritualist who does all her tapping with her big toe—a highly developed big toe, not the sort one finds on most people, but a big toe nonetheless. Could we look at your big toe?"

"You most certainly cannot!" said Mrs. Lancaster.

"All right," said Alice. "I'll let you escape with your big toe unexamined. But there is one more thing." She moved closer to the woman and then suddenly, with a surprisingly quick movement, squeezed her cheeks with one hand and with the other reached inside her mouth. She extracted a small piece of rubbery cloth and, opening it, displayed the imprint of a face. "Annie Chapman," she announced. "Excellent sleight of hand and control of your jaw muscles for that trick."

Mrs. Lancaster, the tip of whose aquiline nose had turned bright red, grabbed her coat and seemed about to flee the room when a tremor passed through her, and she stopped and turned to Alice. Once again, her angular face seemed to undergo a change, to soften in some inexplicable way. Although she spoke in her own voice, the words came slowly, as if they were being dictated. "He says he's sorry," she said, her eyes staring at Alice's face, which had suddenly gone very white. "He says as he didn't know what to do with a girl like you, so quick and nervous and bright. He appreciates the care you took of him at the end, but he couldn't stay. He's sorry, he says, he couldn't give you what you needed. His heart aches for it."

The two women stood for a moment in complete silence, staring at each other dumbly. Mrs. Lancaster then shook herself. Her soft gaze hardened into an angry glare, and turning on her loose pumps, she walked rapidly from the room.

"What in God's name was that about?" said William.

"Nonsense," said Alice softly.

"You'd think she was giving you a message from Father," said Henry. "Not that it was particularly specific. 'He's sorry.' What parent, I'd like to know, isn't sorry?"

"Yes," murmured Alice. "Anyone might have come up with that."

"I have to say that you did an impressive job debunking her," continued Henry, "though your method was a bit foolhardy. The woman could have bitten your fingers off."

"You certainly humiliated her," said William gruffly.

"Humiliated *her*!" Henry exclaimed. "She had the audacity to try to dupe *us*!"

"It may be more complicated than that," said William.

Alice looked at her brother and seemed to pull herself out of a stupor. "The woman is a fraud," she pronounced tersely. "She makes her money by taking advantage of people who are bereft or desperate or simply, like us, seeking the truth. How is that complicated?"

"Because there may be some truth mixed with the falsehood."

"That's absurd. The whole thing with the child reporting on what Annie Chapman said—there was a logical fallacy in it. Annie was dead after her throat was cut, and the premise of these things is that the spirits can report only what they saw while alive. But the child said Annie had been cut down below. That happened later and completely destroys the premise."

"I noticed that," said William. "But I also noticed the strange way in which she reported on the murderer's hands. There was something oddly compelling there, almost as though she was being forced to tell the truth."

"That *was* a dramatic touch," piped in Henry. "The stained hands. I should like to use it in a story."

"I say it's all nonsense!" said Alice, addressing William irritably. "You cling to the notion that there is something beyond the simple reality of our existence; I am reconciled to the fact that there is not. I do not believe in fairy tales, but I do believe in evil men. And this one must be caught. Unfortunately, no spirit from another world is going to help us do it."

CHAPTER 18

THE NEXT MORNING, WILLIAM and Abberline met, as agreed, at Paddington Station before sunrise. They had both brought their breakfasts, wrapped in brown paper, thus revealing a similarity in habit that made them glance with amusement at each other.

When William had proposed that they visit the Broadmoor Criminal Lunatic Asylum, the inspector had initially demurred. "I've sent many a man there," he said, "but I don't see what kind of good it would do talking to any of them."

William argued otherwise. He had read in the police reports that one of the early Ripper suspects, John Pizer, known throughout the East End as Leather Apron, had been sent to Broadmoor. Even after the police had verified Pizer's whereabouts at the time of the murders, there were people in Whitechapel who remained convinced of his guilt; after all, they said, the devil could be in two places at once.

"So you want to interrogate a criminal because people associate him with the wrong crimes?" scoffed Abberline.

"I do," William replied seriously. Indeed, this was precisely the point as he had worked it out.

He had been cultivating an idea on the subject for some time. The perverse impulses that resulted in criminal behavior must, he believed, have utility for the criminal, as a response to trauma or stress that might otherwise be insupportable. The key was to find the context in which the behavior appeared logical, even necessary. William looked down at his fingernails, which had been bitten raw. Wasn't his compulsion a kind of perversion, developed to keep his demons at bay? In cases of sociopathic perversion, like that of Jack the Ripper, the principle was the same. The murders, in this sense, were like nail biting, only on a spectacular scale, a means by which the killer protected himself against some profoundly debilitating pain.

This idea was behind his determination to speak to Leather Apron. He not only wanted to study the man who had been mistaken for Jack the Ripper; he wanted to ask him for his help. Wouldn't someone who had terrorized women be in the best position to understand what might propel someone else to do the same? Wouldn't such a man, mad though he was—indeed, in being mad—know more about the twisted motives of the Whitechapel killer than the most seasoned policeman or psychologist?

These were William's thoughts, but all he said to Abberline was, "We might learn from one madman how to catch another."

The inspector surprisingly acquiesced. There was trouble at headquarters, he muttered, and he might as well get out of the office. A trip to Broadmoor would at least be a diversion, if not an especially pleasant or productive one.

As they sat together on the train, finishing their breakfast, Abberline pulled an envelope from his pocket and handed it to William. "This is as good a time as any to show you this," he said. "It was delivered to headquarters yesterday."

William looked at the envelope. It was postmarked East London and addressed: "The Boss, Scotland Yard, London City." Previous Ripper letters, he recalled, had been addressed to "The Boss" at the Central News

Agency. He opened the envelope and extracted the paper inside. The writing was a raggedy scrawl.

Tell your professer to keep his nose out or be sory for it.
My minds not disesed but he can get the knif too
if he dont watch out—ha ha.

William stared at the message. "Is it authentic?" he asked softly. He had a sudden recollection of the shove that had sent him careening in front of the curricle on the way to Sidgwick's club.

Abberline shrugged. "There are points in common with some of the other letters. The paper has the mark of Pirie and Sons, for example. But then, Pirie is a popular stationer in London; no need to make too much of that. And previous letters have been publicized enough to explain the similarity of locution. It's odd, regardless, that you're singled out for a joke of this sort. Who do you know who's aware you're investigating this case and might have let the word out?"

William furrowed his brow. There were, he realized, plenty of people; Sidgwick and Mrs. Lancaster, to begin with. The Sargents. His brother, Henry, with his general tendency to blab. And something might have come out from their visit to the East End.

"The letter most likely comes from a colleague of yours," explained Abberline, "perhaps a rival in your line of work, who's having malicious fun at your expense."

William could not imagine a colleague doing such a thing, except possibly one of the French.

"As I say, it may be a nasty joke," continued Abberline, "and chances are, it is. But my advice, Professor, is to take care. Our man is a lunatic, but a cunning one, and if he has his eye on you, I'd make a point to keep out of his way."

CHAPTER 19

THE BROADMOOR CRIMINAL LUNATIC Asylum was located in a remote terrain on the edge of the Berkshire Moors, thirty miles outside of London. Its only neighbor was an orphanage for wayward boys, society favoring the placement of the madman and the orphan conveniently out of sight of meddlesome politicians and reforming ladies.

The asylum itself was a massive stone structure in which two broad turrets flanking an archway seemed to stand open, like a giant maw, to swallow its occupants. The building's placement in the ancient moor and the worn look of the gravel path leading up to it made William feel the weight of entrenched and unchanging experience. He could imagine written above the wide arch the lines from Dante's great poem: "Abandon hope, all ye who enter here."

Yet Abberline explained that the asylum had been built relatively recently, after a group of altruistic ladies got it into their heads to visit the Bethlehem Asylum in London. The conditions at "Bedlam" had appalled the ladies, and a wave of reform had followed. The result was the construction of more humane asylums like Broadmoor. Of course, a humane asylum was a relative thing. Broadmoor was not squalid or unhealthy in the way that Bedlam had been. There were provisions for proper exercise, diet was regulated, and sanitation was modern enough, but that was the end of it. If the bodies of the inmates were treated better here, their souls were no better tended than they had been before.

Entering through the vast portal, William and Abberline were met by a burly guard who instructed an orderly to take them to the director of the asylum. The orderly had sloping shoulders and a lazy eye and looked to William exactly the way an orderly in a lunatic asylum should look. If, as he had written, "to laugh was to be happy," then perhaps "to have a lazy eye was to be a lunatic," or at least, an attendant of lunatics.

They followed the lazy-eyed attendant through a large courtyard, where in one area, a sullen group of men were in the process of taking exercise. Under the supervision of another burly attendant, the inmates were linked arm in arm, walking in rote fashion back and forth. At intervals, someone would break off from this chain and loiter in a corner, at which time the attendant would walk over and strike him on the back of the legs so that the man would scurry back to rejoin the group.

"Do they engage in corporal punishment here, then?" asked William. "I thought it was a humane institution."

Abberline grunted. "A swat on the legs is humane enough when compared to being pummeled senseless, and I suppose they do that too if they feel the need."

William stood for a moment watching the inmates, their heads bowed, walking back and forth in a patient shuffle. Were they in identical states of torpor, or were they merely resigned, after months or even years of this routine, to submerge whatever sparks of selfhood they had into private reveries? Once again, he was bothered by the basic philosophical paradox of where the individual began and ended, of how social conditions and personal habits shaped the self, and how the worst aspects of character could be imposed on an individual as the result of the best intentions.

He and Abberline were finally led into a room that had been equipped with some of the amenities of normal society. An effort had been made to add color in the way of a carpet and a variety of bric-a-brac, but the effect was unwelcoming. The room was too large for its furnishings, and a quality of emptiness and desolation prevailed.

In one corner were several armchairs positioned around a low table. In the other corner was a large desk, strewn with papers and files, and behind the desk sat a scholarly-looking man of about William's age, who rose as they entered and stiffly put out his hand. "Henry Maudsley," he said. His handshake was overfirm in the manner of someone used to controlling situations, or at least determined to do so.

William felt a leap of pleasure at hearing the name. Henry Maudsley was a respected figure in the field of psychological research, someone allied with the materialist school, which believed that abnormal mental processes could be entirely explained by physical causes. Although William faulted the materialists for refusing to consider nonphysical aspects of mental illness, he valued their work for supporting the connection of mind and body, albeit from one direction only.

He therefore shook Maudsley's hand with enthusiasm, and in introducing himself, expected that his host would respond to his name with equal pleasure. Maudsley, however, merely nodded and set about explaining his presence at the asylum with a pontifical air. "I am here at Broadmoor on an interim basis, following the retirement of the venerable Dr. William Orange. I find that the institution provides ample subjects for my research." Abruptly turning to William with an accusatory air, he then said, "You hold to a nonmaterial view of mental debility, don't you, Professor James? I reject that. My latest research, in keeping with Darwinian principles, shows that lunacy is the result of neurological deficiencies—debilities of mental process that cause images and ideas to take distorted and unnatural forms."

William bristled. He had hoped to find common ground with Maudsley, despite their differences in approach, but the man's confrontational manner put him on the defensive. He began to argue, somewhat shrilly, that social, cultural, and indeed spiritual factors certainly *did* contribute to mental illness.

Abberline intervened. "We are here to meet with an inmate by the name of John Pizer," the inspector said curtly. "As you may know, he was an early suspect in the Whitechapel murders and would have been hunted down and torn to pieces had he remained in the community. Fortunately, he also happened to be mad. It's a dire state of affairs when we have to send people to a lunatic asylum for safekeeping."

Maudsley seemed to become more reasonable in the face of this professional exposition. He pulled out a file from the cabinet near his desk and read aloud, "'John Pizer. Age: thirty-two years. Residence: East End, London; specific address unknown. Trade: Boot maker. Diagnosis: Mania alternating with melancholia. Treatment: Spinning, blistering, immersion in cold water.'" Maudsley glanced up. "That was the treatment prescribed by Dr. Orange; I have discontinued it." He closed the file. "It's a fairly routine case of mental imbalance. The patient has periods of lucidity but is given to unpredictable ravings and disorientation. No doubt there are lesions on the brain. But you're welcome to speak to him if you think it will do you any good."

He took a set of keys from his desk drawer and led the men from his office. As he approached the doors that led to the patient area, he paused. "I should like to take a detour before we proceed and have you visit someone you might find of interest. He's mad enough, but he hardly fits the conventional mold of the madman." Maudsley addressed William now with more consideration than he had shown formerly. They had reached the end of the corridor, and he motioned to a door. "We don't bother with the locks in this case. This man poses no danger. He killed someone years ago, but here, as you'll see, he's found a modicum of peace."

He knocked on the door and then opened onto a spectacular scene. The room was far more spacious than expected; in fact, it was two cells, the wall of the adjoining one having been removed to accommodate the prisoner's needs.

In a small corner area was a bed and the accompanying hygienic necessaries, but by far the larger space was occupied with an oak desk, positioned in front of a window and affording a lovely view of the moorland. On either side of the window were bookcases, reaching to the ceiling and crammed with books, and above the desk was a cabinet made up of small cubbyholes. William could see that each cubbyhole was marked with a letter of the alphabet and was crammed full of papers. Books of various sorts were also piled on the floor, some open, some with multiple markers inserted in their leaves. The effect was of a vast and complicated scholarly enterprise. It reminded William of his study at home, though his own space, he acknowledged to himself, was not as well organized.

It took a moment, amid the great volume of books and papers, for the figure of a very thin man in his fifties with white, flyaway hair to come into view. He was hunched over the desk with a lamp at his elbow that infused the room with a strong odor of camphor. He had his spectacles low on his nose and was reading intently from a large book, which William saw had to do with the etymology of birds.

"William Chester Minor," said Maudsley, "our resident lexicographer. William James, professor of philosophy and psychology at Harvard College."

Minor looked up. "Professor James!" he exclaimed. "*Psychic, psychologist, psychosis, psychological, psychosomatic*—all words gleaned from your papers and relayed to my correspondent, Sir James Murray, editor of the *Oxford English Dictionary*, currently in the process of being compiled, and for which I am an indispensable resource. I also understand that I am afflicted by a debilitating psychological disorder, for which work on the dictionary, intense and unrelenting, has been a soothing and reclamatory activity."

"You have medical training?" William asked. He sensed that the man understood his own affliction in a way that a mere layman would not.

Minor, whose hands had been rifling nervously through the pages of the book before him, paused a moment and then spoke in a surprisingly measured, thoughtful manner. "Yes, I am a trained physician. The training itself posed no problem. Indeed, I was a superlative student. My difficulty came with the practice. There, you see, there were problems of another dimension. In the end, I found them insuperable."

William gazed at Minor with fascination. "The human dimension," he murmured.

Minor's hand shot to his forehead, as though he had suffered a sudden pain there. "It requires a kind of…thought. I must confine myself to the rote and the methodical, that which imposes order on that great furnace that produces our souls, be they our souls or merely the engines of our being. I cannot rest if I think on it. I cannot think on it, or I go mad." His gaze remained fastened on William as he spoke, as if to say, *You understand.*

Indeed, William did. His own work on mental process, a huge enterprise on which he had been laboring for years, was a compendium of sorts, a way of organizing the chaos of mental life for the underlying end of preserving his own sanity. He knew to be true what Minor said, to think too much outside established forms and habits was to see the chaotic—and demonic—potential of the mind and be catapulted into the abyss.

William felt himself recoil at the kinship he felt with Minor, who, reciprocally, seemed disturbed by the human connection he had fleetingly established with his visitor. The calmness with which he had spoken began to give way to physical signs of distress. His shoulders twitched, and he shifted uncomfortably in his chair until, finally, shaking himself, as if throwing off a confining garment, he ducked his head and returned to his books.

"He is helping compile a dictionary?" William whispered to Maudsley as they backed away from the desk.

"It appears so," said their host. "There is regular correspondence between Minor and this Dr. Murray. I wonder if Murray knows he is writing to an inmate in a lunatic asylum. His letters are simply addressed to Broadmoor, Crowthorne."

"And you see no reason to illuminate him on the matter?"

"No. The work should speak for itself."

William nodded in agreement and continued to gaze around the room, impressed by the care and method with which Minor had organized his materials. He would have liked to examine some of the bits of paper in the cubbyholes, but Abberline was looking impatient.

Leaving Minor's room, they climbed the stairs to the floor assigned to prisoners believed to be dangerous. The atmosphere here was different from below—the air hot and stale, and the cells arranged closer together. Sharp, unsettling eyes peered out through some of the barred windows; invectives were hurled at them as they passed, and behind some of the doors, loud shrieks were punctuated by angry, garbled speech. Occasionally guards would enter a cell; there would be a few heavy thuds, and then silence.

"We put Pizer up here," explained Maudsley, "less because he has proven to be dangerous than to protect him from others. He nodded to Abberline. "As you mentioned, many still hold to the idea that he is Jack the Ripper, though he's been under lock and key since the second murder. The poor man—and I use the adjective with a certain latitude—is the victim of a kind of thinking that keeps half our population mired in falsity and superstition. They hit on an explanation that supports their prejudices and, despite all proof to the contrary, are unwilling to let it go."

William nodded. In this, he and Maudsley were in complete accord.

They came to a cell at the end of the corridor. Maudsley knocked and then turned the key. A man of short but powerful build was sitting on the cot in the corner of the room. He had a broad, flat face and a shaven head with small eyes. His lips were closed in a thin, straight line, except when they twitched spasmodically to reveal a set of even yellow teeth. He did not look at the visitors directly. His gaze moved restlessly about the room.

It seemed to William that the man resembled a snake. He had a feverish alertness and a hard, coiled muscularity. He was not a prepossessing-looking individual, but confined to the small space, there was something profoundly vulnerable about him, much as a beast in a cage seems vulnerable in its uncomprehending captivity.

Maudsley introduced the visitors, but Pizer made no acknowledgment. He sat unmoving, only his eyes continuing to dart about the room.

"Perhaps if I could speak with him alone," suggested William. It occurred to him that the presence of three men, one a police inspector and one the head of a lunatic asylum, was not conducive to intimate chat.

Maudsley considered this request and then nodded. "We'll wait outside with an ear open in case you need us," he said, and he and Abberline left the cell.

William sat down on the stool near the bed and addressed the inmate gently. "I want to speak to you about the Whitechapel murders," he said.

The side of the man's mouth twitched, but he said nothing.

"I came here in the hope that you might help us find the man responsible."

Pizer's eyes darted up for a moment.

William continued. "You were called Leather Apron and suspected of these crimes yourself. Could you tell me why?"

"Bloody sows'll say anything," Pizer burst out in a guttural accent.

"You are referring to…?" prompted William.

"Disgusting pigs, the lot of 'em," Pizer snarled.

William paused. "Is your mother alive?" he finally asked, thinking this might be a way forward.

"Don' know," said Pizer morosely.

"Do you remember her?"

Pizer shrugged.

"What about your father?"

"On'y saw the bloody bastard when 'e was drunk and came round t' beat me."

"Who raised you?" asked William.

The man gave a shrill laugh. "Bloody pigs raised me."

"Pigs?"

"Whores. Indentured to whores. I'd kill 'em all if I could."

"You worked for prostitutes?"

"Washed their chamber pots. Beat me if I didn't make up their filthy beds. And the gentlemen were worse. Kicked me if they felt like it, bloody, stinkin' bastards. Saw 'em do filthy things, but they treated me as if I was the one as was dirt." The man's eyes darted about the room angrily.

"How old were you when you worked at the brothel?" asked William.

"Who knows? Too young to do nothin' else."

William tried to look sympathetic, but the man was so unsavory in his appearance and manner that it was hard to feel sympathy.

"But then I got strong, and they couldn't do nothin' more to me," Pizer continued, having apparently lost his reticence. "I could make 'em do what *I* said. Jus' show 'em a knife, and they done it."

"You carried a knife?"

"'Course I did. Everyone feared Leather Apron."

"Why were you called Leather Apron?" asked William.

"'Cause I wore a leather apron," said Pizer with what William had to admit was impeccable logic.

"And why did you wear a leather apron?"

"'Cause I was a boot maker," said Pizer, as though any moron should know that.

"Did you like your trade?"

"I liked usin' a knife," snarled Pizer. "Needed to, to cut the leather. But I'd rather 'ave used it to cut somethin' else. That Ripper has it right, there."

"Did you…know…Jack the Ripper?" William asked, suddenly taken with the idea that the two might be friends. Did demonic killers have friends?

"Didn't know 'im, though they say as he wrote my name in one of 'is letters." He noted this with a touch of pride. He then said scornfully, "But I wouldn't 'ave done it his way, myself. He's too fancy for me."

"What do you mean 'too fancy'?" asked William, intrigued by this comparative notion.

"All that slashin' and cuttin' up. I likes my knife," growled Pizer, "but I use it spare. Ain't that the point of a knife?" His eyes darted up at William in stating this professional view of the matter.

"So you feel Jack the Ripper cuts more than is necessary?"

Pizer snorted. "Don't need to be fancy to cut shoes. Nor throats neither. Cut 'em clean and simple, I say."

William pondered the idea a moment. What did that signify, to cut more than was necessary? There was something to be said for Pizer's observation that the point of using a knife was to be economical in the realm of killing. But then, it wasn't to kill these women that Jack the Ripper had cut them; they were dead when most of the cutting happened. Why, then, the need to cut more, to be "fancy," as Pizer put it? Pizer had learned to cut sparingly in his trade as a boot maker. Even a surgeon was economical in his use of a knife. Under what circumstances, then, would fancy cutting be appropriate? He was back to the idea that the key to understanding a madman was to find the context in which his madness made sense, became, that is, perversely rational.

Pizer had resumed talking. "Not as I need a knife to do 'em harm," he boasted. "I could use these." He flexed his blunt fingers. "Did it once too."

"You strangled someone?" There had been suspicion among the people of Whitechapel that Pizer was a killer, but no proof of it, as far as William knew.

Pizer did not respond to the question but snarled, "Can't treat me like a dog! Cleanin' up their messes, smellin' their stench, emptyin' their piss, makin' me do filthy things so they could laugh at me."

The man had again returned to the scene of his childhood, and William suddenly had a vivid image of the boy forced to perform all manner of ungodly acts for the amusement of his employers. But what had prompted him to kill later in life? "The person you strangled," he pressed. "Why did you do it?"

Pizer seemed not to hear. "Can't treat me like a dog. Can't make me do that no more. Nobody gonna make me!"

William was staring with an expression of curiosity and disgust. "The person you killed…wanted to make you do something?"

Pizer began to twitch, and his speech grew rapid and wild. "Can't make me! Can't make me! Can't shame me like that! Ain't gonna be shamed no more!" His voice grew shrill with fury. "Ain't shamed by you neither!" He fastened his eyes on William's shoes and stared at them fixedly. "Even with yer nice shoes, you don't shame me!"

"I'm a doctor!" William said sharply. "I'm here to get information about your condition, nothing more."

Pizer was not listening. His eyes were again darting about the room. "All dressed up in good leather to do filthy things! You're a stinking, bloody fraud with your fine shoes!"

"I'm Professor James from Boston," William felt compelled to assert. He could sense that Pizer had lost track of where he was, if he had ever known.

His voice incensed Pizer further. "I can make 'em do as I say if I wants to," he growled and flexed his fingers again. "I can make 'em, as they made me!" His eyes focused again on William's shoes, and he stared at them for several seconds in a state of rapt attention. His face then contorted into a grimace.

It was then that William understood his shoes, bought before he left Boston from a very good boot maker at the insistence of his Alice ("A Harvard professor must have a good pair of shoes," she had scolded), must put Pizer in mind of the men who had scorned and abused him. "Calm yourself!" he said sharply.

The sound of his voice seemed to be a trigger rather than a palliative. The man grimaced again, and William stood up in sudden awareness of the threat, but too late.

Pizer leaped from the cot and placed his hands around his visitor's neck.

William felt a searing pain from the pressure on his throat, and a thought darted through his mind: *This is how I will die, interviewing a madman, with a policeman standing outside the door,* but the next moment, Abberline and Maudsley rushed into the cell. Abberline adeptly pried Pizer's fingers from his neck, while Maudsley ran back into the corridor to call for help.

Within a few seconds, a guard twice the size of Pizer and with eyes even more snakelike entered the cell and, with a sweep of his arm, knocked the man onto the bed. "Don't worry, sirs. I'll have him in hand in a jiffy," said the guard. "You best get yourselves out of the way."

As Maudsley went off to get a compress for William's neck, and Abberline helped him stagger out of the cell, they could hear the blows falling inside.

"So what did your visit do for you besides almost getting you killed?" asked Abberline, when they were once again seated on the train back to London.

William touched his neck and felt the dull ache of the bruise. He had fortified himself with a shot of whiskey in Maudsley's office and had left Broadmoor with an improved feeling about his host. However much the two men differed in basic precepts, they shared an understanding of the horrors of mental illness. Perhaps more to the point, Maudsley's guilt regarding the attack had softened him toward his visitors. It seemed that Pizer had never exhibited violent behavior before, despite his reputation for being violent in the East End. It was another case where salient information had been discounted. If the people of his neighborhood were convinced that he was Jack the Ripper, certainly there must be a reason for their conviction. William suspected that Pizer had not been violent at Broadmoor because no one had spoken to him long enough to elicit violence.

"What did the visit do for me?" he mused in response to Abberline's question. "It taught me that shame is a powerful impetus for action, perhaps the most powerful. Pizer spent his childhood in a brothel, abused by women and men too. I reminded him of the men who frequented that place and used to demean him. His humanity was stolen from him as a child. It seems almost logical that he would become an animal himself, driven to abuse those who shamed and abused him."

"You're saying that Jack the Ripper kills out of rage for having been shamed?"

"I'd say killing of the sort he does must stem from extreme humiliation. It's a frenzied kind of retribution. No knowing whether the initial trauma was even intended as such; it may have been accidental, a matter of circumstance, but I suspect there was shame involving a woman at its origin."

"A prostitute?"

"Possibly, but not necessarily. Perhaps the women he kills remind him of someone in another sense. But like Pizer, I surmise it's a pattern of substitution. We substitute in the present for people in the past. What happens with men like Pizer—and I suspect, Jack the Ripper—is that love and hope turn to resentment and hatred. Who knows what instigates this transformation, trauma or abuse or simple abandonment. Whatever it is, the emotions continue to haunt the victim and can be relieved only through violation of something that stands in place of the original source of pain."

He paused a moment and then added, "There's something else as well. Pizer's attack was triggered by my shoes. He had worked as a boot maker, and his job became a conduit for his rage. Minor's case is an example in reverse, of how gratifying work can relieve and rechannel destructive tendencies. Our vocation, in large part, makes us who we are. Pizer learned to use a knife as a boot maker, and it gave him his name, Leather Apron. One would want to know what this murderer did for a living and how it informs his crimes."

Abberline considered this information. "There may be something to your ideas," he acknowledged, "but I can't say I'm convinced. Who among us hasn't been shamed in some way? Or frustrated in work? I have, and I daresay you have too."

"And both of us might have become murderers had our shame and frustration been great enough," asserted William. "We were fortunate to have been loved enough to counteract our shame, and to have our work become a source of gratification and pride. Had that not been the case, who knows? Evil men are not born, but made."

"You Americans think tolerance and justice can change things," said Abberline with a touch of scorn in his voice. "It's a pretty theory, but I've known plenty of evil men in my time, and it's my opinion they came into the world that way."

They had arrived at an impasse and, realizing that no amount of talk was going to make them budge in their views, retreated into silence for the remainder of the journey back to London.

CHAPTER 20

No sooner did William walk in the door of Henry's flat than his brother announced that a man had been by to report an arrest in the Whitechapel murders. William was half inclined to ignore the message. He was tired from his journey and had become familiar with false leads and the sort of mistakes the police were prone to make. He had just spent the day with Abberline, who had not mentioned that anyone was under investigation. And since when would a serious suspect be apprehended when the inspector was out of the office?

Henry insisted that the man had come directly from Abberline, though, who had made a point of requesting that William report to police headquarters at once to observe the interrogation.

When William arrived at Scotland Yard, he found that, indeed, an interesting scene was in progress. A swarthy young man with disheveled hair, hollow cheeks, and dark, flashing eyes stood flanked by two officers in one corner. He was wearing a long, shabby coat that suggested that he was a university student, a Jew, or an anarchist, and since the uniform of these groups overlapped, the young man could conceivably belong to all three.

On the other side of the room, some four or five officers were attending to an older man in uniform with a puffed-up manner. He was barking orders, and they were scurrying in and out of the room, handing him notes and official documents.

In the midst of this scene, William spotted Abberline seated alone in a corner. He walked over to the inspector. "Is it possible that you have a suspect?" he asked.

"*I* don't have a suspect," replied Abberline testily, "but our assistant commissioner, Sir Robert Anderson, apparently does. He has just come back from the Continent and assumed control of the case. Commissioner Warren is perfectly satisfied to hand over the reins, so long as he isn't bothered. The result is that Sir Robert," Abberline spit out the honorific, "has arrested someone who suits the cut of his prejudices. I thought you might find his methods of interest, given your work in psychological deviance."

He made this assertion with a sneer but seemed disinclined to say more, and William felt it best to leave him alone and mix among the officers nearby. He did this, as he sometimes did at professional meetings when he wished to get a sense of prevailing opinion or pick up salient facts. He walked about with an indifferent air, peering casually over the shoulders of the milling officers, glancing at the documents in their hands, and eavesdropping on their conversation.

After an interval of perhaps a quarter of an hour, Anderson suddenly spoke to the assembled group. "Welcome, gentlemen," he began in the pompous, affected tone that William had come to associate with higher ranking officials in this country. "In the short time I have been back on English soil, I am pleased to have made significant headway in the Whitechapel case that, until now, has baffled some of our allegedly best officers." He glanced superciliously at Abberline, who glared back at him. It was clear that the two men loathed each other.

"I now present to you Mr. Benjamin Cohen, a suspect whom we apprehended only this morning." Anderson gestured with a flourish in the direction of the young man in the long coat who had been led to the center of the room.

"Upon what evidence do you arrest this man?" demanded Abberline angrily.

Anderson turned to the inspector and spoke slowly, as though to a dimwit. "A plethora of evidence, sir, which I will now enumerate for you." He gave a nod to one of his officers, who handed him a sheet of paper. "First, Mr. Cohen's knowledge of medicine. He is said to have helped a local physician with stitching and dressings and to have accompanied the local midwife on some of her cases."

Abberline mumbled under his breath, "No good deed goes unpunished," but Anderson ignored him and moved on. "Secondly, Mr. Cohen has frequented Zionist meetings and, not satisfied with the extreme forbearance of our government toward his people, has protested at various rallies regarding what he deems the ill use of his race. This deep-seated hostility toward Christian society conforms to the message that was written on the wall near the site of the Eddowes murder."

Abberline seemed about to speak, but Anderson continued without pause.

"Thirdly, there is the suspect's socially incendiary tendencies. I have the exhibits here of the books found in his room." He again nodded to the officer next to him and was handed a number of books that he held up by way of demonstration. "Darwin, Marx, Fourier. He is also a member of a Masonic society and is a known freethinker."

Abberline muttered, "First a religious zealot; now a freethinker," but was ignored.

"Finally," pronounced Anderson, casting a triumphant glance at Abberline, "we have an irrefutable piece of material evidence in our possession." He motioned in the direction of another officer, who came forward and handed him an envelope. Anderson opened it and extracted its contents. "I will pass among you these two photographs, one that was found on the premises of Mr. Cohen's business and the other that you may recognize from the newspapers if you did not see it here already."

He handed the photographs to the officer to his right, who passed them to Abberline. He and William looked down at the photographs together.

The first was of a woman seated on a chair. She was naked, though her posture was rather formal and unrevealing, the body positioned sideways, so that only one breast was discernible, and the legs crossed in what might even seem like a prudish posture. The face, however, was turned directly to the camera and registered no embarrassment. The woman was not pretty and not young, but her expression commanded attention, as though, for the purposes of the photograph, she held herself in some esteem.

The other photograph was of a woman stretched out on a slab in the London morgue, her eyes closed, her head thrown back. A line of stitches across the throat indicated where the head, almost severed by the knife's incision, had been stitched back into place. It was not immediately evident that the two photographs were of the same woman, but a moment's inspection made clear that they were. It was Polly Nichols.

Anderson stood in smug silence as the photographs were passed around the room. Finally, he spoke again. "If more evidence is needed, we also have a witness. Mr. Nathan Rosenzweig, greengrocer, has provided us with an excellent description of the man who conferred with Polly Nichols on the night of her murder. 'A thin individual, five foot seven or five foot eight, with dark hair.' Benjamin Cohen to the letter. We have Mr. Rosenzweig here to make the identification."

A small, neatly dressed man had been led into the room and was pushed forward.

"You saw the perpetrator speaking to Polly Nichols on the night of her murder?" asked Anderson.

The man looked about him nervously. "I saw someone speaking to someone who might have been Polly. I knew her only in passing. She sometimes sold flowers near the Aldgate Market. Can't say I knew her."

"But you thought it was Polly."

"It might have been Polly. She weren't the most distinctive-looking girl, and it was dark."

"And you saw the perpetrator talking to her," said Anderson, ignoring this caveat.

"I saw her talking to a gentleman. Whether or not he was the perpetrator is another matter," clarified Rosenzweig.

"A somewhat slight individual of medium stature, dark hair."

"I suppose that's right," said Rosenzweig sulkily.

"This man?" The assistant inspector pointed to Cohen.

Rosenzweig looked at the suspect for a moment. "The man I saw was light complected," he finally noted. "This man is dark."

"You said he had dark hair."

"Dark hair, but fair skin," Rosenzweig insisted. "It's not an unusual combination."

"It *is* unusual among your people!" snapped Anderson and then motioned for the suspect and the witness to be ushered from the room. Once they were gone, he blithely addressed the gathering. "I rest my case, gentlemen. The final proof is in this man's recanting of his former testimony in the face of a Jewish perpetrator. It is clear that he knows the man is guilty but will not turn against one of his own race."

William had been watching Abberline's face as Anderson made his comments and could see that it had gone from being very pale to very red and that his lips were trembling with anger. He seemed about to voice his objections and, one could tell by the livid expression on his face, that the result would be impolitic—or worse.

William cleared his throat and rose to his feet. "Excuse me for interfering, sir." He addressed Anderson with exaggerated deference, having found that a bumbling manner, when combined with his gangly, unkempt appearance, could disarm more belligerent sorts of people. "Do you know me? I don't know if you do, but I'm Professor James from Cambridge, Massachusetts. I was summoned here to help with this case by Sir Charles Warren, who seems, for reasons I hardly warrant, to have a high opinion of my abilities." He shrugged and assumed a puzzled air, as if to demonstrate his humility.

"My professional expertise is in the new field of psychology, which is, you know, something we Americans have pioneered in our limited sort of way. Seeing as I'm here at some expense to your government and would want to be of help, I feel inclined to make a few observations and pose a few questions, if you'll indulge me." He looked around innocently, and as no one said anything, proceeded. "First, it would be helpful in the case of an identification of a suspect to arrange a line of men of similar general appearance from whom he might be picked out. It's something we've learned to do regularly on our side of the Atlantic, seeing as we have so much experience with violent criminals, ours being a more lawless and uncivilized society."

He paused, allowing this observation to sink in, and then continued. "Could you tell me Mr. Cohen's business?" He had overheard certain details relating to the investigation while mixing among the officers earlier that he now judged to be relevant.

The officer holding the folder coughed before responding. "He is a bookseller," he finally said.

"A bookseller?" William lifted an eyebrow and looked around him in mock surprise, wondering, as he did so, if he ought to have pursued a career in the law (it was one of the few professions he had not considered, which, by itself, was something to recommend it).

The officer felt prompted to add, "There are quite a number of small book dealers in the Jewish quarter of the Whitechapel district."

"I see," said William, nodding encouragingly. "And where was the photograph found?"

The officer coughed again. "It had been found in one of the books in his shop."

"A book that was for sale?"

The officer acknowledged that it had been in a book for sale.

William appeared to ruminate on this fact for a moment. "It would be odd, don't you think, for a criminal to place on sale a book with a photograph of his victim in it?" he finally queried no one in particular. "And why were you looking through the books?" he asked abruptly.

There was a good deal of shifting and murmuring among the officers attached to Anderson.

"We were seeking evidence of the man's conspiratorial activity," said the officer under interrogation. "He had been involved in a protest against labor practices at a London factory, and we had been asked by the proprietor to investigate."

"An employee labor squabble, of course." William nodded. "And you have hit on an excellent pretext to put him out of commission as an agitator for workers' rights." He delivered this last observation with a bluntness that he had not displayed until now.

"Excuse me, sir," said Anderson angrily, "but that is an unwarranted supposition."

"I beg your pardon," said William, resuming his previous humble tone. "What I meant to say is that it seems perfectly logical to assume that someone who agitates in one area might have socially aberrant impulses in another. I myself would have assumed as much until I became involved in psychological studies that contradict it. But our research has shown that the social protester, though an impediment to many established interests in society, is of quite a different mental composition from the psychopath. As to the witness you brought forward to support the identification, he never pretended to have seen either the victim or the perpetrator clearly."

"The clannishness of these people is well-known," insisted Anderson, whose face had grown as red as Abberline's.

"Again, that sort of supposition is subject to debate. Indeed, to rely on it is likely, in my opinion, to instigate an insurgency among the Jewish population of the East End that might prove inconvenient and costly to your government."

"You doubt that the perpetrator is a Jew?"

"Yes," said William, assuming an authoritative tone. "I believe that the writing near the murder site is the result of Jew baiting rather than Jewish conspiracy." He had, in fact, as Alice had recommended, queried a professor of Hebraic studies at the University of London as well as a local pawnbroker and been told that the misspelling of Jews had no correlation to any secret spelling in the annals of the race.

Anderson glared at William for a moment and then turned to the officer on his left. "Let Cohen go, but put him under watch. We will see where it leads us," he instructed curtly and then gave a stiff nod, turned, and left the room, a phalanx of officers following sheepishly at his heels.

As soon as they were gone, Abberline stood up and shook William's hand. "You have saved me from an outburst that might have ruined my career."

William brushed aside his thanks, but Abberline insisted on explaining the reasons for his anger. Sir Robert Anderson had a deep-seated distrust of Jews and Catholics and had devoted his career in government to blocking parliamentary efforts to give these groups a greater voice. He had been involved in the false implication of Parnell in the Phoenix Park murders in an effort to thwart Irish Home Rule. His present vendetta against Cohen was probably connected to discrediting the admission of Jews to Parliament. "These people have a network of spies and coconspirators,"

Abberline concluded. "Anderson has ties to the foreign office and is probably fed much of his material through that channel."

William recalled that Mrs. Lancaster, the medium, was married to someone in the foreign office; she too had tried to finger a Jewish subject, although there had also been that odd moment when she veered off from this line, almost, it seemed, against her will. He could not forget her insistence on the killer's stained fingers.

His thoughts turned to the nude photograph of Polly Nichols. He remembered the odd expression on the face of the woman in that picture who would become Jack the Ripper's first victim. He was now convinced, with Abberline and Mrs. Lancaster, that Polly *was* the first, not the second. Despite her nakedness, she had looked dignified, even proud, in the photograph, not the usual expression of a prostitute who sold her body for money. William sensed this piece was important, though he did not know why. Where was the photograph taken? Who had taken it? And how had it gotten into Benjamin Cohen's shop?

"The picture of Polly Nichols—I want to study it," he said to Abberline. "And the address of Benjamin Cohen. Could you please make it available to me?"

It seemed he would get his chance to visit the bookstalls of Whitechapel after all.

CHAPTER 21

ALICE WAS PERUSING THE letters that William had handed over, jotting down occasional thoughts between dozing, when there was a knock at her door, and Archie peeked in, a parcel under his arm.

"Pardon any disturbing of you, mum, but a man was by from Mr. John Singing Sargent who said as how I should give it to you."

Alice beckoned to the boy to approach her bed and took the parcel, which she supposed was the painting John had promised to brighten up. She must remember, she thought to herself, to refer to John in the future as "John *Singing* Sargent."

"Sit here a moment, Archie," she said to the boy, patting the bed, "and keep me company for a moment. I get lonesome sometimes, you know."

The boy perched himself on the side of the bed. "I have some tricks for keepin' the lonesomeness away if you wanna hear 'em, mum," said Archie.

"Please," said Alice.

"Well, when my mum would leave me alone for days and days, I would tell myself stories. I'd make as I had friends comin' by and ud tell 'em the stories bit by bit, like in them *Arabian Nights* that the ol' lady told me 'bout later. It passed the time. But I don' suppose you'd need that, seein' as how you have your books and newspapers, and your brothers too. That's nice to have family."

"Do you miss your mother and father?" asked Alice.

"Can' say I miss what I never 'ad," said the boy. "Not as I blame 'em, havin' all the troubles they did; they couden very well think on me. I kep' track of 'em, though, 'specially my mum." The boy's face grew dark, and Alice suspected that he might blame himself for her death.

"What do you mean you kept track?"

"I were always good at followin' people, without them knowing, that is. So I used to follow my mum when she went places. Not as she went out much, 'specially toward the end. But that day she did, an' I followed 'er. She went to the church and lit a candle for me brother as died, and stayed there for a long time. It was the las' thing she did afore she done away wi' 'erself. I used to follow my dad too. Mostly 'e went to those places where they lie around with pipes lookin' like they're dead."

"Opium dens," said Alice matter-of-factly. "I'm told they can ease pain and misery, but at the cost of deadening the mind. You must never do that, Archie. We must bear whatever pain we have and keep our minds sharp."

"And why's that, mum?"

"Because our minds are the one thing we have that is truly ours—that no one can take from us. To be able to think is a rare and precious thing, to be protected, no matter what happens to us."

"I can see that, mum."

"So you've gotten along without parents," said Alice. "You're a strong boy."

"It's not as I diden wanna have 'em," said the boy. "I saw other chaps whose mums worried 'bout whether they 'ad a hole in their trousers or a button gone. I used to say, 'My mum's gonna whup me for losing that there button,' jus' so it would look like someone cared as I lost it. But no one did."

"Well, we care here," said Alice. "And if you lose any buttons, you will have me to answer to. I hope you can begin to feel at home with us."

"I do, mum. I feel I got a home now more swell than any a the rest of 'em. Sally, she's like a sister, only stric' like a mum. I likes it when she yells at me, which is jus' as well, as she yells at me a lot."

"Well, that's good to hear," said Alice, feeling that she ought to have the boy leave the room before she burst into tears. "Tell Sally that she is to continue to yell. And now, I think, I'll rest a bit. Please close the door quietly when you leave."

After he had gone, Alice took Sargent's parcel from the bed table, where she had placed it. Under the brown wrapping, the painting had been wrapped in newspaper. She carefully spread the paper out on the bed to reveal the picture. Sargent's masterful rendering of the woman in the red cloak shimmered with new luster under the application of a fresh coat of varnish. She let her gaze rest on the painting for a few minutes, and then her attention wandered to the newspaper on which it lay. Her glance stopped with a jolt. "Of course," she muttered excitedly to herself, her eyes fastened on the page. "Of course. I understand now!"

CHAPTER 22

TWO HOURS LATER, WHEN the brothers arrived at Alice's apartment in response to her message to come at once, they found her in bed nibbling on a brioche. Her eyes were very bright.

"You're in time for tea—or rather coffee, since that's what we're having this afternoon. And you must try one of these," she said, motioning to the basket of brioches next to a dish of fresh butter and a jar of preserves. "They're as light as air, thanks to a recipe that Katherine got from Fanny Kemble, and that Fanny got from the divine Sarah Bernhardt. It's a brioche with a dramatic genealogy."

The brothers sat down at the little corner table and began eating the brioches and sipping the Moroccan coffee that Sally poured into the large mugs that had been given to Alice by her friend, Mrs. Humphrey Ward. Mrs. Ward had an idolatrous admiration for the late Dickens, and the mugs, which she liked to give as gifts, were painted with characters from Dickens's novels. Henry found the whole thing very gauche (though perhaps he was jealous). He had at first refused to drink from a mug until Alice said that if he didn't, it would make more work for Sally, at which he relented and took the one with the picture of Mr. Micawber on it.

They drank their coffee, while Alice kept silent as Henry maligned the mugs and William noted that strawberry preserves were better in America. Suddenly she burst out, unable to contain herself any longer. "I called you here on such short notice because I have an idea about the murders."

The brothers looked at each other.

"We await illumination," said William.

"We are all ears," said Henry.

Alice ignored their facetious tone and continued excitedly, "It began with certain observations that I made while studying the letters. I examined them closely after that horrible Lancaster woman left and was struck, first, by the handwriting. We've already discussed the misspellings as exhibiting what William called 'disingenuous illiteracy.' The handwriting appears to show a similar tendency; it is artificially awkward."

"Yes," said William impatiently. "As I said, it's clearly the work of someone trying to disguise his hand."

"But it's more than that!" exclaimed Alice. "It's not the sort of handwriting in which the writer is simply trying to deceive. It suggests someone accustomed to using the pen in unorthodox and original ways. The writing is more graphic than it is orthographic, if you follow me."

"Not really," said Henry.

"Let me clarify, then, with something I discovered this afternoon. Look at that." She pointed across the room, where Sargent's painting had been hung back on the wall.

"One of John's Venetian scenes," noted William.

"Not among his best," said Henry.

Alice ignored them and proceeded. "John took that painting home the other day because he said it looked dull and he wanted to revarnish it. When he sent it back, it was wrapped in newspaper. Some of the varnish dripped onto the paper. Look here." She took a piece of newspaper from the bed table and indicated a few small shiny spots on the surface. "I sent

Katherine to the Sargents' to inquire about it. The substance is called megilp, a mixture of linseed oil and turpentine commonly used to varnish paintings. Now," she said, taking one of the Ripper letters from her bed table with a flourish, "look at this!" She pointed to the spot on the page that they had noted before.

"They resemble each other," acknowledged Henry.

"It's a shiny, clear substance," said William peevishly. "It could be anything."

"I've had Katherine purchase a variety of gluing materials. Nothing except megilp dries this way. So the question is this: why would our writer have reason to employ megilp? This brings me to another observation. The reddish smudge on the other letter that you said yourself did not resemble dried blood. It does, however, resemble dried paint." She took out a sheet of paper, on which there were multiple splotches in a variety of reddish hues. "While Katherine was at John's, I asked her to have him put together a sample of some of his reds, which he did with his usual thoroughness. Kindly take a look. This one on the right, which John has marked 'dark amber,' is an excellent match. I will have to show him the smudge for verification, but it seems to me reasonable to assume that the smudge on the letter is paint."

"Let me see that," said William, grabbing the sample sheet. He had fleetingly considered that the smudge on the Ripper letter might be paint when he first saw it. He knew what dried paint looked like; he had been a painter, but he had instinctively pushed the idea out of his head because he had no wish to recall that period of his life. He knew the mind could work that way. Elements relating to one thing could slip, without one's awareness, into affecting another.

"So the murderer is an artist," ruminated Henry. "It would explain the fair Lancaster's assertion that his fingers were stained!"

Alice waved her hand. The idea of giving credence to a spiritualist almost made her want to dismiss her theory.

"It would also explain this," said William quietly, taking the photograph of Polly Nichols out of an envelope in his pocket.

Alice studied the picture a moment. "Where did it come from?" she asked.

"From the police. They found it in a book that a Jewish bookseller had for sale in his shop. It was probably delivered to him by one of his vendors. I will try to find out where he got it."

"Please do," said Alice. "There's no mark of a photographer's shop on the back. I suspect that it was taken by the murderer."

William nodded. As soon as his sister had mentioned her theory, he realized that it could account for the pride on Polly Nichols's face in the photograph. She was posing in the manner of a painter's model and was proud to be using her body in the service of art.

He mused, "Mary Wells said Polly used to do something in the area that she thought was refined, but came back with her sweater misbuttoned."

"She was posing for an artist who decided to kill her," agreed Alice. "It explains the gashes under the eyes of Catherine Eddowes and the symmetrical gashes on the abdomens of the other women."

"He was painting her body with a knife," concluded William softly. The idea was grotesque but stunningly obvious. It amazed him that he had not made the connection before.

"Do you think all the women killed by Jack the Ripper were his models?" asked Henry.

"Not necessarily," William responded quickly. "Polly could simply have set the acts in motion." He realized that his sister's revelation was compelling, not only because it fit with the pieces of evidence they had gathered, but also because it resolved his theory about the inner workings of perversion, the way it repeated itself in the form of a habit and linked to the instruments associated with the perpetrator's vocation.

"If the murders are the work of an artist, what does that tell us?" asked Alice, as though she were quizzing a group of bright students.

"Artists are inclined to sign their work," suggested Henry. "They crave recognition."

"The letters reflect this," she agreed.

"And every artist has a distinctive style," William noted.

"So what is Jack the Ripper's style?"

"Hardly traditional, I would say," said William. "He'd be in the modern impressionist school."

"But not one of the pretty impressionists," qualified Alice. "Not lily pads and sunsets."

"No," agreed William. "His palette would be dark. We will have to ask John Sargent. He knows everyone."

"Yes," Henry added, bemused. "We can certainly trust John. His pictures are pretty, he loves his sister, and he is too fastidious to commit murder."

"Though sisters may drive even the most fastidious man to murder," William couldn't resist noting.

"This is no time for jokes," Alice intervened sternly. "This is an important discovery, and we must act on it, quickly, each of us according to our abilities." She spoke with the authority of a commander laying out a plan of battle. "I will continue to study the evidence and consider how it may bring us closer to the murderer. William, you are to learn what you can from Scotland Yard and trace the source of Polly Nichols's photograph. Henry, you must inventory the art world and consider who has the motive and opportunity to commit these crimes."

"But Wilde's dinner party is tonight," complained Henry. He suddenly imagined being trundled off to thumb through the membership lists of the minor art clubs and having to dine late on Mrs. Smith's unprepossessing fare.

Alice happily contradicted his assumption. "No need to miss your party," she said. "I want you in society, mixing with the fashionable world, but alert, if you don't mind my adding, which means indulging in less wine than you are probably used to." She gave him a severe look and continued. "Wilde has a wide circle of friends and knows artists, high and low. Keep your eyes and ears open for anyone who seems suspicious. As a novelist, you have an instinct for the incongruous detail; bring this to bear now, where the stakes are the highest."

Having spoken, she laid her head back on her pillow. The exertion of the past hour had taken its toll. "We are dealing with an artist of murder," she murmured. "We must use our much vaunted intelligence and creative skill to catch him."

CHAPTER 23

DESPITE THE MOMENTOUS DISCOVERY of the afternoon, the identity of the murderer was far from Henry's mind as he prepared to attend Wilde's party that evening. He had heard from some of his friends that his countryman, Samuel Clemens, had just arrived in England, and that Wilde, who had met Clemens during his American tour, had invited him to be the promised surprise guest. As much as Henry enjoyed Wilde's dinners, the thought of sitting across the table from this much touted personage did not appeal to him. He did not like the homely demeanor that Clemens affected, and he liked even less the man's great success with it. Clemens was selling books and giving lectures, while Henry had stacks of unsold volumes moldering in a warehouse somewhere and had not been asked to lecture to anyone.

When he arrived at the Albemarle Club, the bohemian enclave that Wilde favored for his more festive gatherings, Henry made his way to the private dining room where the party was being held, ordered himself a brandy, and surveyed the company. Wilde had not yet made an appearance, but most of the other guests were already seated. There were a number of pedigreed women and the usual literati with whom Wilde liked to ornament his dinners. A surprising addition was the venerable Robert Browning, who was fielding questions on the subject of his late wife. How awful, Henry thought, to have to drag around someone else's literary reputation and have it eternally eclipse your own.

There were a few Germans talking loudly about the scientific study of aesthetics (leave it to the Germans to turn art into science), and a contingent of Frenchmen looking superior for no other reason than that they were French.

Also present was a diverse sampling of artists. A handful of eager Pre-Raphaelites were listening with rapt attention to their mentor, Burne-Jones, who seemed to be lecturing them on the china plate. Two members of the Newlyn school, who specialized in Cornish landscape, were whispering about two members of the Marble school, who specialized in neoclassical subjects. Du Maurier was there, sketching a cartoon on his napkin, and a few minor portraitists were looking jealously at Sargent, who had just received a handsome commission for his portrait of a Liverpool factory owner's wife. He had earned it through his ability to give her the eyes of a duchess and remedy her lack of a chin.

Henry considered his sister's hypothesis. Were any of these people capable of a grisly series of murders? It seemed unlikely, though appearances could be deceiving.

He had ordered himself a second brandy and was beginning to relax when there was a bustle near the door, and Wilde finally appeared with his entourage, which included a number of young gentlemen with the comfortable air of stupidity that seemed to accompany hereditary privilege. Several others entered as well, and Henry caught a glimpse of a face that seemed both familiar and strange. Before he had a chance to take it in, his attention was diverted to a middle-aged man in a checkered suit with wild hair and a bushy, oversize mustache. Clemens. The very sight of this homespun creature was annoying.

"*Attention mes amis,*" said Oscar, tapping his spoon to his glass. "*Bienvenue, à tout le monde.* I want to offer a special welcome to our special guest, Mr. Samuel Clemens, or as we know him on the page, Mark Twain. He has just arrived in England and is already the toast of Europe."

Henry winced. He had been in Europe for more than a decade and was still not the toast of it.

"I'm mighty glad to be here," said Clemens, in what Henry believed was an affectedly flat, nasal accent, but by which the company appeared to be immediately charmed.

"What inspires your writing, Mr. Clemens?" asked one of the pedigreed women.

"Alcohol, my dear…and debt," answered Clemens, to appreciative laughter.

"Do you think that your writing suffers from your country's dearth of history?" asked an eager Pre-Raphaelite.

"Not at all," responded Clemens. "I wish we could continue to avoid history, but I suspect we will soon have some of it."

There was more laughter.

"I was struck by the use of dialect in your novel about the young boy and the runaway slave," said a bluestocking woman who had lately taken up linguistics. "Did you study the structure of American Negro speech?"

"No, ma'am," said Clemens. "I did not study Negro speech; I listened to it."

A group of young men, normally intimidated by the bluestocking's erudition, found this comment hilarious.

"Do you Americans have any women poets of note?" queried the great Browning.

"We have our poets in petticoats," acknowledged Clemens, "but we try to avoid reading them."

Browning looked taken aback, but Clemens proceeded to soften the remark in his genial drawl. "You see, we are a vast, untamed country and so tend to favor a more rugged style for the present. I am sure we will have our women poets in time, but for now we are carving our literature out of mud and rock."

Henry felt his mood growing increasingly sour. It was grating to hear Clemens turn his country's demerits into badges of honor. One could laud what was low and vulgar as much as one pleased, but that hardly prevented it from being low and vulgar.

Fortunately, the soup, lobster bisque, arrived as a momentary diversion. Henry was seated across from a group of young men of very slight appearance. "Are you partial to the Uranian school?" one asked him softly.

"Uranian?" asked Henry, confused. Sargent whispered that the Uranians worshipped boys, and Henry shook his head vigorously and turned away.

The meal progressed slowly. There was talk at the other end of the table about the relative merits of New York and London, Grover Cleveland and William Gladstone, Lillian Russell and Lillie Langtry. Clemens explained the American electoral system and the issues in the upcoming presidential election. He spoke about his business ventures, the advisability of reparations to former slaves, and the hoped-for production of a play he had written with his friend, William Dean Howells. These topics showcased his ingenuity, beneficence, and collaborative energy, thereby causing Henry's mood to deteriorate further. That Howells, his own good friend, would collaborate with this creature—and not approach him first—was especially irritating.

During the discussion, Henry remained quiet and, despite Alice's admonition, repeatedly motioned for his wineglass to be refilled. At one point, he turned to Sargent. "Did you know Alice thinks Jack the Ripper is a painter?" he asked abruptly. He had wanted to build gradually to this revelation, but the proceedings of the evening had caused him to lose patience.

Sargent opened his eyes wide with surprise. He and Emily had wondered why Alice had wanted samples of the different reds, but had been too discreet to ask.

"She has amassed considerable evidence to support her theory," said Henry smugly.

Before he could say more, Clemens was at it again, regaling the company with his adventures as a steamboat captain on the Mississippi River. Sargent, diverted by the Clemens account, murmured that he looked forward to learning more about Alice's intriguing theory and shifted his attention to the other end of the table.

Henry was disgusted. Here he was with news that a diabolical murderer might be loose in the Royal Academy, and Sargent was more interested in hearing stories about paddling down a muddy river. He made no effort to speak again.

The courses came and went. There were chicken cutlets that he thought were overcooked, a mutton chop he sampled and left on his plate, a poor selection of jellies, and a mediocre poached turbot. He drank copiously and filled himself up with potatoes. He was becoming very sullen and very intoxicated.

As the meal drew to a close, Wilde called for his honored guest to give a toast. They all rose.

"To the mother country," declared Clemens, "from which my compatriots and I are still trying to free ourselves."

Henry had lifted his glass but put it down. There was only so much of this sort of thing he could take.

"You will not drink to that, Henry?" asked Wilde, pleased at the prospect of a quarrel.

"No," asserted Henry, "I do not share Mr. Clemens's desire to sever my ties to England."

Clemens lifted a bushy eyebrow. "It is my understanding that we fought a war of independence for that purpose," he said.

"Political independence is one thing; cultural independence, another," intoned Henry. "We have much to learn from our European brothers, and we would be remiss to deny it."

"We will have a native literature only when we do," said Clemens.

"Then we will have a *bad* literature," asserted Henry. "I count on my European ties to lend weight to my writing."

"And your writing sinks under it," murmured Clemens.

"Your meaning, sir?" Henry took this up sharply.

"My meaning is that your prose could use more native air."

Henry sputtered. "And yours, sir, could use more art!"

Clemens paused, as the company waited for his rejoinder. "There is such a thing as too much art," he finally said. "I fear that Mr. James's novels suffer from that defect. When I put them down, I find myself incapable of picking them up again."

There was considerable laughter, and it fleetingly occurred to Henry that he and Clemens were making spectacles of themselves in front of the Europeans, which was just what vulgar Americans were expected to do. Still, he could not stop himself and countered stridently, "Sir, no person of breeding would find your writing more than a burlesque diversion."

"Breeding?" Clemens scoffed, looking around him with mock wonder. "Who are these persons of breeding? Are they men…or horses?"

The laughter had grown very loud. Clemens's wit—if one could call it that—was being well received.

"I…resent that!" Henry declared lamely. He had gotten very red.

"Shall we have a duel?" demanded Wilde. "Shall I get out the sabers or the pistols?"

"Dueling is an old-world custom." Clemens laughed. "In my country we would have a boxing match. Does Mr. James box?"

Henry felt vaguely panic-stricken. Clemens was baiting him, impugning his manliness, using vulgarity to place him at a disadvantage. What should he do? He felt ill-used and humiliated, and the prospect of being punched did not seem entirely outside the sphere of possibility. He had always had a horror of physical violence.

He looked with dismay at the company; all seemed to be paying close attention and smirking. Even the French had been roused from their Gallic indifference, eager to see what would happen next.

"I don't think our American guests should fight," a clear voice intruded in the background. "They are both indispensable to our cultural life by showing us the world from different angles, the high and the low. Our literature would be poorer for the lack of either of them."

Everyone turned to the speaker, a fair young man with a square jaw and hard, glittery blue eyes. Henry felt a welling of gratitude.

"That settles it, then." Wilde laughed. "We must not allow you Americans to hurt each other. Now sit." He pulled at Clemens's sleeve. "We will drink some more wine. Our wine at least is better than yours, which is reason enough to settle here."

Henry dropped into his chair. As the wine was poured and the ices served, he pondered the episode that had just transpired. Who was it who had intervened? He looked to the front of the room and saw that the young man who had saved him had moved off to the side and was combing through a bag of what looked like costume apparel. Henry felt suddenly light-headed. Was that the face he had seen and remembered at the beginning of the evening? For weeks he had been trying to recall something from the dinner party at Gosse's (if it had been Gosse's). He believed this young man had been there. Indeed, he was certain he was. A memorable face. How had he forgotten it?

Once the ices had been cleared and the Madeira served, Wilde stood up and raised his glass. "To art and song," he said. "I promised on a recent occasion that we would perform some musical hall turns. We have rehearsed something for this evening." He motioned to the young man, whom James had been watching in the corner, who stepped forward. He was holding a wig and a piece of drapery. He placed the wig on his head and wrapped the drape around his shoulders, curtsied, and smiled. Even in this makeshift ironic garb, he had managed a transformation. There was now a pretty young girl in place of a handsome young man. *A natural gift for mimicry*, thought Henry admiringly.

"We shall perform 'Oh, False One, You Have Deceived Me' from *Pirates of Penzance,* by our friends Messieurs Gilbert and Sullivan," announced Wilde.

There followed a lively rendition of the song, a call and response of the conventional farcical variety. Wilde sang with requisite brio, and the young man, with a sweetly coquettish lilt. Light musical numbers were not to Henry's taste, but he granted that Oscar and the young man performed well. Especially the young man.

At the end, Wilde bowed low, and his partner curtsied and pulled off his wig. There was enthusiastic applause by the guests—even the blasé Frenchmen seemed to have been entertained.

Henry joined vigorously in the applause. It seemed the young man was looking directly at him. Perhaps he wanted a sign of thanks for having intervened in the encounter with Clemens. He nodded an acknowledgment, but the young man did not blink. Perhaps he was not looking at him at all. Still, Henry could not avert his own gaze. He was transfixed by the young man's eyes, which were glacially blue. He felt a shiver pass through himself.

"Who is he?" he whispered to Sargent.

"Walter Sickert. An apprentice to Whistler."

An artist! "Is he any good?"

"Talented but macabre."

"How's that?" asked Henry sharply.

"Dark palette. Tawdry subjects."

Wilde motioned graciously to the young man. "My friend here is even more gifted as a painter than as a music hall performer. You must all go see his work. Buy it or write about it, and make him more famous than Whistler. Do your imitation of Jimmy's laugh again, Walter."

"'Ha ha!'" said the young man.

"That's Jimmy!" cried Wilde. "'Ha ha.' You do it better."

Henry caught his breath. It came back to him in a rush. They had talked of Jack the Ripper at that dinner party the night of his ordeal. This Sickert had been present at that occasion and had noted that the "ha ha" in the letters put him in mind of Whistler. He had imitated Whistler's laugh, then!

Sickert. The name was suggestive. Dickensian, if Henry wanted the name for a murderer. Not that he did. Indeed, a feeling of warmth for the young man competed with a feeling of dread.

It had been an extremely stressful evening, one Henry would not want to repeat, but he had learned something of importance, though he did not know what it was. If his logical faculties were weak, his instincts were strong. He had found a germ. He would have to bring it to Alice and see what she could make of it.

CHAPTER 24

A T THE SAME TIME that Henry was preparing for his dinner at the Albemarle Club, William was in a hansom cab heading to Mansell Street in Whitechapel. He had in hand the address of Benjamin Cohen that Abberline had gotten for him. It was unclear whether it was Cohen's business establishment or his home—possibly it was both. From what he had discerned of the area, distinctions of home and work were not pronounced in the East End.

When William descended from the cab, he soon found that the address coincided with one of the small bookshops that cluttered the area and that he had wanted so much to peruse during his first visit to Whitechapel. But while most of the other shops were still open or just closing for the night, this one was shuttered and padlocked. When William gazed through the shutters, he saw that the shelves were bare, the fixtures removed from the walls, and the place apparently abandoned.

His first response was a lurch of panic. Had Benjamin Cohen been guilty after all and escaped justice due to William's interference? A sense of dread began to rise in him, and he pulled himself back to reason by force of will, summoning to mind what had caused him to act in Cohen's defense:

the man's intelligent and rational demeanor, the obvious scapegoating by Anderson, his own instinct regarding guilt and innocence.

He had calmed himself somewhat with this line of thought and decided to inquire about Cohen's whereabouts of a group of men standing on the opposite corner, speaking animatedly in the Jewish tongue. The men were dressed in the conventional prayer shawls and skullcaps of the sect, perhaps waiting for sundown when they would hold their evening service. In the course of his research into comparative religion, William had been present for some of these ceremonies, which he had found at once exotic and familiar. All religion, as he saw it, was propelled by the same impulse: a need to believe in something larger than oneself. He saw the impulse, regardless of its manifestation, as an ennobling element in human nature, and the longer he lived, the less the various trappings that distinguished one religion from another made a difference to him.

He was about to cross over to talk to this group, but before he could do so, he found a figure blocking his way. The person was dressed, like the men across the street, in a fringed shawl and skullcap, but he was more than six feet tall, and his chest was so large that it pulled the coat that covered his vestments to bursting.

"What do you want here?" asked the sentinel pugnaciously. "Usually your kind comes round when it's dark."

William hadn't realized that someone in a shawl and skullcap could look threatening, but this person did. He surmised that the man was assigned to keep watch on the street, a practical precaution, considering the level of crime in the area, not to mention the recent Ripper murders.

William pointed to the shop and mentioned the name of Benjamin Cohen.

"And what's your business with him?" The man seemed to scowl more deeply.

"I'm not the police, if that's what you think," William explained quickly. "I'm a friend. Or at least, I'm someone in sympathy with…" He paused, trying to determine exactly with what he was in sympathy with regard to Cohen. "I am in sympathy with his position," he finally finished vaguely.

The man eyed him with new interest. Perhaps he was sizing up the possibility that William might, after all, be a Jew of the exotic American variety. Or an anarchist. There had been mention of Cohen's incendiary political activity, and William's hair and beard were unkempt enough for that.

"My name is William James," William clarified further. "I'm a professor of philosophy visiting from America."

The man's face cleared at once. As if thinking on the subject, he commented lightly, "'Replace religion with philosophy,' Ben says, 'and the world will be a better place.' That's rubbish if you ask me. But it's his soul, and yours too, for that matter. You'll find him at the pub round the corner at one of his meetings."

William nodded, wondering why the man had changed in his manner so abruptly, and turned the corner. The pub was indeed just a few yards down, although he would not have known it was there without being told. The sign hanging from the door was so ingrained with dirt as to be unreadable, and the establishment itself was located not on the ground level, which was occupied by some sort of pitiful shop—most of the merchandise of which seemed to consist of torn clothes and broken crockery—but at the bottom of a rickety set of steps in an area that resembled a dank cave. As he entered, William saw that a group of young men were seated toward the back, and that as soon as they saw him, they rose quickly and ducked out the door directly behind them. It was obviously a political gathering, possibly an anarchist cell that was plotting an act of defiance, if not outright destructiveness with regard to their society. He was again struck by the possibility that Cohen could have political reasons for having committed the murders, as Henry had originally suggested with his talk of cabals and Masonic societies.

Cohen remained at the table after the others dispersed, though, and rose with an expression of excitement on his face. "Professor James," he said, his eyes bright. William noted what he had not noted at the police station, that the man was extremely thin and looked malnourished.

"You know my name?" asked William in wonderment. He recalled that the vigilante had also responded with immediate deference to his name.

"I might have recognized you from the photograph in some of your books," Cohen explained, "but I had the additional help of seeing you at police headquarters this afternoon."

When William looked puzzled, he continued. "There are members of our faith even on the London police force, and so news of your defense of me following my arrest came through those channels. I've admired your work for years. To have you to thank for intervening on my behalf makes me almost believe in God."

As he spoke, he had taken William's arm in an appropriating gesture and led him, without commentary, out of the pub. A kind of nervous energy emanated from the man, which William found at once endearing and unnerving. With Cohen's hand on his arm, the two men walked briskly around the corner until he came to the closed shop that he had surveyed earlier. Cohen took a key out of his pocket, unlocked the padlock, and motioned for William to follow him inside. The shop had indeed been stripped bare.

"You are leaving your business?" asked William.

"I have decided it is no longer worth trying to effect social change in this country," said Cohen, waving a nervous hand at his ramshackle surroundings. "I am going east to abet the Revolution."

There was a note of repressed hysteria in the man's voice, and William wondered again if he were an unstable and possibly dangerous personality.

Cohen had by then opened a door at the back of the shop that led into a space hardly bigger than a closet. There were no windows; in the corner was a cracked washbasin and a small cot covered with a ragged blanket. The room would have been cramped and airless under any circumstances, but what made it more so was that every spare inch was piled with books. These were the remains of Cohen's trade, books he had not been able to sell or with which he was not willing to part.

As the two men moved as best they could into the room, Cohen suddenly grabbed a volume at the top of one of the piles. "You must be familiar with the ideas of the German philosopher Marx," he exclaimed, waving the book excitedly. "He exposes the oppression of church and family and calls for the transfer of economic control to the people." He pressed the book into William's hands. "Read his *Capital*, and you will be converted. You are a utopian, Professor James, though you may not know it." He paused as if to scour his memory and then recited, "'This universe will never be completely good as long as one being is unhappy, as long as one poor cockroach suffers the pangs of unrequited love.' It's from one of your essays."

William laughed, surprised. "I had no idea I had a disciple who could quote me on the subject of cockroaches," he noted uneasily, "but I fear you distort my ideas. I believe in social justice, but my political views are moderate—"

"But you haven't given it enough thought," Cohen interrupted impatiently. "As an American, you are removed from the kinds of misery that people like myself see on a regular basis."

William nodded; there seemed to be no point arguing with Cohen. Passionate belief—whether religious or political—was a form of lunacy. One stayed sane by keeping passion in check and by refusing to feel too much about anything. He understood the trade-off; he had made it years earlier.

Cohen waited for William to put the copy of *Capital* into the breast pocket of his coat and then reached under his bed to retrieve another book, obviously placed there for safekeeping. "I was hoping you would come, not just so I could discuss philosophy with someone whose work I respect, but also to give you this." He passed the book to William. "I believe it may be evidence in the case for which I was arrested, though what it means I have not been able to decipher."

William looked at the cover, which was printed in embossed gold lettering, *The Complete Writings of Thomas De Quincey, Volume Four*. He glanced up inquiringly.

"It was from the pages of this book that the police extracted the photograph of the murdered woman in that unseemly pose," Cohen explained. "They had already found enough Marx and Fourier to indict me as a syndicalist and revolutionary. The photograph was an added bonus. I would have assumed they planted it, had I not seen with my own eyes one of the officers find it in this volume. At first, they simply took it as evidence of my degeneracy, after they'd ogled it themselves, of course. I don't think the connection to the Ripper victim would have been made at all if someone at headquarters hadn't seen it. By then, no one remembered the book in which it was found."

William opened the De Quincey volume.

"Notice the first essay," prompted Cohen, as William turned to the Contents page.

"'Murder Considered as a Fine Art,'" recited William.

"A suggestive piece of writing in which to place a photograph of a murder victim, don't you think?"

William nodded. He knew the essay—it had appeared some fifty years earlier in the popular literary magazine *Blackwood's* and had circulated widely since. He recalled that he had once praised its cleverness in a conversation with his father, who had responded with surprising vehemence. "It's easy to make clever claims for degeneracy," Henry Sr. had said, "but it takes a deeper talent to show why evil must be strenuously countered by the force of good. An argument like De Quincey's gives no counterforce to evil and therefore shares in the degeneracy it mocks."

The validity of his father's position now struck William with particular force. De Quincey's argument fit with Alice's theory that the murderer was a perverted sort of artist.

"Look through the article itself," instructed Cohen.

William flipped through the pages and stopped where a line had been lightly underlined in pencil. "'...as to old women, and the mob of newspaper readers, they are pleased with anything, provided it is bloody enough. But the mind of sensibility requires something more.'"

In the margin, also in pencil, was a kind of tracery in the style of an ornate graphic. "What is it?" asked William, pointing to the notation. "A code of some sort?"

"I've studied it, and it looks to me like letters. *P/W* but with an *X* superimposed."

William squinted down at the graphic. "Quite right." He nodded. "Initials crossed out? The slash—if it is that"—he noted a kind of curl in the line between the letters—"might be a slip of the pen. It could refer to someone the reader wanted eliminated."

William had made quick note that none of the victims had the initials PW before shifting his attention to the volume itself. He examined it more closely. It was in good condition, bound in red leather, and the frontispiece said it was published in 1854 as part of a twenty-volume set.

"Do you have the other volumes?" he asked Cohen.

"No. I often get hold of strays like this. The trick, if you want to make money, is to know where the rest of the set is."

"And do you know?"

"Yes—or at least where it was once." Cohen took the book and flipped to the inside of the back cover, where he indicated a small stamp with the initials *A* and *S*. "It stands for Abrams & Son," he explained. "Asher Abrams is a dealer of some note in the city. He used to have a pawn brokerage in this neighborhood, but he's gone up in the world since. No doubt this volume became detached from a set he purchased, and it was sold to me by one of the area dustmen. Normally I would try to sell it back to him, since the set is worthless if it's not complete, but in this case, I thought it best to give it to you. It might be helpful in catching the maniac who is preying on the poor and unfortunate."

William looked at Cohen suspiciously. Was the man being disingenuous? He could not bring himself to believe it. Though clearly at odds with his society, he seemed the sort of person who might wreak havoc, not out of calculation, but out of idealism and purity of motive. It was true, moreover, that Cohen couldn't very well bring this evidence to the police, who had already arrested him under suspicion of being Jack the Ripper.

"Abrams has a shop in Soho and lives in one of the fashionable districts," Cohen continued. "Your friends will know of him, since his trade is with gentlemen collectors and established artists. I've seen his daughter in Whitechapel now and again, though I can hardly imagine what business she has here. A real beauty; carries herself like the queen of the Nile." Cohen seemed to find the image of Abrams's daughter momentarily diverting, and then, as if recalling the larger social context, never far from his mind, summed up contemptuously, "But beauty and riches won't do her any good when the Revolution comes."

CHAPTER 25

WILLIAM AND HENRY WERE seated at the little table in their sister's bedroom the next morning. Henry was eating a large bowl of the oatmeal with brown sugar that Sally had made for him (Archie, Sally had announced proudly, had already eaten two bowls). William ate a banana (as part of his Fletcher diet), and Alice, excited to hear her brothers' news, had eaten nothing, despite the protestations of Katherine that she must keep up her strength if she were going to expose a murderer.

She listened to Henry's account first. He tried, as far as he could, to relay the sense of importance he felt attached to Sickert's imitation of Whistler's laugh. Katherine and William didn't see much in it, but Alice was more encouraging. "Henry's instincts are the most developed in the family," she asserted. "If he senses something worth pursuing in this Sickert, then it must be respected. Interesting how we seem to return to Whistler; but you say that he's out of the question as a suspect?"

"Yes," said Henry. "He's in Paris on his honeymoon and hasn't been in London since July. I have ample correspondence from Bourget and others to that effect. Besides, someone who laughs like Jimmy is hardly likely to render laughter that way in writing."

Alice nodded. "You're saying it's laughter *someone else* might notice and imitate. It's the parodic aspect that struck you."

"Precisely," said Henry, pleased to have it put so well. It was indeed the element of parody that impressed him in the Ripper letters and that the young Sickert had echoed in his verbal imitation.

"Sickert," Alice ruminated. "A name worthy of a murderer. William says that we mold our personalities to our physical characteristics. Why not to our names? Had I been named Dolly or Daisy, I'm sure I would have been gay and pretty instead of grim and plain." She sighed and returned to the topic at hand. "You also said Sickert had a gift for mimicry and comfort with costume and that he is an artist with a dark and macabre palette. It's all very suggestive."

Henry nodded complacently. It was pleasant to have his sister's approval, especially as her subsequent response to William's findings was less enthusiastic.

"How do you know that the essay is even related to the photograph?" she said, looking skeptically at the book that William handed to her. "Perhaps one of the police planted the picture in order to frame this social revolutionary Cohen."

"It's possible," acknowledged William. Cohen had said he saw an officer find the photograph, but sleight of hand was not to be discounted.

"The essay is fairly well-known," continued Alice. "It's likely to elicit interest on a purely academic level from many readers."

"Gosse often mentions the piece," piped in Henry. "His father used to read it to him as a child. Scared him half to death."

"But the underlined sentence and the initials," insisted William, pointing to the volume. It had seemed compelling at the time. Now it seemed less so. Could Cohen himself have introduced the volume in some effort to throw the police off track?

"Have you been able to make sense of the initials?" asked Alice. "PW crossed out?"

"No," said William. "None of the murder victims have those initials."

"There's a mark between the letters," noted Henry, peering over his brother's and sister's shoulders. "Perhaps an ampersand. Sickert's first name is Walter. Polly and Walter," he suggested.

"Then, the *X* would make sense," agreed William grudgingly. He was always somewhat annoyed by his brother's quickness. "Though it is a bit infantile. The sort of thing a child might carve into a tree."

"And our killer is too sophisticated for that." Alice smirked. "He only carves up bodies."

There was silence as the three of them pondered the conundrum. Katherine, who had been sitting quietly in the corner of the room, then spoke up. "Walter Sickert is married to Ellen Cobden," she said.

Everyone looked at her, surprised.

"Jane Cobden's sister," she clarified. Katherine and Alice were both friendly with Jane Cobden, daughter of the noted liberal reformer Richard Cobden. He had four daughters, all known for their beauty and intelligence, of whom Jane was the most politically engaged and the best known to Alice and Katherine.

"That's interesting," said Alice. "How old is Sickert?"

"Quite young," said Henry. "Late twenties at the most."

"Jane is my age, and Ellen is older by a few years, isn't she?"

"Yes," agreed Katherine. "I haven't met her, but I know she's older than Jane."

"That would put her close to forty," said Alice. "So much older than her husband—and the age of the Ripper victims."

They all considered this information a moment. Henry then shifted uncomfortably as he began to turn against the idea he had originally proposed. "Just because Sickert said 'ha ha' doesn't mean he murdered five women on the East End."

"Of course not," said Alice.

"And theatrical talent means nothing. We don't suspect Henry Irving."

"Certainly not," said Alice.

"And because the fact that his wife is older than he is shouldn't be held against him."

"On the contrary," agreed Alice.

William intervened. "None of this is of any consequence unless we can find a motive that ties it all together. If our speculation about the murders is true, that they represent a kind of frustrated artistic expression, then there must be something to bear that out in this man's career."

"Sickert appears to be quite successful," noted Henry. It struck him that he had more of a motive than Walter Sickert, if one went by that.

"External success and internal fulfillment can differ widely," warned William. "He may feel himself inhibited or overshadowed in some way that we do not know."

"The relationship to Whistler," proffered Alice.

"Jimmy is overbearing and egotistical," agreed Henry, "but this Sickert doesn't seem the type to be intimidated."

"Vulnerability is not always apparent on the surface," William noted again. "Or at least not on the surface that we are aware of. One has to see the context thoroughly before passing judgment on a subject's mental health." He glanced at his sister who, by all accounts, was a strong-minded woman, apart from the fact that she could not get out of bed.

"We must find out more about Walter Sickert," concluded Alice. "I will make it my business to speak to Jane Cobden about him. It is up to you to research his past—his career, his education, his friendships. He is no doubt entirely innocent. But…" Her face clouded. "What if he's not?"

"I will ask Abberline to place him under watch," said William.

Alice nodded. "One more thing," she added casually, as they were about to leave. "I must meet him."

The brothers stopped at the door.

"It is the surest way for me to know if there's anything to it. Henry, you must have a dinner party to honor our brother's visit to London, and you must invite Walter Sickert, perhaps as a stand-in for Whistler. I'm sure you and John Sargent can come up with a convincing pretext. Arrange it for Sunday evening," she instructed peremptorily. "We cannot afford to waste time."

Henry looked uneasy. He doubted very much if Mrs. Smith would be up to a dinner party. Especially on such short notice.

"Katherine will help," said Alice, as if guessing his concern. "I know it is not in your line to host such things. It isn't in my line to attend them. But we must both exert ourselves."

The prospect of doing so, however, had already brought on a headache. She waved her hand to indicate that the visit was over. She would exert herself, as she said she would, to find out if Walter Sickert was involved in these heinous crimes, but that would be later; for now, she would rest.

CHAPTER 26

ASHER ABRAMS?" SAID SARGENT. "Of course I know him. He's a dealer but also a generous patron. I've painted his family half a dozen times and been very well paid for it."

William had explained his desire to trace the source of the De Quincey volume that had been stamped with the imprint of Abrams & Son, and Sargent had quickly gotten him an invitation for Friday dinner at the Abrams home on Connaught Square. "If you do not get satisfaction in your search," his friend promised, "you will at least spend an entertaining evening. Asher Abrams has a lively family. They may not have pedigree, but they have life. Everything about them is colorful."

As Sargent had promised, the Abrams home, into which William was ushered by a white-capped Irish maid, was a feast for the eyes. It was not just that the furnishings were lavish, though they were. There were marble floors and crystal chandeliers and furniture, rugs, and drapes of the most luxurious and costly variety. But there were also more exotic items mixed profligately with this opulent fare: inlaid furniture from Persia, screens and wall hangings from China and India, and large numbers of ornaments and relics—candelabras and samovars, scrolls and urns. Most compelling amid this riot of rare and exotic things were the pictures. Asher Abrams's walls were covered in every possible space with paintings of the highest quality. Many featured biblical scenes, not just from the Old but the New Testament (for Abrams, art had obviously been uncoupled from its religious associations), but there were also still lifes and portraits by recognized old masters as well as paintings by more modern artists of note—the French Corot and David, the English Gainsborough and Reynolds.

As William was gazing at a painting by the hand of the Dutchman Vermeer, a young woman entered the room and walked with a purposeful stride to greet him. On Mansell Street, he had experienced a jolt at the thought that Cohen had fled the area; now, at the sight of the figure before him, he experienced another sort of jolt. The woman was young, in her early to midtwenties. She had dark, straight eyebrows, large, heavily lashed eyes that looked to be a bright violet, a coil of shiny black hair atop her head, a rounded face, square jaw, rather pointed chin, and an ample mouth that managed to be both extremely sensual and extremely refined. The nose was prominent and dipped slightly in the fashion he associated with caricatures of the Jewish physiognomy, but in this case, the effect was astonishingly appealing, giving a touch of dramatic vulnerability to the otherwise large, regular features. William thought of the Song of Solomon, that ode to female beauty. It must surely have been written to someone who looked like this.

The effect of the face on William was both delightful and disturbing, and he realized that this combination of feelings carried him back to his youth. When he had begun his medical training and linked himself in matrimony to his Alice, there had been a welling of relief at disaster averted. He had, after much thrashing about in turbulent waters, finally found the shore. But there had also been a residue of regret. He had left indecision and solitary search behind; had chosen science over art, the stability of the mind over the sensuality of the body. It was the exchange required for his sanity. Yet there were times, wandering through a museum or sitting at the opera, when he felt a surge of desire for the life he had not lived. It even struck him sometimes that his impatience regarding his brother's writing was connected to his own buried past.

Looking at this woman brought his unsettled youth back to him in a rush. He did not know why he associated her face with that past life. Perhaps she reminded him of one of the artist models during his failed apprenticeship as a painter. Or perhaps her exotic beauty and her ethnicity suggested something forbidden, outside the realm of the familiar New England world in which he had settled. Or perhaps it was simply that her face, even at first glance, was so expressive that it seemed to have a capacity for the kind of deep and powerful feeling he associated with his younger self. Whatever it was, the face was arresting in its beauty and vibrant humanity in a way that drew him up short. Added to this was the disorienting impression that he had seen it before—an impossibility, surely, but an impression, nonetheless, of which he instantaneously felt certain.

As the woman approached, the contradictory feelings she aroused of both otherness and familiarity made him almost lose his balance, and he grabbed the back of the armchair close by.

"Are you well, Professor James?" she asked, raising a dark eyebrow as she registered his distress. "You seem agitated." Her voice was low, and there was a touch of the melodious foreign lilt that William had noted in many Jews, even those native to a locale.

William assured her that he was fine. "Have we met?" he asked, trying not to stare but doing so all the same.

"We have not," she replied. "But I was pleased to hear from Mr. Sargent that you wanted to meet us. I am familiar with your work and admire your attempt to connect philosophy, a science devoted to the general, with mental operation, a science concerned with the individual. It is something that Hebraic law—perhaps all religious law—attempts to do in its clumsy way. But you give it secular expression, which strikes me as useful. We may worship different gods, but we must all live on the same earth together, and it would be best, if we could, through the establishment of certain principles of behavior, transcend the sectarianism of any particular religious system of belief."

William continued to stare at the speaker. It was rare for a woman to have an opinion on such matters, much less to speak about them with this sort of eloquence. His sister was possibly the only woman he knew capable of doing so. But here was a stranger who had performed the impressive feat of simplifying his philosophy in terms that were at once accurate and unique.

"And with whom do I have the honor of speaking, who knows my philosophical goals so well?" he asked, trying to keep his voice as detached and casual as he could.

"Ella Abrams," said the young woman. "Or rather, *Miss* Ella Abrams. The English are very keen on letting a gentleman know one's marital status at once." She spoke jauntily, and William was not certain whether she was being dismissive of the practice or subtly flirtatious—possibly both.

"I assume you are here because you have an interest in something that my father has to sell," she continued. "That's generally why gentlemen come to dinner. We are not yet at the stage where our visits are purely social. Except for Mr. Sargent, and even he has an interest in us as exotic specimens, though of course we are also great friends."

With the mention of Sargent, William suddenly realized where he had seen the girl before. It was at a gallery show in Boston the year before. It had been Sargent's first American exhibition and had featured some two dozen paintings, mostly portraits of dowagers and society debutantes, but with a few Italianate scenes and one of a striking young woman in Persian costume, now identifiable as Ella Abrams. He recalled at the time staring raptly at that painting, until his Alice pulled him away, saying that she was growing jealous of the model. He had assured her that it was the brushwork that intrigued him—only John could do so much with the color black—and had even convinced himself that it was true. But now, looking at the woman in front of him, he realized it was the face that had mesmerized him on canvas as it now did in life.

She was wearing a dark blue velvet gown, very simple but well cut, with a sapphire necklace that matched the dress and accentuated the sweep of her long neck. She turned to take his arm and lead him into the dining room, and he was aware of the pressure of her fingers and the proximity of her body to his. Every fiber in him seemed alert to her presence and her touch. They walked through the drawing room, then through a long hall, lined, William vaguely noted, with a collection of the new impressionist painters—Asher Abrams's taste was obviously for the new as well as the old—and into the dining room, where once again, he was dazzled by the spectacle that confronted him.

If he had been struck by Sargent's painting of Ella Abrams at the Boston exhibition, he now saw the same effect multiplied. On the walls of the spacious room, in which a large table had been elaborately set for dinner, were five life-size portraits of the Abrams family, all unmistakably by the brush of John Singer Sargent.

"It *is* a bit extreme," admitted Ella when she saw William's expression as he gazed at the collection of paintings around them. "My father believes that without a dramatic showing, we are likely to be swept under the carpet. As it is, although we may be accused of questionable taste, we cannot be ignored."

William felt the force of this statement. It was not just the number and size of the paintings that were arresting. It was also the unique appearance of the subjects and the unconventional way in which they had been painted. The Abramses had not held Sargent to the standard of propriety favored by most of his clients. Perhaps they did not understand that standard or did not like it. The figures represented in each of the paintings had vibrancy and color that seemed excessive. These were unruly, possibly indecorous people, though the paintings also made clear that they had a great deal of money and life.

The family members were all present in person as William entered the room, so that the relationship between the paintings and their subjects was immediately thrust upon him. Ada and Greta, the Abramses' eight-year-old twins, who had been rendered by Sargent with their dog, as though they were three small animals playing together, were quarreling obstreperously under the table. Fiona, sixteen, was fidgeting near her seat, dressed in an extravagant evening gown of gold silk that accented her unaccountably blonde hair, the dress similar to one that her likeness was wearing on the opposite wall. Sargent had painted her in a double portrait with Ella. The two girls, their arms around each other's waists, stared boldly at the observer, a study in dark and light. Alfred, the son and heir, who stood looking bored in the corner, had been portrayed holding a palette and brush (Sargent had mentioned that he was a painter, or at least an aspiring one). The red lips and supercilious expression on both portrait and man branded him the petulant aesthete. Esther Abrams, the matriarch, appeared in person precisely as she had been painted: a small, straight-backed woman in black with an expression of what could be described only as fierce timidity. She gave William a quick, frightened smile and turned to whisper something to her son.

In the midst of this tumultuous scene, in which life and art seemed to be vying for priority, stood the patriarch, Asher Abrams, directly below his own portrait. Sargent had painted him in the formal evening dress he was wearing now, but in the painting he held a ledger book as if to emphasize that, though a gentleman, he was never beyond the call of his business. The image, like the man, exuded power and cunning, a combination that William supposed was precisely the way Abrams wished to be portrayed. As Ella led William over to meet him, Abrams's canny eyes surveyed his guest much as he might appraise a piece of good furniture or a fine picture.

"This is Professor James, Father," Ella said, "the man Mr. Sargent wrote to you about."

Abrams nodded, as if he had already taken his guest's measure. "A friend of John Sargent's is bound to be someone we will like," he said, extending his hand in greeting. "And we are pleased you have chosen to come to us this evening. It happens to be our Sabbath. We are not strict practitioners of our faith, but we hold to its basic rituals, which I hope you will find of interest."

William murmured that he was more than happy to be included, and Abrams motioned for him to take a seat beside Ella. "Mrs. Abrams will now light the Sabbath candles and say the *barucha*, the prayer to commemorate the beginning of the day of rest," Abrams explained for William's benefit.

"Not that we rest," muttered Fiona, clearly at odds with her family's decision to maintain a footing in the Old World. Ella darted her sister a disapproving glance, and Fiona bowed her head.

Esther Abrams moved forward with a large taper, pulled up her shawl so that it draped over her head, lit the candles, and recited the prayer in mumbled Hebrew. William noticed that the twins were kicking each other under the table and that Ella had to pinch one of them to stop.

"We start with a chicken consommé with egg noodles," said Ella, taking over the narration from her father and motioning to the maid to bring the soup. "I hope you like chicken consommé."

William said he did, though he found he had little appetite. The atmosphere around the table was not serene. A good deal of fighting was going on between the twins, and a dispute had erupted between Fiona and her father over her curfew that evening.

"You will be home by ten," pronounced Asher Abrams. "You are only sixteen, and this is London, where Professor James will tell you that it is not wise for young ladies to be gallivanting late at night."

"I won't be gallivanting," protested Fiona petulantly. "I will be with Billy Sassoon."

"So much the worse," said Asher. "Boys of that type are entirely untrustworthy."

"Billy's mother was Jewish," protested Fiona.

"Yes, but she has forgotten it. We have not."

Fiona pouted, obviously wishing that they had.

"It is very difficult, Professor James, to raise a child in our circumstances. I want my children to be English, but I do not want them to forget their ancestors. Can you understand that?"

William said that he did. There had been a similar kind of balancing act in his own home, where the intellectual aspirations of his father had rubbed up against the more mundane social realities of their wealth and position. The result of this dual pressure had not been entirely successful, if judged by the condition of his younger siblings, not to mention certain facets of his own mental health.

A brisket with apricots and crisply fried potatoes had made an appearance, along with greens and haricots verts. The food was served in the American style, he noted, which might well be the Jewish style. Ella had passed him the potatoes, and his hand had brushed hers; his skin seemed to burn at the touch. The idea was ridiculous, yet he found himself unable to turn his head to look at her.

Mrs. Abrams, whose presence had been inconspicuous, suddenly spoke. "Do you have a family, Professor James?" she queried.

William noticed what he sensed from the portrait—that she had, beneath her timidity, something of the same shrewd perspicuity as her husband.

"I do," said William, looking down at his plate as he spoke. "I have three children. A fourth was lost to us three years ago. Otherwise, a healthy brood, I'm pleased to say, like yours."

"And your wife joins you here?"

"No," said William, wondering if he was speaking with more emphasis than the question demanded. "She is at home with the children. Our youngest is barely two and therefore in need of her care."

A bread pudding arrived, followed by coffee and liqueur. Alfred, who had pushed away his food and leaned back in his chair, announced that he wanted his father to contact a dealer in Paris on his behalf.

"You can contact him yourself," said Abrams irritably.

"But he won't listen to me," retorted Alfred.

"He'll listen if he thinks you have talent."

Alfred's face hardened. "That's hogwash." He spoke scornfully. "Everyone knows that success in the art world is about money. Get someone rich and powerful to back you, and everyone concludes you're a genius."

"I beg to differ with you," said Abrams. "Success as an artist requires talent and work."

"And *I* beg to differ with *you*," mimicked Alfred. "What do you know about art? You know how to buy and sell things, I admit. You know what will bring a good price and how to wrangle it from your clients. But you wouldn't understand a work of originality and vision that has not acquired a niche in your marketplace. So don't start giving me lectures on my career. If you want to help, contact your friends on my behalf. If not, keep quiet. I don't need your philistine advice."

There was something so harshly denigrating in this speech that even the formidable Asher Abrams seemed cowed. "I'll make some calls," he muttered, at which Alfred rose abruptly from the table, kissed his mother perfunctorily on the cheek, and left the room.

Watching this embarrassing scene, William was reminded of how cruel life inside a family could be. Alfred Abrams might seem, to the untutored observer, to be spoiled and ungrateful, but he knew how a formidable father could sap the manhood and confidence from a sensitive son. The scene disturbed him, because he knew that blame could not be neatly apportioned. Both parties had suffered, and both had inflicted injury.

After Alfred left, the twins clattered to be excused, and Fiona, after some additional quarreling about her curfew, also took her leave. Mrs. Abrams began supervising the clearing of the plates, and Abrams was diverted by the entry of a bespectacled young man who seemed to be relaying information regarding the framing of some paintings that he was putting up for sale. Business did not wait, apparently even for the Sabbath.

In the midst of all this activity, William felt he should turn to Ella and make conversation. It was something he profoundly wanted to do, yet he had avoided turning his head to look at her during dinner. Her beauty and intelligence unnerved him and made him feel like he ought to say something important or brilliant. Looking at her now, however, he saw that the sharp, inquiring expression that had infused her features earlier in the evening had been replaced by a soft, dreamy look. He guessed that she had gone off into a reverie during her father's unpleasant exchange with her brother, and she had not yet returned from her escapist dream. The expression made her look distant but also vulnerable, and he felt more emboldened to address her. "Do you study philosophy?" He hit on this as a way to begin, since she had spoken so knowledgeably about his work earlier in the evening.

She met his eyes, and he felt her seriously considering her reply.

"I don't know that I study," she finally said, "but I read."

"Isn't it the same thing?"

"I don't think so. Study is a concentrated activity in which the subject matter is allowed to take precedence over everything else. I don't have the luxury of that. I spend most of my time in more practical occupations." She motioned vaguely to the room around her. Whether she was referring to household management or to the paintings on the walls was not clear.

Abrams, who had finished his consultation with the bespectacled young man and seemed to have caught the tail end of this reply, directed a look of pride and affection at his eldest daughter and clarified her response. "Ella is my trusted assistant," he interjected. "My son has relinquished that role in the hope of becoming the next Whistler…or Monet; his style changes so often, it is hard to tell. But Ella serves in lieu of a son. That is, until she is married and settled."

Ella gave a slight grimace, but Abrams appeared not to notice. He lit a cigar and took a contented puff, settling back in his chair. He then gave William another appraising look. "So tell me, Professor. What can I do for you?"

William had placed his satchel, which contained the De Quincey volume, under his seat, and he reached down to take it out. He almost regretted having to get to the point of his visit; it meant that it would soon be over. The meal was done, though, and it was clear that Abrams expected to do business.

As William took the volume out of the satchel, Ella, who had bent her head to look down at what he was doing, suddenly moved quickly back and straightened in her chair.

"I wonder if you know anything about this volume?" He handed it to Abrams, who gently rubbed his fingers on the binding, opened it, and examined the inside cover, where the imprint of his shop was stamped.

"It passed through our hands, obviously," he murmured, "but I see so many things. Ella, do you recognize it?"

Ella seemed hardly to glance at the volume. "I don't know," she said abruptly. "It's probably part of a set we got years ago. I don't recall seeing anything in red leather recently."

"There was the Coleridge," said Abrams ruminatively. "And that set of Dryden. Both were red leather."

Ella shrugged. "I can't say I recall."

Abrams looked at the book again. "If you're looking for a set of De Quincey, I can put word out and see what I can find."

"No," said William. "I want the particular set associated with this volume. I have my reasons."

Abrams examined the book again, and William could see him riffling his memory as Ella shifted uncomfortably in her chair. "I remember," Abrams said finally with decision. "It came with the Coleridge and the Dryden from that Cheshire estate sale a year or so back. I remember it because it was an American edition. I hadn't seen a full set of De Quincey before and was surprised the Americans had put one out. Don't you remember, Ella, you were especially eager to acquire it?"

"No," said Ella curtly. "I really can't say I do."

William leaned forward inquiringly. "How might this volume have found its way into a Whitechapel bookstall?"

Abrams shrugged. "There, I can't help you. I buy only complete sets. A collector wants completeness, whether in china or etchings or books; it represents a level of control. If a set is dispersed—and a missing volume is all it takes—the items become virtually worthless. I can surmise only that we sold the set to someone who was careless with it. It's not uncommon for an unscrupulous employee to lift a volume and then conspire with a confrere to sell it back to the owner for a substantial sum. Perhaps the thief in this case misplaced the merchandise, got sidetracked, or was sent off to prison. We can certainly tell you to whom we sold the set, if that would be helpful. Abrams & Son—or rather Daughter—keep excellent records, don't we, Ella?"

"We try," said Ella, her voice uneasy.

William glanced at her. He could tell she was undergoing a disturbance that the book had initiated. It struck him as both unsettling and intriguing. What could the volume possibly mean to her? "I would greatly appreciate knowing to whom the set was sold," he said to Abrams.

"Then you must visit the shop Monday morning and have my clerk review the records. You will have only to tell him that we have spoken, and he will be sure to accommodate you."

Out of the corner of his eye William could see that Ella had regained her bearings and was sitting less stiffly in her chair. "I would be glad to assist Professor James," she announced lightly. "It would give me the opportunity to continue our discussion of philosophy."

"I should like that," said William, realizing that he would like it more than he wished to admit.

She gave him a quick sidelong glance and removed a card with a gold border and black script from her waistband. "Here is the address of the shop. I shall see you Monday at eleven." She rose, a cue for him to do the same. "Be sure to send my regards to Mr. Sargent. Tell him I shall be over next week to dress as a Persian princess, as he requested."

Abrams laughed and added, "You can tell your friend Sargent that he must paint me again as well. He's already represented me in the proper costume of an English gentleman." He motioned to the portrait behind himself. "Now I should like one in the more splendid accoutrements of a Venetian doge. We could place it in the shop, don't you think, Ella? It might encourage trade." He laughed again, and William thought that the cunning businessman was perfectly aware of how he was perceived by the society in which he lived. He would play the expected role, but he would not be a dupe to it or pretend to take it seriously.

CHAPTER 27

IT WAS PAST TEN p.m. when William left the Abrams home on Connaught Square, and it was a beautiful night. In general during his visits to London, the weather was foggy or rainy, a contrast to the refreshing climate that he associated with his own country. But tonight was an exception; the gray limestone of the buildings, so different from the bold newness of Boston's red brick, shimmered under the soft moonlight.

He considered hailing a cab and then decided that he would walk to Henry's flat across Hyde Park. It was not a long walk, and he felt energetic and ebullient as he strode under the lush autumn foliage. He knew, the habit of self-scrutiny being well developed in him, that his high spirits were the result not only of the weather but also of the feelings engendered in him by Ella Abrams. Her vibrant beauty had impressed itself upon him forcefully. Even her unease with regard to the De Quincey volume intrigued him, suggesting something withheld and secretive that added to his fascination with her. He was a husband and a father, a devoted one on all counts, a man who would never dream of wandering from the path of righteousness, yet he felt, as he strode into the park, that there was no harm in the feeling of attraction he was experiencing. So long as it was not to be acted upon, it was a natural sort of thing. Ella Abrams, with her dark eyes and full mouth, her darting intelligence and humor, her exoticism and mystery, stoked his imagination and made him feel vital and glad to be alive. He would see her again on Monday, and the thought pleased him—that was all there was to it. There was a degree of self-deception in his thinking—he knew that—but he did not care.

It was quite dark as he entered the park and made his way along the main path. A few couples were walking arm in arm, and there was a smattering of beggars of the West End variety, well brushed in the manner of gentlemen fallen on hard times. They murmured discreetly their need for a bit of assistance, and William gave each of them something; he was in a magnanimous mood.

When he approached the center of the park, he veered off onto one of the side paths that would lead him to the avenue nearest to his brother's flat. The gas lamps that lit the main path did not extend to this one, so the area grew darker as he moved farther along. The sounds of the street began to recede, and the trees seemed to grow thicker and more luxuriant. It was nice to have such lush greenery in the center of the city. New York had Central Park, and Boston had its Commons, but Hyde Park was different in the degree to which it could suddenly seem remote from the urban hubbub that surrounded it. Only the English could feel confident enough to allow the wild to encroach so far within a civilized space. It was the first time that he had acknowledged that this country might surpass his native land in some respect. Perhaps he would take a flat in London after all; so much coming and going to conferences and meetings was wearing. And it would be convenient to be near Henry and especially Alice, given her condition.

He paused to be sure that he still had the card for Ella Abrams's shop in his pocket. It pleased him to finger it and remember its gold border and simple black script: "Abrams & Son." Despite the appellation, the card put him in mind of Ella; gold and black were colors one would associate with her. He recalled the painting Sargent had done in which her arms were encased in gold bracelets, and her hair, emerging from a colorful scarf, was jet-black with flecks of white. It was Sargent's hallmark to do hair that way so as to suggest thickness and glossiness and thus flatter his sitters, though in this case, there was no need to flatter; if anything, the representation fell short of the original.

He was thinking of how much nicer Ella's hair was in reality than it was in Sargent's painting, when he heard it, and the lurch of fear it precipitated was greater, in coming in the midst of such pleasurable calm. What he heard was breathing, soft and regular, faint yet distinct. There was no body attached to it, no evidence of anyone in the vicinity, no footsteps. If someone was near, it was someone who had matched William's tread so as to follow unnoticed. Only now, pausing, he could hear the soft intake and outlet of breath.

Where was this person? William's mind raced. He must be very near, in the trees a few feet away. He might be only a thief, he tried to assure himself, yet he knew it was unlikely. His mind had gone immediately to the letter Abberline had passed on to him. Until now, he had pushed that threat to the back of his mind. It was the familiar reflex of denial, a defense against the kind of morbid thinking that had engulfed him at the time of his breakdown, yet he ought to have understood that to push the possibility of danger out of consciousness was as foolhardy as to see danger everywhere.

He began to walk faster, panic beginning to mount in his body. No one was about. The prospect of calling out would be of no use. His hands reflexively burrowed in his pockets, but all he found there was the card for Ella's shop. He felt a welling of sadness as the thought occurred to him that he might never see her again—not her, not his wife and children, not his brother and sister. He felt his shirt grow hot with perspiration against his chest, and for a moment wished only to be able to remove his coat and jacket. What a relief it would be to strip off these clothes, to stop planning and desiring and thinking, to be done with it all at last.

He realized that the predator was holding off attack until the edge of the path, where, at the turn, he would be enclosed entirely by trees. In the shrubbery, the violence could take place with no possibility that a passerby would see. He could picture his own death in his mind's eye, the pale throat beneath the thicket of whiskers suddenly spurting bright red. His hand automatically went to his neck, touching the solid flesh that might, in a few seconds, be ripped open. The image brought a wave of pity for his own frailty. He felt his skin turn cold under the wetness of his perspiration; his teeth began to chatter, and his head grew light as the pressure in his body dropped.

He slowed his pace. He could make out over the din of his pulse that the person behind him was light-footed and agile. He could hear the other's breathing, loudly now; he even imagined he could feel the breath on the back of his neck.

The turn was less than twenty feet away. He had perhaps three seconds before he reached the spot where he would be set upon. In the nightmare ordeal of his youth, when he had suffered from a lack of will, the crisis had been long and difficult, a slow and fitful return from numbness and inertia to active life. But there was no time for such a recovery now. He must either fight against what threatened him or succumb to it. It was the simplicity of the choice that galvanized him.

It happened with remarkable speed. He spied a large branch on the side of the path and made a quick lunge to reach it; then, with it firm in his grasp, he swung. It was the same movement he had once used in his youth to swing a baseball bat. The movement had been embedded deep in the memory of his muscles.

As he pivoted on his soles, turning his body almost completely around, he saw the figure who had stalked him, enveloped from head to toe in a thick cloak. From the folds of the cloak an object flashed, sweeping in countermovement to his own. There was a tremendous crack as he completed his swing. The figure staggered back.

William dropped the branch and ran, not stopping until he had reached the other side of the park. When he glanced down, he saw there was a tear of about four inches across the breast pocket of his coat. The copy of Marx's *Capital*, the gift from Benjamin Cohen, had been sliced neatly in half.

Even as the horror of what he had escaped coursed through him, he felt gripped by a sense of wonder. How fortuitous life was, how sublime the conjunctions of divine intervention: American baseball and a German utopian philosopher had saved his life!

CHAPTER 28

ALTHOUGH IT WAS LATE, William immediately sent a message to Abberline to meet him at his office in Scotland Yard. He realized that the attack might result in clearing the suspect—or incriminating him. If Sickert had been kept under watch that evening, he could not have staged the attack. If, on the other hand, the police had lost his trail in the vicinity of Hyde Park, his guilt would seem all but certain.

Neither situation turned out to be the case. When William arrived at the precinct office, Abberline's face was taut with anger. Anderson, he explained, had taken all his men off surveillance that night to suppress a demonstration in favor of Irish Home Rule. "It was a quiet gathering that he chose to call an unruly mob," fumed Abberline, "which means that we have blundered on two fronts: we have falsely characterized a public event and we have lost evidence that might have identified our murderer."

Abberline was diverted from his tirade, however, when he saw the tear in the breast pocket of William's coat. "It's the work of a medium-sized, sharp knife, the sort that killed the Whitechapel women," he said with concern. "You are clearly the target of this maniac. I have put the watch back on our suspect, but that doesn't guarantee your protection. You must take special care."

William assured him that he would take care, but the reflex of denial was already reasserting itself, his mind recoiling from the memory and blocking off the dread that had engulfed him less than an hour earlier. In the future, he would be more alert, avoid isolated settings, and try not to walk alone at night. But he would not tell Henry or Alice what had happened, and he would not think more about it.

☦ ☦ ☦

The next morning he and Henry rose early and headed for Gower Street, where they had an appointment at the Slade School of Fine Art. Henry had learned from an English art club catalog that Sickert had attended the Slade, a fact William thought was worth investigating. "One can learn a great deal about a man from his professional training," he said.

Henry agreed. Hadn't many of his own choices been made in opposition to his earliest teacher, his brother?

The Slade was a relatively new building with no particular distinction, and they might have passed it by, had they not seen several young men lugging large canvases entering its portals. Inside was a series of cavernous rooms connected by narrow, chilly corridors, not at all the sort of space likely to inspire the muse. Not that this was unusual, William thought, recalling his own experience as a student; the aim of most education seemed to be to strangle the creative impulse as efficiently as possible. The current director of the Slade was the French master painter Alphonse Legros, whose concern for upholding the school's reputation ensured that it taught nothing that deviated from aesthetic convention, and thus nothing that anyone would care much about.

Henry stopped a young man shouldering a canvas depicting the *Rape of the Sabine Women* and asked where they could find the director, and the young man pointed to a room at the end of the hall. "He's in the classroom," said the student, who was very pale and looked like he would do well to spend some time painting en plein air.

"He's teaching a class?" asked William.

"I don't know about that," said the young man laconically, "but that's where he is."

The two men walked to the end of the hall and opened the door of the classroom. There were perhaps ten students seated at easels set up around the figure of a young African male who was standing in a javelin-throwing position and did not have on a stitch of clothing.

"Oh my," said Henry. "Perhaps we should come back later."

Legros motioned impatiently for them to enter. A tall, bearded man with a sour expression, he was standing behind one of the students' easels. He indicated with a gesture that they sit in the chairs in the corner, while he peered through a monocle at the canvas before him. The student had applied large blocks of color from which he apparently intended to delineate the figure.

"What is this?" Legros barked loudly, glaring down at the work before him. "Where is the sketch *preliminaire*, Monsieur?"

The student explained that he had decided to begin by laying the paint down directly on the canvas.

"And you did this for what reason?" demanded Legros in an outraged tone.

"A preliminary drawing can be inhibiting," explained the student.

"Inheebiting?" Legros repeated this word with scorn, making sure to mispronounce it. "You think that to make the painting *correctement* is *inheebiting*? Perhaps you think that the paint and the canvas are *inheebiting* also? Perhaps you should make your pictures on the buildings using the soot?" He cast a glance around the room, as though expecting the other students to laugh, but they only looked down at their brushes in embarrassment.

"I don't think that's a comparable idea," protested the student.

"Not *comparable*! But it *is comparable*, Monsieur! You want to miss the *fundamentales* and make yourself the *maître*? You want to do as you please?"

"But many established artists use this method now," protested the student feebly.

Legros rolled his eyes with scorn. "Established they may be, but they are wrong! If you desire to learn to paint under my *auspice*, then you will do as I say! Start again, Monsieur!" At this, he took the canvas off the easel, flung it to the ground, then turned and calmly crossed the room to greet his visitors.

"Pleased to see you, Messieurs James," said Legros, making a short bow before seating himself with a flourish. "How can I be of assistance?" He did not appear in the least perturbed that they had been privy to his tirade.

William found himself unable to respond. The scene had upset him, recalling instances in his early career as an aspiring painter that he did not like to remember.

"We are here to gather some information about a former student." Henry took the lead, seeing his brother's unwillingness to respond. He too, however, was distracted, finding it difficult to keep his eyes off the model in the center of the room, who, given where they were seated, presented himself squarely in their line of vision.

"I am afraid that I must respect my students' right to privacy," said Legros with pompous formality.

William could not help wondering how such respect conformed with having just berated a student in front of the entire class. His also noted that Legros's French accent had become distinctly less pronounced now that he was no longer acting in his pedagogical capacity. "We are here on special assignment from Scotland Yard," William declared coldly. He produced a letter from Abberline giving them official authority to ask questions.

It was only a few sentences, but it took Legros several minutes to peruse. Finally he handed the letter back. "I am at your disposition," he said, bowing his head.

"Might we retire to your office?" requested Henry, whose discomfort was increasing, as the model appeared to be eyeing him directly.

Legros gave a nod and led them through a side door to a wood-paneled office. Over the desk was a large painting by Poussin, the neoclassical master who epitomized the school ideal of appropriate subject matter, craft, and decorum.

"It's about a student who was enrolled here two or three years ago," explained William without further preliminary. "His name was Walter Sickert. I wonder if you could tell us your impressions, if you remember him."

"Sickert," said Legros sneeringly. "Of course I remember. An insufferable young man. No respect for tradition or convention. No patience or discipline. An egoist of the first order."

"You threw him out?" asked William.

"I would have done," said Legros, obviously irritated that he had not had the chance. "He saved me the trouble by leaving. Whistler took him up."

"Whistler saw something in him?"

"Whistler sees things in unlikely places," said Legros dismissively. "But then he is *eccentrique* and blind to degeneracy.

"Degeneracy?"

"Any falling away from the truth is degenerate. It is not the first time Whistler takes our leavings. I warned him, but he says, never mind, he can manage this Sickert."

"Manage him?"

"Keep him from making trouble."

"What kind of trouble?"

"Sickert is ambitious."

"And that is bad?"

"It is bad for the tradition and the profession. Such types destroy anything they think is established and correct. Their aim is to kill the art of the past. They are dangerous because they inspire others to do the same."

William saw what he was dealing with here. Legros perceived any deviation from tradition to be a form of degeneracy. His ideas about art were so rigid and prescribed that he was close to mad himself.

It was disheartening to realize that the head of a prestigious school was a lunatic, and yet William was not altogether surprised. It took an exacting sort of personality to head up an institution, and if the institution was devoted to the dissemination of rules and precepts, then the person leading it was likely to veer toward the extreme in his support of them. If Legros were mad, his madness was organically connected with his role as the director of the Slade School of Fine Art.

Perhaps, thought William, allowing his perspective to widen in characteristic fashion, all deliberate choice of vocation was a lure to madness, at least to the extent that such devotion to craft was also a kind of crippling. It placed the self into a mold that was not natural to it. The results could be glorious or disastrous, based on factors too numerous and complicated to fathom. There was no telling, really, what the consequences might be.

CHAPTER 29

WHEN THE BROTHERS LEFT the Slade, Henry announced that they should take a hansom cab to Chelsea and make two visits that would be helpful in their investigation. Oscar Wilde and John Sargent, both acquainted with Walter Sickert, lived on Tite Street, practically across from each other, which meant they could interrogate both in the space of a few hours. Henry was pleased to be able to propose it. As boys, it was always William who took the lead, and he was obliged to follow along or remain behind. But here, he knew the terrain and could have the ideas.

As they descended the hansom cab on Tite Street, Henry warned that Wilde might not be home. That he had a home at all, and with the appurtenances of a wife and children, was in itself surprising, so it was little wonder that he was rarely there. Today, however, he was, because he was suffering from a cold. The brothers entered the drawing room to find him reclining on the sofa, two children in blue pinafores playing quietly in the corner, his wife knitting by the fire. It might have been a stage set in which Wilde had been plopped or a scene out of Dickens of the precise sort that Wilde liked to make fun of.

But he was in no mood to make fun. He was wearing a rumpled dressing gown, and his hair, usually glossy and neatly parted in the middle, had a dull, unbrushed look.

"You catch me en famille," he said, waving a limp hand in the direction of his children and wife. One might have thought that they had caught him in a compromising situation, which, given his reputation for the unconventional, they had. "You know my lovely wife, Constance." He motioned toward the woman knitting nearby, who smiled weakly. She was a pale woman with a coronet of flyaway hair and a long, arched nose that strikingly resembled her husband's (it was sometimes given out that Constance was really Oscar in petticoats, since they were so rarely seen together). To Henry, however, the resemblance was not surprising. If someone like Wilde was going to marry, he would try as far as possible to marry himself.

"Get them some tea, my dear," he ordered his wife. Constance went off to get them tea.

"You see before you the domesticated Wilde," said Wilde, blowing his nose in a large handkerchief. "It is very nice to have a wife when one is sick."

Henry could not disagree; the problem, he thought, was having a wife when well.

"To what do I owe the honor of this visit from America's most gifted brothers?" continued Wilde through his stuffed nose.

William explained that he had wanted to relay the best wishes of his countrymen, who had been so taken by Wilde during his American tour. (He and Henry had agreed on this excuse for the visit, knowing that it would appeal to their host's vanity.)

"So they still remember me there?" said Wilde wistfully. "Tell me more."

"Oh, they talk about you continuously," said William, hoping that he would not be expected to name names. "They say you are the epitome of sophisticated wit."

"It's true, I am," agreed Wilde, "though I'm not as acclaimed for it here, which I suppose is to be expected. I've considered moving to your country, you know, but then I'd have to perform myself brilliantly every minute of the day. It would be tiring." He sniffled into his handkerchief, as he considered that prospect. "Here, at least, I can relax from time to time in the domestic enclave." He looked around him and then sneezed, as though he were allergic to what he saw.

There was a pause, as Constance came back with the tea and then, at a gesture from her husband, ushered the children out of the room.

Henry saw an opportunity to move toward the desired subject, even though it meant referring to someone he would have preferred not to discuss. "If you came to America, you would soon surpass Clemens in popularity," he noted.

Wilde looked even more pleased. "It's nice of you to say, but I hardly think so." He then took the bait Henry had planted, his rheumy eyes sparkling maliciously. "Clemens was in rare form the other night, don't you think? I feared that he would pummel you."

"Yes," said Henry, wincing. "I am grateful for the intervention of that young man, what was his name?"

"Sickert. Walter Sickert."

"That's it. Walter Sickert. Are you intimate with this Sickert?"

"Not intimate," said Wilde, winking.

"I mean…are you good friends?"

"Oh yes, great friends. We perform together, as you saw."

"Do you know his family?"

"I'm a great friend of his mother and sister. They dote on me almost as much as they dote on him."

"And his father?"

"His father is a minor painter. A Prussian."

"Severe? Autocratic?"

"Not really," said Wilde. "Can't say I know the man well, but he seems benign enough."

"And Sickert's wife?"

"He doesn't spend much time with her. Goes off to do his painting... Cornwall, Dieppe, and the East End. He has a number of studios there."

"That's odd."

"No. Whistler did the same."

"It must be hard for him, dealing with Whistler."

"Not really. They seem to get along. Jimmy says he has talent, which constitutes high praise from that quarter."

Henry felt frustrated. Aside from the fact of East End studios, which were not uncommon among artists these days, he was not getting the sort of information he would have liked.

"But you should ask him these questions yourself"—Wilde sniffled insinuatingly—"since you appear to be so interested in each other."

Henry looked surprised. "In each other?"

Wilde paused to blow his nose and then continued, "After the party, Walter asked me about you. Wanted to know all about William and Alice too."

"Really?" Henry and William exchanged glances. "Do you have any idea why?"

"None at all, dear boy. You know I don't pay attention to other people; I'm too interested in hearing what I will say next."

William cleared his throat. He, for one, had no interest in hearing what Wilde would say next.

"I'm afraid we must be off," said Henry, taking William's cue.

"So thoughtful of you to stop by." Wilde sniffled. He seemed to want to say more but sneezed instead. There was something to be said for Wilde with a cold.

CHAPTER 30

"JANE COBDEN IS HERE to see you," said Sally, as a woman in a serge skirt and tweed cape swept into Alice's bedroom. Jane Cobden was a regal figure, unusually tall with thick red hair and dark blue eyes that seemed to be focused slightly beyond whomever she was talking to, as though her sense of the world could not be satisfied with the here and now. She had a lean, straight body that would have looked austere, had it not been for an unusually large bosom.

"It must be quite a burden for her to be saddled with those things," Katherine had once noted, and Alice, considering this, had suggested that the physical attribute might reflect an animal side to their friend that, under certain circumstances, could be let loose to surprising effect.

For the time being, however, Jane Cobden seemed to be devoted unswervingly to social amelioration. Her father, Richard Cobden, had also been a noted reformer, but of the old school of gentlemanly diplomacy, chatting and lingering with his friends to get a bill passed or a charity supported. Jane's style, by contrast, was more vehement and direct. Her life seemed entirely without the element of leisure or laxness, and her visits had the single and unique aim of raising money and awareness for the cause of social justice. In the face of such relentless energy, Alice always felt particularly useless.

"I was told you wanted to see me," said Jane in a brusque tone. "I came immediately, though I can't stay long. I am arranging to get qualified teachers for a school outside of London where none of the children are being taught how to read. The single most important issue with regard to alleviating the condition of the poor is literacy."

"Let me know if you need me to contribute," said Alice quickly.

Jane gave a short nod, and Alice knew that in a day or so she would receive a note in Jane's precise block script requesting some small sum for the cause just discussed.

"Since you are busy, I'll tell you at once the reason I asked your here," said Alice, knowing that further chitchat was unnecessary. "I want information about someone, and I can't tell you why. I hope you will accept those conditions."

"I trust you have good reason for what you want to know," said Jane, who had the additional virtue of having no interest in anything that didn't relate to her causes.

"It's about your sister's husband, Walter Sickert."

Jane's face seemed to go blank for a moment; then her brow furrowed. "An impossible man," she said shortly. "Why Ellen married him is beyond me."

"She must have seen something in him."

"Of course she saw something. He's a seductive flirt. All my sisters were in love with him and were surprised when he chose Ellen. Maggie is just as pretty and much closer to his age."

Alice looked curiously at Jane. It was a passionate diatribe, and Jane usually reserved these for the plight of the poor. "You don't like him," she said.

"I disapprove of him," clarified Jane.

"They say he has talent."

"I have no idea." Jane's face had grown flushed, presumably at the notion that such a man might have redeeming virtues. "All I know is that he makes Ellen miserable."

"Could you be more specific? How does he make her miserable?"

Jane coughed uneasily. "He disappears. Sometimes for weeks on end. Ellen says he has studios, 'hovels,' she calls them, throughout the East End, where he paints his 'subjects,' the more squalid the better. Here I am, trying desperately to help the poor, and my brother-in-law wants only to paint them."

"Does your sister know the location of these studios?"

"No, she knows nothing about his whereabouts when he leaves for one of his 'artistic sojourns,' as he calls them. He gives her no warning and no sense of when he will return. Yet she always takes him back. It's beyond me why she does."

"Perhaps she loves him."

"That's what she says," said Jane, her face growing redder. "It wouldn't matter so much if she had work of her own. But she was always a clinging, romantic-minded sort of person. Even when Father was alive, she worked out of devotion to him, not for the causes themselves. She says she cannot think in generalizations the way I do, only in particulars. That would be fine if the particular that she settled on had a bit more to recommend him."

"But perhaps that's the appeal," mused Alice. "She views the particular the way you view the general—as a vehicle for reform."

"She'll never reform that man. He has no…moral compass."

"Why do you say that?" asked Alice softly.

"He's an artist, and artists don't think in terms of usefulness or justice. It's not a commendable vocation, in my opinion, as much as some people worship it."

"Have you seen his work?"

"I don't care for pictures," said Jane curtly. "But as I say, his subjects are the people I try to help, the more squalid and miserable, the better. He does portraits too, for income, though those he paints can't expect to be flattered. They hire him because they've heard he has talent and that he may replace Whistler and fetch high prices in a few years. Art is a commodity in this society, like everything else, and what people pay for it rarely corresponds to what it's worth."

Alice wondered if Jane would be joining one of the communities that had begun cropping up, where wealth was shared and the children were cared for in common. It struck her as an unpalatable sort of life, but she could imagine that it might produce healthier human specimens.

"You have been extremely helpful," said Alice, for whom the excitement of what she had learned had begun to make her head ache. She was relieved to think that Jane was probably as eager to go as she was to have her go. "You must come to dinner when you have more time."

"I never have more time," said Jane bluntly, "and I don't take regular meals."

The idea of not taking regular meals made Alice's eyes open wide. She herself relied upon regular meals, even if she didn't eat them, to structure her day.

"But I will send you a prospectus on the project I mentioned earlier. There's also a woman's suffrage bill that might interest you."

"I could write letters," agreed Alice. "It's the least I can do, given that I cannot be a crusader like you."

"We each serve as we can," said Jane matter-of-factly. There was no hint of irony in her makeup, a fact which Alice, who had grown up in a household thick with irony, much appreciated. Indeed, Jane's response to Walter Sickert had been helpful not only in supplying a number of suggestive details regarding his life but also in calling into question his character. Other people might have ulterior motives for their dislike, but with Jane, one didn't worry about such things. One felt confident that she spoke what she believed, plainly and without subterfuge. If she was not a particularly amusing companion, she was a trustworthy one, and that, Alice knew, was a markedly rare attribute in the human population.

CHAPTER 31

LEAVING WILDE'S HOUSE, THE brothers crossed to 13 Tite Street, where Sargent had both his home and his studio. His was probably the most auspicious house in the neighborhood. It had originally been built by Edward Godwin, the architect, for himself and his wife, Beatrice. James Whistler had bought it from him. It was an irony not lost on his friends that Whistler had taken over Godwin's house and, then, with Godwin's death, had taken over Godwin's wife, a kind of double usurpation very much in the Whistler style. A few years back, however, he had decided to decamp from Tite Street, and the house had eventually been purchased by Sargent, who had transformed the space entirely to his own use. There seemed to be no prospect that he would ever leave.

It was a large house, commodious in its design, that had been made even more inviting through its current owner's tasteful furnishings. It was Sargent's great talent, as Henry often noted, to do everything beautifully without appearing to try. Every item associated with him, from the cut of his waistcoat to the position of the pillows on his bed, seemed to be just what it should be, no more, no less. This was the case with the drawing room that they entered. It was a well-proportioned space, paneled in cherrywood, beautifully accessorized with raw silk curtains of a champagne color. There was a sofa of salmon velvet, a carpet in pink and green, a set of delicate tea tables in an indeterminate French style, and a collection of worn but elegant easy chairs scattered carelessly about.

The men were let in by Sargent's butler, Niccola, a former gondolier whom Sargent had taken into service during his last trip to Venice. Niccola was also enormously decorative and, though not the best servant, apparently good enough for Sargent.

In the corner of the drawing room, Sargent was having tea with his sister. Emily did not live with him, but she dropped by all the time, so that no sooner did she leave than she seemed to come back. William and Henry made chitchat with her for a while until she said she had to go, and after a good deal of fussing about when she would return, she finally left. It had been agreed between the brothers that Sargent should be apprised of their suspicion of Sickert. He was a clearheaded observer of life, an invaluable resource as a testing ground for ideas.

"I can't see Sickert as a murderer," Sargent responded after William presented the idea.

"But that's the point," said Henry. "If you could, he would be locked up by now."

"I don't see that as an argument for his guilt," countered Sargent.

"We're just saying that a man's nature is not necessarily transparent," explained William. "And this Sickert is a good actor. It's one of the elements that makes him suspicious, though there are quite a few more." He proceeded to tick off the various items that had been gathered, to which Sargent listened with close attention. He was not impressed by the "ha ha" episode or the studios in the East End or the age of Sickert's wife. There was only one thing that seemed to interest him: the *P/W* crossed out in the margin of the De Quincey volume.

"Could you draw what the notation looks like for me?" Sargent asked, handing a pencil to William, who drew, as best he could, the letters as they had appeared in the margin of the book. "There is a line between the letters, though not a straight line. We can't make much out of the thing," William explained after he finished the drawing.

Sargent had hardly glanced at the tracery before he rung for Niccola. "Could you get me the sketches in the bottom drawer of the cabinet," he instructed the servant, who gave a lazy nod and went off.

"Whistler had this house before me," explained Sargent, "and things were left here that I've been meaning to send back to him. I think they might shed light on your theory." His voice was uncharacteristically excited.

Henry and William waited expectedly for Niccola to return. When he finally did, he was carrying a sheaf of drawings. Sargent immediately spread them out on the table in front of them. There were half a dozen sketches, mostly crude and incomplete. One, however, was finished—a pastel drawing that both brothers could see was an accomplished work, though not the sort of thing one would necessarily want in one's home. It showed a woman leaning against a wall, her hair wild, her dress falling limply off her shoulders. The face was painted—the lips and cheeks in bright red chalk—and there was a sign behind her, a poster for some sort of performance. The piece was executed in the style of one of Degas's homey ballet scenes, except the setting was more tawdry. This was an English music hall performer shown in a moment of weary dishabille between shows, or perhaps having lost her position on the stage.

"Not an appealing subject," noted Henry, "but it seems to be well done. Is it Whistler's?"

"No," said Sargent. "Not Whistler's, Sickert's. I recognize the hand. An excellent draftsman, with a wonderful, if morbid, sense of composition."

"And what is it doing here?" asked William.

"That's precisely the point. When this was Whistler's studio, Sickert worked here as an apprentice. He has since graduated to a more elevated position as assistant and leading apostle. He gets to sign his own name."

"Is this piece unsigned?" asked Henry. He could see that there was a scrawl in the right-hand corner.

"In a manner of speaking," said Sargent, the excitement mounting in his voice. "It's signed in the way Whistler's apprentices conventionally sign their work." William and Henry bent their heads over the sketch. Written in graphite were the words "pupil of Whistler."

"*P* of *W*," whispered Henry. "The line between the letters could convincingly be 'of.' And the crossing out?"

"Pupil no longer."

"Perhaps an expression of frustration at having occupied that role and still being attached to the man?" suggested William.

"You'd think, if he had murderous instincts toward Whistler, that he'd direct them there," mused Henry.

"Not necessarily," said William. "Often the impetus for pathological anger is too daunting to confront directly. The deranged mind strikes out against someone who is available, weak, and perhaps fills some other need for release."

Sargent had assumed a pensive expression. "The initials you drew resemble Whistler's butterfly imprint, which he often uses as a signature. They're a parody of it, in a manner of speaking—much like the ha ha in the letters, as you suggested, was a parody of his laugh…" He paused to consider his own observation and then leaned back in his chair and stretched out his legs. "There may be something to your theory after all."

✢ ✢ ✢

Sargent suggested that the brothers stay and talk to Ellen Terry, who was expected to come for a sitting within the hour. He had been commissioned to paint Terry, the reigning diva of the English stage, by Henry Irving, director of the Lyceum Theater and her latest official companion. Irving was so pleased with the arrangement, which allowed him to rehearse any time during the day or night, that he had commissioned the portrait to hang in the lobby of his theater.

"Ellen knows Sickert," explained Sargent. "He had some bit parts in her company a few years back. It's possible she can shed light on his character."

They had passed from Sargent's living space to his studio, which was, in its way, as delightful as his drawing room—more so insofar as its decoration was more unrestrained. Colorful rugs in bright colors scattered the floor, and tapestries and drapes in velvet and satin swung from the long windows. There were armchairs and divans, as well as screens and large sequined pillows for lounging by models in an Oriental pose, or by visitors who wanted to take a nap. There were also large trunks containing costumes with a wide range of garb, from ropes of pearls and ruffled blouses to gypsy shawls, plumed hats, and tambourines.

The riot of colors and textures was supplemented by the numerous paintings, with their lush brushstrokes, propped up against the walls, some of them in an unfinished state, some completed but waiting to be framed and picked up by a buyer. Most of the paintings displayed face forward were genre scenes and landscapes, while the ones, by far more numerous, facing toward the wall were portraits, with the exception of the notorious portrait of Madame Goutreau—renamed Madame X to protect the lady's dubious reputation—which was prominently placed, facing forward, directly behind the easel. Although Sargent had initially been upset by the controversy surrounding this painting, berated in some quarters for its purple skin and plunging neckline, he had eventually adopted it as his greatest promotional asset. People came to him now asking him to paint them in the style of Madame X. "Wait long enough, and all judgments will turn into their opposite," Sargent liked to say, pointing to the portrait by way of example.

"It helps if you can afford to wait," Henry would grumble. He supposed his books would eventually sell very well—but he would be dead by then.

As Sargent set out his brushes in preparation for Ellen Terry's sitting, William began looking around the studio, furtively examining the paintings facing the wall.

"Are you looking for something?" asked Sargent.

"No," said William quickly. He was in fact looking for a portrait of Ella Abrams. The trunks full of costumes were enticing his imagination; he could imagine her in a fringed shawl leaning against the cushions. He had hoped that she might be posing for Sargent that day; thus the feeling of being disappointed, given that he had dwelled for some time on this fantasy, was all the greater. He wanted urgently to ask his friend about her but dared not mention her name for fear that he would betray something—what, he could hardly say.

Sargent had begun taking out the canvas on which he was painting Terry. He had already laid down some blocks of color (the method, William noted, for which Legros's student had been berated), and began to prepare his palette. Niccola entered to announce that Ellen Terry had arrived and was changing into her costume in the next room.

In a few minutes, an imposing woman of about forty swept in. She was dressed in a green brocade robe and matching cape, had a thick gold belt around her waist, and a red wig, plaited into two long, heavy braids, on her head. She allowed them all to kiss her hand and assured them they were free to stay and watch the artist at work. "It's the costume I wore for Lady Macbeth," she explained with a grand gesture at her attire. "John suggested it, and I trust him absolutely." (Sargent had recently confided to Henry that the trust of his clients—which was really the trust that he make them look young and beautiful—was beginning to wear on his nerves.)

"Do you like the wig?" she asked Sargent, who had been eyeing it approvingly.

"I do," he said. "I wouldn't have thought of it myself, but it adds something. Did you wear it in the role?"

"No," said Terry. "It was a last-minute inspiration, lent by a friend. Where's my crown?"

Sargent retrieved a large gold crown from one of the trunks, which she took and placed on her head.

"No," said Sargent, "hold it above your head. We want the sense of *desiring* to be crowned, not being so."

"Excellent," said Terry, holding the crown up. "But it's tiring to hold this way."

"For art, my dear," said Sargent, and Terry ceased complaining.

"How's Henry?" asked Henry, referring to Henry Irving.

"He's fine," said Terry indifferently. She had had so many male companions in the course of her career that she had ceased to think much about any of them.

"I suppose he's always on the lookout for new talent," Henry continued. He had a fleeting thought of his own talent, since he had long wanted to write a play and had drafted a dramatization of one of his novels, as he had told Alice a few days earlier. He did not mention this, however. Instead he said, "I was telling William about a wonderfully talented young man I saw the other night performing a musical hall turn with Wilde. They say he's a painter. I didn't catch his name."

"I wonder who it could be?" said Sargent.

William and Henry looked at each other. Sargent did everything so naturally that when he did something calculated, as in the present instance, the effect was ludicrous.

Terry, fortunately, was too preoccupied with holding the crown to notice. "You must mean Walter Sickert," she said. "He and Oscar perform all the time. He's the one who lent me the wig. He has loads of them."

Sargent, William, and Henry looked meaningfully at each other.

"Tell me about him," said Henry casually. His ability to be disingenuous was much more developed than Sargent's.

Terry sighed. "Walter could be a great actor, but he refuses to be patient, so he's turned to painting, where he says he won't have to wait as long. Perhaps he's right. He may be as great a painter as he could be an actor. He is also handsome and charming. And professes to be madly in love with me, which means he has excellent taste." She had assumed a wistful expression, suggesting a dalliance in that quarter and confirming that Sickert's appeal to the ladies was impressive; Terry had her pick of aspiring actors.

"Is there any area in which he falls short?" asked William.

She considered the question. "He's not reliable. He disappears, and one doesn't know where to find him."

"How mysterious," said Henry.

Terry shrugged. "I imagine it's a strain for his wife. It's one reason I'm content to have him adore me from afar."

"You suspect...romantic trysts?" asked William, an unaccountable tremor passing through him at the mention of the idea of illicit lovemaking.

"I suppose." Terry shrugged. "Though I don't know why he needs to be so discreet. I once saw him in the East End with a woman, and he turned the corner to avoid meeting me. It seemed silly. Even if she were a disreputable sort, he could always pass her off as a model."

Henry, William, and Sargent exchanged another look. Not, their eyes said, if she happened to be Polly Nichols, Annie Chapman, Elizabeth Stride, or Catherine Eddowes.

"When did this happen?" asked Henry.

Terry had had enough of the conversation. "God knows! Gossip is such a bore; I really can't abide it. Speaking of tiresome—how long do you want me to hold this crown, John? My arms are beginning to ache!"

CHAPTER 32

THE GUEST LIST FOR the party at Henry's flat, scheduled for Sunday night, had taken some work to assemble. Henry, though he had originally balked at the idea, had predictably gone overboard once he got used to it, and Alice and Katherine had to persuade him to curtail the number of guests, given the limited space and the need for a certain degree of intimacy. Reducing the list had then involved some bickering and hairsplitting as to who should be included. Du Maurier and Wilde had been forwarded, but their wit was judged to be dangerous in such small quarters. Also suggested was Emily's friend Flora Priestley, who was known to be enormously shy and finally deemed expendable, since she would say nothing. There had been some dispute about inviting Violet Paget (who had lately, in rebellion against her femininity, renamed herself Vernon Lee), but for the opposite reason that she was never silent. It was eventually decided that Violet (or rather Vernon) might be useful in keeping the conversation going. Henry had wanted to invite Henry Irving for the sake of his dramatization, but that would have necessitated inviting Ellen Terry, who might find it odd to see Sickert among the guests, when Henry hadn't known his name a few days earlier. Instead, they settled on the infirm but gentle Fanny Kemble, who could be counted on to talk about theater if that were necessary to draw Sickert out. Unfortunately, Edmund Gosse, always a dependable staple, was out of town. Constance Fenimore Woolson, known for mysterious reasons as Fenimore, was forwarded as his replacement, since she was in love with Henry and thus would make an effort, along with the Sidgwicks, because they were so fond of William and could distract Vernon Lee with talk of philosophy, if she became too voluble. Emily and John Sargent would round out the guests—Emily would be cheerful and accommodating, while John would be calm and observant, being the only person outside the family privy to their suspicion of Sickert.

Sickert had been sent a note saying that the Jameses had heard much of his developing talent and were eager to meet him and his wife, whose father, Alice made sure to mention, had been a great friend of their own. By Thursday, all the invitations had been sent, and by Saturday, the responses had been received. Everyone could come, except Ellen Sickert, who, Sickert wrote in a large, easy hand, sent her regrets; she was assisting one of her sisters during her confinement.

"From what I hear, she is often indisposed," noted Sargent. "I don't think he likes to be hampered on the social front."

"Why marry, then?" asked Alice.

"My sentiments exactly," said Henry.

Katherine had come to Henry's flat on the morning of the party to confer about the dinner. She drew a diagram of the table and tried to explain it to Mrs. Smith. "Note the arrangement of the silver," she said. "Make sure to place the smaller pieces on the outside and the little spoon at the top here, as I'm sure you know." She glanced at Mrs. Smith, who it was doubtful knew anything of the kind. "Napkins, wineglasses, water goblets," continued Katherine, pointing to her diagram, to which Mrs. Smith appeared not to be paying attention. "The condiments here, the ices here; please take care to keep the trifle away from the fire, or it will get soggy. Wash the strawberries thoroughly; you don't want any dirt. And have your husband be sure to pour the wine from the left."

Katherine was a calm, mild-tempered woman, but even she was beginning to grow irritable at the other woman's lack of attention. After Mrs. Smith had left to go into the kitchen, presumably to start preparing the trifle, Katherine voiced her disapproval. "What does she do?" she asked Henry.

"Oh, this and that," he said with some confusion. "I assure you she keeps busy."

"I have no doubt that she keeps busy," said Katherine, "but does she do any work?"

"Work, well…" Henry began to sputter.

Katherine felt it best to drop the subject. She would send Sally over to help in the kitchen, though Sally, who had just turned sixteen, could only do so much.

‡ ‡ ‡

Alice had been preoccupied for several days with the question of what she would wear. She had feared at first that she had nothing and would have to resort to the dressing gown of the séance. But a bit of digging had located the black dress she had worn to her father's funeral, and that could be made to look less funereal by removal of the material around the neck and the addition of a panel of pink and gray lace that Katherine found in a shop on Oxford Street. To this was added a set of pearls and black slippers. When she was finally done—dusted with rice powder, cheeks pinched, hair put up with a set of silver combs—she viewed herself in the large mirror in the sitting room and was so enamored of what she saw that she couldn't take her eyes away. "It's not that I look good," she explained, "it's just that I look so much better than I thought."

Emily Sargent, who had come early to help her dress, said she looked beautiful, which Alice found annoying. "I don't want to look beautiful," she said. "I want to look normal. 'Conventionally plain,' for example, would be good. Or 'rather ordinary.' I've always felt like such a freakish sort of person, too pale, too weak, too odd in all respects. To pass for ordinary would be a wonderful change of pace."

Katherine and Emily said she looked beautifully ordinary.

The carriage was finally called, and they got to Henry's flat just as the other guests were arriving. The Sidgwicks were already present, chatting with William, when Vernon Lee came in with a strapping young woman in tow—it was like her to bring a guest without alerting her hosts. Katherine ran into the kitchen to tell Mrs. Smith to lay another setting.

"I'm Kit," said the strapping young woman breezily, gripping Alice's hand so tightly that she winced in pain.

"She's one of the Anstruther-Thomsons," said Vernon, as though this explained everything. "We're working on a new theory of aesthetic philosophy."

"Really?" said Alice. Kit Anstruther-Thomson looked more suited to fox hunting than aesthetic philosophy.

Everyone clustered in the hallway, waiting for someone to take their coats, until finally Mrs. Smith came out of the kitchen, her bonnet askew, and exasperatedly gathered them up.

By nine o'clock, when dinner was supposed to be served, everyone had arrived, with the exception of Sickert. The siblings looked at each other in consternation as they registered the possibility that he might not come, and the entire event—tiring, noisy, and expensive—would be for nothing. But at 9:15, he was announced. Was a murderer about to make his appearance?

Sickert entered the room. He had a sharp, fine-featured face; rather thin lips; a profusion of curly, light brown hair; and a wiry, agile physique. His eyes were even bluer than Henry remembered. He was wearing a tweed coat, yellow gloves, and a soft-brimmed hat and carrying a cane. He gave his hat and cane to Mrs. Smith, who curtsied as she took them (something Henry couldn't help noticing that she never did for him), and then he walked directly to Henry to apologize for being late; he had been delayed at his studio, waiting for a canvas to be delivered. "My framer is not reliable," Sickert explained jauntily, "but as we trained together and he does good work, I make allowances." He winked at the company, as if to say that allowances often needed to be made for *him*.

Henry had been anxious about the encounter, less because Sickert might be a maniac than because of the incident with Clemens, which he felt obliged to acknowledge. "Thank you for saving my life the other night," he muttered with some embarrassment.

Sickert did not laugh as expected. "You must take more care in the future," he said seriously. "You were lucky you weren't pummeled to death."

Henry was taken aback. Did Sickert know something about Clemens's boxing prowess that he did not? To deflect further discussion, he led his guest to his brother across the room.

William had been standing off to the side in a state of nervous anticipation. The thought that he was about to meet a man who might be the cause of four women's brutal deaths, not to mention an attempt on his own life, made him shudder. But Sickert approached him with apparent ease and expressed praise for his writing. *So he reads philosophy between his rampages*, thought William sourly. He shook the hand offered, paying close attention. It was the right hand, he noted. The blow he had delivered with the branch in Hyde Park had been to his assailant's left. There was no evidence of debility, but he couldn't help wonder if Sickert was carrying himself a bit stiffly. Was it the theatrical posture or the stiffness born of injury? In all respects, the man seemed charming and easy—too much so, perhaps. Sociopathic personalities could be extremely congenial in ordinary settings.

"I am intrigued by your theories concerning the plastic nature of human character," said Sickert with the casualness of someone at home with ideas. "I agree with your hypothesis that we can shape ourselves in any number of directions."

"Shape ourselves within limits," murmured William. "There are biological constraints, not to mention habits formed in early childhood that seem impossible to revise."

"Yes." Sickert nodded. "But such things can exist apart."

"Apart?" asked William, looking at their guest inquiringly.

"Relegated to the private sphere…or to other corners of life."

"I don't know about that," said William, furrowing his brow. "Certain impulses cannot be fully buried."

"Oh, not buried," Sickert corrected, "compartmentalized. What is acting, after all, but the performance of character, devised from the tool case of one's experience and fashioned for a given occasion?"

"But actors assume a temporary mask that they put on and off. Don't you believe in an *essential* character?"

"No," said Sickert blithely. "Why should character be singular and not multiple? The latter is certainly more entertaining…and more convenient."

"Isn't it a function of art to provide an outlet for contending impulses?" queried William, who recalled how alive, though also how fraught with anxiety, he had felt during his early years as a painter.

"Admittedly, art serves this end to some degree," agreed Sickert. "The painter dabbles in different styles; the actor and writer inhabit different characters. But there are impulses that cannot be contained by art, or at least not by art as we commonly know it. The true artist is one who finds an accommodation for his disparate impulses. The more original the impulses, the more ingenious he must be in the form he adopts."

William blanched. The speech, which dovetailed with some of his own theories about the mutable nature of consciousness, struck him as sinister coming from the individual before him. Wasn't murder an accommodating form for impulses that might not find a home elsewhere? He did not respond, and Sickert, sensing the conversation was over, nodded politely and moved away to chat with Sargent about the latest art club gossip.

Dinner was served. Mrs. Smith had paid no attention to the diagram, so the forks and spoons were in the wrong order. Mr. Smith, breathing heavily and limping (he had both asthma and gout), began pouring the wine from the right. The soup was brought in; it was tepid and was followed by trout that had not been properly deboned. Katherine felt obliged, for the purpose of safety, to warn the guests to be careful, and the prospect of bones in the fish immediately set Henry's nerves on edge. He had once been at a dinner where an elderly gentleman had choked on a chicken bone, and the idea of a choking death in the presence of Jack the Ripper struck him as particularly infelicitous.

Potatoes and hashed beans, a large filet *de boeuf*, overcooked, and a pork pie that appeared to have no pork in it, followed. Vernon Lee stopped suddenly midsentence in her discussion of utilitarian theory to announce that the potatoes were raw. Fenimore, determined to support their host at all costs, insisted they were fine, popped one in her mouth, and then spent an inordinate amount of time chewing it. Finally, when she had gotten the potato down, she began lauding Henry's latest novel. "It was so moving! The young hero killed himself at the end."

"No need to read the book now," grumbled Henry.

"But why did he have to kill himself?" asked Emily, who liked happy endings.

"He had no choice!" insisted Fenimore. "The boy had been assigned to commit a murder by his anarchist friends. He could not face having failed in his pledge. What else could he do?"

"He could have committed the murder," suggested Sickert lightly.

The siblings exchanged glances.

Sidgwick began telling the company about Mrs. Blavatsky, the medium that the Society for Psychical Research had recently discredited. "I still maintain she has powers beyond the ordinary," he said. "She found Nora's mother's locket."

Nora Sidgwick nodded. "I never thought of looking under the dormer."

"Did she levitate anything?" asked Emily. "John and I once saw a lady levitate a blanket. Except John said there were mirrors. Am I right, John?"

"There most certainly *were* mirrors," said Sargent.

"Kit levitated herself once," said Vernon Lee.

Everyone looked at Kit with curiosity.

"Almost," amended Kit.

"Kit has a gift for the amplification of stimuli," explained Vernon. "As you can see, she has a magnificent physical instrument."

Everyone stared at Kit's physical instrument.

"And how did Kit *almost* levitate herself?" asked Alice.

"It was the influence of a painting," explained Vernon. "A Titian. We were both struck dumb, but Kit was affected most strongly. The uplift in the vertical lines combined with the buoyancy of the reds almost lifted her off the ground."

Everyone pondered this.

"And does Kit have other…gifts?" asked Alice.

"Oh yes," said Vernon, "she feels all sorts of things. Isn't that so, dear?" She turned to Kit, who was buttering a roll but who put it down to address the company.

"I feel the forces in this room," she asserted loudly. "My head is high and my legs rooted, but I feel myself drawn hither and yon." She began to sway. "Divergent impulses among the company: doubt, suspicion, possibly dread. The vibrations course through me." She gave a gasp and a shudder. Then she took a bite from the roll.

"Kit could be an invaluable resource if properly exploited," explained Vernon. "She could anticipate earthquakes, floods, and mining disasters, not to mention evils of the social variety. She has a special feeling for the suffering poor, especially in the area of abused womanhood. The

Whitechapel murders, for example. I'm sure she could help the police find this Jack the Ripper if she put her mind to it."

Henry, who had just taken a gulp of wine to wash down a raw potato, was caught off guard by mention of the individual they suspected might be present. He gagged on the potato and snorted wine out of his nose.

A hubbub ensued, as Fenimore pressed a glass of water to his lips and William slapped him on the back. "The poor man has a problem with esophageal spasms," he explained to distract the company from what might have prompted Henry's response.

"Yes," Alice hastened to add. "We wouldn't want to lose him prematurely to choking death."

Everyone looked at Henry with concern, and even Henry, who had forgotten why he had choked, looked alarmed on his own behalf.

Finally the conversation resumed. "You were speaking of Kit's response to the Titian," Alice prompted.

"Yes," Vernon took up. "The effects were duplicated with a Raphael and even a minor Mantegna…increased respiration and elevated heart rate. There was also an enlargement of soul that cannot be recorded but to which she attests through her sentiments and behavior. Last week she was inspired to a great act of charity after an hour in front of an Etruscan bronze."

Kit nodded complacently. "It's true. I wanted to give all my money away."

"And she would have done it, were it not held in trust." Vernon looked admiringly at her friend, who had started in on a second roll. "But what interests us is not Kit in herself, extraordinary though she is, but her representative nature as the human specimen writ large. Her example demonstrates that great art is literally a source of uplift; it can inspire great acts of charity and mercy."

"And bad art?" asked Sickert with amusement. "Can it inspire great acts of rapacity and murder? If so, I know quite a few painters who ought to be placed under arrest."

There was a titter of laughter, and the siblings exchanged glances again.

Mrs. Smith had come in with the ices, which had melted, and Mr. Smith refilled the wineglasses, shakily. His nose had grown very red. There was some general toasting to William's visit, followed by discussion of the latest Royal Academy show, which everyone agreed was disappointing.

"Except for John's painting of Mrs. Marquand," noted Emily.

"A handsome woman, Mrs. Marquand," noted Nora Sidgwick, "but John made her handsomer."

"John always paints his subjects' ideal selves," explained Emily.

"Their complexions are certainly flawless," agreed Nora.

"That's why they pay me so much," noted Sargent. "I'd cut my fee in half to paint a wart."

As the conversation veered off to a discussion of warts on Mrs. Marquand, Alice turned to Sickert. He was seated to her right, but they had not yet spoken directly. "How do *you* paint your subjects, Mr. Sickert?" she asked quietly.

"I paint them as they are," he said succinctly, "or rather, as I see them."

She paused. "But you apparently do this very well. I have heard excellent things about your work."

"Is that so?" He smiled and waited for her to elaborate.

"I am told you can hold your own against Whistler. And have the talent to surpass him."

Sickert did not refute this fact. "Are you interested in pictures?" he asked, his blue eyes taking in Alice's dress and hair and then settling with interest on her face. The survey was swift but thorough, and for some reason, though normally she was terribly uncomfortable with being looked at, she did not mind.

"I am interested in everything," she responded a bit smugly, "though, sadly, I cannot act on my interests. I am not a well person, you see, not so much in body as in mind. I am obliged to view life from a distance."

"We are alike in that," said Sickert.

Alice looked at him quizzically. "Your mind is not right?"

"To be sure, my mind is not right." He laughed. "No interesting person is sane. But I also view life at a remove. As an artist, I am by necessity an onlooker."

"But I rarely get out of bed," insisted Alice.

"You surpass me there," he said, bowing his head slightly. "And what conclusions do you draw from that vantage point?"

She considered this a moment. "That life is hard. That we all suffer."

He nodded. "I'll grant you that. But is there nothing else? Do you ever laugh?"

"Oh, I laugh all the time."

Sickert laughed in response and seemed to examine her even more closely. "I should like you to see my paintings."

"As I said, I don't go out," said Alice, tossing her head. "Tonight is an exception. I do it in honor of my brother's visit from America. I am sure to pay for it with a week's worth of headaches."

"I hope it will be worth it."

"I hope so." Her tone was saucy. For the first time in her recollection, she was flirting with a man—if she didn't count the teasing that she and William had done as children.

He kept his gaze on hers. "I could always give you a private viewing… bring my pictures to *you*."

She returned his gaze. "I think I should like it better if you painted my portrait. I am told you are gifted but morbid, just the sort of painter who could do me justice."

"I think I could," murmured Sickert. "Though, as I said, I am not inclined to flatter."

"I don't want to be flattered," said Alice lightly. "But you will have to paint me in my bedroom, since as I said, I rarely leave it."

"I would be delighted to be invited into your bedroom—in any capacity you please."

His eyes flickered with amused insinuation, but Alice could not feel insulted. On the contrary, she looked at him with similar amusement and told him it was settled. "But you will have to hurry," she warned. "I cannot keep the headaches at bay for long."

"Then I will come on Tuesday after luncheon."

She nodded her head slightly and turned away. The headache that she had felt coming on early in the evening had disappeared, and despite the unaccustomed activity, she felt surprisingly well.

✣ ✣ ✣

"You what?" said Henry and William together, after the guests had left and Mrs. Smith had tidied up, not very well.

"I have asked him to paint me," Alice repeated.

"Are you saying that you have abandoned our idea? That you think he is innocent? "

"I don't know about that." Alice shrugged.

"My God!" said William.

"It *is* a terrible thing to say, I know. How could one like a murderer? But I did like him, and I don't know if he's innocent. I want him to paint my picture, both because I think he would do it well and because I think it would help me decide. He's coming Tuesday, so I think I should go home and get some rest." She was feeling uncharacteristically lighthearted. "An excellent dinner party, Henry," she added, as Katherine helped her on with her coat. "Tell Mrs. Smith that she outdid herself."

CHAPTER 33

WHEN WILLIAM HURRIED INTO Abberline's office at nine a.m. the next morning, he was surprised by the state of things. The inspector's desk was generally orderly in the extreme, reports and documents arranged in bins that William had laughingly compared to the cubbyholes Minor used for his dictionary definitions. But today, the desk was submerged in an avalanche of unruly papers. Abberline was seated stiffly in front of them, making no effort to set them right. As soon as he saw William, however, he gave the papers an irritable shove and stood up.

"This is what the newly materialized assistant commissioner would have me waste my time doing." He gestured contemptuously at the pile of papers. "Sorting through reports of infractions by members of our labor syndicates. After that, he is likely to have me interrogate the rabbis of London. Sir Robert maintains that a cabal is behind the Ripper murders and will not rest until he has expended great amounts of time and energy chasing an illusory conspiracy. It worked for him before, when he accused Parnell of involvement in the Phoenix Park murders, and he assumes it will work again now."

"But Parnell was found innocent of those charges," noted William.

Abberline snorted. "Truth and falsehood are inconsequential in such cases. The aim is to establish a reputation, and for that, it's better to make a great false claim than a small true one." He took a breath and realizing that he was being goaded by Anderson in a way he disliked, tried to address William more calmly. "You are earlier than usual this morning. Our coffee isn't even ready." It had become a ritual for them to share a late-morning coffee, fortified by a generous dose of brandy.

"No coffee today," said William. "I am en route to an errand elsewhere, but I wanted to give you this." He took a small envelope from his pocket. "I'd like you to examine it alongside the Ripper letters."

Abberline took the envelope and extracted its contents. It was the note Sickert had sent in response to Henry's dinner invitation. It was written in red ink on heavy, cream-colored vellum.

"As you can see, the stock is familiar; it bears the mark of Pirie and Sons." William had noted this point as soon as the letter was delivered to Henry's flat, though he had not mentioned it to his brother or sister. It could mean nothing, and would only have upset them.

Abberline examined the note for a moment. He did not seem unduly impressed. "As I told you, the paper is too common to allow us to draw a conclusion. My wife uses it for…whatever it is she uses it for. But I'll have the note looked at, since you believe there is reason to suspect the writer. It will at least divert me from this." His lip curled as he waved at the pile on his desk. "Do you have time to go with me to consult our 'experts'?" Abberline's "experts" were a ragtag troop of petty forgers who had traded a year in prison to assist on the Ripper investigation. These individuals, some of whom had proven more competent and astute than many on the police force, had sifted through the hundreds of letters sent to Scotland Yard and the Central News Agency and come up with the handful of specimens that William had shared with Alice.

Normally William would have enjoyed consulting with these gifted specimens of criminality, but today he could not linger. Indeed, glancing at his watch, he saw that he was already running late. He therefore promised to stop back for a report on Sickert's note and apologized again that he would miss their morning coffee, which was to say, their morning brandy.

It was forty minutes before eleven, later than he had intended, when he arrived by hansom cab at Asher Abrams's shop, a neat brick structure located at the end of a well-swept cul-de-sac in Soho. The words "Abrams & Son: Art, Antiquarian Books, and Reliquaries" were traced in gold script on the large plate-glass window that fronted the street.

He had wanted to arrive well before the hour Ella Abrams had established they would meet, since he wished to consult with the clerk before she got there. As much as he wished to see her again—and the idea excited him more than he wanted to admit—he was also convinced that she had something to hide with respect to the De Quincey volume.

The inside of the shop was even more impressive than its exterior. The bookcases, which reached to the ceiling, were of a polished mahogany wood decorated here and there with brass plaques to mark the kinds of volumes assigned to each shelf. There were sliding ladders to reach the higher collections, and interspersed with the books were colorful ceramics, bowls, and tiles exhibited behind glass cases. Gilt-framed canvases in oil, watercolor, and chalk hung on the walls that did not have bookcases. A fireplace, in which was a carefully tended fire, was in one corner of the room, in front of which were two armchairs. The room was like an opulent and extremely comfortable drawing room, and William couldn't help thinking how nice it would be to sit in those armchairs with Ella Abrams and converse quietly before the fire.

An older man in an apron greeted William as he came in. When he stated his errand and explained it had been sanctioned by Asher Abrams, the clerk led him to a large room in the back of the shop where artifacts awaiting inventory were stored. There were piles of books with elaborate bindings, picture frames without pictures, pictures without frames, mirrors of various sizes, furniture in various states of disrepair, and sundry other objects reaching from floor to ceiling within the cavernous space.

The man led William to an area in the corner where there was a shelf containing rows of ledger books. He glanced at the paper that had been handed to him on which Asher Abrams had written "Complete set of De Quincey, red leather binding, from Cheshire estate sale." The man considered the notation for a moment, then ran his index finger over the ledgers, located one, and thumbed through it. "Here it is," he finally said, with satisfaction. "De Quincey. Twenty-volume set. Bound in red leather." He squinted down at the notation. "Not sold," he commented succinctly. "Miss Ella took it off the market."

"Took it off the market?" asked William.

The foreman responded, "Took it for her own use. Or to give as a gift," he added without inflection. "As her father's surrogate in the business, it is her right to do as she pleases with the merchandise." William glanced at the ledger and saw that a thin line had been drawn through the item. On the opposite page, he saw another line through an item listed as "small Greek urn, possibly second century," and above it, a line through "silver cigarette case, gold filigree."

Before he could ask more questions, however, the front door could be heard opening and closing, and Ella appeared at the entrance to the room. William thought that she looked, if possible, even more beautiful than she had the other night. Her expression, however, was not pleasant.

"It was rude of you not to wait for me," she said, her mouth set in an angry line and her face flushed. The clerk, seeing that it was a matter that did not concern him, put the ledger back into the bookcase and retired to his desk, where he became immediately engrossed in cataloging a set of ceramic tiles.

William walked over to where Ella Abrams stood, realizing that he wanted desperately to regain her good opinion. "I thought it might be best to get here early," he explained apologetically, "though of course I intended to wait for you. I hope you can still spare me a moment of your time."

She gave a sigh, turned, and walked into the shop, where she settled into one of the armchairs and motioned for him to take the other. She did not speak for a moment; then, having regained her composure and abandoned both her anger and her furtiveness, spoke bluntly. "My father says you have a deep understanding of people."

"And how does he know that?"

"He is something of a psychologist himself, you know. Indeed, he has many talents, though, unfortunately, he must apply them all to one end— that of making money in order to prove that he is as good as other English gentlemen. Of course, by concentrating on that task, he succeeds only in proving that he's not. It's a paradox that it will take another generation or two to overcome. Then we will have the luxury to appreciate art and philosophy as you do."

"*You* seem to appreciate art and philosophy."

"I have an interest," agreed Ella. "But what is that? A woman can take an interest in things, but she cannot do them. You must understand that, having a sister…and a wife. And as a Jew, I am handicapped further, though I suppose it gives me a perspective on things. John Sargent says that women and Jews are the great observers of culture. I, being both, observe quite a bit, you see."

"You are dissatisfied with your life?" William asked, discerning the bitterness in her voice.

"Dissatisfied?" mused Ella. "I suppose I am. I wish to represent myself in some way in the world."

"John Sargent has painted you."

"Yes, he finds me exotic and is taken with the play of light on my hair. Others have delved deeper. But inspiring art is not the same as creating it." There was a pause. "I gave the De Quincey set to a friend."

William sat very still for a moment. "I have reason to want to speak to the owner of the set," he finally said quietly. "Could you put me in touch with him?"

"We are no longer in touch, but you can contact him on your own. He has, I believe, a rising reputation in the art world; his name is Walter Sickert."

William felt his throat tighten, and for a moment he thought he would faint. His distress must have shown on his face, for Ella spoke sharply. "You are shocked that I had an intimate relationship with a man…and a gentile at that? I am an independent woman. I will no doubt marry a Jewish banker of whom my father approves, but until then, I do as I please. As I said, I do not have the resources that you have to accomplish anything of significance, so I resort to attaching myself to accomplished men."

William recalled the other items that had been marked in the ledger, all tokens of affection from Ella Abrams to Walter Sickert, he thought. "You were…in love…with this Sickert?" His voice sounded muffled to his own ears.

"Whatever I felt is over," said Ella, looking at him with calm directness. The sun streaming through the window had burnished her skin so that it looked like polished bronze. The dark, shiny hair; the chiseled face; the bright, intelligent eyes all seemed to be set off by a radiant cloud of light. He was reminded of Sargent's portrait, but as she had implied, the picture was a superficial appreciation; it made her into a sensual surface rather than the complex, restless being he saw before him.

He couldn't stop looking at her, gulping down the smooth planes of her face and the lights in her hair. He was staring, he knew, but he couldn't help it, though he also felt inhibited, constrained in ways he had not felt before.

"I have no doubt that the person I mentioned will be helpful with regard to assembling the completed set," she said softly. "I have no idea how the single volume may have become unattached."

"Why did you stop seeing him?" William had forgotten about the volume; he was thinking only about the relationship that had been revealed to him between Ella Abrams and Walter Sickert. The idea of such a relationship made him feel sick.

Ella paused to fully consider her answer. "I misjudged his character," she finally said.

He knew that he should ask her what she meant, interrogate her as to the nature of the man with whom she had been intimate, but he could not. The idea of speaking about Sickert now repelled him. He would have to see to her again when he was calmer and more prepared to probe the subject. Perhaps the desire to see her again was what prevented him from asking questions now.

She had risen from her chair, and he did the same. They stood opposite each other, close, though not so close as to touch, and yet he felt the presence of her body, in its suppressed energy, and imagined it pressing against his. He had an almost irresistible urge to give himself up to his feelings and knew that if he did, she would respond. He could feel her desire for him radiating back at him. He did nothing, though, merely continued to hold his gaze on her face. When she finally put out her hand, he looked down and took it, grasping the soft palm in his. He did not know how long he held it, but it was a long time before he finally mumbled farewell and hurried out the door into the bustling streets.

CHAPTER 34

I DON'T THINK YOU SHOULD go through with this," said William, as he, Alice, and Henry sat together in her bedroom. She had, he saw to his consternation, already gone to some trouble to prepare for Sickert's visit. She had had Sally purchase her a new cap, and she had changed the coverlet on her bed to the lace one that had belonged to their mother and that she generally kept in storage. She had also made Archie move the armoire so that there would be room for Sickert's easel and paints.

The idea that she was looking forward to the visit upset William considerably. Ella Abrams had succumbed, and now his sister, of all people, was showing herself to be susceptible. What was it with this man Sickert, and more to the point, with the women who found him alluring?

He had tried his best to explain to Alice why Sickert's ownership of the De Quincey volumes strongly supported his guilt, but she stubbornly refused to be convinced.

"I agree that it's a coincidence," she said, "but we remain unsure of so many things: whether the photograph was planted in the book and whether the owner might not simply have notated it without any intention to kill. It's a popular essay, and someone who finds it of interest isn't necessarily a murderer."

"But the initials!" insisted William.

"Who's to say that they refer to 'pupil of Whistler'? It's an ingenious but unsubstantiated assumption. They could mean anything. And"—she spoke with a certain knowing emphasis here—"perhaps they were put in the book before the set was given to Sickert by your young lady. We don't know how the volume became separated from the set."

She was making excuses on his behalf, thought William angrily; she was engaging in the sort of rationalizations one heard from an infatuated woman. As much as he might deny it, he had always found secret comfort in the fact that she had never seemed to care for men. Her friendship with Katherine had pleased him in this respect, alleviating any need to be jealous in a conventional sense. But now he was both jealous and afraid.

"I insist on being present during the sitting," he asserted vehemently. "There's no telling what that maniac might do alone with you in your bedroom."

"I am quite sure he will not ravish me…unless I cooperate," said Alice, ignoring the shocked expression on her brother's face. "And he couldn't possibly cut my throat. Everyone is within shouting range. Your inspector's man will be keeping watch outside."

"You must have Katherine with you, then," said William, sensing that Alice's companion was a bar of more than a physical sort to any kind of emotional entanglement.

"Katherine is off to nurse her sister in Sussex. And it is just as well. If I am to arrive at any sort of conclusion, I must see him alone."

"We can't condone it," William fumed. "Can we, Henry?"

Henry, who had been sitting off to the side musing, was not prepared to agree unequivocally with his brother. "I don't know," he said. "Sickert seems rather a nice sort of fellow."

William looked disgusted. "Of course he's nice. It's his modus operandi to be nice." He was half in mind to tell them about the attack on his life, and then thought better of it. It would only upset Alice without necessarily convincing her of anything.

"If you insist on worrying, you can keep watch from my closet," said Alice finally, indicating the small room off to side that contained a commode and a large washbasin that could be moved into the back hall.

It was, William concluded, not a bad idea. The space connected to the bedroom by way of a little door with slats that could be adjusted so its occupants might see what was transpiring in the next room.

"I realize that it's not very dignified to hide in a loo," Alice noted with amusement, "but it offers a good vantage point on the proceedings."

William said he did not care about his dignity, and Henry, who had roused himself to become involved in the discussion, said he didn't either. He could not think of Sickert as a murderer, but the idea of spying on him seemed an exciting prospect from which he was not about to be excluded.

"It's too cramped for both of us," protested William, looking at his brother with annoyance.

"I think there's plenty of room," countered Henry.

"Why should the two of us keep watch?"

"Because I may catch something you miss."

There was some truth in this point, William grudgingly admitted to himself. His brother had a way of seeing things that never ceased to surprise him. There was no denying that Henry could be an astute observer, and that the nature of their respective vision was often complementary. William therefore nodded curtly in acquiescence.

They brought their chairs into the little room, arranged the slats on the door, and took their places.

"It's moldy in here," complained Henry, sniffling.

"Then leave."

"I was just making an observation."

William glared at his younger brother. "If you insist on being here, I ask only one thing: that you keep quiet!"

✢ ✢ ✢

Sickert was late. William had begun to shift restlessly, and Henry, though he had kept his mouth shut as stipulated, was sniffling from the mold in the closet when the visitor finally made his appearance at almost four p.m.

He arrived weighed down with easel, paint box, and canvas, which he placed in the corner of the room, and then he came directly up to the bed, took Alice's hand, and kissed it gallantly. His lateness, he explained, was because he had to wait for the canvas to be stretched. For this purpose he relied on a man who was often out on errands, yet here Sickert was, and the canvas was just as he liked.

He sat for a few moments on the edge of the bed, holding Alice's hand and looking at her closely, as he had done at the dinner party. The brothers peered through the slats. There was hardly room for both to look at once, so there was some jostling and elbowing. Sickert's closeness to Alice and the silence in which he gazed at her struck William as sinister, but his sister did not seem to mind. She returned his gaze, smiling.

"I was beginning to think that you had second thoughts about painting me," she said.

"On the contrary. I have been looking forward to it all day." He moved his head closer to hers and touched the strings of her bonnet. "But I think you should remove the cap." With a quick stroke, he pulled the strings and unceremoniously took the cap from her head and threw it on the floor.

"It's a new cap," protested Alice.

"So much the worse for it. I'm not painting the cap." He smoothed her hair with his hand, and she did not protest.

Henry elbowed William sharply to get a view through the slats, and William elbowed back, his teeth clenched in anger at the sight of Sickert with his hand on his sister's head.

Sickert moved his hand to her cheek and held it there a moment, then got up, walked back to the easel, and stood looking at her from that vantage point. "Unclasp your hands, please," he said. "Place them at your sides."

She did.

"Now close your eyes."

Alice paused. "You want to paint me as if I'm sleeping. Or dead?"

"No," said Sickert. "I want you to relax your face. Close your eyes and then open them again."

She did.

"You look more relaxed already."

"I never relax," protested Alice.

"We'll see."

"I am not a picturesque subject," she added.

"I don't care for picturesque subjects."

Her face dropped slightly. She had expected him to say that she *was* picturesque.

He did not speak for a moment as he prepared his palette, and then he finally said, "I care for interesting subjects, not picturesque ones. Beauty, in the conventional sense, is not interesting." He began to daub the canvas with paint, moving back and forth, looking at her with his bright blue eyes and then bringing his brush to the canvas in quick, sharp jabs.

William poked Henry to observe the manner in which Sickert was applying the paint.

"You do not care for beauty?" Alice asked, a touch of rancor in her voice.

"I said I do not care for conventional beauty. You are beautiful."

"Yes, I have a beautiful soul."

"I don't believe in the soul," said Sickert drily.

"Morality holds no interest for you?"

"I didn't say that. But I have no use for conventional morality either. I follow my own morality."

"And what does that consist of?"

He paused. "I don't judge human desire, and I don't deny my own."

"But do you consider other people?"

He paused again. "Others must occasionally be sacrificed."

"Sacrificed?"

"Inevitably, there is pain."

Alice had grown pale and motioned to the door. "Can you call for some wine?" she said softly. "I feel a bit faint."

Sickert put down his brush, went to the door, and called down the stairs. Almost immediately Archie appeared with a glass of wine. He handed the glass to Alice and stood waiting at the side of the bed as she took a few sips.

Sickert watched him curiously. "How old are you, young man?" he asked the boy.

"Twelve or thereabouts," said Archie.

"You seem very attentive to this lady."

"I does my best, sir. She been good to me."

"And how did you come to this employment, may I ask?"

"Milady took me on after me mum died," said the boy matter-of-factly.

"I see," said Sickert gently. "You seem a very bright and responsible young man, if I may say so. I think your mother would be proud of you."

The boy looked up but said nothing.

"You can go now, Archie," Alice instructed. Her eyes lingered on Sickert as he returned to the canvas and picked up his brush. "I thought you didn't believe in morality," she said as he began to jab at the canvas again. "You seemed to feel for the boy."

"Of course I feel for the boy," said Sickert with some annoyance. "I'm not a monster or a stone."

Alice nodded. She would have to tell Jane Cobden that her brother-in-law, despite his neglect of her sister, was kind. Watching his short encounter with Archie, her feelings had undergone a change, or rather had settled into a kind of certainty. She felt she had seen into Sickert's character and could put aside any doubts she may have entertained about his guilt. A man who could speak with such simplicity of feeling to a child could not, she was convinced, be capable of murder.

"Tell me about your wife," she said.

Sickert put down his brush as if contemplating how to answer. "I have great affection for her," he said.

"But you are not faithful." Alice completed the thought.

"I follow my inclinations."

Inside the closet, William had become flushed with anger. The man was shameless, acknowledging his depravity so boldly. Who could doubt that he had murdered those women in the East End? He poked Henry again, to register his outrage, but his brother was not paying attention. The mold in the closet was seriously irritating his sinus cavity, and he had begun to sniffle loudly. Suddenly he sneezed, the sound reverberating beyond the closet into the adjoining room.

"I think you have a chaperone," noted Sickert.

"He heard you," whispered William furiously. "Go out there. Come up with an excuse."

Henry stumbled out of the closet, taking a notebook from his pocket and nodding to Sickert. "Hello," he said vaguely. "I was doing a little writing in the"—he motioned behind him and waved the tablet—"an enclosed space excites the imagination, you know." He sneezed again. "But it's moldy."

Sickert laughed and offered his handkerchief, which Henry pressed gratefully to his nose. It was of fine cambric and smelled faintly of lavender.

CHAPTER 35

After Sickert left, William burst out of the closet looking distraught. Henry had already seated himself at the little table and was pressing the handkerchief to his nose.

"There!" exclaimed William to Alice. "That finishes it! It's clear we need to have Abberline arrest the man and formally begin interrogation."

"What are you talking about?" asked Alice.

"He's Jack the Ripper! He as good as confessed. You saw it! You almost fainted!"

"I had a moment of trepidation, I admit, but I was mistaken. Walter Sickert is as innocent as I am."

William stared at her.

She continued. "The man is incapable of calculated brutality. He is a philanderer, to be sure—no doubt a source of misery to his wife—but he would never commit murder."

"He has seduced you! Even as we watched, he exerted his animal magnetism and caused you to lose your reason."

Alice laughed and protested that her reason was entirely intact. She had, she admitted, found Sickert appealing; for the first time in many years she understood the attraction that a man could hold for a woman. Indeed, though her condition made it impossible for her to act on her inclination, she could understand how other women might. She felt for Ellen Cobden, the long-suffering wife, but one ought to know what one was getting oneself into when marrying this sort of man. He belonged, one might say, to womankind.

William listened with mounting astonishment and disgust. He had never dreamed that his sister would espouse the notions of unfettered love or make excuses for an adulterer. But here he was, listening to her do so.

"Will you make her see reason, Henry?" he insisted, turning to his brother.

Henry, who had been pressing the handkerchief Sickert had given him to his nose (he had finally put it together and recalled the scene of his near death in the East End that night), looked up with surprise. "Oh," he said dreamily, "Walter Sickert couldn't possibly have killed those women in the East End. He's a capital fellow. He saved my life."

⁜ ⁜ ⁜

Sickert was not late the next day. He arrived at three p.m. as he had said he would. It was, Alice suspected, more than a matter of professional punctuality; he wished to see her again as much as she wished to see him. And why should this be surprising? Although she was not young or pretty, she was interesting. Why wouldn't a man of exceptional sensibility enjoy her company? William could not be expected to understand it; his opinion of other men was too low to imagine that anyone might be as discriminating as he was.

Her conviction that Sickert was innocent of anything beyond excessive appreciation of the opposite sex had solidified, and in the face of her conviction, she had forbidden her brothers to spy on her. "If you want to come in to greet the artist and exchange a few words, you may," she intoned regally, "but I will not permit you to stay."

William knew that he was helpless to change her mind. From child-hood on, there had been certain edicts that she would not allow to be breached; thus, when Sickert arrived for his next visit, William remained downstairs in the kitchen, fuming and pacing.

Henry, on the other hand, made a point of coming into the room to offer thanks to the man who had saved him from attack in the East End some weeks earlier. "I had no idea it was you," he explained with a mixture of gratitude and embarrassment, "given my…confused…state of mind. But yesterday I recognized the scent of your handkerchief and then realized that was the event you were referring to when we spoke at dinner the other night."

Sickert smiled affably and had the good grace to shift the focus of discussion from the victim to the attacker. "It was an unfortunate combi-nation of circumstances," he said. "You found yourself in the wrong place and collided with the wrong man. Such people are dangerous, because they want more than your money."

"What do they want?" asked Henry.

"They want attention. They want to be heard. But they don't know how to express themselves except by beating you senseless."

"I see," said Henry. "So you think my attacker was trying to express himself. And would you say the same for all criminals…for this Jack the Ripper, for example? Does he want to express himself by killing those women in Whitechapel?"

"Most assuredly," said Sickert. "All that carving up of the bodies. It's clear something is being expressed."

"Something sexual, you mean," said Alice, interested in hearing Sickert elaborate.

"No, I wouldn't say that. The murders do not seem to me sexual in nature. Creative, but not sexual."

"You call murder creative?" asked Alice, surprised to hear her own views echoed so succinctly. "What do you mean?"

"All human beings are creative. They may not express their creativity as your brother and I do, by painting or writing, but they find an outlet in some form."

"It puts me in mind of that De Quincey essay, you know," said Henry casually, shooting a glance at his sister.

"Oh yes," said Sickert. "'Murder Considered as a Fine Art.'"

"I'm fond of De Quincey," murmured Henry, "though I haven't read everything."

"I have a complete edition, given to me by a friend," noted Sickert. "I'd be glad to lend it to you."

Henry said he was grateful and would consider the offer.

"And how does someone who is bedridden express her creativity?" asked Alice returning to the original topic.

"With her illness, certainly," said Sickert. "It takes a certain amount of creative energy to be sick."

Alice laughed. "Precisely what I've always believed. Henry has explored it in his fiction. Some of his most interesting characters are sick. But William does not approve. He sees the invalid as someone who hasn't exerted his will sufficiently. It's the American Puritan in him," added Alice. "His touchstones are spirituality, exertion, and restraint. He doesn't approve of Henry and me."

"Then he certainly wouldn't approve of me," noted Sickert.

CHAPTER 36

WILLIAM WAS SEATED IN the public house off Whitechapel High Street waiting for Ella Abrams. He had arranged the meeting in order to interrogate her on the subject of her former lover. The thought made him twitch with repulsion, but he was determined to gather ammunition in his case against Walter Sickert. His brother and his sister had turned against him. Abberline was useless.

He had stopped in to see the inspector that morning and received the report of Abberline's forgers on the subject of Sickert's note. "They say there's no proof that it *wasn't* written by Jack the Ripper," Abberline asserted, "but no reason to believe that it *was*."

Under other circumstances, William would have accepted the verdict that the note was a potential piece of evidence that had come to nothing, but since his meeting with Ella Abrams in the shop, his attitude had changed dramatically. Suspicion of Sickert had hardened into conviction, and the note seemed to be irrefutable evidence. It was apparent to him now, for example, that the ink was the same ink used in the "Dear Boss" letter, that the *r*'s were formed in precisely the same way, and that the flourish under the signature looked exactly like a line near the bottom of that notorious letter. He had made his case to Abberline, noting that the use of Pirie and Sons paper became significant in the context of the other factors. Surely, there was more than enough evidence on which to base an arrest.

Abberline had disagreed. "My forgers assure me there are no definitive points of resemblance," he insisted, "and they are experts in these matters."

"Experts!" William sneered. "They are criminals, not to be trusted!"

Abberline looked surprised at the vehemence with which his colleague spoke. "I assure you they are trustworthy in this arena at least. Honor among thieves and all that."

William grew incensed by Abberline's light tone. "They are protecting their own livelihood," he spit out. "The longer they delay the resolution of this case, the better for them. It's doubtless the same for you," he added tersely. "You have you own interests to protect. Sickert is a man of standing in society…or at least he knows people of consequence. This keeps you from arresting him."

Abberline drew back, surprised. He and William had spent many days together by then and had acquired some understanding of each other's character. The accusation seemed to come out of nowhere. "I assure you I have no reason to protect my social superiors." He spoke proudly. "I would be prone, if anything, to take the side of my own class over those above me. But I advocate only for justice. I will pursue a murderer, whatever his class, and will make an arrest when there is evidence to warrant one."

William was hardly listening and instead continued arguing in the same line in which he had begun. "When you grow up in a society in which the privileged are protected, you are conditioned to follow suit."

Abberline stared at his colleague. It was as though William had lost touch with reality and retreated into his own world. He spoke slowly, as if to a child. "I would be the first to arrest this man, were there evidence against him. But I see no evidence. Only a desire on your part that he be guilty."

"A desire on my part?" exclaimed William. "And why would I have such a desire?" His voice had grown shrill.

"I have no idea what motivates you; only you are privy to that. I will continue to keep your Walter Sickert under watch, but will do no more without additional reason to suspect him."

William had not argued further but had turned on his heel and left. He felt eaten away by anger and resentment, even as he knew, behind the turmoil of his emotions, that Abberline was right. Ella Abrams had once loved Walter Sickert. That fact fed an irrational, morally ignoble jealousy that undergirded his conviction of the man's guilt. He knew this fact at the same time that he could not disentangle what he knew from what he felt.

As soon as he left Abberline's office, he had sent a note to Connaught Square, requesting that Ella meet him that afternoon. Perhaps the evidence he craved lay with her, or perhaps he sensed that seeing her would assuage his agitation. She had immediately written back that she would meet with him in Whitechapel, as she had business in that area. She designated a public house and an hour at which she would be there.

He had arrived early, still smarting from his encounter with Abberline, but the place had a soothing effect on his nerves. The large downstairs room was practically empty and, unlike rowdier establishments in the neighborhood, was clean and quiet, with a comforting lack of distinctiveness. He could have been anywhere, in a limbo outside of time and place, where nothing he did mattered, where he would not be held to account for his actions. He chose a table toward the back and waited for her to come.

He had been waiting almost an hour when a figure in a cloak rose up before him, causing him to jump in alarm. He had been so engrossed in his own thoughts that seeing the cloaked figure had brought back the visceral terror of the attack the week before. But in a moment, Ella pushed back the hood and revealed her face. The relief and pleasure of seeing her was as great as the initial terror, merging into what he could only describe, based on his readings from some of the Germans, as a sense of the sublime. Her beauty dazzled him, made him feel literally dizzy with euphoric wonder, as it had on the two previous occasions when he had seen her.

"It's good of you to go out of your way at such short notice," he said, his voice sounding muffled and unnatural to his own ears.

Ella sat down and faced him. "It's not out of my way," she said. "I was delivering some canvases for framing to a shop nearby. And I wanted to meet you."

She draped her cloak over her seat and looked at him with a frankness unusual for a woman. It occurred to him, seeing her here, how much she lived between worlds: rich and poor, Jewish and gentile, male and female, and he wondered if this fact wasn't a large part of her fascination for him. He too lived between worlds, or had swung between them, if one considered the chaos of his younger life and the settled nature of his present one. And of course, he maintained oscillation in his work. He was constantly sliding out of one field and into another, finding he could not get a grip on the discipline as it existed and needing to reshape it in light of something else. Was the mark of a certain kind of character its inability to fit into the grooves that life had established, either because of happenstance of birth or temperament? Was this the nature of the philosopher and the artist—as well as the malcontent and the misfit?

Whatever was behind it, he felt he was being pulled off the hinges of his conventional life by the sight of her. He could feel himself swerving and careening, and he clutched at something practical. "I asked you to come," he said, trying to keep his voice level and calm, "because I wanted to know more about that...man...to whom you gave the volumes. Walter Sickert. You said you misjudged his character. What did you mean?"

Ella looked surprised. "Didn't you meet with him?"

"Oh yes," said William. "He is painting my sister."

He must have registered distaste in saying this, because she smiled wryly. "And you disapprove?"

"I didn't say that," said William defensively. "She has commissioned him to do her portrait. I was simply curious about your comment regarding his character, since he visits her house now every day."

"I think if he is painting your sister, you know what my comment means," said Ella. "He only paints women he admires. I'm sure your sister enjoys his admiration. Of course, she must be prepared to share it."

"My sister has no interest that way," said William sharply. "She is an invalid, and he is a married man." He spoke, realizing that he himself was a married man, though he was sitting with a strange woman in a public house in Whitechapel.

"Yes, he is married. I didn't mean sharing him with his wife."

"You mean that his immorality goes beyond simple adultery?"

"Simple adultery, as opposed to complex adultery?" said Ella with amusement. "Yes, I suppose that *is* what I mean."

"In other words, there are other women," William said pointedly and then paused. "And that's all?"

"All what?"

"All you meant when you said you misjudged his character."

"I should think that would be enough."

William nodded. She knew no more, then, than that Sickert was a philanderer of the worst sort. It was not what he had been looking for, and yet why did he need more to convince him that the man was a degenerate and, by extension, a murderer. He cleared his throat nervously. There was no point talking about Sickert any longer. "I hope you don't feel I've wasted your time."

"No." She smiled. "I don't see how you can waste something in such plentiful supply. I am flattered that you would want to see me again. I certainly wanted to see you."

He felt himself flush but hurried to disguise his pleasure. "It's good you had an errand to do," he said lamely.

Ella shrugged. "There are always errands for me to do."

"Tell me about them." He wanted to know more about her life.

"Oh, business for the shop. And chores for the household." She paused. "I must make visits and receive them. My mother wants me to get married."

"And is that what you want?"

She shrugged again. "It would be a change."

William laughed. It was odd to think of marriage as the means to "a change," but in a sense, that was what it was. Marriage allowed the sameness of one's original family to be opened up, to detour from its static, familiar course.

"I should like to have children," she mused. "There might be satisfaction in being a mother. But for that, I must find someone to marry. And so far, I have found no one suitable."

"And whom do you consider suitable?"

"Oh, he must be Jewish and rich, and I suppose moderately attractive and interesting to talk to."

"That's a rather exacting set of requirements."

"I'm sure your wife conforms to an exacting set of requirements," she said drily.

William acknowledged to himself that she did. His Alice shared his religion and his interests and had been fully approved by his parents.

There was silence between them for a moment. He could think of nothing to say, and part of him did not feel inclined to talk. For some reason, the feeling of nervousness and discomfort he had felt when she arrived had disappeared. He sat looking at her, and she looked back without embarrassment. She then laid her arm on the table, the palm open.

It was odd how a simple gesture—an arm on a table, an open hand—meaningless in other contexts, could be so eloquent. He looked at the hand in its roundness and softness, the long fingers with the smooth nails, which had been filed so that they tapered into little white moons showing above the rosy, darker flesh. It was a hand not so different from other hands, and yet infinitely different. And it had been placed on the table expressly for him.

He gazed at it. The attraction he felt for her was intense; it was as though he were underwater, breathing through a filter. His senses felt muffled but also preternaturally alert, attuned to the presence across from him. He took his hand from his lap and placed it on her hand, his fingers intertwining with hers. It was as though he had caught a small animal that might jump away if he did not hold it tightly. Every nerve in his body was vibrating with life, his mind in a kind of frenzy of excitement and desire as he felt her pulse drumming under his fingers. He clasped her hand more tightly, and it remained still under his.

The rest was a kind of dream. A wizened little barmaid showed them upstairs without the trace of a question and opened the door to a room. It was almost bare except for a bed and a night table, but cleanly swept. Ella placed her cloak on the end of the bedstead and stood before him. He put his hand out, touched her cheek, and then let it fall to the button at the top of her dress. It was a simple dress with buttons leading from the top of the neck to the waist, where there was a wide embroidered sash. He imagined that he would unbutton each of the buttons to the waist and then, in a great sweep of his hand, pull the sash so that the whole edifice that encased her would open up suddenly, and she would be released into his arms. It was just the sort of dress he would have imagined for her—sleek and unadorned, yet intricate with its buttons from neck to waist. Everything about her was simple and strange that way—contained and quiet but also dramatic, intense, excessive.

His fingers touched the top button of her dress. A button, he thought, was itself simple but strange, a mere twist and it was undone, yet it held through all sorts of buffeting. Human skin was like that too, the way it covered the body in an unbroken casement, so solid and yet so susceptible to harm, so protective and enduring, except in cases where it was penetrated, and then there was nothing one could do. He had a sudden mental image of the photograph of Catherine Eddowes, her body opened up in a thicket of carved flesh. But the image was engulfed with the image before him: disgust eclipsed by desire.

He looked down at Ella, whose face was flushed but who registered no sense of shame. She was looking at him, and he knew that she felt the same intense desire that he felt. His hand moved, twisting the button free of the cloth. He placed his hand on the flesh of her neck, feeling the heat of her throat pulsing beneath it. She moved closer to him, her body nestling into his. He smelled the London damp on her dress mixed with the odor of her strangeness. How astonishing it was to be entangled with another body to whom one had no past, no formal relation. And yet the wonder was also that for all the strangeness of her—the difference in nationality, religion, experience of people and events—she had come to him here as he had come to her. Hadn't it seemed from the first moment they saw each other that they were destined to embrace? So much of life was unsynchronized, where one person desired more, and the other, less. Could it be wrong to feel such mutual desire? Could it be anything but good to desire alike, so different from the case of the murderer, that incarnation of evil? For what was murder but the denial of reciprocal feeling, the imposition of one will at the expense of another's life? He and Ella were that miracle of mutually desiring beings in the midst of a universe that was too often unbalanced, unruly, and cruel.

His fingers twisted the next button on her dress and released it from its hold, exposing the full sweep of her throat. His hand brushed against her flesh, and now his fingers moved quickly, opening the line of buttons until the thick cloth of the dress opened like a flower and revealed not nakedness but what, in its way, was more intimate than nakedness: the stiff encasement of her corset. He put his hands to the tightly laced garment, feeling the heat of her body underneath. Above the ledge of the bodice, he could see the top of her breasts, rising and falling. Beads of perspiration dotted the skin of her throat. His own clothes felt thick and confining. He would have liked to stop to strip off his waistcoat and shirt, but instead he moved his hands to the back of the corset and, with the instinct bred from years of married life, found the hook holding the laces in place.

It was that instinctual motion that brought him back, for the movement of his fingers suddenly transported him to the space of his bedroom at home. He heard whispering inside his head, the words that had roused him to laughter a week earlier when he had fumbled with the laces of his Alice's corset. "Female suffrage is all well and good," she had said, "but liberate us first from our corsets."

"Liberate us first from our corsets." Why did he have to recall those words now? The recollection of his wife's voice in its familiar cadence, the laughter they had shared, the image of his bedroom with the child's crib in the corner caused his fingers to freeze. The desire he had felt for the woman pressed against him seemed to evaporate. His hands fell from her back, and he was overwhelmed with the enormity of the crime he had been about to commit. A vision of his Alice, gentle but accusing, engulfed his consciousness. He saw her, the way her hair curled under her cap near her ears, the way her eyes half closed and her head bent when he embraced her. He desired Ella Abrams more than he had desired any woman before, but his Alice was his life. She was the mother of his children, she shared his grief over their dead Hermie; she had cared for him and listened to his litany of complaints about colleagues and work; she was waiting for him at home.

He wondered, was the desire he had felt really the opposite of the murderous desire of the killer, or was it a variation on the same thing? The opposite of murder was not desire, but love—the steady, willed love that one felt for wife and family. He looked at Ella's face. It was the most beautiful he had ever seen, but beauty, like ugliness, was a great seducer, an objectifier of the human.

He stood frozen for perhaps a minute until Ella slowly moved away and began to button her dress. When she had finished, she straightened her hair in the small mirror near the door, took her coat from the chair, and touched William's arm as if to register that she was not angry. He had remained rooted in place, in a kind of stupor, horrified at what he had almost done and awash with regret at what he had failed to do. When he finally roused himself to look around, she was gone.

CHAPTER 37

THE PORTRAIT OF ALICE took longer to complete than expected. Sickert had originally said he would need her for four sittings—or rather lying downs, given her condition—but at the third, he announced that he would need more time, at least two more days, probably three. This was despite his arriving every day promptly and remaining for more than two hours.

Alice had forbidden her brothers to enter the room again, and Katherine remained out of town nursing her sister until the following Sunday. Occasionally Archie or Sally came in with a tray of biscuits or a decanter of port, and Sickert charmed them both by performing snippets from his music hall numbers. But these interruptions were short-lived, and for most of the time Sickert was present, he and Alice were alone.

The week they passed in each other's company, Alice secretly understood, constituted a romance. She knew that people would laugh at the idea. She was ten years older than he was, bedridden, and plain. She existed, moreover, in a comfortable relationship with Katherine that resembled a long-standing marriage. But her feeling for Sickert was different, closer to the kind of pulse-quickening feeling that she had read about in books and had believed she would never experience.

At the end of each visit, after he put away his paints and covered the portrait with a sheet, he would come over to her bed, take her hand in a rather formal manner, and kiss it, lingering a bit longer than was necessary. The scene, to a superficial eye, was conventional enough. This was a charming young man, handsome and pleased with himself, used to getting women, no matter the age, to fall in love with him. Yet Alice felt that, appearances notwithstanding, he desired her as she desired him. The idea would be too ludicrous to utter aloud, and yet she knew it to be true.

When the picture was finally done, Sickert covered it and prepared to take it away. "I don't want you to see it until it is framed," he explained. "The frame marks the end; it says with finality that this bit of reality has been set aside and can no longer be altered. But I should warn you," he added, "seeing your portrait for the first time can be a shock."

"I'm sure I will like it," said Alice. "I am not vain."

"It's not a matter of vanity; it's seeing yourself as someone else does. I've known people who say that it's like seeing themselves in their coffin. I don't agree. But it can be strange to see how another sees you."

"I should like to see how you see me."

"Then be patient." He was, he said, off to Cornwall for a few days, where he had agreed to meet with a group of old school friends, fellow artists. When he returned, the portrait would be framed, and he would drop it off so they could look at it together.

He walked over to the bed to say good-bye, but this time he did not take her hand as he generally did, but touched her face as he had that first day. He held his hand against her cheek for a long time until she turned her head and kissed his palm. She looked up, and he lowered his face almost to hers, holding it there for a long time. For a moment, she thought he would kiss her, but she flinched slightly, and he pulled back.

"I look forward to seeing how you see me," she repeated, her voice wistful.

He did not respond but rose from the bed, took the easel in one hand and the painting in the other, and left without another word.

It was just as well that he had gone, Alice thought. Katherine was due back the next day.

CHAPTER 38

WILLIAM LAY AWAKE THAT night in an agony of self-recrimination and relief. Although he had contemplated an act of monstrous betrayal, he had abstained from committing it. He had come to the brink, yet he had stepped back. Should he lament that he had been tempted, or celebrate that he had resisted temptation? The disparity between thought and deed was at once great and negligible, depending upon one's perspective. But as always, his perspective was multiple, so he could not find rest. He was racked with guilt and driven to rationalization.

The struggle continued through the night, and only close to dawn did he fall into a fitful slumber. He slept until midmorning and would have gone on sleeping, had he not been awakened by a clamor in the outer room. A minute later, Mrs. Smith appeared at the door to his bedchamber. She had the obsequious manner she assumed when she wasn't being surly and uncooperative. "There's a man from Scotland Yard who wants you to come with him right away, Professor James," she simpered.

William stumbled out of bed and dressed quickly. When he entered the parlor, he found a stocky, red-faced officer waiting impatiently. "Inspector says you should come," the officer asserted bluntly.

Remembering the mistake made with Archie's mother, William asked if the man was certain that the situation wasn't a false alarm.

"Certain as the devil," was the reply.

They drove in silence to the East End, where they descended in front of a two-story house of discolored brick. Next to the house was a shabby yard, where a sickly looking dog, barking feebly, had been tied to the gate. The building looked to be a multiple dwelling, perhaps a boardinghouse for people who had yet to fall into outright indigence. In front, a collection of official carriages stood, blocking the narrow road.

He followed his guide up to the second floor and through a narrow doorway. Abberline was standing with a circle of police officers and a white-smocked medical examiner. He acknowledged William when he came in—a short nod with a mere flicker of his eyes; no more was needed.

William stood near the door. He had always prided himself on seeing things clearly, on being less abstract and more clear-sighted and practical than his European peers. As an American, he had the energy and courage to look life straight in the eye.

Yet just as he took hold of what he saw before him, his grasp of it seemed to slip. The very act of thinking and articulating transformed the thing before him into something else, something already labeled and filed away: old, known, detached from his perception of it.

Death. What did it mean? He had seen his father's and mother's weakening conditions, his Hermie's racking coughs and fevers. But the death that came ultimately to these loved ones had been based on words already in circulation: death from circulatory disease, death from pneumonia, death from whooping cough. These people had disappeared from his life, but it was as though "death" had been affixed to them at a crucial point and blotted them out. Their actual demise was a blank.

He had seen the photographs of the dead women of Whitechapel and understood the modus operandi of how and when they had died, but had he truly grasped the fact of their deaths? Even the body of Catherine Eddowes and of Archie's mother were only the ghastly residue of something already out of sight and beyond comprehension. How close to actual death was it possible to get? Only so close before the thing swerved away into a diagnosis, an idea, an abstraction.

William averted his gaze and then looked again. The scene was too terrible to hold in view for more than a few seconds. It was a plain room—or was it? He assumed it was plain because it was in a squalid part of town; the public houses and pensions of Whitechapel were not likely to be fancy, devoted as they were to sleeping, eating, and the animal acts that people engaged in either as their only diversion or as the source of their livelihood. His mind shifted suddenly to the thought of himself in such a room with Ella Abrams, his hand on the button of her dress, and then his thoughts were wrenched back to the scene before him.

No, one couldn't say whether the room was plain. There was no knowing what it had been like. It could have been a nice room. The occupant could have arranged it with some taste, perhaps sought out colorful fabric for the bed and pillows and kept it neat and swept. Perhaps there had been flowers on the night table.

But he could not see the room for what it had been. It was awash in blood. The word "awash," with its suggestion of a great, engulfing flood, was apt, yet it was also wrong. There was too much flourish to it, too much of a vague suggestion of the Great Flood. The place didn't need to be compared to something else, didn't need to be helped along by literary props and foils. Blood was not metaphorically present in this room; it was literally so, and it was everywhere. Could one body produce so much of it? From a purely scientific point of view, it was interesting. It raised the question of how much blood was needed to produce such an effect, perhaps less than appeared by virtue of spattering and seeping. Painters diluted their paint and used quite a little to cover large canvases; they made washes that could stretch for, really, miles.

His mind was drifting again, finding a way to detour from the fact of the scene into the academic and the metaphorical. He mustn't do that. The room was soaked with blood. Take a dozen cans of paint and throw them about, and one could not do it. It was not just the horrific extent of the coverage, but the differing thicknesses of the globs and stains, the gradations in color—bright red here on the sheets, duller on the walls where the spatter was thicker, brick red on the curtains and the shades, where the globules were round and glistened like giant teardrops; a jewel-like beading in vermilion on the side of the lamp.

Central to the spatter and stain was the body. "Body." The word was an absurd descriptor for the mutilated thing on the bed, yet there was no doubt that it had been a human being only hours before, a woman once named Mary Jane Kelly. The name had been whispered to him by one of the officers near the door. But a woman's body was precisely what the murderer had tried to erase. For the body was a canvas for such extraordinary viciousness that horror alternated with wonder. It was the feeling one had in front of great art. One could not take it in.

He tried to make an accounting of what was before him. The lower torso of the woman's body had been hacked entirely open. The blood filling the body cavity had created ponds of fluid that had spilled over to soak the sheets and drench the walls and the floor. The puncturing of certain organs must have resulted in geysers, for even the ceiling was spattered. The upper torso too had been hacked and seemed to float in a sea of vermilion. Although in places the fluid had congealed and turned almost black, here the pools of color were bright and grotesquely festive.

The face, what had been the face, had been mutilated beyond recognition. Catherine Eddowes's face had been treated delicately by comparison. Here, the nose was cut off, the ears, the eyebrows, the cheeks slashed. And most appalling of all: this grotesquerie was propped up as if the murderer had wanted to present it for particular inspection, to make it the focus of ghoulish appreciation.

William could hear Abberline speaking softly to his assistant in a dream-like colloquy off to the side. "Multiple mutilations to arms; abdomen and thighs flayed; labia, right buttock cut off." The inspector motioned to the night table, where William saw a drenched clump of red-stained flesh, firm but dripping, like bloody wedding cake piled near the lamp. "Breasts hacked off." (Now he could see that the upper body was in fact two connecting puddles of blood where the breasts should be.) "Kidneys, uterus, one breast placed under the head." (He glanced to see that there was another bloody clump propping the head up in its ghastly pose.) "Other breast, part of it," Abberline pointed to the left of the body. "Spleen." He indicated the right. "Liver." He motioned to a lump between the legs.

William had almost fainted at the sight of Catherine Eddowes's body, but now he felt strangely calm. The degree of mutilation was so extreme that the mind could not possibly—

"In all my years…" he heard Abberline mutter.

"'In all my years.'" It was a useful phrase. Other phrases came to mind: "an atrocity of extravagant proportions," "a grotesque demonstration of human depravity." Such statements would inevitably be applied. They would remain in use until someday another murder would be referred to as "even worse than the Ripper murder in '88." That's how it worked, language; it organized, compared, and placed things in categories from which they could be taken out and examined in the future. Words were the first line of defense, the most subtle and most elementary abstraction. Use words that had been used before. Putting the unspeakable into words, the reality receded.

However much one tried to take hold, it happened. One killed the poor woman again by describing her death. It was the fundamental paradox that one had to kill again and again in order to live. And the paradox went further when one thought about the killing itself. For one might say that Jack the Ripper's escalating brutality was a means of confronting the reality of death rather than obscuring it with abstract notions or averted glances. Each murder required that he keep it from receding into the unreal, and each time, it required greater ingenuity, greater viciousness to do this. It made the murderer not just an artist, William thought bitterly, but a philosopher. A murderer was perhaps by definition an applied philosopher.

He could feel his mind moving in the direction he feared most: forgetting the distinctions that constituted life, forgetting the scale of things, making everything into some version of the same. Morality was predicated on distinction and scale. He must never forget that. To forget was the path to madness.

CHAPTER 39

ENRY HAD BEEN WORKING on his novel, practically without pause, all week. It was like that with him. Everything else was embroidery and diversion; writing was the center and foundation of his life. *Bounded by a nutshell*, he sometimes thought during these intensive, almost maniacal periods. He might get up for a cup of tea and a biscuit, but it was only to carry them back to his desk, too excited to stop working and eat properly. Now, for example, he sat, absently picking at the buttered crumpet that he had put down near his chair, contemplating the sentence that he had just written. *We must recognize our particular form, the instrument that each of us—each of us who carries anything—carries in his being. Mastering this instrument, learning to play it in perfection, that's what I call duty, what I call conduct, what I call success.* Was he overdoing it? Perhaps he was, but the character who was speaking these words was flamboyant and extravagant, and the sentiments expressed were true.

After putting aside the idea of writing about murder and tabling his dramatization, he had decided to work on a story about art and theater, more congenial and familiar subjects. His heroine was an actress; his hero, a painter. Ellen Terry and Walter Sickert were not far from his mind;

Wilde was in there; and his brother too was an oblique inspiration. He had glimpsed in William over the last few days a resurgence of the conflicted loyalties that had besieged him during his youth. He had watched with fascination as the struggle, muted by age and experience, replayed itself. He himself had never had such a struggle. After a brief and unpleasant dabbling in the law, he had plunged, with certainty, into his vocation as a writer. It had been simple for him. He could not do most things, and what he could do, he did. But William had always been capable of many things. The stress of choice had weighed on him.

In the novel Henry was working on, the hero would be like that—a man drawn to the artistic life who felt obligated to pursue a political career. With William, of course, the loyalties were different—more tangled and confused—but that was as it should be. One didn't want art to imitate life. As deep as his characters were, they were never as deep as real people. To go that deep, one would drown.

He was engrossed in his work, scattering crumbs on the floor and spotting his notebook with butter, when a clamor was heard in the hallway, and Alice's girl Sally pushed into the room.

"She wouldn't wait to be announced, sir," said Mrs. Smith, coming in behind huffily. Despite her own frequent lapses, she was always shocked by a lack of decorum in other people.

Sally, however, did not register Mrs. Smith's protests. She had thrown off her usual timidity and, breathless and distraught, ran to Henry and pulled at his sleeve. "You must come at once," she cried. "Your sister needs you."

Henry required no more incentive than the girl's frightened words. He rose hurriedly from his desk and followed her to the waiting carriage. As they drove the few blocks to the other end of Bolton Street, Sally could say only that Alice had been wild with fright, though the girl had no idea why.

It was only when they were in the carriage that he realized that it was nearly four p.m. and he had not seen William all day. Engrossed in his writing, he had lost track of time. Now it occurred to him to wonder where his brother was and why he had not heard from him. He told the driver to drive faster.

CHAPTER 40

ALICE HAD SPENT THE morning listening to Katherine's report on her sister: Louisa's appetite was back, and she had put on weight, all the result of Katherine's diligent care. Hadn't she done the same many times for Alice—nursed her back to relative health from the brink of hypothetical death? That was Katherine's genius after all, to make people make an effort and continue living their lives.

Generally, Alice was jealous when Katherine spoke about her sister, who was, though fragile, fortunately not as fragile as Alice. But today, she listened patiently. She was grateful to have Katherine back and was willing to indulge her more than usual. They had had a pleasant reunion the night before, dining together over a mutton stew that Sally had whipped up entirely on her own. The girl had begun to put ingredients together, a sign, they agreed, that she could think for herself. "Perhaps she will be a cook," said Alice, "and Archie can be a footman." They had laughed delightedly at the idea. Despite her reformist impulses, Alice agreed with Henry that the lower orders had no reason to aspire to the occupations and desires of the higher ones. Comfortable servitude seemed to her to have much to recommend it.

On the subject of Sickert, she had said little to Katherine except that her portrait was done, and the artist would deliver it in its frame in a few days.

"I look forward to it," said Katherine shortly, and Alice was glad that she did not pursue the subject. Her relationship with Sickert seemed too private to discuss even with—indeed especially with—her most intimate companion.

After an early luncheon, Katherine left to do errands, and Alice turned over in her head what ought to be done with regard to the Ripper investigation. It was wearisome. They were going to have to start again, comb through the membership lists of the art societies, look through the exhibition catalogs, interrogate John Sargent about the gossip in the art world. She still believed that the murderer was an artist, but everything else they had assumed before now struck her as dubious. Convinced as she was of Sickert's innocence, she could hardly say that the idea of a Whistler connection carried much weight. *P* of *W*—"pupil of Whistler." It was, upon consideration, a silly hypothesis. The line between the letters might not be "of," and PW could stand for anything.

She had been jotting some notes in her diary and dozing, when Archie came to the door with a package.

"This here been dropped off for you, milady," he said, presenting it with the characteristic flourish that Alice found both amusing and pathetic. He would be less charming, she thought, when the novelty of his circumstances wore off, and yet she could only hope that they would, that he would forget that he ought to be grateful for regular meals and people who cared about him, that he would come in time to take such things for granted.

"Who left it?" she asked, looking curiously at the box on which her name was scrawled, not very tidily, in red ink.

"Don' know that," said Archie. "It was lyin' on the mat when I went out to wash the stoop. I was out an hour afore to shake the rug, and it weren't there then, so I'd say it were left within the hour."

"Thank you, Archie. That shows good reasoning. You can take the afternoon to play if you like. Just be sure you're back by dinner so that Sally won't be left shorthanded."

The boy seemed to find this warning to his liking and trotted away, presumably to win more marbles off the neighbor's boy, who had lost almost all of them to him already.

Alice turned to the package. It was small, no more than four or five inches long, and very light, so it was not books, which was what people usually sent her. There was no address, which meant it must have been placed by hand on the stoop where Archie had found it. She took the letter opener on her night table and slit the top, which had been glued together using brown paper. She opened the flaps of the box. What lay inside took a moment to take in. First she felt her throat constrict, and she gagged. Regaining her breath, she screamed.

Inside the box, nestled in tissue paper that had been soaked crimson, was a bloody piece of a woman's breast.

CHAPTER 41

EVERYTHING HAPPENED QUICKLY. KATHERINE returned as Henry arrived and administered a few drops of laudanum. William came in soon after with news of the murder and immediately sent Archie out with a note to Abberline.

Alice had not allowed anyone to open the box and refused to say anything about it. She had placed it near the bed, but out of her direct sight.

When Abberline arrived, she mutely pointed to it, and he took it into the small drawing room and shut the door. He was gone for several minutes, and when he returned he spoke to the assembled group. "The package that Miss James received appears to contain part of the left breast of Mary Jane Kelly," he announced. The suspense had been so great for the others that even this shocking information was a relief. Most helpful, however, was the professional tone of the inspector, for he simply stated the facts with grim simplicity: "A portion of that organ was missing when the body was examined by Dr. Phillips. The question now becomes why it was sent to Miss James."

"It's obvious," asserted William, who had been sitting off to the side, tapping his foot in restless anticipation. "The man who painted her portrait has just murdered another woman in the East End. He must know I'm involved in the case and assumes this is the way to scare me off."

But Alice, who had been leaning back weakly against her pillows, rallied herself. "Walter Sickert is incapable of murder," she declared. "And besides, he has gone to Cornwall."

"You hold to that line," sneered William.

"We have brought Mr. Sickert in for questioning," said Abberline, waving a hand, "and will see what he has to say for himself."

Alice had turned chalk white.

"Not in Cornwall, apparently," said William gloatingly. "I assume the officer assigned to watch him has evidence of his whereabouts last night, though why he couldn't stop the attack is another matter."

"We do not know that he committed the crime," continued Abberline. "All we know is that he went to a public house in Whitechapel on Wednesday evening. He was accompanied by a woman."

Henry, watching his brother and sister, was struck by the reversal. William turned pale, while Alice regained a degree of color and life. Something had shifted for each of them. He had no idea what it was, but it was interesting to watch.

Abberline continued, "He arrived with the woman at around ten p.m., but he did not leave before the murder. She, however, did. At approximately one a.m. My man noticed because the other women leaving the public house at that time of night were, let's say, not of a reputable sort, and she, by contrast, was."

"And when did *he* leave?" asked William sharply. It was Abberline's turn to be discomfited. "My man appears to have left the scene when news of the murder became known. When he returned to the public house, Sickert was gone."

"And who was the woman?" asked Alice.

"We have questioned Sickert on the subject, and he will not say."

"What did she look like?" asked Henry. William had retreated into a tense silence.

"She was fairly tall and wore a long cape. He could not see her well when they arrived, though he said she was well featured and wore her hair in a thick plait. Leaving, he could see nothing. It was dark, and her hood was up."

CHAPTER 42

ALICE WAS IN A state close to collapse. The package had shaken her, but what she felt now was different—and worse. After Henry and Abberline left, William had remained behind and spoken to her, his voice shaking with emotion. He had said that the evidence was clear. Sickert had murdered those women and had used one of his many conquests—he spit the words out with a venom she had never seen him express before—as a means to escape detection. He had also told her about the attack on himself a few weeks back. A man in a cape, covered from head to toe. The cape, he said, though he had not realized it at the time, might well have been borrowed from a woman.

"And how do you know it wasn't a woman who attacked you?" asked Alice. It had been a reflexive sort of question, her way of expressing doubt that it was Sickert who had committed the crime.

The comment had elicited an unprecedented response from her brother. At first he stared at her, his eyes glazed, his face flaccid, almost idiotic. For such a brilliant man to look like an idiot was a transformation she was not likely to forget. He stared at her like that for a few seconds and then, shaking himself, exploded. "You're a fool! You sit there in your bed, reading books and talking about politics and the poor. But let a man pretend to admire you, and you lie down at his feet like all the rest of them."

Alice was too shocked to respond. She had never dreamed that her brother could speak to her like that, and could not fathom what had provoked him. She poured some laudanum into a glass and began stirring it with a trembling hand.

William was not yet done; he continued to speak with increased venom. "You'd run after him if you could. Why don't you hide him here, under the covers of your bed, and maybe he'll do what you want before he cuts you up!"

The color had drained from Alice's face. Was this her brother, the man she trusted and loved more than anyone in the world, for whom she would be willing to sacrifice her life? Had he become a raving lunatic?

"Please leave," she said softly, pointing to the door.

"You want me to leave, but you'd welcome him." William sneered, his face contorted with anger and disgust.

She did not tell him again. He had finished his tirade and slumped in his chair, all will and energy sapped. She turned her head on the pillow and closed her eyes, trying to regain a measure of calm. They remained like this for a long time, opposite each other, saying nothing, sunk into morbid thought, when Alice was roused by Sally, who had entered the room to announce that Jane Cobden was below and wanted to see her.

"Tell her I'm indisposed," she responded dully.

Before this message could be relayed, Jane, who had apparently followed the servant up the stairs, hurried in, rushed to Alice's bed, and knelt down beside it. She was trembling violently. Her thick red hair, usually fastened neatly at the back of her head, was loose and disheveled, and her large bosom within the plain serge dress was heaving with exertion and anxiety. "Please help me," she said, grasping Alice's hand and raising a tearstained face in supplication.

What was going on? thought Alice, in a spasm of panic. Had everyone gone mad?

William was sitting in the corner, slumped slightly, hardly paying attention.

"You must help me," Jane Cobden repeated. "And him."

"Him?" asked Alice, surprised.

"Walter Sickert. My brother-in-law."

Alice, who was still holding the glass of laudanum in one hand, dropped it to the floor so that it shattered, but neither she nor William seemed to notice. They were both staring at the woman who had just spoken.

"I was with him last night, at the public house. I spent the night there; I left early in the morning. I know they've arrested him. I know you and your brothers have suspected him of those murders. But of course, he's innocent of killing anyone, though not of other crimes, of which I hold myself more guilty than he. If he is an adulterer, I have betrayed my own sister. If Ellen knew…" She broke off and put her face in her hands.

Everything had suddenly changed. William had sprung from his chair and gone over to Jane Cobden. He raised her to her feet and began assuring her excitedly that he understood; flesh was weak, and sometimes even the most stalwart and upright tripped and fell. She could count on his discretion. He remembered her father and knew of her good works. He was in the counsel of the inspector on the case and would do his best to keep things quiet.

He had her write down a statement about what had happened, and after he put it in his pocket and saw her to the door, he returned and faced Alice. He did not hesitate to abase himself for his behavior. He had spoken rashly, said things that were unforgivable and cruel; yet he begged her to forgive him. He had been jealous—that was the crux of it, seeing his beloved sister so taken with a man known to be a libertine, though obviously a very talented and charming individual.

As he spoke, he appeared to Alice to have returned to his familiar, rational self. He was deferential, kind, articulate, yet she also recalled how he had sounded before Jane Cobden came in. He had said he was jealous of her affections; she believed him. She had often been jealous of him; why would he not be of her? But she also knew that there must be more that he was not revealing. He had gone mad for a time, and though the originating influence had dissipated, she could still sense the undertow pulling against his rational speech. She would never hear him speak again without a sense of that undertow. It existed, she knew, in everyone, but she had always thought of her brother as the most exemplary of beings, capable of keeping that side of himself at bay. Now she knew otherwise.

She would have to face what she should have known to be true all along: that on the stage that was her life, there were no other principal actors. She was entirely alone.

CHAPTER 43

WILLIAM WAS SEATED IN Abberline's shabby office, going through photographs of the murder scene. Sickert had been released upon delivery of the statement by Jane Cobden, and William and the inspector were back where they started: a vicious killer on the loose and no apparent suspects. The delivery of the gruesome specimen to Alice, which had initially seemed to William a sure indication of Sickert's guilt, seemed now to have a different connotation. After all, it was widely known that William had been asked to consult on the case; a little digging by the cunning murderer would have revealed that he had family in London. What better way to mock his efforts than to terrorize his invalid sister?

Abberline returned to the office that afternoon and immediately began to study the details of the Kelly murder, poring over the photographs of the scene that had been delivered by the police photographer a few hours earlier.

"What's the point of looking at photographs when we saw the room firsthand?" asked William.

"Because," Abberline explained, "at the scene of a crime, it is impossible to see things in any perspective. The details overwhelm the whole, especially in a case as vicious and bloody as this one."

William nodded, remembering his difficulty taking in the room when he had first arrived on the scene. He also recalled the tirade he had earlier directed at Abberline. Seating himself at the table where the photographs were spread, he gently touched his colleague's shoulder. It was his way of apologizing. He sensed that Abberline understood that he had briefly gone mad and had now come back. There was no need to speak about it.

William saw at once the value of the photographs. They presented an entirely different view from what he had looked at that morning. At the time, his mind had moved in and out, from horror to a kind of reverie, incapable of engaging for any sustained period with the scene itself. The pictures, however, placed him squarely in a middle ground—at once more bearable and more horrible. He had felt it when he had looked at the photographs of the other victims. Here, the effect was amplified. He had the image, freshly imprinted on his memory, of the scene as it had actually existed; these pictures were a kind of overlay on that. He saw again, though more clearly now, the hollowed-out eyes, the pools of blood where the breasts had been, the carved-up torso, the bespattered room. The photograph eliminated color, texture, odor—all the distracting variables that had overwhelmed his senses. It provided instead a simple clinical representation: the body laid out, the head propped up, the left knee bent, and the tatters of nightdress showing here and there amid the blackness that designated the soaking blood. He was again struck by the paradox of what constitutes reality. The photograph was a representation, without color or dimension, much of the detail subsumed in darkness or blurred images, yet it made the scene available in its entirety in a way that being there could not.

He and Abberline stared together at the image of the eviscerated woman in the darkly shadowed bedroom. It was like peering through a keyhole into hell.

CHAPTER 44

TWO DAYS AFTER THE murder of Mary Jane Kelly, Sickert appeared at the door of Alice's bedroom holding Archie's hand. The boy had let him in, and they had come up to the room quietly, "as a surprise," Sickert had whispered, placing his finger to his mouth.

Alice, propped up in bed writing in her journal, looked up over her spectacles as though her visitor's presence were the most normal thing in the world.

"Our young man informed me that you were awake," said Sickert jauntily, "so I told him that we should sneak up on you. But you do not seem surprised."

"Do you want me to be surprised?" she asked, returning automatically to the teasing tone that she had been used to taking with him. So much had happened in the interval, and yet at the sight of him, it all seemed to melt away.

"I don't know if I want you to be surprised," said Sickert, "or to be so anticipating my visit that you are not. Since you're not, I'll assume the latter."

"You look well," said Alice.

"I've had a hard few days, but I'm recovered."

"And how was Cornwall?"

He held her eyes for a moment. "Oh, I didn't go as planned. Something came up. But I'll be leaving tonight; this time it's certain. Still, I wanted to drop this off before I left." He held up the canvas, its back facing to her. "I promised to hang it on the wall for a proper viewing, and I try to keep my promises, when I can."

Without further explanation, he took out a hammer from his satchel and a nail from his pocket and strode over to the wall opposite the bed. He stood back a moment to establish the position and then hammered in the nail. "Now, close your eyes," he said.

"I recall your telling me to do that once before," said Alice, complying. "You said it would relax my face."

"And it did. As you'll see. Now open."

She opened her eyes and looked at the picture. It was dark. She had heard he had a dark palette. In this case, he had painted her as though it were twilight. Much of her figure was blurred in the impressionist manner, but the head, though not in the style of high realism, had been delineated with a greater attention to detail. The face itself was pale and stood out against the dark background. The eyes were bright and hooded, and the mouth straight, but with the faintest touch of a smile. Her head was bare; he had painted the cap where he had thrown it to the right of the bed. The effect was of her having uncovered herself for the observer, if only in a slight way, but with a certain passionate determination.

"It's an interesting portrait," she noted ruminatively. "I look like one of those ecstatic saints or martyrs." It was true that the frame of the bed might have been an altarpiece, and flecks of yellow used to highlight the dark background gave a suggestion of fire.

"Do you think I have made you look spiritual?" asked Sickert.

"You have made me look otherworldly," said Alice.

"But you *are* otherworldly," he insisted. "You are a woman beyond my reach."

She laughed.

He had been looking at her as she looked at the painting, and Alice felt herself shiver slightly under his gaze. Neither one of them had noticed that Katherine had entered the room until she crossed over to seat herself in the chair next to the bed.

"And what do you think, Miss Loring?" said Sickert, with a trace of irritation in his voice.

"It's not my place to say," said Katherine in her usual mild tone. "It's Alice's portrait."

"You don't like it!"

Katherine shrugged. "We see the subject differently."

"And how, pray tell, do you see her?" He asked the question automatically, as though not really wanting to know the answer.

"I see her as an island of reason in a world of irrationality, cruelty, and turmoil," responded Katherine.

"An island of reason who lives her life as a professional invalid?"

"It's how she pays for her rationality," said Katherine quietly.

"And how do you think Mr. Sickert sees me?" Alice asked, intervening and addressing her companion.

"As a feral animal, caged," said Katherine shortly.

"I thought he made me look like an ecstatic saint."

"Perhaps it's the same thing," said Sickert. He turned quickly to Alice. "I'm sorry that I have not pleased your friend, but perhaps that is inevitable. One cannot please everyone." His voice had grown distant, and he seemed to have become restless and less at ease.

"That's true," murmured Alice.

Sickert was not listening. He had reached for his hat. His impatience to be gone had become almost palpable. "I'm afraid I must bid you ladies good-bye."

Alice looked at him, but he did not look at her. His eyes grazed the room, and a look bordering on disgust seemed to cross his features. Katherine had disturbed something. Or the portrait, being finished, had brought the disturbance. Whatever it was, Alice felt the bond between them had dissolved, leaving nothing but the painting behind. Perhaps it was at the root of his art—that the past held no meaning for him once the work was through; that his relationship to life was entirely a matter of impressions and observations as they occurred in the present. He had connected profoundly with her because she had consumed his imagination in the act of painting her, but the painting was done. She had become what ostensibly she had always been: an invalid spinster taking up his time. It was as though a spell had lifted.

But not just for him. Looking at him within the circle of Katherine's cool gaze, she saw an arrogant stranger. What could she possibly know about this man's character and motives? She felt herself blushing at the thought of what she had once felt. It was time, indeed, that he left.

"Thank you for the portrait," she said, taking Katherine's hand and leaning her head back on the pillow. "You should hurry, or you'll miss your train."

CHAPTER 45

I T'S A SIDE OF you," said Henry. He was sitting at the little table in Alice's bedroom, assessing the portrait and eating a scone with blueberry jam that Sally had made from her own recipe. William was expected. They had agreed to meet to discuss how they would proceed with the case, if indeed they would. The idea of more women being killed filled Alice with dread, but how could she, a bedridden invalid, really be of any use in hunting the killer?

"It was the Whistler connection that threw us," said Alice. "It got us thinking in the wrong direction. You with your 'ha ha.'"

"It was a normal sort of connection," said Henry huffily. "I still say Whistler laughs that way."

"We made too much of the '*P* of *W*,'" continued Alice. "It could stand for anything."

"That's true," he agreed. "The Prince of Wales, for example."

"Exactly," said Alice. It was as likely as anything else.

"And it's not as though Whistler didn't have other pupils," noted Henry. "Legros said he had a habit of taking the Slade's leavings."

"There you are," said Alice.

Before they could say more, they heard the downstairs door open and the sound of footsteps coming upstairs. William had arrived.

He strode into the room and over to the bed and then bent down and kissed Alice on the cheek. They had been exaggeratedly affectionate to each other ever since his "mad scene," as she secretly referred to it to herself. She had always believed she understood him better than anyone, better even than his wife, but his outburst had surprised her, causing her to conclude that she had missed something—or been kept in the dark. The fact discomfited her, but on the surface she behaved as though nothing had happened.

"What do you think?" she asked, motioning to the portrait as he seated himself on the other side of the bed.

He turned to look.

"Do you like it?"

He did not respond. He was studying the painting more closely than would have been expected, his brow furrowed. "What's that doing there?" He pointed with sudden vehemence to the bonnet in the lower left of the painting.

"It's my bonnet," said Alice, peeved by his focus on a minor detail. Although the floor and the bed had been painted in the impressionist style, the bonnet was, like the face, delineated rather clearly. "It's a joke," she explained irritably. It did not seem very funny to her now. "I expected he would paint me with it on, but he said he wanted to see my hair." She touched the cap on her head, recalling the incident in which he had thrown the cap to the floor and put his hand to her head. "Why do you ask?"

William again did not respond, but his face was deep in concentration and then seemed to shape itself into a grimace. "Your friend Sickert…do you know where he is?"

"He's off to Cornwall," said Alice with a certain indifference. "This time I believe he means it."

"He must be stopped."

Alice looked at him quizzically.

"We have let a guilty man get away." William's voice was high with restrained emotion. "The bonnet"—he pointed to the canvas—"there was a cap on the floor in precisely that spot in Mary Kelly's bedroom. It struck Abberline and me at the time as an odd sort of thing for a woman of that type to have lying about, but I wouldn't have noted its position had I not just seen the photograph of the crime scene this morning. And I understand it now. None of the other murders were in a bedroom, with the victim in a nightdress. This was different because it was inspired by someone in particular." He looked at his sister, who was staring at him uncomprehendingly. "Don't you see? The killer placed the cap on the floor of Kelly's room in an effort to re-create the scene in your bedroom. I hadn't realized until now how similar that room was to yours. And Kelly was your age, considerably younger than the previous Ripper victims."

"Are you saying that Mary Kelly was killed because of me?" Alice asked. Her face had drained of color, and she was staring fixedly at the picture opposite her bed.

William nodded. "What we find to love or to hate comes to us as a substitute for something else. It wasn't safe for him to attack you directly, so he found a way to duplicate the scene and put someone else in your place. But his need for substitution has given him away. Sickert must be Jack the Ripper. No one else would know about the bonnet."

The three siblings were silent, taking in this conclusion.

William rose abruptly, strode across the room, and took the painting from the wall. "I must go immediately to Scotland Yard and present this as evidence," he said. "We have allowed a murderer to slip through our fingers once; it would be unconscionable if we did so again."

Before Alice could intervene—for an idea had flashed into her head—he was gone. Henry, however, was still with her, brushing the crumbs from the scone off his lap. She beckoned to him to pull his chair closer to the bed. "There is something I want you to do," she said, keeping her voice as even as she could. "Now listen carefully."

CHAPTER 46

ALPHONSE LEGROS GREETED HENRY in his office. There were no classes that day, and he was sitting, looking weary and a little sad, under the large painting by Poussin, that exemplar of the neoclassical style he was constantly exhorting his students to study and imitate.

Unlike his brother, Henry felt sympathy for Legros. It was hard work protecting the artistic establishment against the corrosive forces of the new. He himself sometimes felt prompted to say "no more" when he heard about some of the latest experiments in literary expression: the lady who decided to eschew use of the comma; the young man who insisted on describing fornication. An artist was an individual, but also part of a social system, and thus had a responsibility to stem the tide of vulgarity as far as it was possible to do so. Of course, the new always looked vulgar until one had moved on a bit. Who could tell, but the very things that seemed outrageous now might come to seem routine in time? Knowing this kept Henry from wagging his finger too vigorously, yet he could sympathize with, even envy, Legros for being without such foresight.

Legros proved far more congenial that day than during Henry's last visit. Perhaps he was feeling lonely and was pleased by the distraction.

Whatever it was, he shook his guest's hand with enthusiasm, offered him a brandy, and bid him take the most comfortable armchair in the room. Best of all, he praised Henry's work, making special mention of his early novel, *Roderick Hudson*, whose hero was an artist who had gone to Italy to paint. "I am a strong advocate of the Italian *séjour*," said Legros. "I shall recommend your novel to my students."

Henry felt himself swell with pleasure. He was as vain of his books as other people were of their children, and he could listen to them praised for hours. But not today. Alice had sent him on an errand, and there was no time to waste. He hurried to get to the point.

"I have come to ask about a statement you made when my brother and I visited you a few days ago. You said that Sickert was not the first difficult student Whistler had hired as an apprentice. You said that he had 'taken the Slade's leavings before,' or something to that effect. What were the leavings you were referring to? Was there someone in particular?"

Legros shifted in his chair. "Yes," he said carefully, "but it was a shocking case."

"You can rely on my discretion," Henry assured him.

"Well then," said Legros, settling back to embark on the story with a certain prurient relish. "The student's name was Peter Newsome, a boy of modest circumstances from East London. During his early months, he showed considerable promise, copying the head of a Raphael Madonna extremely well. I recall making a note of it." He paused.

"Go on," prompted Henry.

"There was no reason for concern until the life-drawing class during our winter term. It seemed to disturb his…*équilibre*." Legros paused again.

"Yes?" prompted Henry.

"Some of our students are always unsettled at first." Legros cleared his throat. "They have never seen a woman…uncovered. But a woman, a man—in the end, it is the same thing. We teach them to see the body as it has been rendered through the ages, as a matter of proportions and properties. Generally, they become…habituated."

"But this Newsome did not become…habituated?"

"No," said Legros.

Henry had begun to feel vaguely alarmed. "And?" he prompted again.

"And one day we found him…in an indecent posture after one of the classes."

"An indecent posture with the model?"

"*Mais non!*" said Legros, as if this would have been far more acceptable. "An indecent posture…with himself!"

Henry drew a breath. It was as he had somehow expected. "And what was done to the student?"

"His belongings were removed from the premises, and he was asked to leave at once for fear of contamination. It was a great humiliation for the school, though we tried to keep it quiet. It would be assumed that the boy's career would be over, but Whistler, as I said, took him on."

"Whistler knew the circumstances?"

"It seems likely that he did. But then, it was Whistler's way to court scandal and to thumb his nose at established ideas. But he could do nothing with Newsome."

"Did Newsome…abuse himself again?"

Legros shook his head scornfully. "I have no doubt he continued on the course he had begun, but that was not the issue. Apparently the abuse began to affect the man's brain and, with it, his art. Whistler wanted no part of him when he found he could no longer draw."

"He ceased to be a 'pupil of Whistler'?"

Legros nodded. "It was around this time that he took on Walter Sickert as an apprentice."

"And what happened to Peter Newsome?"

Legros shrugged. "I cannot say. Perhaps he continues to live off his poor father. Or perhaps he is on the streets or in the workhouse. But as is well-known with regard to such cases, it is only a matter of time before he descends into madness and finds his way to the lunatic asylum."

CHAPTER 47

WILLIAM RUSHED INTO ABBERLINE'S office with Alice's portrait under his arm. "We were wrong to release Walter Sickert," he announced breathlessly, propping the painting against the wall and motioning to it excitedly. "He was painting this portrait of my sister just prior to the death of Mary Jane Kelly. It was clearly her room that inspired the murder. Don't you see?"

Abberline looked at the picture and shrugged. "I see a woman in bed, and Kelly was in bed. But then, most women do go to bed on occasion," he noted drily.

William waved his hand. "You're missing the point! Look at the configuration of the room; look at the bedstead; look at the nightdress. My sister even resembles the victim in age and appearance. And look here." He gestured to the bonnet that had been painted on the floor to the right of the bed. "My sister said he flung her bonnet on the floor before he painted her. Don't you recall the photograph we examined together? There's a bonnet on the floor in precisely the same spot. You noted it and said it was an incongruous sort of thing for the victim to wear."

Abberline got up and studied the painting closely for a few minutes.

"I admit the presence of the bonnet is odd, and the similarity of placement is provocative. But it could well be a coincidence. A night bonnet on the floor, after all…" He broke off and then chewed his lip for a moment. "There were items of women's apparel in Sickert's studio, no doubt bonnets among them. Such things are of course commonly in the possession of painters who use female models…" He paused again and then said, "But it does bring to mind another line of thought." His voice became more excited. "Seeing as this Sickert had in his possession a variety of women's clothes, it could be that he dressed himself in some of them to make his escape. We concentrated on the idea that he might have left in the cape worn by the woman he came with, which proved to be false, since your friend Miss Cobden said she left at the hour our man saw the caped figure leave. But perhaps Sickert dressed like another sort of woman—like a harlot, for example. The officer on duty that night said he saw women of dubious reputation coming and going throughout the evening. But it never occurred to him—and I can't say I blame him—to imagine that one of them might be Walter Sickert."

"Most certainly," William agreed encouragingly. "We know Sickert was fond of performing music hall songs for his friends. Dressing in female garb of that sort was par for the course for him."

Abberline nodded. This idea seemed to him of more importance than anything else he had heard. He tended to look at things from a practical standpoint. Where an alibi existed, it was useless to concoct a theory. But where there was no alibi, or an alibi destroyed, then one could begin to do some work.

There had been plenty of circumstantial evidence to link Sickert to the murders if one wanted that. As William had noted earlier, his notepaper was watermarked Pirie and Sons, the mark on some of the alleged Ripper notes. And then there were his paintings—they had been of precisely the sort of women that had been killed. Indeed, several of the subjects in his "music hall series," as he had referred to them flippantly during interrogation, had resembled in age and physical appearance the murdered women. And there were his studios in the East End, providing ample opportunity for the man to know the area and to be known, so as not to elicit suspicion.

But Abberline had not given any of this much credence. He had learned from experience how easily a person could be led in the wrong direction based on predisposition and circumstantial evidence. William's insistence on Sickert's guilt had struck him as too adamant and therefore likely to be influenced by emotional factors irrelevant to the case. So long as Sickert had an alibi, he existed outside the realm of suspicion.

But things had now changed. Sickert's alibi had proven to be less than sound, and as a result, what had previously been dismissed now seemed freighted with meaning. Abberline did not quarrel with his colleague this time but hurried to gather his men and send them in pursuit of their suspect.

CHAPTER 48

WILLIAM RETURNED TO ALICE'S flat to find his brother and sister sitting together. He knew that neither was convinced of Sickert's guilt and was thus prepared to be patient with them in discussing the case. But before he could speak, Henry motioned excitedly to him to approach the bed.

"I have a delicate question to ask you," he said, glancing conspiratorially at Alice. "Popular wisdom has it that self-abuse causes insanity. Do you agree?"

William looked at his brother with surprise and exasperation. "This is neither the time nor the place to discuss your personal neuroses."

Henry waved his hand. "This has nothing to do with me. It pertains to the case."

William looked puzzled but responded, "The enlightened medical view is that the act of self-pleasuring is natural enough if there are no other outlets for such urges. Although anything to excess bears looking into," he added with his usual tendency to caution. "Still, I can't see what relevance this could possibly have—"

"Then where did the theory come from?" Alice intervened.

"From the fact that we stigmatize children and young people for the act, and the trauma that results can have lasting pathological effects. It's a common logical fallacy of reversed cause and effect. But again, I can't see—"

"Lasting pathological effects!"

"Did Sickert abuse himself?"

"Not Sickert," said Alice, for whom everything had now become clear. "Henry just visited Legros, who told him that not long before Sickert left, a student named Peter Newsome was expelled from the Slade. He was caught abusing himself after a life-drawing class. Whistler took him on and then let him go when he found he could no longer draw. That's the 'pupil of Whistler' we should be looking for."

"Another 'pupil of Whistler'?" said William. "But you're forgetting the room and the bonnet on the floor. We've established that the murderer of Mary Jane Kelly had to have seen your bedroom. Only Sickert was here."

"It's true that only Sickert saw the room," said Alice quietly, "but you are concentrating on the wrong element. It's the mistake you just mentioned… what did you call it? 'A logical fallacy of reversed cause and effect.'"

"I don't follow," said William.

Alice and Henry looked at each other as though enjoying the uncharacteristic slowness of their brother. "Don't you see? The murderer didn't have to see the room…if he saw the painting."

CHAPTER 49

THE STATEMENT STRUCK WILLIAM with the force of a blow. As always, when he got something wrong, he felt how narrow and stupid he had been. He had forgotten the primary factor necessary in solving any human problem: the element of motive. There had never been one with Sickert, just an array of contributing circumstances and a desire on his own part to find the man guilty. He felt shame for his stupidity, but also for his excessive emotional involvement in the case; the former had followed directly from the latter. One became stupid when emotion blocked reason.

But now, Alice's news had had an amazingly equilibrating effect. The sense of feverish excitement he had felt only moments before had receded, and he felt he could see plainly for the first time in a while.

"Did Sickert show your painting to anyone after he finished it?" he asked Alice. His voice had returned to the calm, measured tone of the academic researcher.

"I've been considering that," she responded. "I'm sure he didn't show it in any general way. He said he didn't like a portrait to be seen before it was framed."

"But did he frame it himself?"

"*That* is the key," she agreed. "I don't know, but he did say the picture would be framed by the time he returned from Cornwall. He didn't go to Cornwall, as it happens, but I do think he dropped it off somewhere for the purpose."

"We know that he used someone to do his framing," piped in Henry. "I recall he was late to my dinner party because he was waiting for a framed painting to be delivered. He said he had gone to school with the framer."

William nodded. He had already known that the theory would be confirmed. He had accepted it at once, as soon as Alice had uttered it. It was that way with a scientific truth: one tried and tried to understand how something in nature worked, and then once one did, the process became entirely evident, as transparent as glass.

The atmosphere in the room had changed; the sense of disagreement and distrust had evaporated. For a moment, William felt great exhilaration, less regarding the case than because of the sense of reunion with his brother and sister. It was as though his family, long fractured, had been repaired.

William seated himself on the edge of the bed, Henry drew his chair closer, and Alice leaned forward so that their heads were almost touching. Calmly and carefully they pieced the thing together. A young man named Peter Newsome, studying under Alphonse Legros at the Slade, was caught abusing himself after a drawing lesson. He was thrown out of the school and shamed terribly. Whistler took him on as an apprentice. But the trauma affected the boy's mental state, which in turn affected what was most important to him: his art. He could no longer draw. To make a living, he resorted to framing pictures, since it was something he could do, yet he continued to try to paint. Meanwhile, Sickert became the new "pupil of Whistler." He had met Newsome at the Slade; perhaps they even overlapped in their apprenticeships. In any case, Sickert employed his colleague to frame his work, and that work became a source of envy and frustration to Newsome. Whenever he saw one of Sickert's paintings, it reminded him of his earlier promise and prompted him to attempt something similar. Polly Nichols posed for him because Sickert had recently painted a woman of Polly's general appearance and profession. There was the music hall sketch in Sargent's studio, no doubt preliminary to a series of paintings in that line. The other victims reflected the same impulse.

"Perhaps all the murders were inspired by Sickert's paintings," noted Alice. The idea seemed grotesque yet logical. It had the added element of making Sickert complicitous, if not consciously so, in the murders.

"It's possible," agreed William. "But no doubt your portrait is a special case, since Newsome knew that I was involved in the investigation and wanted to retaliate against me as your brother. That would also explain the gruesome package. But the key to everything is the strength of the motive—extreme shame and loss of vocation, with a trigger in the form of a successful artist with whom he continued to be in contact."

"The friendship also gave Newsome access to Sickert's stationery and inks," speculated Henry.

"And to the De Quincey volume," said William. He thought of Asher Abrams. Perhaps Sickert had introduced Newsome to Abrams, who employed him as a framer. He recalled that Ella had met him in Whitechapel on that shameful day because she had business with a framer.

The siblings had fallen silent. If their hypothesis was correct, Newsome would have had access to everything within Sickert's sphere. No wonder they had made the mistake. Sickert was the successful incarnation of what Newsome wanted to be, and Newsome was Sickert's obverse self, his doppelgänger.

They sat together thinking about this for a few minutes, until Alice spoke abruptly. "If what we suspect is true, we are wasting valuable time. We must alert the inspector. Walter Sickert is temporarily out of reach for questioning, since he is in Cornwall. Who else can lead us to the suspect? Who else knows Peter Newsome?"

Ella Abrams, thought William. Ella would know where to find Newsome. He felt a tightening in his throat at the idea that he would have to contact her again.

Before he could speak, there was a rustle in the corner of the room. It was Archie, who had been napping under the table and was roused by the urgency in Alice's voice.

"Peter Newsome?" He looked around, bleary-eyed. "I knows Peter Newsome."

CHAPTER 50

EVERYONE LOOKED AT ARCHIE with wonder.

"How do you know Peter Newsome?" asked William.

The boy had gotten to his feet and come to the side of Alice's bed. He stood there as he often did, waiting for her to pet him and offer him sweets. Katherine had warned that he ought not to be fed so much sugar; it ruined his appetite and would rot his teeth, but Alice explained that the psychological benefits of a piece of candy outweighed any physical harm it might do.

"'E's a friend of Mr. Sickert and an artist too," said Archie, eyeing the two chocolates on the little dish next to Alice's bed.

"And you know him?" Alice asked quietly.

"Well, sure. 'E's been by when Mr. Sickert was painting, to drop off brushes and such. 'E told Sally she'd make a fine subject for a picture. 'E's paintin' 'er now."

There was a hush in the room.

Sensing that he had said something wrong, Archie spoke quickly, as if to cover his tracks. "I told 'er 'e probly couldn't draw a pot and sure couldn't make such pretty things as Mr. Sargent or sing songs like Mr. Sickert, but she says as she don't care. She wants to 'av 'er portrait painted like the mistress. That's all."

He paused and looked around him and, seeing that the faces of the adults remained taut and anxious, added quickly, touching on the subject that he assumed was the source of their concern. "She said takin' yer clothes off fer an artist ain't bad. Even the fine ladies does it. So's I believed 'er."

"Where did she go, do you know, Archie?" asked Alice. She had taken hold of his arm and was gripping it tightly.

He did not answer but sniffled loudly and squirmed under her grasp.

"Can you tell us where Sally's gone?" William asked sharply.

The adult behavior must have reminded him of calamitous events in his former life, for his eyes darted about, as if looking for a means of escape. "I hope Sally ain't come to no 'arm," he wailed.

Henry interceded. He held out the plate of chocolates and waited calmly for Archie to take one, and then he spoke with stern directness. "We need to find Sally so she *won't* come to harm. We need you to help us. Can you do that?"

The boy nodded, though he continued to sob. He forced himself to speak. "I followed 'er once. I knows I'm not supposed to spy. But I did it with my mum, so I do it automatic." He whimpered in fear.

Henry assured him that in this case they were happy he had spied. "Now, we need you to tell us where you followed her. Is it far?"

"Far enough. It's near to where me mum died." Archie whimpered. "I thinks," he amended.

"Would you be able to find it if we took a hansom cab to your mum's street?" asked William.

"Dunno," said Archie. A look of panic crossed his face again. "Don' want Sally to come to no 'arm!"

"Can you remember how to get there by foot?" asked Henry, realizing that the boy would be best going the way he'd gone before.

Archie nodded, still whimpering.

"Just lead us there, then," said Henry. "Don't worry about how far it is. Go the way you went when you followed her. I'm sure you can remember."

The boy nodded, his face white, as the brothers urged him down the stairs and to the door. William paused only to instruct Katherine, who had been busy in the kitchen, to go immediately to Scotland Yard and alert Abberline. "Tell him to look for the shop of a framer named Peter Newsome in the vicinity of where the poor woman killed herself last week," he explained. "Tell him to waste no time."

There was hubbub as hats and coats were hastily put on, the front door noisily opened and shut, and then, silence. Alice was left, propped up in her bed, alone in the flat. As always, it was her fate to stay behind and wait.

CHAPTER 51

IT WAS STRANGE THAT Henry was able to keep up. William maintained a daily regimen of exercise and diet and was in shape to make the trek from Mayfair to Whitechapel on foot, but Henry, corpulent and sedentary, would have been expected to lag behind, perhaps to give up the chase altogether. But he did not. Indeed, he continued in the lead, following Archie through the park, up the embankment, and into the winding streets of the East End. As he strode through the various neighborhoods and saw the houses grow shabby and the streets dirty and rubbled, he recalled that awful night when he had been attacked and saved by Walter Sickert. It was perhaps the sense of dread he felt then that made him hurry to the aid of the girl now.

They entered a narrow path in the vicinity of Spitalfields, and Archie began to move more slowly, trying to recall where he had gone the day he had followed Sally. He paused for a moment at the crossroads of two streets, cocking his head, like a dog trying to follow a waning scent, and then moving forward with more certainty. They had arrived at a maze of small muddy paths, and Archie seemed to be surer as he moved into this labyrinth, turning left and right and left again until they found themselves

at the end of an alley at which stood a tall, brick structure with the sign
that said "Frames, Canvases, Art Supplies" hanging from the cornice. They
tried the front door; it was locked. Henry had already gone to the back and
returned to say it was locked too.

"We've got to get inside," said William.

Archie looked at the brothers and then took a metal wire from his
pocket and poked it into the lock until it clicked open.

"Where did you learn to do that?" asked Henry.

Archie shrugged. "I knows I'm not supposed to, but you says we gotta
get in."

"Yes." William nodded. "There are exceptions to every rule. Now quiet
as we can; we don't want to scare Sally."

They entered the shop. It was very still.

"Maybe they've left," said Henry.

"Or we're too late," whispered William. "Keep a watch on the boy. I
wouldn't want him to find her if she's…" He could not complete the thought.

The front room, where the principal operations of the shop were carried
on, was a large space lit by high windows. Canvases in the process of being
framed were laid out on a long table, and others, not yet framed or already
completed, were propped against the wall. There was a great variety of
pictures, including some that appeared old and valuable, no doubt the
property of wealthy collectors like Asher Abrams.

The space itself was exceptionally neat and well organized. There were
separate areas where the frames were cut, carved, and painted, with the
necessary tools placed carefully at each station. The frames were stacked in
orderly rows, saws and files were kept together, and varnishes and paints
were lined up neatly on the shelves.

The three passed to the back of the room, and William tried the door.
It was locked, and he nodded to Archie, who took out his piece of wire
and again fiddled with the lock until it opened. They entered another

room. Here there were no windows, so the area was dim. Henry gripped Archie's hand, both because he genuinely had trouble seeing and because he feared they might find something from which he would need to shield the boy.

Despite the dim light, the contrast to the front room was immediately apparent. The place was a jumble of disorder. Scores of canvases lay about in unruly heaps, making it difficult to pass. At first it seemed like these might be additional inventory that would eventually make their way to the outer room for framing, but as the brothers moved farther into the space, they could see that what lay there would never be framed. The pictures had been destroyed, cut to tatters, so that the linen hung in strips from the wooden stretchers. They had once been paintings of women. Here and there one could make out an arm, a breast, or a torso that had escaped the knife, although mostly one saw only flesh-toned strips hanging from the wooden supports like flayed skin.

"My God!" said Henry with horror. To create under any circumstances was arduous—his worst moments as a writer came when he had to discard a work that refused to thrive. But to have one's work fail again and again as it apparently had for Newsome—no wonder the man had gone mad. "It's a graveyard," he murmured.

"Newsome and the girl must have left," said William, looking around the appalling space with relief and leading them back to the main part of the shop. They were about to leave when Henry pointed out a low door behind the framing table that they had not seen when they came in.

William walked over and turned the knob, which opened onto a steep flight of steps leading into a dark basement. A light from a lamp flickered below.

"Someone's down there," said William, trying to fight back a sense of dread. "Stay here." He took a file from the table—it would serve as well as anything for a weapon—and descended the stairs. It was eerily silent, though the light from the lamp continued to shine dimly from somewhere in the recesses below.

At the bottom was a cavernous space dominated by a large wooden table. Rolls of cloth were arranged on shelves behind it, and piles of wood were bundled on the floor beneath. Hanging from hooks on the wall were knives of various sizes for cutting the cloth and wood for the creation of new canvases. If the space above were a graveyard, William thought, this was a birthing room. Each new canvas was like a life that had not yet been shaped by choice, a tabula rasa for the imprint of the imagination. Yet how fragile and short-lived was that innocent state. One touch of the brush and it was lost.

The light from the lamp was coming from the far end of the space, and William crept quietly to what he soon saw was an alcove, hardly bigger than a closet, abutting the far end of the room. He took a breath and looked inside.

The girl Sally was seated on a stool at the back of the alcove. She was undressed, not comfortable in being so, yet not ashamed either. She held herself with the sort of awkward pride that William recalled in the photograph of Polly Nichols. It was amazing how the idea of art aroused an instinctive reverence in people.

Hunched at an easel in front of the girl stood a slight man in glasses. Although he was turned so that only part of his face was visible, William knew at once that he had seen the man before. He was the bespectacled youth who had conferred with Asher Abrams about framing during dinner. There was another piece to the puzzle, then. Newsome must have overheard his questions about the De Quincey volume and then attacked him in the park afterward. He had had the image of Sickert as the attacker in his head for so long that it took him a moment to adjust to this revised image. Indeed, for the space of a few seconds, he could not do it. He could not replace the one figure with the other in his mind's eye.

Newsome was painting in concentrated silence, yet even from the distance at which William was standing, he could see that the results were not promising. Newsome had drawn a preliminary sketch in keeping with Legros's precepts, but the outline was shaky and uneven; it might have been the work of a child. And the brush, subject to regular bursts of movement, seemed beyond the control of the artist. William remembered having seen this sort of spasmodic activity in patients fixated on certain basic acts—washing their hands or buttoning their jacket—as if some outside force were compelling them to do these things against their will.

Sally turned her head. Perhaps she had heard a creak in the floorboards or was tired of holding one position, but whatever it was, her gaze shifted so that William entered her line of vision. She gave a sharp cry of surprise, scrambled from the stool, and grabbed for her clothes.

Newsome stopped his jabbing motion, his brush poised in midair. He seemed about to ask the girl what she was doing, and the look on his face seemed quizzical, until he suddenly registered the presence of an interloper. He turned sharply and faced William. "What are you doing here?" he demanded in a thin, reedy voice. It was a frightened whine, hardly the voice one would associate with a murderer. "Can't a man paint a picture in peace?" His voice was pleading, and for a moment, William felt a great welling of sympathy for the slight figure before him and, with that sympathy, a fleeting doubt as to whether this poor soul could be guilty of such horrible crimes. There was hurt and fear in Newsome's face, but not malevolence. Could the whole scene be an innocent one, a young man, sadly without talent, struggling valiantly to produce art?

Sally had run from the alcove and across the larger room to where Henry and Archie stood at the top of the stairs. The boy threw his arms round her.

"Go to Scotland Yard and tell them where you've been," William called out loudly. "Wait for us there." He had spoken with shrill authority, and he saw that his words had brought about a change in the visage of the figure before him. Newsome's face, which had looked only sad and confused a moment earlier, contorted into an angry grimace.

The children had clambered out of the shop, but Henry descended the stairs into the basement and was approaching the area where Newsome stood. What happened next was rapid and dreamlike. With a quick, surprisingly determined movement, Newsome darted from the alcove, took a knife from a hook on the wall, and grabbed Henry by the collar of his jacket, pressing the knife to his throat. William did not have a chance to raise the file he had been holding. He remained planted where he was, his face blank with shock.

Henry too had no time to register what had happened, only to realize suddenly he had a knife at his throat. He could feel it there; indeed, it was so sharp that it had already made a shallow incision, and a trickle of blood had run onto his collar. Mrs. Smith would have a job with that, he couldn't help thinking, even as he felt the sting of the cut and a sense of dread rise in him. Perspiration gathered on his forehead, and his body began to shake. He looked across at his brother. Countless times on the playground of their youth, William had come to his rescue, pushing the offender aside or saying something in his sharp boy's voice that had the same effect. But what could William do for him now?

Newsome pressed the knife harder against Henry's throat, and there was another trickle of blood. How much of this could he take? Henry wondered desperately. Was the maniac going to hack him to death by degrees? He tried to remain still to avoid more pressure from the knife, though he was perspiring heavily and feared he would collapse, which might well cause the knife to slide down his throat, with God knew what result.

William, who had remained frozen, staring at the scene before him, roused himself from his stupor and addressed Newsome. He tried to keep his voice calm and authoritative, though he could feel the effort as a physical strain on the muscles of his body. "What good would it do for you to hurt him?" he asked softly. "I'm the one you want. I'm the one investigating the case."

Henry murmured agreement. "Just tagging along," he muttered faintly.

Newsome did not appear to hear. He continued to grimace. Henry, fearing that the knife would slip, tried to hold his breath.

"Haven't you done enough?" William exhorted.

The question seemed to agitate the attacker further, who, for the first time, raised his voice. "How do you know?" he cried. "Did they tell you? Did they advertise it?"

William was confused. Hadn't Newsome advertised his deeds himself with his letters to the newspapers and Scotland Yard? "You know that everyone knows what you did!" he exclaimed.

Newsome seemed to grow wilder with this statement. His eyes darted about, and he pressed the knife closer. Henry's teeth began to chatter.

William recalled what had happened with Pizer during his visit to Broadmoor; he had somehow provoked the man to attack him. It was the same now, except it was not himself but his brother who was in danger. This fact made him feel sick with guilt and fear.

"You need to go where you'll be cared for," he pleaded with Newsome. "You need to be helped."

"Helped?" The man's voice had grown louder and more shrill. "Where they'll know and stare? Like you and him and all the others!" He spit out the words wildly and pressed the knife with still more force against Henry's throat. Henry's eyes rolled up in his head.

William paused. What he was doing wasn't working. Indeed, it was making things worse. He must reevaluate, rethink the context in which he was responding. This was how he came up with original ideas: reseeing a situation from another angle, one that had been ignored because of convention or habit. Except it was one thing to resee in the pleasant confines of his study in Cambridge, Massachusetts, and another to do so in a dark basement where a deranged killer had a knife at his brother's throat. But this was precisely what he had to do. What use were his powers of thought if they could not be employed now, when Henry's life was in danger?

He willed himself to concentrate, to block out everything but the problem before him. What was inciting this man to such a frenzy? What was he afraid of? Suddenly he saw why Newsome was painting in a dimly lit basement alcove; why he painted with spasmodic, uncontrolled brushstrokes and responded with fear and then fury at being interrupted. He had not been following the pattern of the man's increasingly enraged responses. Newsome's mind was not on the women he had killed; they were only the by-products of the initial trauma of being discovered in the act of self-abuse.

Brand a man a deviant, and you are likely to make him one. Newsome could not recover from what had happened to him that day at the Slade. He replayed that traumatic episode every time he tried to paint a picture, and it was the failure to paint that must have driven him to kill. The murders were repetitions too—furtive and performed with the repetitive stabbings that he had seen in the bodies of Catherine Eddowes and Mary Jane Kelly. They too were a reenactment of that original trauma. At the root of it all was shame. That had been the root of Pizer's rage. The lesson was clear: deprive a man of his humanity, and be prepared for the consequences: a human being capable of God knows what.

William addressed Newsome slowly and carefully, trying to incorporate his new understanding into his words. "I didn't mean to disturb your privacy," he said. "I was worried about Sally."

Newsome continued to press the knife to Henry's throat, blinking rapidly behind his spectacles.

William continued. "We are all of us prone to do things that are...

unseemly. What you did was unfortunate, but in no way deviant or unnatural. It was wrong to shame you." He spoke gently, no longer as an investigator or even as a conventional scientist, but as a psychologist and a human being who could not only explain but soothe the turbulence of a disordered mind.

Newsome blinked again and then spoke in a wavering voice. "I didn't mean to do it. I wouldn't have done it if I'd known anyone was there. I thought they'd all left."

"Of course you did."

"They called me an animal."

"We are all animals. But like us all, you are a human being as well. What you did then was hardly the worst thing a man can do." He did not say that Newsome had gone on to do the worst.

Newsome gestured desperately toward the alcove, and his voice became a pitiful groan. "I can't paint!"

William considered this; then he walked slowly to the easel and turned the painting over. "There," he said. "Now no one can see."

Newsome's face relaxed.

"Please take the knife from my brother's throat. I know you don't want to harm him."

Newsome loosened his grip, and Henry staggered over to William's side. Released from the pressure of the knife, he felt a surge of well-being. There was something to be said for having your life threatened; you appreciated being alive afterward—if you got away.

The atmosphere in the room had become almost serene. The man's spiritual being had been awakened, William thought. He had been deprived of his humanity, which had destroyed his vocation, an irrevocable loss, deeply connected to who he was. William could understand this. He had suffered his own crisis of vocation, and it had almost cost him his sanity. For Newsome, it had, and worse—it had driven him to kill.

William looked at the man before him again. How could this quivering mass of fear and insecurity have brutally killed those women? He felt again a momentary doubt. It was ridiculous to doubt, when Newsome had just threatened to kill Henry. He had seen the man's capacity for violence with his own eyes. Besides, Newsome had a motive, a psychological profile that explained the Whitechapel murders with an admirable completeness. And still, the shifting tendency of his own mind, his incapacity to arrive definitely at any solid conclusion frustrated and unnerved him. Couldn't he ever be sure? How was it that others seemed to settle on things and be done? Of course Newsome was Jack the Ripper. Everything pointed to it.

"What should I do?" Newsome asked simply. He still held the knife, but he seemed more like a child than a threatening killer.

William would have liked to tell him to pray—a minister would tell him that—but he was not a minister. He said nothing. He only stared at the man before him, not knowing what to do or what to expect.

It was Henry who knew. As a novelist, he trafficked in endings, and he had found that life and art were not so very different in that respect. Besides, he had heard the sound of shouts outside the shop and could see that Newsome had heard them too. Abberline had found them; he would be inside in a moment, but it would be too late.

Henry averted his eyes, but William, who did not realize what would happen, saw it, in what seemed slow motion: the glint of steel against the pale throat, the slash, first only a sweep of the hand, then a red line, then a gush of vermilion.

By the time Abberline and his men clambered down the stairs, Peter Newsome's body, his hand still clutching the knife, lay slumped on the floor beside a pile of newly stretched canvases.

Jack the Ripper was dead.

EPILOGUE

London. 1911.

HENRY GAZED AROUND THE gallery, looking for people he knew. Some seemed familiar. Perhaps he had met them at dinner parties or seen their pictures in magazines, but they were so young; really, too young for him to know. Beside him stood Sargent, his tall frame more hunched than usual. It was clear that John would have preferred not to be there at all.

"You know I don't like to go out," he had told Henry when the invitation had come. He had grown reclusive since the death of his mother and sister, content only during his sojourns to America, when he was painting the ceiling of the Boston Public Library. It was as though all the portraits he had painted had soured him on people's faces.

Henry, by contrast, craved society even more now than he had in his youth. He had purchased a home in Sussex, where he lived most of the year, but he looked forward to his visits to London. The social chitchat was a relief from the locutions of his writing, which had grown more complex as he grew older. The weight of his verbiage was like his physical weight. It too grew greater every year, as Alice would have noted with disapproval. There was the weight of loneliness as well. Life in the country exacerbated it. When he wasn't working, he had a tendency to brood, to recall a past that he could not change, that unlike his writing, he could not qualify or amplify with words.

The invitation to this event had been particularly welcome. It had brought to mind the great adventure of twenty-three years earlier. Henry touched his throat retrospectively, recalling the madman's knife. How dreadful it had been, but how wonderful, a sublime interlude of family solidarity, a return of sorts to a childhood idyll.

They were both gone now, his brother and sister. Alice had been first; she had succumbed to a cancerous lesion on the breast, a paradoxical ailment, given the gruesome memento she had received from that notorious killer. But when the diagnosis had come, she had seemed almost pleased. She said she welcomed an illness that had the good taste to be real and malignant. "All those years in bed with nothing wrong with me. It's a relief to finally suffer in a way that people can understand."

In the time that remained, she had rarely spoken of the Ripper investigation. When reference was made to the case, she changed the subject or announced she had a headache. And though Sargent would occasionally bring over his paintings for her to look at, she lost her interest in the fine arts. She ceased to follow the gallery shows and exhibitions or ask for the art-world gossip as she used to.

One incident during this period stood out for Henry. It had occurred one afternoon toward the beginning of her illness. She already understood the gravity of her condition, but the pain had not yet become debilitating, and the sickness seemed to make her, if possible, more alert than ever. They would spend some of their pleasantest moments together during this time, whiling away the hours, as she macabrely put it, awaiting the Angel of Death.

On this particular day, she was propped up in bed sipping a cup of tea in which she had added a generous quantity of brandy. Henry sat nearby reading the paper; he had taken his brandy without the tea. There was an air of mild debauchery in the air. Katherine was off visiting her sister's family, and the siblings both felt free to drink not only earlier, but more than they normally would.

The girl, Felicity, had entered the room with the post. She had replaced Sally, who a few months earlier had taken a position as a downstairs cook in a grand establishment, where Archie, under the guise of being her brother, had been employed as well, possibly as assistant to the footman.

Alice had taken the letters from the girl and settled back to examine them. Although ostensibly occupied with his newspaper, Henry watched her out of the corner of his eye, as he often watched people when they were not aware of his doing so. On this occasion, he found his attention repaid. As he watched her flip through the post, he was struck by the sudden hardening of her features and the quick, almost brutal gesture with which she cut open one of the letters, glanced at the card inside, and then crumpled it in her hand. Later, when she went to do her necessaries, he reached under the blanket and found the crumpled card. It was an invitation to Sickert's latest gallery exhibition. Across the top, in red ink, were the scrawled words "Please exert yourself and come—or I shall be desolate. WS."

Her reaction had served as a cue. Walter Sickert would come to represent, for Henry, a private place in his sister's emotional life. He would never know what the actual contents of that place consisted of; indeed, he had no wish to know, only that the place, heavily guarded and under lock and key, was there.

As for William, Henry had seen him at intervals since that exciting time, but these were short visits, hardly more than glimpses. William was much in demand by the scientific world and rarely available. Their longest time together had been a year ago, when his brother had made the crossing to consult a specialist on the Continent. He and his Alice had stopped over to stay with Henry in Sussex. The problem, William confided, was with his heart, an organ one thought nothing of, at least in the literal sense, until it failed. So much of life was like that.

In the final month of his brother's life, Henry traveled to America to wait by his bedside. William had clung to his wife in those last weeks, never wanting her out of his sight, demanding that she read to him, bring him his papers, or take down his thoughts as the whim struck. It should have been trying—Henry could not have stood it—but William's Alice was unstinting in her devotion. She did not complain and, indeed, seemed to enjoy these ministrations. It gave Henry pause. If only one could be certain to predecease one's spouse, it might be worth all the bother to have a woman like that, constant and attentive, to ease the final passage.

It had all gone well enough, considering that it was death and the end. "He's had more dire episodes than this," his Alice had noted. Henry agreed. William's fear had never been of death but of madness. He had always worried that he would succumb to another episode like the one he had suffered in his youth. It had not occurred. He had passed into the great unknown with dignity and quietness, rather in the manner one might have expected of a lawyer or a stockbroker.

His students flocked to the funeral. He was much loved, or at least in theory. Not that William wasn't lovable, Henry thought, only that the many who claimed to love him had no idea what he was really like. But then, who could know another in any essential way? It was the great advantage of the writer to create characters and thereby know them fully. But with regard to real human beings, one saw only the outer shell.

✢✢✢

The invitation to this evening's event had come in a hand Henry recognized at once, though he had seen it only twice: on the card crumpled beneath his sister's bedcover and, before that, in the reply to the invitation to his dinner party those many years ago.

"You are cordially invited to attend the opening of the Camden Town Group Show," and scrawled in red ink at the top, words that mimicked those on the card to his sister: "Please exert yourself and come—for the sake of old times if nothing else. WS." WS, not PW, thought Henry. Sickert was no one's pupil now. He had forged a reputation of note, become an eminence in the art world.

Although Henry had not attended Sickert's previous exhibitions, he was determined to go to this one. It was the lure of the past—not just the literal past referred to in the scrawled message, but the hidden, subjective past that lay buried with his sister. *I must go*, he thought, *in reverence to her*—oddly, since she had not wished to see the man again. But wasn't that precisely the reason? Sickert had meant something of consequence or she would not have been so adamant about banishing him from her life.

There had been some difficulty persuading his friend to go. Sargent was resistant. The art world had changed, he said; the new people newer than they used to be. He feared being heckled or, at best, condescended to. Indeed, the crowd in the gallery did not seem congenial—young men with wispy beards, wiry little physiques, and sharp, unforgiving eyes. In the corner was Roger Fry, who had pilloried Sargent in the press the week before. Near the window was the wild female painter who, along with her sister, the supercilious Woolf girl, was like an Amazon, likely to throw a spear at you when you weren't looking. Where were the artistic lions of yesteryear? Alphonse Legros had died. The bulwark had given way; the deluge had come.

Henry gazed around himself at the paintings in the gallery. There were half a dozen artists on display who called themselves the Camden Town Group. Some were conventional postimpressionists. Such a name. It sounded like a contradiction, but in fact, innovation had become formulaic. The tradition that Legros had championed—scrupulous schooling in the old masters—had been superseded by a rote taste for the primitive, the geometric, and the abstract. "Modern" was the term. Henry himself had been called it in one breath and castigated for not being enough of it in the next. The whole thing gave him a headache.

The paintings around him were not pleasant, and he could see that Sargent, for one, was put off. He peered at a group of canvases by Wyndham Lewis, who stood nearby, surrounded by an admiring throng. Lewis was the great star of the moment, acclaimed far beyond such elder statesmen as Sargent. It must rankle, to have such a young man eclipse you. It was a problem *he* didn't have, Henry thought bitterly; he had never sold well enough to suffer eclipse. Of course, he was idolized by some, he reminded himself. *The happy few*, he thought, *select, discriminating, but sadly few.*

Sargent had been collared by a group of young artists who were likely to bait him like a muzzled bear. It could be painful to watch. Henry wandered to the other side of the room.

A spry, middle-aged man with thick, wavy gray hair and sharp features approached. He was accompanied by a woman of the same age, elegantly dressed with a dark, exotic physiognomy. Her hair was piled fashionably on the top of her head. It was lustrous and black but shot through with a white streak that made her look even more striking. As the man drew nearer, Henry met his eyes and saw they were piercingly blue. Sickert.

"It was good of you to come," Sickert said, smiling. "I would only wish that your brother and sister could have been here too. I deeply regret their passing."

Henry nodded. He could still see the music hall performer in the established artist, the young man in the older one. The change really wasn't very great. There was something sharp edged about Sickert even now, something young and saucy. He was the sort of man who would always appear to be new, no matter how established and successful he became. There was a talent in that.

Sickert gestured to his companion. "This is my friend, Mrs. Cassel."

The woman smirked slightly and extended her hand. "I was a great admirer of your brother's," she said.

Henry bowed. During William's lifetime, a comment like this would have annoyed him, but now he was willing to be magnanimous. After all, he had, in the most literal sense, won that battle in being the one still alive. "He was a genius," he acknowledged.

"I didn't mean his work," said the woman with surprising directness, "though I admired it as well. I was speaking of the man. I knew him, though only briefly, during his visit to London many years ago. We were quite…simpatico."

Henry blushed. Though the woman spoke without shame, he felt that she meant something more than simple friendship. He recalled his brother's strange behavior during the Ripper case and was swept with the conviction that this woman must have had a part in it. The De Quincey volume had been connected with a woman, he recalled.

"Have you seen my work yet?" asked Sickert.

"Not yet," said Henry, looking dazedly around the gallery. "There are so many pictures. Please show me."

Sickert led him over to one wall where a half dozen paintings were displayed. Henry remembered the watercolor Sargent had found in his studio, done early in Sickert's career. It was odd how much these works reminded him of that, done, it must be assumed, when the man had been no older than twenty-two or twenty-three. He had struck his keynote even then, when he was still a "pupil of Whistler." Again, he thought of the appellation that had set them all going, at first, in the wrong direction. His eyes darted to inspect Sickert. Was it so wrongheaded? The man was quick, furtive, comfortable in costume, odd with women. He could, if one had an imagination, be conceived of as a murderer.

Henry turned and looked at the picture before him. It showed a woman in tattered underclothes beside a man in evening dress, skulking—the word seemed apt—in a dark room. He read the tag: "Camden Town Murder."

He shrank back as though slapped.

"What is it?" said Sickert, looking at him with his sharp blue eyes.

"It's a provocative title," murmured Henry.

"It's a subject that interests me," said Sickert, "for reasons that go back. The perpetrator in this case has not been caught either."

Henry shuddered slightly. It was true that Abberline had found it impossible to confirm Newsome's guilt. It required imagination to put it all together, and that, Abberline said, was the problem; the facts were sparse. Nothing in Newsome's shop had linked him to the murders. The gist of the thing lay in his relationship to Sickert, in his access to Sickert's things: the writing materials, the De Quincey volume, the costumes, the goad of the paintings. It required that Newsome be a failed version of Sickert, an idea at once powerful and elusive. In the end, Newsome's death had been judged a suicide due to masturbatory insanity. The siblings had been content to know what others didn't, and to register the implications: no more women hacked to death in the East End. Until now.

Sickert's blue eyes met Henry's. "Perhaps Jack the Ripper is back."

Henry remembered what he had read about these murders. In one article, the inspector—not Abberline, who had long retired—had noted that they were "worse even than the Ripper murders of '88, if such were possible."

"But we must have dinner and reminisce," said Sickert, changing the subject brightly. "Mustn't we, Ella?" He motioned to the woman beside him. "What a shame that your brother and sister can't join us. But then… they are in a better place. I don't believe in the immortality of the soul, as

I once explained to your sister, but that doesn't prevent me from thinking that where she is, is better." He paused, musing. "She was an exceptional woman. I am sorry that we did not keep up our acquaintance. But I blame myself. I am not reliable."

Sickert smiled at the thought and touched his brow with his handkerchief. A group of young artists had beckoned to him from across the room. He took the arm of Mrs. Cassel, made a theatrical bow, and moved off, a faint odor of lavender trailing in his wake.

Henry remained standing in front of Sickert's macabre painting for a moment. *If only Alice and William were here*, he thought wistfully, *they would turn it all over, the three of them. Who knows where it would lead?* But his brother and sister were gone, irretrievably beyond call, and he himself was, quite frankly, tired. Tired and old. It was best, at such a date, to let things go. He looked at his watch. It was late. Time for him to find John Sargent, who had, Henry hoped, not been too violently abused by the younger set, and head home.

But first, he would have another glass of wine.

ABOUT THE AUTHOR

PAULA MARANTZ COHEN IS Distinguished Professor of English at Drexel University in Philadelphia. She is the author of *Jane Austen in Boca*, *Jane Austen in Scarsdale*, and *Much Ado About Jessie Kaplan* and five works of nonfiction, including *Silent Film and the Triumph of the American Myth*, *Alfred Hitchcock: The Legacy of Victorianism*, and *The Daughter's Dilemma: Family Process and the Nineteenth-Century Domestic Novel*.